THE FRAGILE EDGE

Books by Suzanne Chazin

The Jimmy Vega Mystery Series

The Fragile Edge

Voice with No Echo

A Place in the Wind

No Witness But the Moon

A Blossom of Bright Light

Land of Careful Shadows

The Georgia Skeehan Mystery Series

The Fourth Angel

Flashover

Fireplay

THE FRAGILE EDGE

SUZANNE CHAZIN

www.kensingtonbooks.com

KENSINGTON BOOKS are published by

Kensington Publishing Corp.
119 West 40th Street
New York, NY 10018

All Kensington titles, imprints, and distributed lines are available at special quantity discounts for bulk purchases for sales promotion, premiums, fund-raising, educational, or institutional use. Special book excerpts or customized printings can also be created to fit specific needs. For details, write or phone the office of the Kensington Special Sales Manager: Attn. Special Sales Department. Kensington Publishing Corp, 119 West 40th Street, New York, NY 10018. Phone: 1-800-221-2647.

Library of Congress Card Catalogue Number: 2021905340

The K logo is a trademark of Kensington Publishing Corp.

ISBN-13: 978-1-4967-1556-2
ISBN-10: 1-4967-1556-X
First Kensington Hardcover Edition: September 2021

ISBN-13: 978-1-4967-1559-3 (ebook)
ISBN-10: 1-4967-1559-4 (ebook)

10 9 8 7 6 5 4 3 2 1

Printed in the United States of America

To my son Kevin,
my cheerleader and pillar.
Thanks for the story charts and late-night brainstorming sessions.
I couldn't have written this book without you.

We walk on the fragile edge
of a heap of earth.
A wing goes by, anointed with oil,
with purity. But a blow,
falling somewhere I don't know of,
grinds a hostile tooth
out of every tear.

Prologue

He didn't think too deeply about the job before him. He understood that it was necessary. Sometimes people must be punished for their poor choices.

Sometimes they have to die.

He concentrated instead on the particulars. The location of the security cameras in the bus terminal. The fastest route upstairs. The nearest exits. He tried to ignore the reek of diesel fumes, fried food, and sweat that wafted over the passengers swirling around him. The nearness of their bodies. It rekindled the acrid memory of his stepfather, the way he'd come home, stinking of booze, and grab him in a headlock. He was a small boy then, powerless to fight back.

He wasn't powerless any longer.

Everything he needed was in his black backpack, disassembled and wrapped in foam and clothing so it wouldn't jiggle. A twelve-pound bolt-action Nemesis sniper rifle with a holographic scope. Two five-round magazines of high-velocity full metal jacket ammo. A military-grade flash suppressor. He knew the courthouse schedule. Knew when his target would move across the security lot.

In his thirty-plus years, he'd taken many a life. How many, he couldn't say anymore. He was in his teens when he made his first kill. It didn't bother him, though he suspected it might other men. It was never just about good vision and steady hands. It was about something deeper. A dead calm at his center. An impenetrability.

Some men are born to build. He was born to destroy.

Not that you'd know it by looking at him. He was on the short side, a little husky but otherwise unremarkable in appearance, dressed as he was in khakis and a baseball cap. He had deep, close-set eyes that sometimes made people uncomfortable if he looked at them too long. He wore sunglasses to hide them as he took the stairs to the second floor, past the office of the station manager who was always on his phone or playing games on his computer. He made his way through a door he'd already familiarized himself with and headed to the roof. The August day was blistering, and the silvery gray thermoplastic roofing concentrated the heat like a frying pan. The humid air felt gauzy on his tongue. His cheeks itched from the beard he'd glued on this morning.

He pulled a toothpick out of the front pocket of his khakis and chewed on it. Chewing cleared his sinuses. He hated this kind of weather, the way it constricted his nasal passages. Made him feel like he was trapped in a house full of cats and dogs. He was allergic to every kind of animal. Just as well. He didn't like them anyway.

Too unpredictable.

One shot. One kill. That was his MO. Always had been. That's why he used a bolt-action rifle. Semi-automatics were less accurate over long distances and more prone to malfunctions. He'd retrieve the shell casing when it was over and disappear. Everyone checks the adjoining rooftops. No one thinks to look for a shooter positioned a half mile away.

He stayed low beneath the lip of the roof as he unzipped his backpack. He pulled out the rifle receiver, rotated the collapsible stock into place, then inserted the barrel, tightening it with a quick two-finger turn of a screw. He slipped the hand guard over the top of the barrel and inserted a pin to hold it in place. He flipped the bipod down so the cushioned feet balanced the weapon and mounted the scope on top. Then he screwed a flash suppressor onto the muzzle. When he was satisfied with the alignment, he slid a five-round magazine into the well and settled the rifle securely on the lip of the roof. From the scope, he scanned the courthouse security lot and waited for the golf cart to motor into view. Rubber tires kicked up a trail of dust and stopped short of the rear doors.

Three people sat in the cart. One in front. Two in back. He was interested in only one. He waited for the perfect moment to get his subject dead center in his scope.

He fired.

There was a moment of Zen-like stillness after he squeezed the trigger, when the earth seemed to balance on the head of a pin. He didn't hear the screams. From this distance, he had only a vague sense of the blood and carnage he'd unleashed. And yet, for the first time ever, he felt a flutter of uncertainty in his chest. A tremor in his hands. Not because of who he'd killed.

But because of who he hadn't.

Chapter 1

"Will the defendant please take the stand."

Defendant. In nineteen years as a police officer, Jimmy Vega never expected that term would apply to him.

He rose from the safety of his lawyers' table and walked to the witness stand. He could feel the jury's eyes on him as the court clerk lifted her bifocals from a chain around her neck, then produced a well-worn Bible and swore him in. Juror number two, a balding white man in a New York Jets football jersey, wiped a handkerchief across his sweaty pate and yawned. Juror number three, a Black woman with long, beaded braids, folded her arms tightly across her chest and eyeballed Vega like he'd just ticketed her for jay-walking.

"Detective Vega," the plaintiff's attorney, Bernard Carver, began in his TV doctor's voice. "You've been a homicide investigator with the county police for three years now. Is that correct?"

"Yessir." Vega resisted the urge to loosen his blue polyester tie or remove his JC Penney suit jacket even though the air was dense and humid. The courthouse was old. Its high ceilings and ancient air ducts did little to quell the heat of such an oppressive August day. The hot breath of so many sweaty bodies didn't help. In the gallery, Vega saw reporters he recognized from the local news outlets, along with representatives from the police union and members of various anti-police groups united in their singular hatred of him.

"Before your stint in homicide, where were you?"

"I was a detective in the narcotics division for five years," said Vega. "And a patrol officer for eleven years before that."

"What was your primary assignment in the narcotics division?"

"I worked undercover, infiltrating drug rings and gang operations."

"I see." Carver nodded like this was news to him, even though, as opposing counsel, he'd likely spent the last two months combing through every detail of Vega's life, from his statements after the shooting to who was in the courtroom supporting him this morning.

Joy. Adele.

Vega slid a sideways glance at two faces seated directly behind the defense table. His nineteen-year-old daughter, Joy, and his girlfriend, Adele Figueroa. Vega hoped Carver wouldn't find a way to drag them into this case. Especially Adele. Here she was, director of one of the most influential immigrant advocacy organizations in New York State, dating a cop who'd shot and killed an unarmed immigrant. True, the man had been a suspect in a home invasion at the time of the shooting eight months ago. Vega was cleared of any criminal wrongdoing. But in the court of public opinion, the taint never really left him. And now this civil trial was stirring things up all over again.

"During your time undercover," Bernard Carver continued, "did you ever step out of your role to make arrests or serve search warrants?"

"Occasionally," said Vega. "Usually, my superiors didn't want me to blow my cover."

"But it happened?"

"Yes."

"Did you just show up and"—Carver made a tumbling motion with his left hand—"bust down someone's door?"

"I never just *busted down someone's door.*"

At the defense table, Vega's attorney, Isadora Jenkins, made a subtle patting motion away from the jury's view. Vega got the drift. He was losing his temper. That was a ten-million-dollar mistake he couldn't afford.

Vega cleared his throat and clarified. "There were rules. Procedures."

"Can you educate the jury a little about such . . . *procedures*?" Carver made the word sound like code for something illegal. Vega forced himself not to rise to the bait. *Be honest. Be humble. Be sincere.* Those were the instructions Isadora Jenkins and the county's attorney, Henry Zaroff, had given Vega this morning before court. Among many others. *Don't wear sunglasses. Juries hate cops in shades. Dress neatly but not expensively. Shine your shoes. Stay off your phone. Make eye contact with the jury.*

Vega tried the last piece of advice now. There were six jurors—not twelve, like in a criminal case. This was a civil suit. It was all about money. How much the county could be squeezed into paying in recompense for the man's death. The more they paid, the less of a future Vega could expect in the department. No one came out and said that, of course. But every cop knew it.

"In the cases where I was involved in an arrest or search," Vega explained, "I would notify my sergeant, who would dispatch a patrol to assist."

"A patrol?" Carver leaned a hand on the witness stand, the sort of subtle invasion of space Vega himself used on suspects. The light caught the soft sheen of silk in Carver's gray suit. Vega noticed, too, that the man's nails were buffed. He probably had a personal stylist. One for him and one for the dead man's widow, a full-figured Latina in her late thirties with dark eyes that watered on cue. *Lucinda Ponce*. In all the months Vega had gone over the case in excruciating detail, not once had anyone mentioned Ponce having a widow back in Honduras.

"When you say that your sergeant dispatched a patrol to assist," Carver continued, "do you mean uniformed officers?"

"That's correct."

"Why uniformed officers?"

"So the suspect understood that we were the police."

"In other words, Detective Vega, you had concerns that the people you were trying to arrest might not realize you were a real police officer."

"Objection!" Isadora Jenkins rose from her chair. She was a tiny, wizened Black woman with close-cropped white hair and orthopedic loafers, so standing didn't offer much height advantage, but her voice more than made up for it. She had the vocal range and depth of a Pentecostal minister. "Mr. Carver is asking Detective Vega to speculate."

"Sustained," said Judge Edgerton.

Carver offered a slight bow. "Your Honor, I'll rephrase the question. Detective Vega, isn't it standard operating procedure for plainclothes officers to request uniformed officers to assist in an arrest?"

"Yes."

"Yet, on the night of December fourth of last year, you violated your own department's procedures—"

"I didn't violate—"

"You just said it's standard operating procedure to request uniformed backup. Yet you didn't do that when you chased Mr. Ponce into those woods."

"I didn't have time."

"*You . . . didn't . . . have . . . time.*"

Carver let the words hang in the air for an uncomfortably long moment. Vega could hear the rumble of air-conditioning through the antiquated ducts and the shifting of jury members in their seats.

"Things happened in a matter of seconds," Vega explained. He wished he could ask the jury to stand in his shoes for a moment. To contemplate a job where every routine encounter had the potential to be an officer's last. A traffic stop. A domestic dispute. Teenagers fighting in a park. He was twenty-four years old when he came on this job and one of his very first call outs was for a triple homicide with a fourth victim—a six-year-old girl—clinging to life. He saved her—and many others since then. But every choice boiled down to seconds. Not hours or minutes.

Seconds.

"So, you made a split-second decision—the wrong one, it turned out," said Carver. "And yet, you've been allowed to return to the homicide unit, a very prestigious assignment in your department."

"I was cleared of all criminal charges and therefore entitled to resume my former duties, as is standard procedure after any officer-involved shooting."

"And now, you're being rewarded."

"Rewarded?"

"Promoted," said Carver. "To sergeant. The official swearing in will be sometime next month, if I'm not mistaken. September twenty-first. At the county center."

Vega's breath caught in his chest. Bernard Carver knew about the promotion. Even before Vega did. Well, officially, anyway. Last Friday afternoon, Sergeant John Simonelli—Forty-year John—turned in his retirement papers, a surprise in itself since Simonelli's nickname was RIP, short for *Retired-in-Place*. He'd stopped working years ago. He just came in for the free coffee.

With Simonelli gone, there was suddenly an opening. Vega's name was next on the promotion list. Every wannabe sergeant knew that list by heart. This morning, right before court, Vega's cell phone began dinging with texts from fellow officers. Texts Vega couldn't answer because Isadora Jenkins and the county's attorney, Henry Zaroff, wouldn't let him check his phone.

"A sergeant's promotion is not a reward," Vega explained. "It's based on a civil service exam I took more than a year and a half ago—"

"Your Honor," Isadora Jenkins cut him off. "Mr. Carver's statement is factually inaccurate. The department is in no way rewarding Detective Vega. If my colleague and I could approach the bench with Mr. Carver to explain."

"Very well." Edgerton tugged at his black robes. "Let's get on with it." The heat was making him irritable. It was making everyone in the courtroom irritable.

The court clerk produced a small step stool and helped Jenkins onto it. Carver and Zaroff flanked her on either side. Her voice was a soothing murmur, soft enough to remain unintelligible to the jury. But Vega, on the witness stand, could hear every word.

"Mr. Zaroff spoke to Detective Vega's supervisor this morning," said Jenkins. "The department is promoting another officer instead. A man named Drew Banks."

Vega felt like he'd just been tossed out a ten-story window. Drew Banks was the next officer on the sergeant's list *below* Vega. What were all the texts on his phone about, if not to tell him he was getting promoted?

Unless . . .

Unless it was to tell him that he'd been passed over.

"Given this new information," said Edgerton, "I will rule with the defense—"

Two court officers burst through the rear doors. All heads in the packed courtroom turned.

"Folks, we need everyone to exit the building right away," said one of the men. "Officers in the hallway will direct you to the emergency stairs."

Edgerton banged his gavel and adjourned court. Vega stepped down from the stand and hustled over to Adele and Joy.

"What's going on?" asked Joy.

"Someone probably called in a bomb threat." Vega put a reassuring hand on his daughter's shoulder. "These things are almost always false alarms."

Vega felt less sure of his words as they followed the crowd into the hallway. There was a coiled, nervous energy to the cops and court officers that didn't look routine as they directed civilians toward the exit stairs. One Broad Plains cop turned away from the crowd and talked excitedly into his radio. Two court officers hugged each other. A civilian with a court employee lanyard around her neck passed by in tears.

"I'm so sorry about the promotion, Jimmy," said Adele.

"Yeah. Me too." The pain was theoretical at this point. It would hurt more later, when the shock wore off. Right now, his mind was elsewhere. He kissed Adele on the cheek. "Get Joy out of here. I'll catch you later."

"You're not coming with us?"

"I want to find out what's going on. Last I checked, I'm still a county detective. For now, anyway."

Chapter 2

It wasn't a bomb threat. It was something much worse.

"Somebody shot a court officer in the security lot," one of the local cops told Vega.

"Who?"

"Darryl Williams." Vega knew a lot of the court officers, but not Williams. "Word is a judge was hit too."

"Which judge?"

"Julia Spruce."

"Is the suspect in custody?"

"Don't think so," said the officer. "It's crazy outside. Everybody's running around."

Vega took the staircase one flight down to the security lot. A blast of humid air assaulted him as he pushed open the door. The midday sun cut into his vision like the straight edge of a razor. He had no gun. No Kevlar vest. Not even a pair of sunglasses. He lacked all the normal things he'd carry as a cop because his lawyer had warned him not to bring them to court.

But that wasn't what bothered him. It was the crowd. The disorder. Courthouse employees were wandering the fenced-in lot, talking on their cell phones or crying and hugging each other. Court officers were traipsing in and out of the building, touching doors and vehicles with their bare, sweaty hands. Nobody was taking charge.

Vega cupped a hand over his brow and stepped closer to the tight circle of bodies surrounding a white golf cart with blood trailing down the front of it. Judge Julia Spruce was sprawled in the backseat. She'd sloughed off her judicial robes, revealing capri pants and a T-shirt beneath, all of it spattered in blood. Her black hair was raked back from her pale white face as she wadded up her robe and held it to her left ear. The robe had the wet, oily, maroon color of soaked blood. A little man in gold-rimmed glasses sat next to her, fanning her with a stack of papers. Her court clerk, Albert Pearsall. He'd been a clerk since Vega was a rookie in uniform. His gray hair was tousled, though he otherwise looked unharmed. His lips were open in horror, his mustache framing them like two parentheses.

On the ground in front of the golf cart lay Darryl Williams. His dark blue uniform shirt was soaked with blood. His face had turned the color of cigarette ash. His lips were nearly white. Another court officer knelt beside him, leaning hard on his chest, trying to stop the blood spurting from a spot below his collarbone. A squeal of sirens in the distance punctuated his efforts.

Vega scanned the perimeter. The fence was eight feet high, slatted in solid metal, rimmed in razor wire—and locked. No way could a shooter have done this sort of damage on the ground and gotten away. The surrounding buildings—a parking garage, a row of delis and fast-food joints—were all one story. Which meant the assailant hadn't aimed from close by, either. This was a sniper attack, accomplished at a distance, with a scope and a high-powered rifle.

If the shooter was still in position, they were all fish in a barrel.

He walked over to a court officer he recognized. Soft, fleshy chin. Chest and arms like a bouncer—useful for keeping defendants in their place. He was a head taller than Vega. Vega didn't remember his name until he read it off his name tag: *McAllister*.

"Hey there, McAllister. Jimmy Vega. County homicide. You've got too many people here. Can you round up a couple of your guys and move them out of the lot?"

McAllister didn't budge. Maybe it was the cheap suit that made Vega look like a defendant. "Our priority is Darryl . . . and the judge."

"You're gonna have a lot more priorities if the shooter's still in position." Vega gestured to the fence. "You've got a potential active sniper out there. He could be reloading as we speak."

McAllister called over to two court officers by the golf cart.

"Gary, Cesar—get everyone out of here who isn't helping Darryl and the judge." He turned back to Vega. "That means you too, Vega."

"I'm leaving. Just one question."

"What?"

Vega pointed to a corner of the courthouse's white stucco facade. Above a surveillance camera sat an electronic receiver that Vega recognized as a ShotSpotter—a device designed to isolate the location of gunfire. "Where's the feed for that go?"

The surveillance room was in the basement of the courthouse. It was the size of a projectionist's booth. Banks of video monitors lined the wall above a desk littered with empty coffee cups and vending machine wrappers. A county dispatch radio crackled with codes and commands. More cops were arriving on scene. The FBI was on its way.

"Don't know what you expect to see," the court officer on duty grunted. He spoke from the side of his mouth, his eyes never leaving the computer screen on his desk. "The

ShotSpotter's wrong. Been wrong before. They spend a fortune on this high-tech crap and it ain't worth a damn."

"You're sure about that?"

"It picked up a single shot ninety degrees due west. There's no vantage point in that direction, plus two people were shot."

"The bullet could have ricocheted after hitting Williams. You have video, right?"

The officer swiveled his chair to face Vega. He had lizard eyes and a paunch barely concealed beneath his Kevlar vest. "I have video for the FBI."

"Pretend I'm the FBI."

"Pretend I give a rat's ass who you are."

Vega pulled a pen and a small notepad out of his jacket. A detective's habit. He always carried it. He squinted pointedly at the man's name tag. "P. Daley," he said slowly, scribbling down the name. "I assume there's only one P. Daley in the courthouse?"

"Why?"

"So that when my superiors at the county police ask why I couldn't see the video, I can give them a name."

Daley exhaled slowly, like he was dealing with an incompetent. Vega suspected he was the sort of cop who referred to officers with college degrees as "professor" and everyone who came on the job after him as "kid." He swiveled back to the screen and brought up the video.

Vega watched a small white golf cart putter into the frame, traveling north from the records building to the courthouse. At the wheel sat a tall, athletic-looking Black man who appeared to be in his late thirties or early forties. Court Officer Darryl Williams. His shaved head glistened with sweat. Behind him sat two figures: Judge Julia Spruce, a white woman in her fifties with long black wavy locks, save for one very prominent strip of white hair down her left side. Vega thought it made her look like a skunk. Next to her, on the inside seat of the cart, sat her clerk, Albert Pearsall. With his neatly trimmed gray mustache and gold-rimmed glasses, he looked like a modern-day Teddy Roosevelt.

Darryl Williams stopped the cart near the rear entrance door to the courthouse and jumped out of the vehicle with an easy stride that suggested to Vega that Williams liked his job. He was probably the sort of court officer who chatted with all the judges and clerks. Maybe he was chatting to them now. The judge appeared to be leaning forward slightly, as if in conversation with him, though it was hard to tell from the security footage. Williams turned to the backseat and bent forward, perhaps to help the judge out of the cart. Then he reared back and clutched a hand to his upper right chest, his face stretched tight with shock and disbelief.

"The shot clearly came from the west," said Vega. "The angle of the shooting confirms it."

"Then it punched a hole through the fence," said Daley. "There's nothing else high enough in that direction."

Vega didn't see any bullet holes in the fence when he was outside. "Can I get a satellite map on your computer?"

Daley rolled back his chair and waved his hand with an exaggerated flourish. "Knock yourself out, *Detective*."

Vega took Daley's seat and settled in at the computer. He forced himself to blot out the turmoil going on outside. The bank of video monitors above him captured it in grainy footage with a fisheye lens. In the security lot, EMTs loaded Darryl Williams's body onto a stretcher. On the courthouse roof, SWAT officers in flak gear took up positions. Out front, local cops redirected traffic. Vega tried to tune out the static bursts of chatter on the dispatch radio and tapped some keys until he found the right screen. He wasn't looking for high-rises. He was looking for something else. A very specific building to the west.

Down the hall, two sets of dress shoes clicked briskly

along the linoleum tile. Only the FBI wore dress shoes to a crime scene.

"You don't need to be here anymore, Vega," said Daley.

"I'm a county homicide detective and this is a county building."

"Yeah, but now the FBI—" Daley stopped midsentence when the dispatcher came over the airwaves and asked for radio silence. Something important had happened and needed to be relayed privately. Vega was pretty sure what that information was. On one of the monitors, he watched an EMT pull a sheet over Darryl Williams's face before he loaded him into the ambulance.

"Goddamn," said Daley, slapping the edge of his desk. "The poor bastard."

Two FBI agents in identical navy-blue windbreakers edged into the doorway of the small room.

"You just heard, I take it," said the shorter of the two agents. "About the court officer?" He had the lean, compact build of a soccer player and dimples that contracted his cheeks, even when he was affecting a somber expression. The agent extended a hand to Daley. "Doug Hewitt. FBI Joint Terrorism Task Force. Special agent in charge." He had boyishly thick chestnut-colored hair with just a wisp of gray at the sides. A dye-job, Vega suspected. He wasn't as young as he pretended to be.

"And this is my associate, Richard Fiske."

Fiske offered no words of greeting or eye contact. He felt like Hewitt's polar opposite. Silent. Dour. With crew-cut white-blond hair and sharp, leathery features. He brought to mind a villain out of Nordic noir.

"And you are?" Hewitt turned his gaze to Vega.

"Jimmy Vega. Detective. County homicide."

"Captain Waring assigned you to the case?"

"I was in the building already." Vega didn't give Hewitt a chance to ask why. "Has the shooter been apprehended?"

"We're working on it." *In other words, no.*

"How big is your search area?"

"We've secured a three-block perimeter around the premises."

"You might want to enlarge that," said Vega. "Officer Daley picked up a shot on the ShotSpotter ninety degrees due west. The only building that could clear the eight-foot-high fence from that angle is the Broad Plains Bus Terminal."

"The ShotSpotter's wrong." Daley jabbed a thumb in Vega's direction. "That's what I've been trying to tell this guy. The terminal's only two stories tall. And it's four blocks away."

"A high-powered rifle could certainly hit a target more than half a mile away," said Vega. "That's four blocks. Plus, the terminal's on a rise. I know, because after nine-eleven, the county police established a command headquarters on the building's second floor. They chose it for its visibility."

Hewitt walked up behind Vega's chair and considered the aerial view on the screen.

"Is the command center still at the bus terminal?"

"They don't use it much these days," said Vega. "They have a newer operation at the county airport. But it's still there. And it's a great vantage point."

"Interesting." Hewitt turned to Fiske. "Enlarge the perimeter to five blocks. Seal the terminal. No buses or passengers may enter or leave."

The Nordic ghost disappeared without saying a word. Vega wondered if he spoke at all. Hewitt swung his attention back to Vega.

"Can you show me this headquarters?"

Vega hesitated. He was a defendant in a ten-million-dollar lawsuit who'd just been passed over for a sergeant's promotion. Not the sort of poster boy Waring would choose to represent the county police. "Sir, it's just four blocks due west. I'm sure the FBI can find it without—"

"Time is of the essence, Detective. I need your help now. We can handle the paperwork with that boss of yours later." There was an edge to Hewitt's words that sent a flutter of alarm through Vega. The last thing he wanted was to get between two powerful men. "What I don't get," said Hewitt, "is why the bus terminal? Wouldn't it be quiet on a Monday afternoon? I would think a sniper would pick a place where he could melt into a crowd."

"You're not from the area, I take it."

"I was transferred about six months ago from the Denver office."

"Broad Plains is a major travel hub for asylum-seekers coming up from the border," Vega explained. "When the buses come in, it's a madhouse."

Chapter 3

Cold, clammy air greeted Vega as he followed Agent Hewitt into the Broad Plains Bus Terminal, now rimmed with emergency vehicles and police posted at every door. Sunlight faded, replaced by the glare of overhead fluorescent lights. An electronic billboard overhead flashed bus arrivals and departures to small towns in the Midwest and up and down the eastern seaboard: Columbus, Ohio. Richmond, Virginia. Schenectady, New York. Lowell, Massachusetts. Lewiston, Maine. All were followed by a single word in capital letters: *DELAYED*.

Nobody was going anywhere.

In the main waiting area, every bolted seat was filled with a warm body, most of them Hispanic-looking. Women nursed crying babies. Men crouched against walls, their eyes nervously scanning the police officers who clustered by the exits. Children stuck close to parents and grandparents, their little fingers holding onto the sleeves and belt loops of adults, as if fearful of being separated.

"It's like a third-world country in here," said Hewitt.

It's like a modern-day Ellis Island, thought Vega. It was the same throughout so many small towns and cities in America. So much hope. So much fear.

"The terminal was slowly dying until recently," Vega explained. "Most people drive or fly or take an Uber these days. For people coming up from the border, however, this is the only means of transportation they have to reunite with family members."

"Speaking of which," said Hewitt, "how's your Spanish?"

"Fluent." It was the language of Vega's youth, the one his mother and grandmother argued and joked with him in when he was growing up in the Bronx. He used to be embarrassed that his grandmother never learned English. Or that his mother never lost her native Puerto Rican inflections, especially when he was still married into Wendy's large, Jewish family. Now, he felt only admiration for how hard they'd worked to give him a footing in both worlds.

"Good to know," said Hewitt. "I might ask you to stick around and help with the interviews."

The two men picked their way across the waiting area, dodging backpacks, overflowing trash cans, and children playing tag. The squawk of police radios intensified as they climbed the stairs to the second floor. There were no passengers up here. Only cops with badges slung around their necks and cell phones plastered to their ears. They spoke in loud, authoritative voices and strutted around with an inflated sense of self-importance, like they were the guests of honor at a party of their own making.

Hewitt scanned the ceiling pockmarked with water stains and plaster repairs. The terminal had seen better days. "I don't see surveillance cameras on this level."

"There aren't any, to my knowledge," said Vega. "Only employees of the terminal or law enforcement are allowed up here."

At the far end of the hallway, a Greyhound manager was pacing in the doorway of the command post. He was nearly as wide as he was tall, with sweat stains encircling the armpits of his bright blue uniform shirt. He was conversing with someone, but he seemed to be doing all the talking. When he turned, Vega felt himself shrink a little as the other man's gaze fell upon him. The man had the straight-backed stance of an ex-soldier and the flinty-eyed bearing of a Depression-era dustbowl farmer, all hollow cheeks and stoic endurance. In the best of times, Captain Frank Waring never looked happy to see Vega.

This was not the best of times.

Hewitt strode forward, working his dimples into a smile that reminded Vega of a game-show host. "Fraaank. Good to see you."

"Doug." Waring nodded. He was never one for bombast or flattery. "Why is Detective Vega here? He's on inactive status." Waring held Vega's gaze just long enough to make him squirm. *Inactive*—that was one way to describe Vega's current situation. Maybe his future one too.

"Detective Vega was the one who suggested that the shooter might have fired from this location." Hewitt pulled a pair of latex gloves from his jacket and slipped them on. Then he crouched down and examined the locking mechanism on the open door. It was a solid wood-core door with a veneer of dark brown finish. Neither the door nor the frame showed any evidence of being tampered with.

The shooter hadn't broken in. Vega was wrong. *Ay, puñeta!* He'd brought the FBI and his own agency here for nothing.

Hewitt straightened. "The door doesn't appear to have been breached. Yet you're still up here, Frank. You haven't pulled your men or called off the search. So that leaves two possibilities. One, the sniper had a key. Or two, the door was never locked to begin with."

Bad news either way, thought Vega. By bringing the FBI here, he'd just highlighted his own department's failure to secure the post—a failure that cost a court officer his life and wounded a sitting judge.

"It has no bearing on the investigation," said Waring, sidestepping the question. "The sniper didn't fire from here." He pressed a set of binoculars into Hewitt's hands and led him past desks with peeling wood veneer and boxy computers that had been written off years ago. The command center hadn't been used since the operation was moved to the county airport. The whole place had a dusty, museum feel to it.

At the window, glazed with years of oils and grime, Waring gestured across the street to two new two-story buildings. They filled up the space that had once supplied a clear view of the courthouse.

"You see?" said Waring. "The shot didn't come from here."

Vega felt a moment of relief that his department's screw-up wouldn't become public, followed by an aftershock of having been wrong. Or was he? The location was right, if only the sniper could clear those buildings.

"What about the roof?" asked Vega. "Is there some way to get access?"

A blast of heat hit the men as soon as they opened the hatch to the roof. The air clung like Saran Wrap to Vega's skin. He made a wide circle, dodging the fan-coil vents and air-conditioning compressors that stuck up like growths from the silver-coated surface. Ten blocks to the southeast, the city rose in a tight knot of towers, all glinting steel and smoky glass. The highway snaked serenely past, diffuse and unremitting as an ocean.

Vega turned his gaze to the two new two-story buildings, their oversized windows mirroring the bulk of the beige concrete bus terminal in their reflection.

"Well, I'll be damned," said Hewitt. He handed Captain Waring the binoculars. "There's a thirty-foot radius, end-to-end, between the two buildings, with a clear view of the security lot. Plenty of space for a sniper with a scope to take out his target."

Waring looked through the lenses, then raked his gaze along the metallic surface of the roof. "I don't see a shell casing."

"If he was experienced enough to shoot his target in a thirty-foot radius from four blocks away," said Hewitt, "he was experienced enough to take the shell casing with him. I want crime scene up here right away."

"Will do," said Waring.

Hewitt kept his gaze on Waring. "Your detective was right."

"If you mean that he suggested a viable possibility, then yes."

Vega cringed. Hewitt was using Vega to humiliate his boss—with no thought of the consequences.

"I'd like your detective to stick around a bit," said Hewitt. "Maybe talk to some of the passengers in the terminal. I understand he's fluent in Spanish."

"So long as you put in the requisition and it's on the FBI's dime," Waring replied.

They were talking about Vega like he wasn't there. Or rather, like he was someone's "boy," mere chattel, available for hire. Disgusted, Vega began walking the roof, searching for any evidence that the sniper had been up here. On the street below, emergency vehicles blocked off the intersections and double-parked along the curbs. It was going to be a long, hot afternoon. Nobody was going anywhere.

Waring sidled up beside him. "I didn't oppose your promotion, Detective. I want you to know that."

Hewitt had gone downstairs. Captain Waring was alone. For the first time Vega could ever recall, his boss looked unsure of himself. The only sound between them was the far-off wail of a police siren and the voice of the county dispatcher relaying commands and codes over Waring's radio.

"Legal made the case for bypassing you," Waring continued. "Chief Lakeworth accepted their rationale. It was a done deal before I was ever involved."

Legal. In other words, the county's attorney, Henry Zaroff.

"Is there anything I can do about it?"

"Not a thing," said Waring. "I asked."

Vega couldn't hide his surprise. He never felt liked by Frank Waring, a man who confused humor with insubordination and seemed to regard Vega as a source of the latter every time he opened his mouth. Vega had none of the attributes his boss so keenly prized: a military background. Disciplined adherence to the chain of command. A passion for procedural detail. Yet Waring had allowed Vega back on homicide after the December shooting. He accepted Vega's mea culpa for being present without permission at a botched Lake Holly police surrender last January. Perhaps Vega had misread his boss. Not that it mattered now. Lawyers run the world. Cops just clean it up.

"You've made quite an impression on Agent Hewitt," said Waring.

"I'm sorry," said Vega. "I didn't mean to—"

"Never complain. Never explain," said Waring. "Just remember that you're not FBI and he's not the county police."

"We work together."

"When you work with the FBI, you work *for* them, not with them. When a man like Douglas Hewitt invites you to dinner, make sure you're not on the menu."

"Is that a personal warning about Hewitt? Or a general one about the FBI?"

"Both," said Waring. "Let's get out of this heat."

Vega fumbled to pull a handkerchief from his pocket to wipe his sweaty face. That's when he saw it. Poking up from a crevice where a caulked vent met the roof flashing. Not a bullet casing.

A toothpick.

Chapter 4

Crime scene bagged the toothpick while Vega questioned the detained immigrants downstairs in the bus terminal. They were packed into the main waiting area, surrounded by bags and backpacks. Babies cried. Children with runny noses and hacking coughs scampered about. The clammy, fetid air probably didn't help. It was laced with a mix of diesel fumes, sweat, and the discarded diapers from overflowing trash cans.

Some of the immigrants were too scared to help. Others tried but had nothing to offer. Many had spent weeks on their journey north, traveling through dangerous lands. They'd long ago learned to tune out all but their own survival needs.

"They're not going to help you," said a familiar voice.

Vega turned to see a lanky Latina with short kinky hair, dusted blond at the tips. She was wearing a black windbreaker with *ICE* printed across it.

"Not with you and your *migra* pals running around," said Vega.

"Actually, they speak to us. They're afraid not to answer questions posed by Immigration and Customs. You?" She grinned. "They're savvy enough to know they don't have to talk to some county dude in a bad suit."

"I had to wear this for court."

Her playful expression turned serious. "How's that going, *mano*?" *Brother*. Well, half, anyway. Michelle Vega-Lopez's kinky curls were nothing like Vega's soft waves. Her body was more angular. Her lips, thicker. Her eyes, less hooded. People said they shared a strong resemblance, but Vega didn't see it. Or maybe he didn't want to see it since any resemblance between them reminded Vega of his two-timing father whom he hadn't seen in years.

"I found out on the stand that I've been passed over for my sergeant's promotion."

"*Ay bendito.*" All the Bronx-girl toughness drained from her face. "They can do that?"

"Since the last contract," said Vega. "The new provisions allow the brass to skip up to two names to promote someone. It was supposed to be a way to encourage promotions of women and people of color. But they can use it any way they like."

"Is the person they're promoting a woman?"

"No. Drew Banks is a Black man. But the next name after Drew is Tracy Romano. A white woman."

"You are so screwed."

He didn't want to talk about this anymore. It was already burning a hole of regret in his gut. "What are you doing here?"

"Two of my colleagues were scouting the terminal for a gangbanger who should have been *deportado* a long time ago."

"They find him?"

"No," said Michelle. "But they stuck around after the shooting to help with security. I was in the area, so I came as well."

That is the problem with law enforcement in the county, thought Vega. *Too many damn agencies*. "You get any information?"

"Directly?" She laughed. "ICE is the last to know anything. But I'll tell you this: That judge, Julia Spruce, was the target. That's for damn sure. Lotta people aren't in her fan club."

"Adele likes her."

"Snowflakes of a feather stick together."

Vega gave his sister a disapproving look. He didn't agree with all of Adele's views, but he didn't like Michelle belittling them either.

"Oh, come on, *mano*. You know it's true. Adele likes Julia Spruce because she's soft on illegals."

"I've heard the judge is tolerant—"

"She's more than tolerant. It's a point of pride with her to ignore our deportation detainers. Know what we call her at ICE?"

"What?"

"Turn-'em-loose Spruce."

Vega grinned. "Catchy."

"You wouldn't think it was funny if you went to the courthouse to enforce an order of removal and your subject had already split because Spruce released him. You'd be as pissed as ICE."

"Maybe the FBI should be looking at one of *your* people for this shooting."

"If one of *my* people was gunning for her, trust me, they wouldn't miss." She pulled out a pack of gum and offered him a stick. He waved it away.

"Look, Jimmy," said Michelle, undoing the wrapper. "All I'm telling you is that plenty of people would like to see that woman off the bench. And not all of them are thinking *retirement*. We keep a whole folder full of her most outrageous cases in our office."

"I'd like to see that."

"And I'd like to keep my job."

"That makes one of us who will." Vega's phone dinged with a text from Hewitt, asking him to come upstairs. "I've got to go," he told his sister.

She put a hand on his arm and gave it a reassuring

squeeze. "I'm so sorry about the promotion." Her words carried the gravitas of a condolence. A part of his career had just died. They both knew it might never come back.

Vega's boss and the local police were gone by the time he walked back upstairs. Aside from the bus terminal manager, Vega was the only one in the manager's office who wasn't FBI.

He felt a certain shyness suddenly, being in a room full of federal agents. Early in his law enforcement career, he'd briefly entertained the idea of applying to the FBI. The credentials and expertise demanded by the agency were daunting. Vega never even finished filling out the paperwork. Part of it was fear of rejection. But another part of him simply wasn't sure he wanted to stay a police officer. He'd backed into the job when his girlfriend—later wife, later ex-wife—got pregnant with Joy and he needed a steady paycheck and medical insurance. He ended up loving the job. Loving how much it mattered and how much he mattered when he was doing it. But by the time he discovered those things about himself, the window of opportunity for something more had closed behind him.

He supposed a lot of ambitions were thwarted that way. You didn't know what you wanted until it was no longer yours to have.

The agents were crowded around a video monitor. Vega loosened his tie and sloughed off his jacket. The room was hot. He felt ready to pass out from the heat of all these bodies. He was dying for a shower. And a change of clothes. He wondered what those poor people downstairs in the waiting area felt like. Some of them had been traveling for days without sleep or showers or anything resembling a real meal.

"We picked up something odd on the terminal's surveillance video," said Hewitt. A sweat-darkened lock of dyed hair, the color of dried blood, drooped across his lined forehead. Vega could see the gray roots beneath. "I'd like to get your reaction." Hewitt nodded to the manager. "Run the footage from the beginning again, please."

A time stamp on the bottom of the footage allowed Vega to track the events second by second. The footage began at 12:43 p.m. It showed a male figure in a baseball cap with a dark, bushy beard and sunglasses walking in the eastbound direction of the terminal area, toward the front exit doors. The man wore loose-fitting khakis, an army-green, long-sleeve T-shirt, and boots. He was on the burly side. Vega estimated him to be about five eight and a hundred sixty-five pounds. Between the beard, cap, and sunglasses, Vega couldn't see much of his face, but he looked to be on the light-skinned side. White or nearly white.

Over his shoulder, he carried a black knapsack—more than big enough for a disassembled rifle.

"The courthouse shooting occurred at twelve-forty p.m.," said Hewitt. "This video was taken three minutes later."

"He looks pretty calm," Vega noted. "Does he show up in any footage prior to the shooting?"

"We have a couple of brief shots of him moving through the terminal," said Hewitt. "But the oddest thing is that after the shooting, he moves again through the terminal. He could have simply left by the fire exit door at the bottom of the stairs. That would have been the fastest escape route."

Vega thought about his conversation with his sister. "ICE was in the terminal before the shooting. It's possible one of their cruisers was parked outside the exit door."

"We'll check that out," said Hewitt. "That plays into what I brought you up to see." He pointed to the screen. The time stamp was 12:45. There was a commotion by the front doors of the terminal. Vega noted the two ICE agents Michelle had mentioned. They were questioning people, looking for that suspected gang member. People tried to move away but they were crowded in by all the baggage and bodies and church volunteers pushing juice carts, creating a blockage that was impossible to traverse.

Vega scanned the crowd for the bearded figure in a baseball cap, but there were so many men in baseball caps, Vega couldn't isolate the right one. He wondered if the suspect had escaped through the front doors because of the commotion with ICE.

And then he saw him, heading away from the crowd in the opposite direction at 12:46 p.m. Only he wasn't alone anymore. He had a young girl by the wrist. Vega estimated her to be maybe ten or eleven years of age. She had strong indigenous features, common to many rural Central Americans. A squarish build. Asian-looking eyes. High cheekbones. She wore jeans and a pink T-shirt with a unicorn on the front. Her dark hair was swept up in a ponytail. The video wasn't good enough to make out her facial expression, but her walk was stiff and hesitant.

She wasn't accompanying the subject by choice.

"Where did she come from?" Vega asked the agents in the room. "Was she alone?"

"We found some earlier footage that indicates she was traveling with a Hispanic woman in her twenties or thirties," said Hewitt. "Likely a mother or other relative. They were sitting in the area where the church volunteers were serving juice and cookies, so we have to assume the two are recent border-crossers bound for family members somewhere in the region."

"Where's the woman?"

"We don't know," said Hewitt. "We suspect perhaps they were taking turns in the bathroom so that one could watch their stuff and keep hold of their seats. Anybody mention this girl to you?"

"No one," said Vega. No one had mentioned anything. How was that possible? he wondered. How could this bearded man in a baseball cap and sunglasses drag a girl by the arm across the terminal without someone noticing? Then again, Vega reminded himself, he hadn't spent the last few months on a perilous journey north. He hadn't witnessed the stuff they had. The rapes. The beatings. The casual inhumanity. If he had, maybe he'd keep his head down too.

The girl and suspect walked out of range of the camera. Two minutes later, another camera picked up the girl near the stairwell, alone. Then she slipped into the crowd and disappeared.

"Where's the suspect?" asked Vega.

"We can't find him on any of the footage after this," said Hewitt. "Not inside or outside the terminal, though we're still looking. We believe the beard was a disguise. He could look like pretty much anyone under all that hair."

Vega replayed the sequence of events. "The subject tries to leave, perhaps via the fire exit in the stairwell, but something outside the door spooks him. He changes plans and walks across the terminal. But ICE officers are near the exit doors. So he grabs the girl. Why? As a hostage? To blend in?"

"We're not sure," said Hewitt. "Our theory is that he grabbed the girl, intending to use her as cover to get out of the building and kill her once he was away from the scene. But she fought back while he was slipping out of his disguise. So he had a choice: get away or get the girl. He chose escape."

"I didn't see the girl in the waiting area downstairs," said Vega.

"That's what I was afraid you'd say," said Hewitt. "Most likely, she and her adult female companion boarded one of the last buses out of here. We're checking the passenger lists now. Fiske is going to enlarge our best shot of her and put a BOLO out to law enforcement. See if we can track her down."

Vega squinted at the girl on the screen in the pink unicorn T-shirt. "If she fought back while he was slipping out of his disguise, she knows what he looks like."

"We believe so," said Hewitt.

None of the agents spoke. The only sound Vega heard was the crackle of police radios and the whir of an ancient fan circulating air through the stifling room.

"A guy who plans and executes a shooting like this, from a well-cased vantage point, isn't about to leave witnesses," said Vega. "I wouldn't make any mention of the shooting in the alert."

"We're not," said Hewitt. "We're calling her a missing person. And hoping like hell we can find her before our subject does."

Chapter 5

"I can't believe we're here!" said Aurelia Rosales. "Safe at last!"

Eli cradled her left wrist and looked back over her shoulder at the exit doors of the bus terminal. Had the man seen her leave? Seen her cross the street? She'd be easy to spot in her pink unicorn T-shirt. Her teeth and gums throbbed from biting the man's palm when he cupped a hand over her mouth. She didn't tell her mother any of this, however. She didn't want to alarm her.

"New York." Aurelia said the words with almost mystical wonder. "They call it the 'Big Apple' for some reason. I don't know why."

Eli didn't see anything that looked like apples. Just a bunch of one- and two-story stucco and brick buildings on either side of the street. A nail salon. A tattoo parlor. A bodega with advertisements in English on the greasy window. None of it felt like the New York Eli had seen on television in Guatemala.

"Where's the Statue of Liberty?"

"I don't know," said Aurelia. "Why does it matter? We'll be with my brother and his family. That's all that's important."

Eli tried to keep her mind off her wrist by thinking about finally meeting her uncle Luis and his family. Her

Aunt Miriam. Her three teenage cousins, Franklin, Christian, and Wilmer. Her whole life, she'd heard stories about her mother's big brother who'd left rural Guatemala at seventeen and become rich in America. Rich enough to support Eli's grandmother. Rich enough to bring Eli and her mother here now, beyond the grasp of her abusive father.

"Will I get to go to school again?" Eli had had to leave school four months ago, after they hid at her grandmother's house, a two-hour bus ride from Nejapa, in the mountains. A mudslide had washed away the bridge to the primary school there three years ago, so she couldn't attend.

"Of course you will go to school, *mi corazón,*" said Aurelia. "That's why we're here. To keep you safe. And get you an education."

Eli cast another glance back over her shoulder. She couldn't wait for *Tío* Luis to get them away from this place. "Where are we meeting him?"

Her mother unfolded the scrap of paper with his cell number on it. She'd borrowed one of the volunteer's phones to call Luis. They didn't have a phone of their own. They didn't have anything but an envelope of asylum petition papers from a judge at the border and two small backpacks of clothes and toiletries that some volunteers had given them at the bus station in Richmond, Virginia.

"He said to walk through a big shopping mall," Aurelia explained. "His car will be on the other side. He told me it's too hard to park near the terminal."

The mall was one block north of the terminal. In the shop windows, Eli saw mannequins dressed in silky shorts and sandals with spiked heels. Their legs were longer than Eli's whole body. Everyone was so tall here. Even young children. Which was probably why people assumed that Eli was ten years old.

She'd be twelve next month.

A blast of cold air hit them as they entered the mall. It felt like they were back in the *hieleras*—the ice boxes—that the border patrol kept them in for days after they turned themselves in. Eli shivered as they walked the white marble floor. They passed a food stand. Eli's stomach rumbled. All they'd eaten for the past four days was chips and cookies and tiny cups of applesauce and canned fruit that the volunteers at the bus terminals handed out. They had no money.

They left the mall at the other end and exited onto a side street. No one was waiting at the curb. Aurelia squinted at the traffic stopped a block away at a light. "He wouldn't leave us," she murmured in a childlike tone, as she clutched the scrap of paper tightly in her hand. She was five years old when Luis left Guatemala. That was twenty-four years ago, when the borders were demarcated with chicken wire and people traveled back and forth with the seasons.

Except Luis didn't. He left Nejapa and never returned, sending money and photos instead. Of his big house. His new cars. His wife and three sons. In their small mountain town, people spoke of Luis Monroy with reverence. He helped bring Guatemalans over to the United States and got them jobs and housing.

Aurelia's only clear memory of her older brother was when he used to carry her on his back to church on Sundays. And one other—the corn husk doll he made for her shortly before he left for the United States. She carried it with her on the journey north, but it got washed away when they crossed the Rio Grande into Texas.

"What does his car look like?" asked Eli.

"He said it's dark blue and big. Like a Jeep."

They waited in the shade of the mall's parking garage. Eli's wrist swelled from where the bad man had grabbed it. Her mother was too keyed up to notice. The minutes ticked past. Each car that slowed gave them hope. None of them were *Tío* Luis.

Finally, a shiny blue Jeep pulled to the curb. It had a big chrome front bumper, polished to a blinding gleam. A man got out of the driver's seat. He was short like Eli's mother, only much broader, with thick, black, fuzzy eyebrows that matched the fuzz of crew-cut hair that covered his head. He was clean-shaven and dressed in a white, short-sleeved, knit shirt, untucked from his jeans. On his left wrist was a gold-colored watch with many dials.

He looked just as Eli's mother had described him: her big, rich, American brother.

"Aurelia." He hugged Eli's mother stiffly. "I wouldn't have recognized you, even from the photos." His Spanish was flat, with only a trace of the Guatemalan nasal twang. He didn't smile. Sometimes people in her country didn't because they were ashamed of their crooked or missing teeth. But this felt different. This felt like he never smiled. He gave Eli the same wooden hug. "And you must be Elizabeth."

"Eli," she mumbled shyly.

"You are in the United States now," he admonished her. "Elizabeth is a better name." He opened the back door of the big blue Jeep. "Climb in. We need to get moving."

Eli poked her head inside the air-conditioned interior with its plush, clean seats and spotless rugs. She expected to see *Tía* Miriam and maybe one or two of her three cousins. There was nobody. Nobody had come to welcome them after their long journey.

They were probably all working, Eli told herself. It *was* a weekday, after all. Things would be different once they settled in.

Aurelia walked around to the front passenger seat and climbed inside. Luis pulled away from the curb. A few minutes later, they were traveling on a highway that seemed to glide effortlessly beneath their wheels. No potholes. No bumps. Eli was amazed how smooth the roads were in the United States. The skyline of steel and glass faded, replaced by much smaller brick and wooden buildings. The hills were full of tall, sturdy green trees and little else.

"Will we see the Statue of Liberty from the road?" Eli asked hopefully.

Her uncle laughed. "You thought you were going to New York City? New York City is a hundred kilometers south of here, silly girl. New York is a whole big state, not just a city."

Eli felt foolish. She said nothing after that and just watched the scenery change. The buildings fascinated her. None had gates around them. How did people keep thieves out? She didn't dare ask. She didn't want her uncle to laugh at her again.

Her mother filled her uncle in on how everyone back in Nejapa was doing. He listened but didn't ask many questions. Eli supposed that he felt shy and awkward with his sister after so many years apart.

"Mami appreciates the money you send each month," said Aurelia, referring to Eli's grandmother, *Abuelita Concepción*.

"Money, yes." Luis tapped the steering wheel. "Everybody appreciates Luis's money." His words hung in the air, like a bad smell that lingers, even after the cause has gone. Eli sensed her mother had touched a nerve.

Luis turned his gaze from the windshield and scrutinized Aurelia in the front passenger seat. "You don't look all beaten up."

Aurelia stared at her lap. Eli could tell her mother was embarrassed to be questioned about such a personal matter. And anyway, it had been months since her father's last rampage, the one that had finally made them flee. All the scars were inside.

"Did you tell the judge that you are running from your husband?" asked Luis.

"I did," said Aurelia. "That was the right thing to do, yes?"

Luis shrugged. "You won't get permanent asylum because you made a bad marriage, Aurelia. Don't count on staying, unless you want to spend the rest of your life running from the police."

"But we can't go back." Eli heard the panic in her mother's voice. "He'll find me and kill me. Kill us both." Aurelia lifted her eyes and set them pleadingly on his profile. "Can't you do something, *mi hermano*?"

"I did. I paid for you to come over. A hundred and sixteen thousand quetzales." He said the figure slowly, as if he'd been counting that money in his head, over and over, ever since it left his pocket. "That's about fifteen thousand American dollars. More money than you've seen in a lifetime."

"Eli . . . *Elizabeth*"—she corrected herself—"and I are very grateful to you."

"Gratitude is for gifts," Luis grunted. "This was not a gift. It was a loan."

"A . . . loan?"

"Yes. A loan. You're not five years old anymore, Aurelia. You make choices. You pay for them."

Silence. The only sound in the car was the soft hum of the air-conditioning. Eli could feel the tension between her mother and uncle. She said nothing.

"But I don't have any money," Aurelia said softly. "You? You are rich. Everyone in Nejapa says so."

"I have money because I worked for it," said Luis. "Every day. Seven days a week. That's why I have money."

Eli and her mother stayed quiet after that. The scenery changed again, from forests cut by small villages to pastures and orchards with only the occasional farmhouse or trailer in between. The hills were rolling and gentle—not like the wall of mountains that surrounded Nejapa.

Luis flipped his turn signal and made a right off the highway. The turnoff showed nothing—just a sign for North Kitchawan, with an arrow. He followed the winding two-lane road onto another road that led through what looked like a town. Eli saw a white steepled church. It sat across from a set of railroad tracks and a couple of streets with small wooden houses packed tightly together. All the roofs were pointy. Eli asked her mother why. Luis answered.

"It snows a lot here in winter. Snow slides off pointy roofs. You've never seen snow, have you?"

"Never," Eli replied.

"Well, one winter here," said Luis, "you'll see enough to last a lifetime."

The Jeep cruised slowly down the main road through town. The buildings all looked like people built them at different times out of whatever they had lying around: brick, wood, aluminum, concrete. Some were pretty, like a bank that sat in a reddish stone building with a year over the door: 1896. Others looked like they were built more recently. A food market with big plate-glass windows advertising specials. A silvery trailer that looked to be some sort of restaurant. A gas station. A building with unfinished wood siding and a beer can sign glowing in a small window. There was a patch of green opposite the railroad track with an American flag on a flagpole and some statue of a man with a gun. A war memorial, Eli supposed.

People in the United States really liked their flags and war memorials. Eli had seen hundreds since they left the border.

At the end of the road, Luis turned right. Eli noticed a red-brick building, two stories tall, with a flagpole out front and a playground on one side. A big board by the parking lot spelled out a message in English. Eli recognized just one word—the one word she had made herself memorize in English: *school.* It looked so beautiful with its paned-glass windows trimmed in white wood and that perfect curtain of lawn. Nobody had lawns in Guatemala. Things just grew. If they grew too much, you paved them over.

"That's the school!" Eli cried.

"That's the primary school," her uncle corrected. "You're too old to go there. You have to be under eleven."

"There's no school for over eleven?" asked her mother.

"It's far away."

Eli watched the school disappear through the back window as the vehicle turned out of town.

"I think," her uncle said slowly, "it would be better if Elizabeth spent some time learning English first. That way, you can both work to pay back the loan."

Aurelia turned to him, incredulous. "You mean . . . not go to school?"

"Not right away," said Luis. "Maybe . . . after you've both worked for a little while."

"But she was a very good math student in Nejapa."

Luis said nothing. He turned up a gravel road, slowing as he crossed a small bridge over a stream. Sunlight slanted through the trees. Their canopy choked off the sky. At the top, Eli expected to see her uncle's house. Instead, there was a collection of old trailer homes and laundry lines.

"Where is your house?" Aurelia asked Luis.

"About ten minutes from here."

"We're not staying with you?"

"There's no room." He didn't look at Aurelia as he spoke. "My oldest is starting community college in ten days. He needs a place to study." He seemed to be fumbling for words. Eli wondered if this was his idea or his wife's. "You'll have your own trailer. Don't worry."

He pulled the Jeep in front of the trailer on the end. It

was white with rust stains that snaked like tears down the sides of the windows. The screens bulged from their aluminum frames. A set of wooden steps, bowed and rotting, led to the front door. Weeds fanned out around the base, some of them deep enough to hide spare pieces of old machinery. The trailer next to theirs had a front porch cobbled out of unpainted lumber. A lumpy couch with frayed armrests sat beneath the metal awning, along with two plastic chairs. Chickens pecked freely in the grass. Eli noticed that someone who lived in one of the other trailers had fashioned a coop.

"Who else lives here?" asked Aurelia.

"Other Guatemalan families," said Luis. "Good people. They work in the dairy farms and orchards around here. I help get them jobs."

"You *help*?" asked her mother, her eyes suddenly hard. "Or they *pay* you to help?"

"They don't pay me," said Luis.

"But somebody does."

"Look," he said impatiently. "Do you want to live here or not? You can find your own place to live. It's all the same to me."

"We'll be fine here, Mami," said Eli, lacing her fingers into Aurelia's. She could see her mother was on the verge of tears. For twenty-four years, Luis Monroy had been an almost mythic figure to her mother. The man her father never would be.

The worst part of building your life around a dream is the day you have to face it up close.

"You're putting us in a labor camp," she hissed.

"I paid for you to come here!"

Her mother folded her arms across her chest. Her voice was flat and cold. "You didn't pay, Luis. You *loaned,* as you keep saying. And how, exactly, are we supposed to pay back this loan so that Eli can go to school? By taking in washing? Selling tamales from a cart?" That was the work her mother did in Nejapa.

"The gringos don't eat tamales. The Guatemalans and Mexicans make their own. And everyone has a washing machine or visits a laundromat. But it's apple season. We have plenty of orchards around here where you can make good money picking."

"We came two thousand miles . . . to pick fruit?"

"You came two thousand miles to get away from that *pendejo* of a husband," Luis shot back. "But since you're behaving like a princess—yes, *mi princesa,* you can pick fruit. And Elizabeth too. When I started out in this country, I could pick twelve bins a day."

Eli's mind was already trying to work out the numbers. Luis said they owed fifteen thousand American dollars. How long would it take to pay it back so she could go to school?

"How much?" she asked her uncle.

He turned to her like he had forgotten she was there. "How much what?"

"How many apples are in a bin? How much does the *patrón* pay per bin?"

"Each bin holds about a thousand apples," said her uncle. "Orchards pay twenty American dollars per bin."

"And how many bins do you think we could pick in a day?"

"You?" Luis frowned. "Four, I suppose. Your mother, maybe seven."

Eli did the math in her head. Five bins would pay $100 in American dollars. Fifty bins, $1000. Five hundred bins, $10,000. Which meant they'd need to pick at least seven hundred and fifty bins of produce to pay off the loan. Times a thousand apples. Three quarters of a million pieces of fruit. Eli's heart sank at the realization.

There weren't enough apple trees in the whole world to pay off such a loan.

Aurelia couldn't do the math, but she didn't need to. She knew it was bad. She stuck her lip out like she was five again. "I'm going to tell Mami how you are treating us!"

"Tell her. I don't care." Luis waved a hand dismissively. "She's not going to do anything to jeopardize the money I send her, and neither are you. Like they say all the time in this country, Aurelia: There are no free rides."

Chapter 6

By the time Vega took leave of the FBI agents at the bus terminal, it was too late to check in at the county police headquarters. Not that he wanted to anyway. All the talk would be about Forty-year Simonelli retiring and Drew Banks getting his spot.

Vega decided instead to head up to Anniston and surprise Adele. She and her colleagues were celebrating the opening of a new community center there. Normally, Vega hated such events. The endless speeches. The smarmy local politicians who dressed up their vote-gathering as selfless idealism. He was a practical man who spent his days dealing with people's worst impulses. Their greed. Their anger. Their propensity to lie and cheat. He viewed human beings—all human beings—as equally capable of good and evil.

No group, in his opinion, had a lock hold on virtue.

But this wasn't about politics. It was about Adele, the woman he not only loved but admired. A Harvard-educated attorney, she gave up a promising legal career to afford immigrants the opportunities her own undocumented Ecuadorian parents had never had. If this center in Anniston was important to her, then it was important to him. He wanted to be there.

Anniston was an old and venerable blue-collar city in the northern part of the county on the banks of the wide and majestic Hudson River. A century ago, it billed itself as the soap-making capital of the world. But the factories had long-ago shuttered, leaving a collection of fast-food joints and autobody shops in their place. The grand Victorians that once graced the hillsides had been bulldozed or repurposed into funeral parlors and social service agencies. The wood-frame triple-deckers had turned swaybacked and arthritic, their porch rails as gapped as an old man's teeth.

Black and white residents formed an uneasy truce until about ten years ago, when an influx of immigrants from Latin America began to move into the city. Their presence strengthened the local economy but changed it too. Delis became bodegas. Pizzerias became taco joints. The school population exploded, forcing officials to redistrict. Overnight, children in the whitest parts of the city began going to school with black and brown classmates.

Tensions reached the boiling point after two Ecuadorians were nearly beaten to death in a hate crime. Community leaders reached out to Adele. She'd brought her own town, Lake Holly, back from the brink of unrest eleven years ago with the founding of La Casa and its central goal of bridging the gap between newcomers and longtime residents. If she could do it in Lake Holly, the leaders of Anniston reasoned, why not there too?

After three years, that dream was finally coming together. Or so Vega thought, until he got within a block of the two-story, blue, wood-frame house that was the new headquarters of La Casa North. The street was cordoned off. A crowd of at least a hundred protesters gathered behind sawhorse barricades and police cruisers, waving American flags and banners and shouting angrily at the little blue house, all done up optimistically with colorful balloons and welcome banners.

No one was on the property's front or back lawns, though Vega was sure the celebration was meant to be both indoors and outdoors, given the warm weather. Vega wondered if Adele and her colleagues were as blindsided by this as he was. Either way, he was worried for their safety.

He parked his truck a block from the commotion and texted Adele. **I'm in Anniston. Came early to cheer you on. *Qué pasa?* There's a mob of angry white dudes with clubs and banners at the end of the street.**

Adele texted back. **Everyone's inside. We're safe. Let the local police handle this. It's too dangerous for you to try to get through.**

Maybe. But he couldn't sit here and do nothing. **Let me see what I can find out.**

He tucked his phone in his pocket and stepped out of his truck. The media had gotten wind of the protest. A couple of television stations were setting up cameras. Reporters were fitting themselves with microphones and finger-combing their hair in the humidity. This wasn't just some gathering of neighbors with a NIMBY complaint. Vega could see that as he scanned the crowd. All of them were white. The majority were men under thirty, though Vega saw some women and older males too. The young men wore quasi-military gear. Camouflage jackets. Army shirts. Khaki pants. Jack boots. They carried shields with insignias painted across them. Celtic crosses and jagged black lightning streaks and more obvious hate symbols too, like Nazi and Confederate flags. Some carried sticks and clubs. Others made the OK gesture with their raised hands in a silent call for white power. They were being led in various chants:

"Rapists and murderers, go home!"

"You will not replace us!"

"White lives matter!"

Vega looked over at the Anniston cops leaning on their patrol car behind the police barricade. Two officers and what looked like a sergeant. All of them white. They weren't making any moves to calm the crowd down. Vega needed to get to the cops and find out what their plan of action was—if indeed, they had one at all. But he couldn't see a way past the protestors without running straight through the gauntlet. A dark-brown-skinned Puerto Rican in a cheap suit would be easy prey. It wouldn't matter if he said he was a cop. No one knew him.

He stood across the street from the protest, at the rear bumper of one of the television-station vans, and watched, waiting for his opening. He noticed the chants were being led by a white man at the center of the crowd. The man looked to be in his early thirties. He was on the short side, muscular and clean-shaven with a shaved head. He wore dark sunglasses and a motorcycle vest with the words *Puritan Pride* and an American flag emblazoned on the back. But it wasn't the man that made Vega draw back in surprise. It was the person standing next to him. A young blonde in denim cutoffs and a pink tank top. She was barely five-feet tall—so tiny, the crowd nearly eclipsed her.

She was the last person Jimmy Vega ever expected to see at a rally like this.

He felt a great disappointment well up within him—as if his own daughter were in that crowd. Kaylee Wentz had been many things in her short twenty-five years of life. A victim. A survivor. A troubled runaway and addict. A hopeful young mother.

What she'd never been was hate filled.

He thought of Kaylee often on sleepless nights when the soft tread of memory carries burdens of its own. He'd had a lot of sleepless nights since the shooting. Nights when the cumulative weight of his work dragged him down with doubts and what-ifs. He'd awaken in a pile of sweaty, twisted blankets, his dog snoring by his side, and stare out the small cabin windows, watching the sky fade from black to blue to faded denim. He'd think back on the people he'd tried to save and the ones he couldn't.

She was supposed to have been one of his saves.

Perhaps his greatest save. Not because he'd kept her alive at six years of age as she hemorrhaged from a gunshot wound her own father had delivered, after killing her mother and brother and then turning the gun on himself. *No.* It was all the intervening years he'd tried to make a difference in her life. To be the one constant that told her she mattered. The Christmases he sent gifts to her aunt's house. The dinners and trips to amusement parks to celebrate a good report card or a birthday. The times he'd interceded with local police when she got caught shoplifting and later, with drugs. That night he'd canvassed the entire county to find her after she ran away.

He had to think back to the last time he'd seen her. It was maybe two and a half years ago. Kaylee's life was finally on track. She'd gotten her GED and was working as a secretary for a real estate firm, studying nights to get her Realtor's license. She'd recently given birth to a little boy and was engaged to be married to the child's father, a steadily employed auto mechanic with no criminal record (Vega checked).

When she stopped returning Vega's phone calls and emails, he consoled himself that she'd finally outgrown her need for him. She'd moved on from her past and he, unfortunately, would always be a reminder of those dark times. It made him happy to think of her as a married mom, selling houses and maybe living in one of her own.

He couldn't reconcile the woman he'd imagined with the one at this rally. The pale, nearly translucent skin that cleaved too tightly to her cheekbones. The stringy blond hair. She looked both older and younger than her twenty-five years.

She looked like she was using again.

She was standing close to this Puritan Pride loser. Was he her boyfriend? Her *husband*? Vega couldn't match him at all to the photos Kaylee had shown him of the sweet boyish auto mechanic who'd fathered her son. And yet it seemed clear that Kaylee and Mr. Puritan Pride were together. Vega watched him clap a hand on her tiny shoulder and shove her out of his way so he could get a better angle to address the crowd. Vega noticed, too, her reaction. The way she shrank from his touch. The economy of her movements, as if long ago, she'd resigned herself to taking up the smallest amount of space possible in the world.

Maybe it was the sight of the television vans with their big satellite receivers—Vega couldn't say. But Kaylee happened to turn in his direction. Their eyes locked for only a few seconds. Her face softened. Vega could almost see the child he'd rescued that terrible night nineteen years ago. In his mind's eye, she would always be six. Corn silk ringlets. Baby teeth like seed pearls. Dimpled hands wrapped tightly around a bright red Tickle Me Elmo. Not the blood-soaked one he found her with that day. No child should have that for a memory. The other one—the one he gave her at the hospital. The one that always appeared in photos her aunt sent each birthday.

Something like shame crossed Kaylee's features. She dropped her chin and turned away.

And then it happened. A scuffle. With the cops? With a reporter? Vega wasn't sure who started it. Mr. Puritan Pride? Someone else? But that was the way crowds turned into mobs. In an instant. The protestors scattered as more police showed up, along with fire trucks and an ambulance. Reporters and camera people tried to capture the action for the six o'clock news. Vega texted Adele: **A brawl just broke out. Stay inside. Lock all doors. Stay away from the windows.**

Ok, she texted back. Vega could tell by the short message that she was scared. He turned back to the crowd.

Mr. Puritan Pride and a couple of other skinheads were in handcuffs. Vega looked for Kaylee. He didn't see her. And then he did. She was cowering behind a parked car. Blood ran down her right leg. She was hurt. She needed medical attention. He skirted the crowd and dashed behind the car.

"Hey," he asked huskily. "What happened?"

That question could cover many fronts.

Up close, he saw how skinny she was. Her arms were sticklike. Her collarbone protruded from her chest.

"It's nothing," she said softly. "I fell and skinned my knee when everybody started running."

Vega felt in his pocket for his handkerchief. He pressed it to her knee to stop the bleeding and flashed on that terrible afternoon all those years ago in the backseat of her family's car. Katharine Wentz had apparently just told her husband, Richard, that she was taking their son and daughter and leaving him.

They were the last words Kaylee's mom ever uttered.

"Let me walk you over to the ambulance," said Vega.

"No, please," she insisted. "That's not a good idea. The bleeding will stop in a minute."

She gently brushed away Vega's hands and pressed on the handkerchief herself. "I'm sorry I'm getting it all bloody."

"Keep it. I don't mind." He straightened and peeked around the edge of the car. Mr. Puritan Pride was handcuffed and being loaded into a cruiser. The protestors had dispersed. Adele and her colleagues inside were safe for the moment. Vega lowered himself to the ground beside Kaylee again.

She opened her purse and pulled out a pack of Newport Lights. She'd stopped smoking the last time Vega saw her. She told him she didn't want her baby exposed to it. She tipped out a cigarette and lit it with a Zippo lighter, inhaling deeply while she regarded him through a haze of tobacco smoke.

"Why are you here?" Her voice was husky from the smoke. She wouldn't know about Adele. Vega certainly wasn't going to highlight the connection and put Adele at risk. Not given Kaylee's choice of companions.

"The question," said Vega, "is why are *you*? You never expressed this kind of hate when I knew you."

"I don't . . . that is, Boyd just feels—"

"*Boyd?* Is that Mr. Puritan Pride I saw you with? The skinhead who just got busted?"

"Oh God." She pushed a strand of blond hair away from her face. Her own color was subtle. The color of spun honey and butterscotch. The shade she was wearing was too platinum. Too brassy. That wasn't all that had changed. She'd had a small butterfly tattoo on her ankle when Vega last saw her. Now, she had several on her arms as well. Hearts with daggers, vines with barbed wire encircling them. Vega hated tattoos. He was un-inked and intended to stay that way. It still bothered him that his own daughter had gotten a heart tattoo on her shoulder last year.

Kaylee peeked around the corner of the car. "Boyd's going to wonder where I am. I've got to go to the police station and bail him out."

"Please don't tell me he's your husband," said Vega.

"Boyfriend."

"Well, now would be a good time to break up."

"I can't," said Kaylee. "Hunter and I are living with him."

Hunter. Kaylee's son would be about three now. She stared at the smoldering ash on the tip of her cigarette, as if looking for a neutral place to rest her eyes. "I know it looks bad. I know he's got some anger issues—"

"*Anger issues?* He's a freakin' white supremacist."

"He just . . . He did a couple of tours in Afghanistan and it messed up his head. That's all."

"Lots of vets did tours in Afghanistan," said Vega. "They didn't come back as white supremacists. You can't *believe* this crap?"

"It doesn't matter what I believe," said Kaylee. "It's the way things are. I'm with him. That's the way it is."

"Well, you can be *un* with him," said Vega. "You want me to find you and Hunter another place to stay?" He'd rescued her many times before. He could do it again. But he saw something in her big blue eyes he hadn't seen since the day of the shooting when she held so tight to his hand, all the way to the hospital: *fear.*

"Please, Jimmy. I appreciate your offer, but that's not a good idea. Wherever Hunter and I went, he'd find us."

"I'll get you an order of protection."

"He'd violate it." She left the bloody handkerchief stuck to her knee to help congeal the blood and stubbed out her cigarette. Then she pushed herself to her feet. "Thanks for the first aid, but I'm okay. Really. I'm not a little girl anymore. You can't swoop in and solve all my problems."

"You're right, Kaylee. I can't. Especially when you won't help yourself." He allowed his eyes to wander from her skeletal face to her knobby shoulders that stuck out from her pink tank top like a dog's rawhide bone. "When did you start using meth again?"

"I'm not . . ." Her voice trailed off. Whatever else she'd become, she didn't have the heart to lie to him. "I'm trying to beat it. I want to get into a treatment program, but I got busted a few months ago for possession and they're talking jail this time."

"Why the hell didn't you call me? I could have interceded. I could have—"

"I didn't want that."

"But why?"

"Because . . ." She brushed the street grit off her denim

cutoffs without looking at him. "You were so proud of me the last time we saw each other. I wanted you to remember me that way."

"I'd always help you."

She finger-combed her hair. "Look, I've got to go. Just . . . forget about today, okay? Just remember that last time you saw me. That's what I want you to remember."

Chapter 7

Vega showed his badge at the police barricade and made his way up the steps of the new community center, which was now crawling with law enforcement. He found Adele in a room full of outdated computers and children's books. The colorful walls were adorned with posters exhorting people in Spanish and English to read to their children and dream big. It was all so hopeful. It did not match the grim reality that was facing the fledgling center.

They'd become an extremist target.

Adele put on a brave face, encouraging the attendees—white, black, and Hispanic—to push forward with their vision for a more inclusive community. Her voice was strong. Her dark eyes held the gunpowder flash of defiance.

She didn't crumble until they were alone in Vega's truck, heading away from Anniston. Away from her colleagues whom she was supposed to catch a ride with back to Lake Holly.

"I let them down," she mumbled softly into her hands. "I've let everybody down."

"How?" asked Vega. "By believing you could make a difference? Build a better community? Get people to treat each other with respect? You have, *nena.*" His endearment for her. *Babe,* in Spanish. "You've brought the town together. Most of those assholes protesting out there today probably aren't even *from* Anniston."

She stared out the window. "Maybe. But they're out there, either way, scaring people. Maybe next week, they'll be doing the same thing to La Casa in Lake Holly."

His fear as well. But there was no point in mentioning it. "Listen." He patted her knee. "Sophia's in Cape Cod with your ex-in-laws for the week. Why don't you spend the night at my house? I'll make dinner. We can watch a movie together and I'll drive you home in the morning."

Adele rarely stayed at Vega's place. Normally, she had her ten-year-old daughter to take care of. Plus, she was allergic to Vega's dog.

"I'll kick Diablo out of the bedroom," Vega promised. "It's summer. We can keep the windows open so your allergies don't get too bad. I've got Claritin in the medicine cabinet. What do you say?" He took his eyes off the windshield and gave her a pleading look. "We've both had a rough day."

"You're right." She took a deep breath. "I'm sorry, *mi vida*. I've been so preoccupied with the protestors; I haven't even mentioned the courthouse shooting or your lost promotion. God, what an awful day. Do they have any leads on the shooter?"

"I'm not FBI," said Vega. "They don't tell me those things."

"Some nut guns down a court officer and wounds a judge in broad daylight. You'd have to think they'd catch him quickly."

"Apparently not or the media would know about it." Vega, too, was surprised. And chilled. There were surveillance cameras and license-plate readers everywhere in Broad Plains. This guy had evaded them all. This wasn't dumb luck. It was preparation—the sort of preparation only someone with a lot of experience could pull off. Someone who had killed before—and could kill again.

By the time Vega pulled onto his gravel driveway, a late-day sun glowed like an overripe cantaloupe through the pines, turning the bungalow's weathered white paint a syrupy color. Vega powered down the windows of his black Ford pickup and drank in the scent of old rowboats on the lake below, mixed with the aroma of damp earth and the ash from someone's campfire. Diablo barked out a greeting from inside.

He was home.

They got out of the truck. Vega went in first. Diablo rushed him with delight, covering his cheap suit in equal parts slobber and dog hair.

"Happy to see you too, pal," said Vega, giving Diablo a scratch behind the ears. The mutt—part German shepherd, part retriever—had come into Vega's life at its darkest moment, right after the shooting. He was a gift from Adele—probably the greatest gift of his life. Diablo loved him when he didn't love himself.

Vega let Diablo outside; the dog never wandered far. Then he vacuumed what he could of the dog's hair and opened the windows. The whole cabin consisted of one big room downstairs, flanked by a stone fireplace on one wall and the kitchen on the other. A set of stairs led to two small bedrooms and a bathroom under the eaves. The vacuuming didn't take long. He must have done a good job because Adele didn't sneeze—not even after she'd showered and changed into one of Vega's old T-shirts and a pair of his track shorts. He greeted her at the bottom of the stairs with a glass of white wine while she still had a towel wrapped around her wet hair.

"I'm defrosting a steak," he said. "After my shower, I'll put it on the grill."

She smiled at him playfully. "You are a man of many talents."

He pulled her toward him. "Some better than cooking, I hope."

"Let's see." She put her glass of wine down on the kitchen counter and slowly began unbuttoning his shirt. The western light streamed in through the windows, framing her in a halo of gold. Vega slipped a hand beneath the shorts and felt the soft warmth of her skin, the way it grew sweaty from his touch. They made love on the rug by the fieldstone fireplace while a soft breeze flitted in through the sliding screen door to the deck.

By the time Vega showered and fired up the grill, the sky flamed a bright tangerine. They ate on the deck, laughing and talking about nothing in particular—which was just the way they both seemed to want it this evening. Then they cleared their plates, grabbed Diablo's leash, and took him on a walk around the lake, which glowed pink as the sun sank low over the hills. In winter, Vega's lake community was a ghost town. Only a handful of people lived here year-round like he did. In summer, however, houses came alive with the sounds of children and dogs. Hamburgers sizzled on grills. Sandcastles and plastic shovels dotted the little lakefront beach.

The children were gone from the beach by this hour. Which was just as well since Diablo could never resist a swim. As soon as they hit the sand, he raced forward and waded in, dog-paddling until he found a stick floating near the shore. He brought it back to Vega for a game of fetch, shaking his fur off at the exact distance calibrated to give both him and Adele a thorough shower.

"I just hope he doesn't decide to dry off by rolling on the sand," said Vega. "I'll be walking on grit for days."

The sky stayed bright, but the earth around them began to fade. They sprawled on the sand—Adele tucked between Vega's legs—and watched Diablo chew the stick he'd fished out of the water. He was so easy to please.

Adele sat up suddenly and patted her chest.

"What's wrong?"

"My Dad's religious medal. It's gone."

"Are you sure you put it on this morning?" She wore it mostly for good luck—not every day. Her father gave it to her when she was a child, to make her feel safe when her parents had to leave her and her sister alone at night to clean offices. Vega could picture the medal now. It was a small gold disk, the size of a nickel, with a raised engraving of a veiled saint bowing her head in prayer. Saint Mariana de Jesús de Paredes, the patron saint of Ecuador. Her parents' homeland. If Vega closed his eyes, he could still feel the delicate links of the gold chain through his fingers and the raised nubs of the saint's halo worn smooth by the years. He could still picture the Spanish words inscribed on the back, lines from the Catholic prayer, Ave Maria: *El Señor es contigo. The Lord is with thee.*

Adele began frantically raking her fingers through the sand. "I put it on this morning. As a prayer for good luck at your trial."

So much for the power of prayer, thought Vega. He touched her hand. "It's not here, *nena*. I'm sure of it. When we made love earlier, you weren't wearing it."

"Oh God."

"Did you have it in Anniston?"

"I don't know." She stopped raking and sat back on her heels, her eyes glassy. Vega knew how much that necklace meant to her. Her father died when she was sixteen. She had so little to remember him by.

"Come on." Vega pulled her to her feet. "I'll bet it fell off in my truck."

It wasn't in the truck. Or on the driveway. The last blush of daylight was fast disappearing over the smoky lavender hillsides. They wouldn't find it now. Mosquitos buzzed in the thickening darkness. A chorus of cicadas rose and fell like waves crashing to shore. Snatches of chatter and music wafted from houses normally silent most of the year. It would all disappear in a few weeks once summer residents packed up for the season. Already, the air felt graced by the first breath of autumn.

"We can search again in the morning," Vega promised. "You can call La Casa North and I'll see if the courthouse has a lost-and-found."

Adele didn't look encouraged. "It's gone," she said wearily. "I'll never find it."

"We will." Vega hoped he was right. He knew this wasn't about a lost piece of jewelry. It went much deeper, to a time Adele rarely spoke about when her parents—both undocumented—left Adele and her younger sister alone at night because they couldn't afford childcare. Every time they left the house, Adele feared they might get arrested and deported, never to return. It was a heavy burden for a child. Vega knew about heavy burdens and how they could shape a young life. He had only to think of Kaylee Wentz.

Later, when they were snuggling on the couch, Vega told Adele about his encounter with Kaylee at the protest.

"*That* Kaylee? The one you saved?" Adele was shocked to hear she was dating a white supremacist. "Does she believe those things?"

"I don't know what she believes anymore," said Vega. "Mostly, she looked scared. Of him. Of her drug charge. Of losing custody of her little boy. She needs help."

"Maybe you should talk to her," Adele suggested. "Now would be a good time while her jerk boyfriend sits in jail on an assault charge."

"Yeah. Maybe tomorrow I'll track her down," said Vega. "She said she lives with the boyfriend. His arrest report would show their address."

Adele's cell phone rang. She frowned at the number. With Sophia away in Cape Cod, she was always on alert.

"It's Rafael." The evening manager at La Casa. A comma of concern settled along one side of her lips. Rafael never called at night for mundane things.

"Put him on speaker," said Vega. He knew as well as Adele that if Rafael was contacting her, it wasn't for a busted light switch or a lack of folding chairs for an evening class.

"Rafael?" Adele's voice came out hoarse and tentative. Rafael's was just the opposite—rapid-fire and breathy as he addressed her in Spanish. He spoke perfect English, but for some reason with Adele, he always used Spanish. Maybe it was because that's what they used mostly at La Casa.

"I heard about that mess in Anniston this afternoon," he began. "Ramona said they were skinheads. White supremacists." Ramona was Adele's assistant.

"They certainly looked like it," Adele replied in Spanish. "The Anniston police arrested about half a dozen of them."

Silence. Vega expected to hear the clack of balls on the pool tables in La Casa's recreation room or the chatter of clients. He heard nothing.

"Rafael?" asked Adele. "Is everything okay?"

"We had to close the center down this evening. Someone called in a bomb threat."

"A bomb threat? When?"

"Forty minutes ago. I called the police and sent everyone home," said Rafael. "A couple of Lake Holly officers searched the center, inside and out. They didn't find anything."

"Are they going to investigate?"

"Detective Greco promised to look into it tomorrow."

Louis Greco. Vega was glad his friend had been assigned to the case.

"Who spoke to the caller?" asked Adele.

"I did." Vega heard the slight tremor in Rafael's voice. He was a social worker, not a cop. He didn't come to work each night thinking it might be his last. "I wish you'd never gotten involved with that community center in Anniston, Adele."

"Did the caller mention it?"

"Oh, he mentioned it, all right." Rafael took an audible breath. "He said to stay out of Anniston or people will die."

Chapter 8

"You look like you pulled an all-nighter at a college frat," said Isadora Jenkins when she met with Vega the following morning before court.

"Hey." Vega pointed to his suit. "You said I should wear the same suit with a different shirt and tie. You said juries want to see humble civil servants—not *Miami Vice*." The jacket felt sweaty and lived in. Vega hoped no one got too close.

"I'm not talking about the outfit. I'm talking about the detective inhabiting it."

"Someone called in a bomb threat to La Casa last night," Vega explained.

"Everyone okay?"

"For now." Vega wanted Adele to close down La Casa for a week or two while Detective Greco investigated. Adele refused. She said La Casa was a lifeline for the community. She was not about to be bullied. The argument that followed led to a sleepless night for both of them.

"Let's hope that's the only bomb of the day," said Jenkins.

The crime-scene tape had been removed from the courthouse security lot, but the place was far from back to normal. In front, the flag flew at half-mast. Court officers wore black mourning bands across their badges in honor of Darryl Williams. Security was beefed up. More searches. More metal detectors. Snipers on the roof. The lost-and-found was closed—had been since the shooting. If someone happened to find Adele's religious medal in the building, there would have been no way to turn it in.

Vega was starting to lose hope—in more ways than one.

"Detective Vega," Bernard Carver addressed him again on the witness stand. "How would you characterize your record as a police officer?"

Make your comments to the jury, Isadora Jenkins had warned him. *Always the jury.*

The now-five jurors and two alternates—four men and three women—looked hotter and more irritable today. Some fanned themselves with a two-for-one Denny's flyer some joker was handing out on the corner. Vega's favorite juror, a heavyset, middle-aged Latina, was gone. She'd suffered a panic attack about coming back to the courthouse after the shooting. The judge had replaced her with one of the alternates—a surly-looking, young white man who gave his occupation as "T-shirt artist." Not the sort of career choice that engenders law-and-order attitudes. Vega was betting he had a few *Bad Cop, No Doughnut* shirts among his merchandise. Vega forced himself to think of the man as open-minded.

Or at least, not ready yet to fry his ass.

"I would characterize my nineteen years with the county police as very good," Vega began. "I have four commendations for undercover work bringing down several major drug distributors in the region. I have a clearance rate of almost ninety percent as a detective. As a patrol officer, I received three community policing citations—one for delivering a baby by the side of the road. Another, for rescuing an elderly man trapped in a burning vehicle. And a third, for providing life-saving emergency aid to a six-year-old after a shooting." *Kaylee Wentz.* Vega wondered if he'd done all that much to save her after all. "I was also recognized as Hispanic Officer of the Month right before I made detective."

Vega expected Carver to cut him off or dismiss his awards as the equivalent of Cub Scout badges. Carver didn't—which surprised Vega. Maybe his awards didn't mean that much to the jury. But hey, how many of them had ever done even *one* of these things?

It's why he became a cop, wasn't it?

Well, no. Scratch that. He became a cop for more practical reasons. But that was initially. As time went on, he grew to love being a police officer. He was proud of helping people in times of crisis and protecting them against criminals and abusers. He didn't like a lot of the old-boy aspects of the job. He wasn't into the control. But he'd made this life his own and he was good at it. Couldn't these people on the jury see what a decent guy he was?

Carver let Vega talk himself out. It didn't take long. Vega wasn't the type to embellish his accomplishments. He'd stated them and that was that. But still, Carver stood there, as if he expected more. The sheen in the attorney's light gray silk suit picked up the silver streaks in his hair and the gloss of his straight, likely veneered, and very white teeth.

"I'm sorry, Detective. I thought you were going to talk about *all* of your accomplishments."

"I just did—to the best of my memory."

"I suppose your memory doesn't include your work with the Lake Holly Police Department."

"I do a lot of work with a lot of local departments in the county."

"I'm referring, specifically," said Carver, "to your work in apprehending a felon back in January. You *do* recall that, don't you?"

Vega felt a slow crawl of acid from his stomach into his esophagus. He shot a panicked look at Henry Zaroff and Isadora Jenkins at the defense table. Zaroff closed his eyes and muttered a curse under his breath. Jenkins laced her fingers together and shot Vega a dark look. Vega read the warning in her eyes: *Don't go there. It's a trap.*

Vega stumbled about for an answer. "That was a Lake Holly Police investigation—"

"But you were there, weren't you?" Carver demanded. "You helped set up the surrender. A surrender that resulted in the police fatally shooting the suspect."

"Objection!" Jenkins was on her feet. "Your Honor, Mr. Carver is discussing a case that my client had no connection to. He did not shoot that suspect, who was armed, by the way. He was not part of that investigation in any capacity."

"Oh, come on, Counselor," Carver retorted. "Do you really intend to insult the judge—insult this jury—by suggesting Detective Vega was a mere bystander? That he just *happened* to be inside a locked Lake Holly preschool on a Sunday afternoon while a police surrender was taking place? And by surrender, I mean, shoot first—ask questions later."

"Objection again!" said Jenkins. "Counselor's remarks are inflammatory and egregiously false. The suspect in Lake Holly was a felon and a convicted rapist who took a civilian hostage at knifepoint. Those are the circumstances of the shooting. And none of it involved Detective Vega."

"Sustained," said Edgerton. "Strike that last exchange," he told the stenographer. "Counselors, control yourselves. We are conducting a civil case here. And I do mean 'civil' in every sense of the word."

"My apologies, Your Honor." Carver gave a courtly bow. "I will move along." He turned to Vega. "Just one more question, Detective. Did you get approval from your department to be present at that surrender?"

Jenkins was on her feet. "Objection, Your Honor. This isn't germane to the case."

"I'll allow it," said Edgerton.

"No," said Vega. "I did not get approval."

"And how about Lake Holly?" asked Carver. "Did the lead detective involved in the surrender get permission for you to be there?"

"You would have to ask Lake Holly."

"I certainly will, Detective." Carver's eyes glinted like knife blades. "But I suspect you already know Lake Holly gave no such permission."

"Objection," said Jenkins. She had to be tired of saying the word. "Counselor is asking Detective Vega to speculate."

"Sustained," said the judge.

"I'll withdraw the question," said Carver. "But let me just ask you, Detective Vega—were you reprimanded in any way for being present at an officer-involved shooting without your department's permission?"

"Your Honor," Jenkins tried again. "Can we please move along from this completely irrelevant line of questioning?"

"The detective will answer the question," said Edgerton.

All eyes settled on Vega. He could have just said "yes" or "no." But neither answer would sit well with the jury. If he said "yes," he would come off as a bad cop who had done something wrong. If he said "no," he would look like the cowboy Carver was painting him to be—a cop who could do anything and get away with it. It was a classic lawyer question. Vega settled on what he thought was the best course of action.

"I was exonerated."

"*Really?* You were exonerated?" Carver's thin lips curved with just a hint of a smile. "Tell me, Detective: How were you *exonerated*?"

"In a departmental hearing."

"A hearing. I see." Carver's smile got broader. Like a kid at Christmas. Vega had no idea why. He was just stating the facts. Without any embellishment.

"Was a stenographer present at that hearing?"

"Objection!" said Jenkins again. "Mr. Carver's questions have no relevance to the case at hand."

"Your Honor," said Carver. "I intend to show this has great relevance."

"Very well," said Edgerton. He looked fed up with both sides. "Detective Vega will answer the question."

"I . . ." Vega stumbled. He sensed a trap but he didn't know what to do about it. ". . . I think so. I don't remember."

"Surely someone must have taken notes."

"Probably."

"And yet"—Carver held out his palms—"we weren't given any notes from this hearing."

"Your Honor," said Jenkins. "I repeat: Whatever did or did not transpire has no bearing on the matter at hand—"

"Which is why the defense is withholding it," Carver shot back.

"We're not withholding it—"

"Then where is it?" Carver walked over to his table and patted the stack of briefs next to a bored-looking Lucinda Ponce, dressed today in a formfitting black pencil skirt and scoop-necked white blouse. She wore a cross in the center of her fleshy chest, fanning herself with a paper Vega hoped wasn't important. She looked as if no one had told her that this case could go on for days.

"I was never given a copy," said Carver. His face mimicked hurt and shock, like a teenage girl finding out all her friends got a party invitation except her. The jury bought it completely.

"It was up to the plaintiff to request all such materials before the trial began," said Zaroff, getting to his feet for the first time in two days. His comb-over was slick with sweat. The hair looked like black magic marker lines someone had drawn across his scalp.

"I can't request what I never knew existed," said Carver. "Detective Vega's actions in Lake Holly go to the heart of our case. They demonstrate a pattern of irresponsibility and a cavalier attitude to authority. I respectfully ask Your Honor to require the defense to make any and all parts of that hearing available to us forthwith."

People think life happens in the big moments. Where you go to college. Who you choose to marry. What sort of work you do. Whether or not you have kids. But really, life happens in those blink-of-an-eye choices you make every day. Diving into a pool that turns out to be too shallow. Crossing a street just as a drunk driver rounds the corner. Accepting help from the wrong stranger. Small decisions with big consequences. It didn't matter if the rest of your life was full of sober, carefully considered choices. Fate was linear. Remorseless.

Two seconds. That was the amount of time Vega had had on that December night to decide whether or not Ponce was about to shoot him.

One. Two.

Two seconds. That was the amount of time Vega had had on the witness stand to answer Carver's question about the disciplinary hearing.

One. Two.

Nineteen years of helping people and putting bad guys in jail. And it had all boiled down to two wrong two-second decisions.

"I'm going to have to give this matter some thought," said Judge Edgerton. "Court will recess for lunch. I will render my decision by the end of the day."

Vega stepped down from the stand and took a seat at the defense table, in between Isadora Jenkins and Henry Zaroff. The judge and his clerk and the stenographer exited through a door behind the bench. The jurors and spectators filed out through the rear exit doors. Vega was glad he'd told Joy and Adele to stay away today. Neither could afford the time off and he couldn't afford the embarrassment.

"I was exonerated," Vega mumbled into his chest. He knew now that that was the wrong answer, but it was the only answer he could give.

"Unanimously?" asked Zaroff.

"I don't know," said Vega. "They don't tell you that."

"But you can guess, can't you?" Zaroff pressed. "Who was on the panel?"

"My boss, Captain Waring. The chief of department, John Lakeworth. And the head of Special Investigations, Greg Lorenzo."

Lorenzo. Captain Doom. He'd been gunning for Vega ever since the shooting. He could have said anything at that disciplinary hearing.

"What happens if Carver gets hold of the transcript?" asked Vega.

"He can subpoena the panel members," said Zaroff. "Force them to corroborate their comments, especially the unflattering ones. He does that?" Zaroff slammed the table. "It's over. No jury's going to side with us no matter what we say."

"But I didn't do anything wrong," said Vega again. "I had no hand in what went down in Lake Holly."

"This isn't about right or wrong," said Zaroff. "It's about legal exposure."

"Legal exposure." Vega gestured to the empty plaintiff's table where Carver had been sitting earlier. "You know about Carver's background, right? This guy made a name for himself after nine-eleven, suing companies on behalf of people who claimed their undocumented relatives had died working in the Twin Towers. He collected millions because the workers all used fake IDs and nobody could prove or disprove whether these people were relatives."

"So? You've done your homework," said Zaroff. "What's your point?"

"My point," said Vega, "is that in all likelihood, Lucinda Ponce is, at best, a distant relative . . ."

"Enough!" Zaroff held up his hand. But Vega continued.

". . . And, at worst, a mail-order widow . . ."

"I said enough!"

". . . I'm just saying," Vega continued. "Everyone in this trial knows it but the jury."

"Now, you listen to me." Zaroff got to his feet, closed his briefcase, and wagged a finger at Vega. He was a tubby man and he wheezed with the effort. "You say one thing like that in front of the jury—*one thing*—and so help me God, I will have your badge."

"I didn't," Vega protested.

"I don't even want you to *think* it," said Zaroff. "I don't want the thought to cross the medulla of your lizard-cop brain. Do you hear me? That's a ten-million-dollar comment we cannot afford."

Chapter 9

"Well, that didn't go well," said Vega after Zaroff stormed out.

Isadora Jenkins played with a charm bracelet on her wrist without saying a word. She always dressed extremely conservatively for court. Dark blue suit. White shirt. Orthopedic loafers. But she had kitschy taste in jewelry. Today, it was a Disney characters bracelet. She was fiddling with the Goofy charm. Vega wondered if it had something to do with him.

"You *do* realize that Zaroff represents the county—not you," she said.

"We're on the same side."

"That's where you're wrong," said Jenkins. "The county wants to limit liability. You want vindication. If Zaroff decides we can't win, he'll settle—even if the jury might have sided with you."

The department would definitely punish Vega if that happened. The punishment could include anything from an unfavorable assignment, to beginning the process of termination. "What do I do?"

"For starters, don't fight with Zaroff."

"I'm sorry about that—"

"Don't apologize to me," said Jenkins. "Apologize to him."

"That's punishment in itself."

"You see? It's that smart mouth that's going to get you in trouble." She pushed herself to her feet. "And don't leave the building. I want to be able to find you easily if I need to."

"Yes, ma'am." Vega wasn't going to leave the building anyway. He had other plans.

He left the courtroom and climbed a flight of stairs. He wandered a hallway under construction until he found himself in an area with unfinished sheetrock walls, scaffolding, and half a dozen cubicles. The temporary offices of the court clerk.

There were six clerks who worked for the office. Each handled a different judge or administrative duty. Vega craned his head to see if Julia Spruce's clerk, Albert Pearsall, was around. He was one of the most senior of the court clerks and was a familiar face to Vega even before the shooting.

Vega didn't see Pearsall, though he saw what he thought was Pearsall's desk—unless there were two court clerks who adored all things British. A Big Ben paperweight weighed down a stack of folders. A Union Jack coffee mug held pens and pencils. Pinned to one of the fabric-covered partition walls was the World War II slogan, *Keep Calm and Carry On*.

It felt especially appropriate right now.

"Can I help you?" asked a woman with a pixie cut of gray-blond hair and large gold hoop earrings that looked as if she'd borrowed them from her teenaged daughter. Vega thought she clerked for Judge Infante but he wasn't sure. He wished he could remember her name.

"Detective Vega, County PD." He wanted to sound as official as possible. He had no legitimate reason for poking around. "I'm wondering if you can look up an arrest for me. It happened yesterday. In Anniston. For assault. The Anniston PD processed it."

"Certainly."

Vega noticed that her cubicle was adorned with photographs of children in Mickey Mouse ears in front of the Disney World castle. Vega had taken Joy to Disney World when she was little too. They'd gotten the same shot, though the rest was a blur of long lines, short tempers, and sunburn that the pictures never show. He read the woman's name on a nameplate above her desk: Lucille Bouchart.

"Name?" She looked up from her screen.

"James Vega."

Bouchart smiled. "No. I meant the name of the arrest suspect."

"Oh." Vega realized he didn't have it. "Boyd is his first name. I don't know his last. He's white, early thirties—"

"I can probably get it by typing in Anniston," said Bouchart. "Here it is: Boyd Richter." She read the arrest report off the screen. "Age: thirty-two. Occupation: truck driver. Residence: three-twenty-two Parkland Avenue in Anniston."

Vega copied the address into his phone as well as the phone number on the screen, though he doubted a guy like Richter had a home phone. More likely, it was Richter's cell.

"What's his status?" asked Vega. "Did he get bailed out yet on yesterday's assault?"

She tapped some more keys. "According to the entry, he's still at the county jail, awaiting arraignment. No bail has been set yet."

Good, thought Vega. He could speak to Kaylee while Richter cooled his heels in lockup.

"Any way you can check for priors from your system?"

"It's not something we normally do here. But let me see." She switched screens and entered a password into her computer. Then she typed in all the identifying data she had on Richter. "One arrest for vandalism six months ago. For defacing the parking lot of a synagogue. He was fined and sentenced to community service. One arrest three months ago on a DV."

A domestic violence charge. Alarm bells started going off in Vega's head. "What was the outcome?"

"The victim dropped the charges," said Bouchart. "Case dismissed."

Vega wasn't surprised. Women often endured multiple instances of abuse before they ever reported it. And when they did finally report it, they often withdrew the charge out of fear of retaliation. Now Vega definitely wanted to speak to Kaylee.

"Can you give me a printout of everything?"

"Of course." She typed a command onto her screen, then excused herself to retrieve the materials from the copier. Vega looked over at Pearsall's desk again. There was no sign of him. He gestured to his cubicle when Bouchart returned and handed him the reports.

"How is Albert doing?"

Bouchart's face darkened. "He hasn't been in. This whole situation is terrible. Just terrible." She tugged softly on one of her gold hoop earrings. "Darryl's family . . . I can't even imagine. He has a wife and two little girls. And poor Albert—he seems to be taking it especially hard. I think he blames himself for not being able to protect the judge."

"It happened so quickly, there was nothing any of the victims could do," said Vega.

"I know," said Bouchart. "But Albert's very loyal to Judge Spruce. They've worked together many years." She cast a glance at the *Keep Calm and Carry On* slogan tacked to his fabric partition. "I think we'll all feel a lot better when the FBI finds the sniper."

"Have you heard any updates?" asked Vega. The only group more gossipy than cops was the administrative personnel who worked around them.

"I heard they were looking for a witness. Some migrant girl at the bus terminal," said Bouchart.

"I thought they would have found her by now," said Vega. Doug Hewitt said the FBI was going to check all the bus passenger lists. Was it possible she never boarded?

"Honestly . . ." Bouchart rolled her eyes. "I hope the FBI isn't counting on some illegal who can't even speak English to hand them their shooter." Vega recognized the disparaging language and casual dismissiveness for what they were: a cop's opinion. Bouchart was probably echoing the words of a Broad Plains officer who'd been working at the terminal.

Vega wanted to point out that the girl and her adult relative were likely legal asylum-seekers who'd been granted a temporary stay by a judge, pending a formal hearing. But most Americans outside law enforcement or immigrant circles didn't care about such distinctions. You're either American or you're not. Besides, the woman's and child's immigration status wouldn't make them any easier to find.

"You don't happen to know when the courthouse lost-and-found will reopen?" asked Vega. "My girlfriend lost a religious medallion yesterday."

"If she lost it during the evacuation, it's probably gone for good," said Bouchart. "Many of our 'visitors' "—she lifted her hands in quotes—"are not exactly of the most upstanding caliber."

"That's what I was afraid you'd say." Vega thanked her for the arrest report. "Don't worry too much about the shooting," he said reassuringly. "I'm sure the FBI's got a handle on this."

He hoped so, anyway.

Chapter 10

It was pitch black when the wind-up alarm clock in the trailer woke Eli and her mother from a deep sleep. Aurelia clicked on a lamp on the floor by their mattress. The bare, incandescent bulb cast shadows across the speckled mold on the ceiling. Outside, the buzz of insects was broken only by an occasional deep-throated croak of a frog. Eli wiped the sleep from her eyes and blinked at the clock.

Four-thirty a.m.

"What's wrong with your wrist?" asked her mother. Eli's left wrist had swollen to the same size as her forearm from where the man had grabbed her yesterday. It had throbbed all night, but Eli didn't want to say anything. Her mother had enough worries already without finding out about that incident in the bus terminal.

"I must have sprained it yesterday," said Eli. "I'll be okay."

"You can't pick fruit like that."

"I'll use my right hand. I'm right-handed anyway."

Her uncle had left them two plastic bags of hand-me-down clothes, but the jeans for her mother were too long and tight. For Eli, they were too big in every direction. So they dressed in the same jeans they wore yesterday and slipped into clean T-shirts. One with an American flag emblazoned across it for her mother and another with cartoon characters for Eli.

Eli couldn't secure her hair into a ponytail with one hand, so her mother did it for her. Then Aurelia rummaged through the cabinets for something to eat. Luis had left them beans, rice, tortillas, coffee, cooking oil, a few bruised apples, and some cereal. They'd eaten the fried beans, tortillas, and rice last night. This morning, her mother settled for mugs of black coffee and bowls of dry cereal with the apples sliced on top.

Aurelia stared out the smudged window above the sink. Her own tired reflection stared back. "This wasn't the way things were supposed to be," she muttered.

In Eli's experience, nothing ever was.

They ate and assembled some beans and tortillas for lunch. Then they slipped into their flip-flop sandals and pushed open the door of the trailer when they heard the rumble of a pickup slowly grinding its way up the hillside. It was the same truck they'd seen yesterday evening, dropping workers back from the fields. It had been filled with men and teenage boys, with a few older women as well. They all looked dusty and fatigued. Their accents were Guatemalan, from the same Chimaltenango region as Eli and her mother, though no one looked familiar. Wherever Luis had recruited these people, it wasn't from Nejapa.

The wood-sided truck lumbered into the clearing. The same driver slipped out from behind the wheel. An old Guatemalan man with no teeth and a pronounced hunch to his back. Workers came out of their trailers, stamping their boots in the predawn chill. The few women present nodded politely to Eli and her mother. The men mostly ignored them. Eli folded her arms tightly across her chest. The thick dew on the weeds was so cold, it made her toes curl.

The people began to climb into the bed of the pickup.

The toothless, hunched driver frowned at Eli and her mother's feet.

"Don't you have sneakers? Boots?" he grunted in a thick, rural accent.

"We lost them," said her mother. They were stolen, actually. On the border crossing. But Eli suspected her mother was too embarrassed to admit it.

The driver cursed under his breath. "Baseball caps? Gloves? Long-sleeved shirts?"

"No." Her mother straightened proudly. "We're not supposed to be doing this work. My brother is Luis Monroy."

The old man laughed. "Is that supposed to impress me? My brother was the deputy mayor of Huehuetenango. Now he's doing fifteen years in prison there."

His words made Eli's mother's spirits sink even further. Her eyes filled with tears. Life had been hard in Nejapa. But it was the life they knew. A life stitched together by the hope that there were better worlds out there. Worlds warm with family, security, and comfort. All of that seemed to be unraveling now.

Maybe it was never there to begin with.

One of the women said something to a teenage boy. He ran back into their trailer and emerged a few minutes later with two pairs of muddy rubber boots. Then another woman ran back and brought out two ripped and faded flannel shirts. Eli's mother tried to wave away their gifts of kindness, but they insisted.

"The shirts will keep the sun off your arms," said one of the women, her skin crinkled like old wax paper, her hands as callused as a man's. "The boots will keep your feet dry and keep your legs from touching poison ivy."

"What's poison ivy?" asked Eli's mother.

"A vine," said the woman. "I will show you when we get to the field. Don't touch it. You will get a terrible rash."

Eli and her mother slipped into the clothes, then crowded with everyone else into the bed of the pickup. The driver made a three-point turn. Then the truck bumped down the hill and through the long stretch of woods to the road. It was difficult to keep from falling in the back of the lurching truck, especially with her painful wrist. Eli braced against her mother, who wrapped an arm around her to steady her. They watched the sky turn bleached through the trees, then dusty orange by the time the truck nosed onto the paved two-lane.

Ten minutes later, a small wooden arrow, pointing left, read *Watkins Farm*. The driver turned and drove along a gravel road, then turned again onto a deeply rutted dirt path. On each side of the path stood rows of apple trees, lined up so straight and even that, as the sun crested the hills, Eli could see from one side of the orchard all the way to the other. Each tree was the height of three men standing on each other's shoulders. Their dark green leaves sparkled with dew. Even from this distance, Eli could smell the sharp sweetness of ripening fruit.

The driver stopped the pickup in front of a white trailer permanently parked on cinderblocks and fronted with an awning. He pulled down the liftgate and everyone got out. To the right of the trailer sat a water spigot. A few feet farther Eli saw two big blue outhouses. She supposed this was the only place to get water or use the bathroom at the farm.

The woman with the wax-paper skin tugged at Aurelia's sleeve. "Whatever you do," she whispered, "don't be alone with Señor Ortega."

"Who is Señor Ortega?"

"The foreman."

The door of the trailer opened and a stocky, brown-skinned man in a tan cowboy hat emerged. He had high cheekbones and a broad, black mustache that trailed down either side of his lips. His light-blue, short-sleeved shirt was starched and spotless. It opened just enough to see a gold cross nestled in the dark hairs of his chest. He held a clipboard in one hand and muttered in Spanish for people to sign in. He smiled too long at Eli's mother as she bent over to write their names.

"You are the new pickers," he said in Mexican-accented Spanish. Eli noticed that the other workers had already grabbed white mesh bags from a crate and were heading into the fields.

"Yes," said Aurelia. "I am Luis Monroy's sister."

"Luis Monroy's sister?" The foreman's voice had a mocking edge to it. "Your brother owes me money, Luis Monroy's sister." Eli assumed her uncle was rich and powerful. Maybe he wasn't as rich and powerful as they had believed.

Ortega said something to the driver in English. They both laughed. Then he pointed to the crate. "Grab two bags, one for each of you. You can start over on the south field, picking the low branches." He turned on the heel of his cowboy boots and disappeared inside the trailer, the screen door slamming behind him.

The driver could see Eli and her mother didn't know what they were doing. So he showed each of them how to fit the white mesh bags across their chests.

"I don't pick anymore," he explained. "My back can't take it. But there are three things you should know," he said, his voice surprisingly gentle. Maybe he felt sorry for them, how ill prepared they were for this. "One, picking is about rhythm. Don't pick one apple when you can pick two. But don't go so fast that you drop things. A bruised apple is an apple you won't get paid for."

"Don't drop the apples," said Aurelia, rephrasing the obvious.

"Two," said the driver. "Don't touch any vines. Encarna, the woman who gave you the shirts, is right about the poison ivy. Also, pesticides and ticks. You may want to remove your shirt because you're hot. But you could get a rash from the plants or the chemicals or the ticks if you expose your skin. You could get sick. So, no matter how hot it gets, keep yourself covered."

They both nodded. Already, Eli could feel the sun's heat like tiny pinpricks, stabbing at her skin right through the thin fabric of her shirt. The air wasn't only growing hotter, it was also growing more humid. Her neck perspired like someone was breathing on it.

Eleven hours. She needed to pick at least five thousand apples in eleven hours if she wanted to earn a hundred dollars to help her mother pay off the loan so she could go to school. She did a rough approximation in her head. Eleven hours into five thousand. That was about four hundred fifty apples per hour. Two hundred twenty-five every thirty minutes. Seven to eight apples per minute. Her mother had to pick eleven or twelve a minute—every day until they paid off the loan. And that assumed no breaks.

"What's the third thing we should know?" asked her mother.

The old man removed his baseball cap and wiped a streak of sweat from his brow. He held Eli's mother's gaze for a long moment before he spoke. "Don't go anywhere by yourself. Either of you. Not even to talk to the señor. Especially not to talk to the señor."

He squinted at the fields. "There's a reason why there aren't a lot of women and teenage girls working here."

Chapter 11

Two expert witnesses testified during the afternoon portion of Vega's trial. A ballistics expert whom Carver had hired to discredit Vega's assertion that he'd fired on the suspect in self-defense. And some psychologist from the Human Factor and Ergonomics Society—whatever that was—to back up the first expert's assertions that Vega had acted outside police norms.

Two experts, back to back, turned out to be too much for the jury. Especially in the oppressive afternoon heat. The white guy—in the Jets jersey yesterday, in a Yankees T-shirt today—must have caught the doubleheader last night. He was snoring loudly in his seat. Even Lucinda Ponce looked fed up. She slumped in her chair, arms folded across her chest like an adolescent being grounded. Carver whispered in her ear, and she gave him a sour look before slowly unfolding her arms and straightening.

Vega kept waiting for the judge to tell them whether he was going to admit the transcript of Vega's disciplinary hearing into evidence. Edgerton said nothing.

"How come he's not giving us his decision?" Vega whispered to Jenkins.

"Probably because Carver's experts are paid by the hour," she whispered back. "Or at least, that's what he told the judge. So, they get to go first. I'll bet he's enjoying every minute."

It wasn't until the experts had finished testifying and being cross-examined by Jenkins that the judge looked at the clock and mumbled something to his clerk. The jury perked up. They knew he was getting ready to dismiss them for the day.

The judge folded his hands in front of him and bounced a look from the plaintiff's table to the defense.

"I've given this matter regarding Detective Vega's disciplinary hearing transcript some serious thought. As much as I always like to give police the benefit of the doubt, Mr. Carver has raised some legitimate concerns regarding Detective Vega's behavior in this other officer-involved shooting. And while I understand he had no part in the shooting itself, clearly his department felt his behavior justified a hearing on his conduct. I believe plaintiff and counsel are entitled to view the transcript of that hearing, so I'm going to allow it into evidence."

Henry Zaroff was on his feet, even before Jenkins could wrest herself from her chair.

"Your Honor," said the county attorney. "The events in Lake Holly transpired nearly two months *after* the shooting in question here. We are talking about an entirely separate set of circumstances that have no bearing on this case."

"I disagree, Mr. Zaroff," said Edgerton. "My ruling stands."

Carver rose slowly, a broad, self-satisfied grin on his TV-doctor face. "Your Honor, I humbly thank you on behalf of Mr. Ponce's widow for your fair and balanced—"

"Counselor, I'm hot and tired," snapped Edgerton. "Don't flatter me. If you have a request, spit it out. If not, I'd like to adjourn for the day."

"Of course, Your Honor." Carver gestured to Lucinda Ponce, who was halfway out of her chair. She wanted this day over too. "My client and I will need time to read through this transcript. Subpoena witnesses. Prepare questions. I would like to request this court consider a two-day adjournment so that I may secure all necessary materials and subpoenas—"

Zaroff began to object. Jenkins put a hand on his arm and whispered something into his ear. Zaroff slowly rose. "Your Honor, defense has no objections to the extension."

"Good." Edgerton banged his gavel. "Court is adjourned until Friday. Let's hope the heat wave breaks by then."

The judge, his clerk, and the court reporter left. The jury and spectators filed out. Vega waited until they'd all gone. Then he turned to Jenkins and Zaroff.

"Are you both out of your minds? *Two days?* Carver will have plenty of time to sharpen every sword in his arsenal."

"This is Isadora's decision, not mine," said Zaroff. "I've got to relay this to my boss before he leaves for the day." Zaroff stuffed his papers into his briefcase. Vega had done as instructed and apologized to the man. It didn't seem to have made any difference to their relationship. He was as cold as ever to Vega. He walked out without a good-bye, leaving Jenkins and Vega alone in the courtroom.

Vega waited for Jenkins to offer some pithy strategy. Instead, she reached into her handbag for her cell phone, tapped in her password, and handed the screen to Vega. On the screen was an extended weather forecast. Thunderstorms were moving through the area on Wednesday and Thursday. By Friday, the heat wave was supposed to break.

"That's it?" asked Vega, handing Jenkins back her phone. "That's your big strategy? Everyone won't be as sweaty, so they won't convict the cop?"

"Never underestimate the effect of weather on mood," said Jenkins.

"What about the effect of that transcript and my bosses

testifying against me? We could have a polar vortex, and nothing's going to change that."

"That's right," said Jenkins. "Nothing you or I do can change their testimony at this point. All we can do is manage the circumstances."

"So, we give Carver two extra days to prepare?"

Jenkins laced her hands on the defense table. "Detective Vega, do you like sports?"

"What kind of question is that?"

"Well, do you?"

He sighed. "I played baseball in high school. I'm a big Yankees and New York Giants fan now. I'll watch the Knicks too, when they're doing well. What's your point?"

"When the opposing team gets on a scoring streak, what's the first thing a coach does?"

"Puts in his best players," said Vega. "You planning to dump me?"

"Don't tempt me." She fingered her Disney charm bracelet again. Goofy seemed to be a favorite when she was around him. "Think harder."

Vega frowned. "I suppose the coach calls for a time-out."

"Precisely," said Jenkins. "The coach calls a time-out to disrupt the other team's rhythm. He can't stop them from playing well. He can't stop them from scoring. So, he takes everything out of play for a short spell. Often, when play resumes, that rhythm is gone."

"You think that by giving Carver two days off, his rhythm is going to be disrupted?"

"Not Carver's," said Jenkins. "The jury's. They're hot. They're bored. They're ready to vote against you because that's the wave Carver is riding at the moment and it will get them out of here faster. We take a break, the weather changes, who knows what could happen?"

"I guess," said Vega.

"Far larger events in history have been decided over such trivialities," Jenkins pointed out. "The French emperor Napoleon might never have met his Waterloo if not for wet weather that bogged down his artillery and hemorrhoids that bogged down his, well, you know." She smiled sheepishly.

Vega laughed. "Carver deserves hemorrhoids."

"There's another rhythm at play here too," said Jenkins. She pointed at Vega's chest. "Yours. Your mind is elsewhere this afternoon, Detective. I can feel it. Whatever's bothering you isn't in this courtroom."

Kaylee Wentz. And her brute of a boyfriend, Boyd Richter.

Jenkins rose and closed her briefcase. "You want my advice? Take the next few days to clear your head. Because if you don't, Carver is going to have it."

Chapter 12

It was almost four p.m. when Vega left the courthouse. The sun had lost its blistering intensity, but the air still felt like dryer exhaust. He walked to the public parking garage, hopped into his truck, and programmed the GPS on his phone for Boyd Richter's address in Anniston. He had no idea if Kaylee would even be home. But he had to start somewhere. Isadora Jenkins was right: He couldn't get Kaylee's situation off his mind.

Parkland Avenue was at the far eastern corner of Anniston, in a neighborhood of vinyl-sided capes, stucco ranches, and wood-framed triple-deckers with mismatched windows and siding. Weeds sprouted from driveways cracked like just-baked cakes. BEWARE OF DOG signs adorned chain-link fences and screen doors. American flags fluttered on porch columns and window stickers and car bumpers. But there were subtler signs of the neighborhood's makeup as well. Some front doors sported wreaths of green shamrocks with *Erin go Bragh* written across them. Muscle cars and pickup trucks had NRA stickers on their back windshields. Here and there, Vega saw darker symbols as well. There was a yellow *Don't Tread on Me* banner in a window and a Confederate flag on a motorcycle.

The message was clear: Only white people were welcome here.

Three-twenty-two Parkland was a triple-decker with faded vinyl siding and three mailboxes running up the side of the porch. A gravel parking lot graced one side of the house. Air conditioners leaned precariously out of window frames. On the sparse grass out front, children's ride-on toys and partially deflated balls lay scattered, their bright colors faded from sun and rain.

Vega parked across the street, a few car lengths from the house, and turned off his engine. He pulled out his phone. He had to be careful here. He didn't want this to backfire on Kaylee. He still had her cell number, even if she didn't answer him these days. At least he could text her. Maybe arrange for a neutral place to meet.

Hey, Kaylee. I had a job in Anniston today. A lie. But he didn't want her to feel like he was stalking her. **Any chance we could get together and talk? Let me know. I'm concerned.**

He didn't know if she'd even answer him. She hadn't in a long time. He was surprised when she texted back right away.

Can't. Sorry. Out of town. XXX

Out of town? With her boyfriend in jail? But maybe that was good, thought Vega. Maybe Kaylee had taken this opportunity to escape. Maybe that was why the message was so brief and cryptic. She didn't want anyone to know where she'd gone.

Vega restarted his engine to head home. He checked his rearview mirror before he pulled out of his parking space. In it, he saw another black Ford truck driving down the street in his direction. It turned into the gravel parking lot adjacent to Kaylee's building. Boyd Richter got out from the driver's side of the vehicle.

Kaylee got out of the passenger's seat.

Vega turned off his engine and slumped down in his truck so no one would spot him. He tilted his rearview mirror in Kaylee's direction. He assumed she had her little boy with her, though she made no move to open the rear doors. She just stood there, eyes on the pavement, shoulders hunched, as Richter strode over to her side of the truck and began frantically waving his arms and shouting at her, repeatedly jabbing his index finger into her chest. Each jab sent Kaylee back half a step, so she had to fight to stay on her feet.

Vega's hands clenched into fists. He wanted to beat Richter to a pulp, then cuff him and haul him back to jail where he belonged. But no. That would only come back to hurt Kaylee. He willed himself to stay in his seat and observe. If Richter threw a punch or slapped her, all bets were off. But instead, Richter tossed the keys into the truck, stormed out of the lot and into the building, leaving Kaylee just standing there. Vega waited and watched.

After a few minutes, Kaylee seemed to compose herself. She pulled a cigarette out of her purse and lit it. Then she fished the keys out of the truck, got in, and made a three-point turn out of the lot. Vega made a U-turn and followed, keeping a good distance between them, so as not to tip her off. She had the driver's side window rolled down, her arm dangling out, with a cigarette attached.

She made a right at the first traffic light and drove past a collection of fast-food franchises and auto body shops, tossing the spent cigarette out the window somewhere along the way. Then she turned left and left again onto another street full of small capes and ranches that looked a little better cared for, parking the truck in front of a small, yellow, one-story house with a blue door and a swing set out back. A sign on the chain-link gate read: LITTLE SPROUT DAYCARE.

She was fetching her son.

Vega double-parked beside her truck and powered down his window. Her big blue eyes widened. "Jimmy? What are you . . . ?"

"Get your boy," said Vega. "Then you and me, we need to talk."

"But Boyd's expecting me. I can't just—"

"We'll work that out," said Vega. "Right now, I need you to follow my instructions."

She nodded meekly and opened the latch gate. She emerged a few minutes later carrying her three-year-old son. His eyes had the sleepy look of a child who'd just woken from a nap. His messy blond hair was curled into ringlets by his ears in the heat. He hid his face on his mother's shoulder as Vega approached.

"Hey there, pal," said Vega. "What's your name?"

The child averted his eyes. Kaylee stroked his hair. "Hunter," she replied. "Boyd's not his . . . that is, my former fiancé—"

"The mechanic," said Vega.

Kaylee nodded. "Eddie's married now and he's not around as much anymore." Vega could see from her eyes that it pained her to say it. Vega wasn't sure if it was because she still had feelings for Eddie or because she felt Hunter deserved better.

"You have a favorite place you grab dinner?" asked Vega. "A pizzeria? Chinese takeout?"

"Hunter likes pizza," said Kaylee. Vega noticed she didn't mention herself. Kaylee had lost her appetite as most meth users did. It showed in the shrunken angles of her jaw, the way her wrist bones protruded like dresser-drawer knobs. She was wasting away before him, a ghost of the lively girl she'd once been.

"We can't . . . that is, Boyd wouldn't—"

"Call the place and order a pizza to take home," said Vega. "I'll pay for it. Tell Boyd that Little Sprout was giving away coupons for free pizzas and that's why you were delayed." Vega was betting that Mr. Puritan Pride wouldn't refuse a free pizza after coming out of lockup.

Kaylee took out her phone, called in the order, and hung up.

"Now what?" she asked. She would always be a little girl with Vega, waiting for him to tell her what to do.

"I follow you to the pizzeria, then get into your truck. It should take about twenty minutes for them to get the order ready."

She buried her face in her son's hair. "I don't know what you want me to say."

"The truth, Kaylee. After all these years, I think you owe me that."

He tailed her to the pizzeria, then drove around the block once before parking at the opposite end of the lot. He waited until no patrons were outside to slip into the front passenger seat of her truck. Hunter was in a child seat in back, playing with some electronic toy that beeped and whirred frantically every few seconds. Vega had forgotten how noisy life with little kids was.

"You have no idea how dangerous this is," said Kaylee. "If Boyd finds out—"

"Then let me help you file an order of protection against him," said Vega. He turned to her, his brown eyes soft and pleading. "Kaylee, I know you called the cops on him a few months ago and then dropped the charges."

She stared at her lap and said nothing. Vega braced himself for tears. He never knew what to do when women cried. He could handle blood better than he could handle tears. But he'd forgotten that about Kaylee. He'd never seen her cry. He wasn't sure she knew how.

"Does he hurt Hunter?"

"No. Only me."

"There's a really good shelter for battered women over in Granville. I can get you in."

She shook her head. "I'm already looking at jail time on the meth charge and losing custody of Hunter. This will only make things worse."

"How can they get any worse?" Here Vega was, turning himself inside out to help her and she was sitting there passively, allowing this asshole to use her as a punching bag.

"Mommy? Can we go home?" came a little voice in the backseat.

"In a minute, Hunter," she cooed softly. "We're waiting for pizza." The boy went back to playing with his electronic toy. Kaylee's phone dinged with a text.

"It's Boyd. He wants to know where I am. I have to tell him."

"Does he do this all the time?"

"All the time," said Kaylee. "When I get on the phone with a friend or my aunt, he puts a two-minute egg timer next to me. I have to be off the phone before the sand runs out."

"You can't live like this!"

"But I do." Kaylee turned to Vega, her voice barely above a whisper. "I don't have a choice, Jimmy."

"Of course you do."

"No. I don't." Her voice dropped to barely above a whisper. "He has guns."

"Guns? *Plural?*"

She nodded. "A lot of them. Automatic rifles. Handguns. All sorts of weapons. Some, he builds out of unmarked parts and sells to people he knows over chat sites."

"Felons?"

"I don't know," said Kaylee. "All I know is they hate anyone who isn't white and Christian."

Her cheeks flushed. She averted her gaze. It must have dawned on her suddenly that Vega was in that category. She probably didn't see him as Puerto Rican or dark-skinned or even a cop. He was her friend and protector on a deep elemental level that had formed before she knew anything about the world.

"You . . . *like* this life?" he asked her.

"It's just the way things are."

"How on earth did you meet this loser?"

"He didn't seem like a loser when I met him," said Kaylee. "He'd just gotten out of the army. He came into O'Rourke's where I wait tables. He told me I was pretty. Told me to stay off the meth." Her face fluttered at the memory. "I knew he was very straight-laced and all. I mean, he hated when anyone spoke anything but American. That's what he calls it. Not 'English.' *American.* I didn't mind the way he talked, I guess. I was alone with Hunter. Tweaking a little. Scared. It felt good to have a strong man in our lives."

"Strong, right." Vega couldn't believe how warped her sense of a "strong man" was. Then again, Vega had to remind himself that this was a woman who'd seen her father blow away his entire family. She had no yardstick for normal.

"At first, things were good between us," said Kaylee. "He got me to cut back on the meth. But then he started spending all his time on these online chat sites. Talking to crazies who told him there was this plot hatched by Jews to breed white Christians out of existence. It made him a little paranoid, I guess. He's a truck driver, so he travels a lot. He started making more guns and selling them to people who can't get them legally. Neo-Nazis and skinheads and people who hate the government. He started drinking more too—even as he told me to stay off the meth. And then the abuse started."

"So that protest yesterday," said Vega, "that's not a one-off, I take it?"

"He's got this group of biker friends," said Kaylee. "They call themselves 'The Puritan Sons.' "

"Yeah. I saw the vest," said Vega. "Puritan pride." The words felt oily on his tongue.

Hunter dropped his toy and whined. Kaylee reached around to fetch it for him. When she turned back, something heavy seemed to settle in her eyes. She traced a finger on the wheel. "They want to start a race war."

"For real?"

"They seem pretty serious," she said. "They want to rid the country of immigrants, but they've got a long list of enemies. Blacks. Jews. Liberal politicians. Universities. The media. Judges . . ."

Vega sat up a little straighter. Something buzzed inside his brain, grating like microphone feedback. He thought of his sister's words at the bus terminal yesterday: *Plenty of people would like to see that woman off the bench. And not all of them are thinking retirement.*

Kaylee misread his stiffness as personal. "I'm so sorry, Jimmy. I know you're Puerto Rican and all. You've been so good to me. The closest thing to a father I've ever had. None of this is about you. I just . . . don't know a way out." Her phone dinged twice. "That's Boyd. And the pizza's ready. I've got to go."

"Kaylee, wait." Vega touched her arm. "Tell me you don't believe this bullshit."

"It doesn't matter what I believe," she said. "I've got bigger problems. The drug charge. Maybe losing custody of Hunter."

Another ding. Another text from Boyd. Kaylee tapped out a reply.

"What if I told you," said Vega, "that I could make all of this disappear?"

"You can't fix this by talking to the cops," said Kaylee. "It's way past that point."

"I'm not talking about fixing anything." Vega chose his words carefully. He'd have just one chance to make his case before she stepped out of his life forever. "There was a shooting at the courthouse in Broad Plains yesterday. Did Boyd mention it?"

"I know he and his friends were really happy about it," said Kaylee. "They hate the judge who got shot."

"Do they hate her enough to want a permanent solution?"

Kaylee went very still. "Look, I've got to go. You don't have to pay for the pizza."

"I want to," said Vega. He slowly fished his wallet out of his pants. He was stalling for time. "Listen, Kaylee—it seems to me like someone in Boyd's circle might know who was behind the courthouse shooting—"

"No."

"I'm not saying he was involved," said Vega. "But he might know who was."

"He doesn't discuss those things with me."

"You could search his computer history," Vega suggested. "Find out who he's speaking to online. What he's discussing. Whether he knew about any plans to target the courthouse. At the very least, you could find out who he delivers his guns to."

"He'd kill me."

"You'll die if things continue as they are," said Vega. "By his hand. Or yours. Kaylee." Vega turned to her. "I'm offering you a chance to work as a confidential informant. To put Boyd and his friends away so they never bother you again. And in return, I will make absolutely sure you get diverted to a treatment program instead of jail so you can raise your little boy safely as a clean and sober mom."

Kaylee allowed a glance in the rearview mirror at Hunter playing with his toy. Her face trembled. Her lips quivered. It was as close to crying as he'd ever seen her.

"I don't want to lose my baby."

"I know you don't," said Vega. "Here's your way out."

"I don't know what I'll be able to find out."

"All I'm asking is that you try."

"Okay." Kaylee exhaled. "On one condition."

"What?"

"I talk to you and you alone, Jimmy. You're the only one I trust."

Chapter 13

Vega sat in his truck, windows open, the sticky evening air making the back of his pin-striped dress shirt stick to the seat. A swirl of gray clouds feathered the sky. He would have loved some rain to cool things down, but nothing came.

He studied the cell number that Special Agent Doug Hewitt had given him the other day at the bus terminal. You don't just call up a man as important as Hewitt and ask to be part of the FBI's case. Not if you're a nobody county detective. You talk to your boss who talks to the chief of department who talks to the FBI.

Vega already knew how that would go.

And yet, he had to do something. Not just because he wanted to help Kaylee—which he did. But because his gut told him that Boyd Richter might very well be involved in the courthouse shooting, either directly, through involvement with the shooter, or indirectly, by supplying the weaponry. And even if he wasn't, Richter was the sort of guy who might be inspired by such a shooting to attempt one of his own.

Hewitt would want this lead. He'd welcome the informant. Which meant he'd have to take Vega as well. Kaylee wouldn't trust anyone else. Nor would Vega. Still, this wasn't the sort of conversation Vega wanted to have over a cell phone.

It was nearly five p.m. Vega searched his phone for a main number for the FBI's Broad Plains office. He put on his most official voice.

"Detective Vega. County PD," he said when the receptionist answered. "I'm trying to reach Agent Hewitt on a matter he asked me to get back to him on. Do you know where I can find him?"

"He's at the medical examiner's office," she replied. Vega suspected he knew why: *Darryl Williams's autopsy.* "Would you like me to contact him for you?"

"No," said Vega a little too quickly. "I'll swing by there myself."

A half hour later, Vega pulled into the parking lot in front of the Office of the County Medical Examiner, a small, unassuming building, tucked away in a corner of the state medical college's campus, across from county dispatch and the teaching hospital. It looked like a maintenance facility from the outside with its collection of roof vents and air compressors. The waiting area was like a hotel lobby with its skylights, soft pastel couches, and profusion of plants. All of it was for the suddenly bereaved, the families of murder victims, suicides, accidents, and traffic fatalities. There were a million terrible and unexpected ways to depart this earth. Vega counted himself lucky that he'd never had to set foot in this place as a civilian.

He showed his badge at the door to a security guard, who buzzed him in.

"Do you know if the FBI is still here?" Vega asked.

"Two of 'em, yeah," said the guard. His name tag read *Perez*. He was a short Hispanic man with a close-shaved scalp and a smooth, pleasing voice like a radio announcer. "They're with Dr. Gupta now." Anjali Gupta, the chief medical examiner. "She's finishing the cut."

There was nothing Vega could do but wait in the lobby and catch Hewitt before he left. Vega was glad he was there alone. Bereaved families made him feel self-conscious. Like he was eavesdropping on someone else's misery. He took out his phone and checked in with Adele via text. He didn't want Perez eavesdropping on him either. She already knew about the trial continuance. He'd called her earlier about that and his lack of luck finding her religious medallion. He was texting her now because he wanted to know if Greco had come up with any leads on the bomb threat.

None, she texted back. **We have extra security at La Casa but everything has been quiet. I have to hope it was a one-time hoax.**

Did you find your medallion? he asked.

No, she texted back with a sad little emoji face. **It's gone.**

He wished he could do something to lift both their spirits, but they couldn't even see each other tonight. Three months ago, Adele had been tapped by a New York State immigrant coalition to write a report on immigrant health services in the region. The report was due next Friday, and she hadn't yet assembled all the research. She wanted to get started tonight.

Call me if you need anything, Vega texted her.

I need another month to put this damn report together, she wrote back. **Thanks for understanding, mi vida.**

He tucked his phone away just as Hewitt and Fiske walked into the lobby, joined by Dr. Gupta, in a white lab coat and lime-green sneakers. She always wore bright-colored clothing, which made Vega smile. When they worked together, he liked to tease her that for a very proper Indian doctor, she had a little bit of Puerto Rican in her blood.

"Agent Hewitt." Vega stood. "Agent Fiske."

Hewitt's noncommittal smile suggested he assumed Vega was here on another case. "Hey, Doc," Vega greeted Gupta.

"Detective?" Gupta looked perplexed. "Did we have some business this evening?"

"Actually, Doc, I'm here to speak to the agents."

"Ah." She nodded. "Then I will bid you all a good evening." She walked back through the security door into the building's administrative offices. Hewitt's eyes buzzed with impatience. Vega wondered what the agents had learned during the autopsy that had fired him up.

"Sir," Vega began, addressing Hewitt, "I've uncovered some information that might be important to the investigation. I'm wondering if I could speak to you for a moment?"

"Go ahead."

"The information is of a sensitive nature. Could we speak more privately?"

Hewitt looked pointedly at his watch. "Five minutes." Vega was of no use to him anymore. He didn't have to feign politeness.

In the parking lot, Fiske, silent as ever, climbed into the driver's seat of a white Chevy Tahoe with a gold FBI emblem on the door. Hewitt joined Vega in back. When the adrenaline had been pumping right after the shooting, Vega felt confident about speaking to Hewitt and giving the special agent his impressions. In the intervening twenty-four hours, he'd lost some of his nerve. He thought back to his insecurities when he considered applying to the FBI. He tried to swallow those doubts and concentrate on Kaylee.

"I've made contact with a potential confidential informant who has inside knowledge of a white supremacist involved in the manufacture and distribution of automatic weapons," Vega began. "My informant believes the subject has been involved in chat sites advocating violence against immigrants, politicians, and—most importantly here—judges."

Hewitt exchanged a glance with Fiske in the rearview mirror.

"Why have you made contact?" Hewitt asked Vega. "Is this regarding a case with the county police?'

"There is no case," said Vega. "The contact was purely coincidental. My informant was a victim in a case I had many years ago. I think the information is accurate and could be useful to the FBI."

Silence. Vega wondered if he was stumbling into an already solved case. "Maybe you have your primary suspect in the shooting already," Vega offered.

"Off the record?" Hewitt pinched the bridge of his nose as if trying to rouse himself from exhaustion. "We're not even close. We've got nothing on any surveillance videos surrounding the terminal. We can't find that girl witness. The lab ran a check on that wooden toothpick you found on the bus terminal roof. It was negative for fingerprints."

"How about DNA from saliva?" asked Vega.

"Saliva was present," said Hewitt. "But the lab found no match to anything in CODIS." The federal searchable bank of DNA. Vega nodded at the implications. Whoever tossed that toothpick had never been convicted of a violent felony or sexual assault. It was possible the toothpick wasn't even related to the shooting.

"We could use someone with inside knowledge," said Hewitt. He gestured to Fiske in the driver's seat. "Agent Fiske has been monitoring right-wing extremist chat sites. There's been an uptick in activity since the shooting. A number of the posters have mentioned Julia Spruce. Your informant's report on this subject jibes with our profile of the likely perpetrator."

"So, you think Judge Spruce was the intended target," said Vega.

"On the record?" Hewitt spread his palms in a folksy way as if he were conducting a press interview. "We're saying the victims were random targets of someone angry at the courts. Off the record?" Hewitt dropped all the mannerisms, his body shrunken and tight, his boyish chestnut-colored hair at odds with the lines in his face. "The suspect fired only one bullet. A bullet type used for big-game hunting. A full metal jacket .338 Federal, capable of accuracy at extreme distances. So yes, the shooter was aiming for one—and only one—victim. Likely, the highest profile of the three: Judge Spruce. We have nothing on Darryl Williams to suggest he was the intended target. It was chance that it ricocheted off Williams and nicked Spruce."

"If the suspect was aiming for the judge," asked Vega, "why not squeeze off a second shot when he missed?"

"We don't know the answer to that one," said Hewitt. "Perhaps he was concerned about getting away quickly. Perhaps the commotion after the first shot ruined his chances of a clean second shot, especially if he was using a bolt-action rifle that he had to manually chamber."

"Do you know which brand of rifle he was using?"

"We think it was customized," said Hewitt. "He was able to carry it in a small backpack, which eliminates many of the more well-known brands."

Hewitt glanced again at Fiske in the rearview mirror, as if, in some alternate universe, Fiske actually carried on conversations with his boss. "In either case, we believe, judging from his choice of ammunition, venue, and overall shooting ability, that the suspect likely has military experience."

Vega thought about Kaylee's comment that Richter had served two army tours in Afghanistan. Vega wished he'd asked her what his job had been over there.

"Who is the white supremacist making guns?" asked Hewitt.

"Boyd Richter." Vega walked them through what he knew of Richter's background and arrest record. Fiske tapped the information into the onboard computer. Hewitt leaned forward between the front seats and stared at Richter's mug shot and vitals.

"You know . . ." Hewitt wagged a finger. "He's the approximate height and body type of the subject on our bus station video. Minus the beard and mustache, which appear to have been fake."

"That's true," said Vega. "And certainly, the FBI could talk to him right now if you wanted. But I suspect you'd only drive his whole operation underground."

Hewitt's jaw set to one side. His eyes narrowed. "What's your informant looking for from this? A reduction of jail time? Some dropped charges?"

"She's facing a meth possession rap," said Vega. "She wants to be diverted into treatment and keep custody of her little boy."

"Give us her name and we'll see what we can do."

"She won't talk to anyone but me."

"A county detective. *Riiight.*" Hewitt was unconvinced. "Why? Because you once scored a little meth from the police station's stash for her in exchange for a tip?"

"Because when she was six, I saved her life."

Chapter 14

Vega told them her name. He had to. It was the only way to save her. Hewitt, who was not from the area, had no reaction. But Fiske swiveled his white-blond crew cut of hair and stared at Vega with those intense Nordic blue eyes.

"You were that rookie?" The first words Vega had heard him speak.

"I was."

Something softened in Fiske's gaze, like he was seeing Vega for the first time.

Nineteen years after the fact, and Vega could still revisit that day in all its clarity. He was fresh out of the police academy, on a routine patrol through Far Hills, the largest of the county's parks. It had a swimming pool, picnic areas, wooded trails, and a small lake where people could rent paddleboats for $5 an hour. It was a hot Sunday afternoon in mid-July. Everyone else in the world seemed to be off but Vega. He could still recall the starchy feel of his new blue uniform. The polyester shirt. The six-pound Kevlar vest that sat between his undershirt and uniform shirt. The twenty pounds of gear on his duty belt. No matter how much he turned up the air-conditioning in the cruiser, he was still sweating his ass off.

He felt like he was playing dress-up, *pretending* to be a

police officer, rather than really *being* one. Twenty weeks of training at the academy had taught him rules and procedures. It had given him a physical semblance of police work. But it hadn't altered the core within him. He was still a twenty-four-year-old kid without a shred of confidence when he wasn't behind a guitar. He felt about being a cop the way he felt about being a father to his newborn, Joy, a husband to his new bride, Wendy. He felt like he was watching himself from a great distance, laughing at his incompetence. His hesitance. The way he'd twisted himself into this image of a steady, predictable family man when all he really wanted to do was ditch the uniform and responsibilities and make for the open road with his six-string.

In short, he felt like a fraud.

He wasn't supposed to have been cruising the county park alone. He was supposed to have his field training officer with him, but his FTO, a guy named Bobby Dutton, had eaten something at lunch that sent him straight to the can. Vega had left him by the restrooms and circled the park without him. He knew it was going to be a while. That much, Dutton made clear. So instead of taking the main path, past the lake and pool and picnic grounds, Vega headed up to the more remote parking lots at the head of the trails. He figured perhaps he'd catch some teenagers drinking beer. Or maybe just grab a few minutes to himself to enjoy the nice summer afternoon. Being a cop meant working nights and weekends and holidays. He'd forgotten the simple joy of having a whole two days in a row to himself.

He was driving to the parking lot of Trail C, a lot that had a beautiful view of the rolling green hills beyond, when he heard what he thought was firecrackers going off. *One-two-three*, and then after a pause, *four*. He sped up. He'd been a teenager himself not that long ago, so he wasn't going to arrest some kid for shooting off a few bottle rockets. He'd just confiscate the fireworks with a warning. Remind them that there were little kids in the park and that they should be more careful.

But as he pulled into the lot, a white couple ran over. They looked to be about Vega's age. Both wore hiking boots and had backpacks over their shoulders. The guy had a bushy beard like he thought he was a mountain man from the 1800s. The girl had very long brown hair and wore a bandana. They waved their arms above their heads like two marooned sailors, trying to signal a passing ship. Their faces showed both fear and relief when Vega slowed the cruiser next to them and powered down his window.

There's a car over there, the woman huffed out, pointing to a dark blue Nissan Maxima parked off by itself, away from the half dozen other cars in the lot. *Somebody inside was just shooting. And now, it's quiet and there's blood everywhere!*

Vega pulled his cruiser at an angle to block any onlookers—and also, to give himself cover in case the shooter tried to take a shot at him. He got on his radio, willing his voice to stay calm as he relayed the particulars to dispatch, along with a request for an ambulance. He had to hope Bobby Dutton would hear the call on his radio as well and find his own way up here.

For the moment, Vega was completely on his own.

He approached the vehicle and remembered, belatedly, to identify himself as "police," which sounded bogus, even to his ears. He wasn't the police. He was a kid pretending to know what the hell he was doing. He was in over his head.

No one moved. He took a step closer and the full carnage of the scene came into view. A white man lay back against the driver's seat, his hand still wrapped around a .22 caliber Sig Sauer pistol, a bullet having ripped off his face.

To his right, in the front passenger seat, a white woman's

bloody head leaned against the window, spattered with brain matter. In the back, two children were folded over. A boy of about eight or nine—it was difficult to tell. He had a head wound that had probably finished him instantly. And a girl of about six—blond ringlets, pale, bluish skin—her arms clutched around a red Tickle Me Elmo doll from Sesame Street, the red of the stuffed figure's body now soaked with a darker and more sinister shade. Blood poured from a single gunshot wound to her chest. It drenched her lacy, white T-shirt and yellow shorts, but her face was pale and angelic, her blue eyes wide and unblinking. She was in shock, hemorrhaging.

She was alive.

Vega tugged on the door handle, but all the doors were locked. He pulled his flashlight from his duty belt and smacked it against the rear passenger window. The safety glass frosted and pebbled. Vega peeled it back like Saran Wrap and unlocked the door.

The little girl didn't cry. She didn't say a word. It was possible she couldn't. Possible her lungs were filling with fluid.

You're gonna be okay, sweetheart, Vega said softly, mustering as much confidence as he could. *I got you. I'm not going to let anything happen to you.*

He ran to the back of his cruiser for his emergency first-aid kit and brought it over to the vehicle. He recalled from his academy training that sealing a gunshot wound to the chest with plastic was important to keep air from getting in, causing a lung to collapse. If that happened, the girl would die in a matter of minutes. But the damn first-aid kit didn't have a chest seal. Back then, gunshot wounds were still rare in the county. When they happened at all, they were generally suicides. The person was dead by the time police arrived.

Stay calm, Vega told himself. *There has to be another solution.* He jammed his fingers into surgical gloves, then opened a pack of sterile gauze. The packaging itself was sterile on the inside and plastic—to keep out moisture. He settled the child's Tickle Me Elmo into her left arm, away from her chest, and lifted her bloody shirt. The wound was no bigger than his pinkie but that meant nothing. It was all about what was happening on the inside, and right now, Vega knew that was bad. Her face was turning blue. She was dying before his eyes.

He wiped the gauze across the wound. Before it could flow again, he pushed the inside of the packaging over the wound and sealed it in place, using his kit's surgical tape. Then he took more clean gauze and pressed it on top to try to stem the bleeding.

The smell of blood and body fluids filled the car in the stifling heat, soaking the upholstery. Soaking him. His uniform was drenched in blood. He tried not to think about what was going on and just keep up a steady, calm, white noise of words to soothe the child: *You like Elmo? I love Elmo. Hey, I bet you know all the characters on Sesame Street. Elmo and Big Bird and Oscar the Grouch. And Cookie Monster. He's my favorite . . .*

The little girl never said a word. She just squeezed her Elmo doll in her left arm tightly and stared up at Vega with her big blue eyes. He knew he should probably check the other occupants to see if they were alive, but he sensed it would be futile. And besides, he couldn't leave this little girl. Not for a minute.

He couldn't recall all the things he said to her. Did he tell her he had an infant daughter? He knew he thought about Joy. How small and precious she was. How unbearable it was to him that anyone could do such a thing to a child. There were a few spectators behind his vehicle, watching him. But he wasn't aware of them in those fragile minutes he leaned over the girl, sweat drenching his three layers of uniform, plastering his hair to his scalp like he'd just come out of the shower.

When you get better, I'll get you a new Tickle Me Elmo, okay? A special one. Just from me. My name is Jimmy. I know you can't tell me yours, but I'll find out. I'll visit you at the hospital. You'll get well. We'll celebrate with cake and ice cream and you'll be fine.

It was a prayer. As much for him as for the child.

It took five long minutes before the ambulance siren screamed up the hill to the trailhead parking lot. It took two more minutes before his FTO, Dutton, finally appeared. The little girl's color was good by then, but she still hadn't spoken. She'd gone from clutching Elmo to clutching Vega. When the EMTs tried to pry her away, her little bloody fingers wouldn't let go of his uniform shirt.

It's okay, baby girl. I'm riding with you.

He didn't leave her side until she was wheeled into surgery. He was there—off duty by then—when she got out. He'd been there, one way or another, ever since. At birthdays and grade school graduations. On street corners and in police holding cells.

She was a year older now than he'd been when he leaned over her that day, sweat-soaked and covered in her blood, bargaining with God to save this child. The doctors later told him that if he hadn't taped that sterile gauze packaging to her chest and kept her breathing calm and even with his steady, soothing banter, she would have died before the ambulance arrived.

He'd saved her. But she'd saved him too. He went to work that morning not even sure he'd last six months in the job. He came home that night with a tiny nugget of understanding that this was what he'd been put on earth to do.

He told Agents Hewitt and Fiske the bland facts of that day. He could never convey their meaning. But perhaps he didn't need to. Something shifted in both men's eyes.

"All right," said Hewitt. "Let's see what she can do to help us. I'll put the paperwork in to your boss and get you reassigned as a liaison to the case, effective tomorrow morning."

"Thank you, sir," said Vega.

"I'd like you to do something else for us as well," said Hewitt. "I understand there's a division inside the county police that handles threats against government employees."

"It *was* a division," said Vega. "Back after nine-eleven, when the county had funding for it. It's down to one sergeant now. A guy named Don Barzak."

"I'd like you to meet with this Sergeant Barzak," said Hewitt. "Find out if Julia Spruce has been the target of threats before."

"Certainly," said Vega. That was one way to narrow down the list of suspects. The other was that witness. "No leads on the girl, I take it."

"She wasn't on the buses," said Hewitt. "We have some footage that indicates she and the woman she was traveling with may have left the terminal on foot. No car picked them up at the terminal so we have to assume they're still in the vicinity of Broad Plains."

"Have you checked with anyone in the local immigrant services community?" asked Vega. "The Hispanic Action Network? Broad Plains United? Urgent Care Español?" Vega knew all of them, both as a cop and through Adele.

"My agents have checked in with all of them," said Hewitt. "No one recognized her."

Vega wondered whether someone *had* recognized her but was keeping quiet so as not to make themselves a target. Especially if this sniper had an anti-immigrant agenda.

"She's gotta be out there still," said Vega. "I mean, you haven't found a body."

Hewitt's eyes tightened. "Yet."

Chapter 15

A cool morning mist fanned the hillsides as the old wood-sided pickup truck bounced and dipped along the dirt road toward the orchard. People held on to the sides and to each other to keep their balance, swaying in unison with every turn of the wheels. Lunch tins and backpacks jostled at their feet.

"Maybe it won't be so hot today," Eli's mother murmured. But already, the mist was thinning beneath a blush sky and the morning birds were leaving the fields for shade.

Eli held her left wrist awkwardly at her side. Her mother had wrapped it tightly in a T-shirt last night. It was swollen and painful. She couldn't use it to pick apples. But she didn't want to tell her mother and worry her.

The truck stopped next to the white trailer where Señor Ortega sat under the awning in his tan cowboy hat and leather boots. Everyone climbed out. Eli knew the routine now: Grab a big white mesh bag. Slip it across your body. Pick as much fruit as you could before the sun got high in the sky. It was hard yesterday, especially with her bad wrist. But at least then, her muscles didn't feel like they were on fire from all that reaching and stooping and carrying. She'd been so tired last night; she'd fallen asleep at dinner. Rice and beans again—along with some carrots and potatoes from the nice neighbor, Encarna, with the wax-paper skin.

"Everybody out," said the hunchbacked driver, herding them out of the truck bed like cattle. Señor Ortega had yelled at Eli and her mother yesterday for picking apples the wrong way. *Use the sides of your fingers—not the tips,* he'd scolded in Spanish. *And don't drop them in the bin. No one will pay for bruised fruit.* The apples were hard as rocks but no matter. They had to carry them like they were baby birds.

Eli had no idea how much money she and her mother had made yesterday. Ortega told them he paid Luis their salary. They could take it up with him.

As the sun rose, the morning grew hotter and more humid. By midday, the air had the weight of glue. They could feel the heat through the thin fabric across their backs and arms like someone was holding a hot iron on the other side. They didn't dare take their shirts off for fear of poison ivy, ticks, sunburn, and the pesticide powder that made their noses and lips sting.

They ate lunch in the fields, eating and drinking as they picked, so as not to waste time. They used the outhouses only once—together—to avoid getting cornered by the foreman. Even with all their care, Eli still got stung by a wasp. She tried hard not to cry as her mother removed the stinger and their neighbor, Encarna, dabbed the spot with white vinegar from a bottle she always carried for this purpose. It helped a little.

"Things will get better," Eli's mother promised softly, more to herself than to her daughter. "Once Luis sees how hard we're working to pay back the loan, he'll take care of us. He'll send you to school. A good school like your cousins attend. He just needs a little time."

Eli bit back the burning pain of the sting, which at least took her mind off her throbbing wrist. Her mother's words frustrated more than soothed. By the time most Guatemalan women reach the age of twenty-nine, like her mother, life tends to make them soft in the body and hard in the soul. They walk around like overripe mangoes—all fleshy and colorful on the outside to hide the enormous pit of ache within.

Eli's mother wasn't like that. No matter what happened to Aurelia Monroy-Rosales, she remained stubbornly trusting. Too trusting, in Eli's opinion. She'd held on to her marriage to Eli's father until he'd nearly killed her. Killed them both. Had her grandmother not pressured Luis for the money to smuggle them here, they might be dead already. And despite all signs to the contrary, her mother still believed her brother was that same boy who carried her on his shoulders and fashioned a doll out of corn husks.

That boy was gone, thought Eli. Life had changed him. Rotted him from the inside. She didn't say these things, of course. It would not only be disrespectful; it would hurt her mother. Instead, she stuffed her thoughts deep inside her chest, in the only spot where her muscles didn't ache, and concentrated on picking the apples to fill those bins and earn her twenty American dollars so that one day perhaps, she could go back to school.

By late afternoon, dark clouds had gathered on the horizon, rolling over the hills, trailing thunder. The rain was more unpredictable here than it was in Guatemala where it could be timed with the seasons. Here, it blew through without warning, catching people by surprise. Everyone kept working under the rounded, deep green leaves. But when the downpour intensified, Señor Ortega, looking silly in his bright yellow rain slicker and damp cowboy hat, ordered the workers to cover the picked produce and retreat under the trailer awning. It wasn't the workers he was worried about. It was the fruit. Wet apples could end up being moldy apples.

Nobody would get paid for bringing in moldy fruit.

Eli and her mother were soaked, like everyone else, by the time they stepped beneath the awning to get out of the rain. There was no place to sit. The ground beneath their feet oozed mud with every shift of their rubber boots. Some of the workers used the opportunity to line up for the outhouses. Others filled their water containers at the spigot. The rest gathered beneath the tin awning in family and friend groups, their conversation spare and quiet from exhaustion.

Señor Ortega retreated inside his trailer. It was built, from the top-heavy looks of it, to be hauled behind a truck, though it clearly hadn't been moved in a long time. The white metal exterior had gone green and black with mold in places. Weeds rimmed the perimeter. A set of concave wood plank stairs led to a screen door that was bowed in the center and frayed at the edges. Norteño music—with its blaring horns and accordion riffs—spewed out the aluminum-framed windows.

After about half an hour of steady, unrelenting rain, Ortega opened the trailer door and announced that he'd called the trucks to take people home for the day. There was no reaction. On the one hand, people could knock off early. On the other, they wouldn't earn as much money.

The air was warm, but people were so wet, they huddled and shivered under the awning. Aurelia clasped Eli close to her. The rain had soaked the T-shirt wrapped around Eli's wrist. Her mother undid the knot to squeeze the water out of the material and retie it. That's when she took a good look at the wrist for the first time. Deep bruises covered the swollen area, along with dark red splotches.

"*Mi corazón,*" her mother gasped. "That's not a sprain. That's a break. How on earth did you break your wrist just going to the bus terminal bathroom?"

Tears stung Eli's eyes. She'd been trying so hard to hold

them back. She couldn't anymore. She sobbed openly. The other workers tried to ignore her, to give mother and child some desperately needed privacy. Only Encarna hobbled over. "*Chiquita,*" she said softly. "The wasp sting will go away."

But already, Aurelia knew this wasn't about physical pain. This was something deeper. Something she'd feared their entire journey north from Guatemala. All this time, she'd kept Eli safe. And now, in a New York bus terminal, it had happened. She gently directed Eli to a corner beneath the awning, away from the other workers.

"What happened in the bathroom at the bus terminal?" she demanded.

Eli was crying so hard, she couldn't get the words out. All she managed was "the bad man" and "he will kill me if I talk."

"Did he touch you?"

"I ran away," Eli choked out. "He grabbed my wrist, but I got away."

"*Dios mío,*" Aurelia whispered, making the sign of the cross. She hugged Eli to her breast, the heat of their bodies doing little to dispel the dampness of their clothes. "You are safe now, *mi corazón*. Thank God, you are safe." Aurelia pulled back slightly so Eli could see her eyes. "We will get you to a hospital. Get your wrist looked at. That's the least my brother can do."

The pickup truck lumbered into the clearing, rain slapping the roof. The driver opened the liftgate. People filed out from beneath the awning and onto the back of the truck. Eli and her mother followed them, the rain beating down on their shoulders and plastering their hair to their scalps. But instead of walking to the back of the truck, Aurelia led her daughter to the cab upfront where the driver sat, warm and dry. Her mother knocked on the window. The man powered it down.

"I need to get in touch with my brother," said Aurelia. "My daughter's wrist is broken. She needs to go to the hospital. I don't have a phone."

The toothless man peered at Eli beneath a frayed baseball cap. His look was accusing, like she'd broken her wrist on purpose to get out of picking apples. He sighed. "Señora, the hospital is many kilometers from here."

"I don't care. I need you to call him."

Slowly, the man pulled out his phone and dialed. Then he handed it through the window to Aurelia. She stood with Eli in the rain, the thick, sucking mud forming puddles around their boots, and told her brother the situation. He didn't sound happy. Then she handed the phone back to the driver.

"My brother said to wait here. He will pick us up. He said there is a clinic nearby where a doctor can treat her."

The driver looked past Aurelia and Eli to the trailer behind them. Something tensed in his eyes. "Okay." He said the word in English. Like he didn't trust their native tongue to convey its full meaning. "Take care of yourself and your daughter, señora." It was the first time he'd ever addressed her formally.

Eli and her mother retreated to the shelter of the trailer awning. When all the people were on the truck, the driver pulled up the liftgate and drove away, splashing through potholes now several inches thick with muddy water. Eli watched the red taillights wink through the trees, then disappear.

Señor Ortega was inside the trailer. The door was closed. Norteño music blasted from within.

"I'm sure Luis will be here soon," said her mother. Her words sounded weak. They huddled together, shivering. There was no place to sit. Mud clawed at their boots like quicksand, making even a shift in their footing difficult.

Eli leaned against the trailer. Her legs felt like jelly. Her wrist felt like it was on fire.

The door to the trailer opened. Señor Ortega stuck his square head out. He wasn't wearing his cowboy hat. A patch of hair had been swept across his otherwise bald scalp, the clumps of black hair following the tines of a comb like a newly seeded field.

"Your brother just called my cell phone," he told Aurelia, his Spanish laced with a strong, rural Mexican accent. "He is going to be delayed. He'll be here in an hour or so."

An hour? Eli didn't know if her legs would last in the mud an hour.

"You are both more than welcome to wait inside the trailer," said the foreman. Ortega opened the door to reveal a warm, dry, paneled interior with a desk and table and some old cushioned chairs. Aurelia looked at her daughter. Eli remembered the driver's warning the other day.

"I'm okay, Mami. We can wait out here."

"Nonsense!" said Ortega. "Why would you stand in the cold and wet when you can wait inside?"

The two women said nothing.

"You are *refusing* my hospitality?" His question had a dark edge to it.

"We would never refuse your kind hospitality," said Aurelia sweetly. She and Eli both knew how touchy men could be about perceived slights. He was their boss. He could make things difficult for them.

Aurelia put a hand on her daughter's shoulder and murmured into her ear. "We're together. We'll be okay."

Ortega opened the door wider and stood in front of it, so that Eli and her mother had to brush past him to walk inside. Their clothes were sopping. Their T-shirts and flannel shirts cleaved to the contours of their bodies. Eli was underdeveloped for her age, her breasts little more than tiny teacups, but Aurelia had all the soft, pleasing curves of womanhood. In Nejapa, men's eyes followed her wherever she went.

The trailer smelled of sweat, cigarettes, and fried food. At the far corner sat a desk with an empty coffee mug next to a crumpled fast-food wrapper and an ashtray overflowing with cigarette butts. Behind a chair repaired in duct tape hung a calendar. August showed a picture of a naked blonde with her legs spread. On the opposite wall sat a counter with a sink, refrigerator, and microwave. Beyond that, Eli saw a door. It was closed.

The foreman offered them two plastic chairs that they gratefully sank into. Eli's feet tingled. Her muscles twitched like they were being held together by stretched rubber bands that were finally being released. A slow ache replaced the tension.

Her wrist throbbed more than ever. She could no longer move it at all.

Ortega opened his refrigerator. Eli felt the blast of chilled air from where she was sitting several feet away. It made her shiver. "A long day of work deserves a cold beer," he said. "And a soda for the girl." He pulled out a can of beer and a can of Coke.

"Thank you, señor," said her mother. "But it's not necessary. We are happy just to wait for my brother."

The foreman put the beer and Coke on the counter, like it was still up for offer. Eli would have loved the Coke, but she sensed the foreman wasn't giving. He was trading. They just didn't know what the terms were yet.

He closed the refrigerator, then leaned against the sink and gave Eli's mother a long, probing look. "This is hard work you are doing out there, señora," he said slowly. "Not just for you, but for your young daughter. This is no life for her."

Aurelia said nothing. This was not a man you opened yourself up to. He reminded Eli of the coyotes who'd smuggled them north. Men with dead eyes and lightning reflexes who measured everything by how little they could offer and how much they could take. It had been a constant struggle not to get molested and beaten. Mostly, it involved being as invisible as possible. Never complaining. Always following directions. Staying with the crowd. Never being alone.

Like Eli was at the bus terminal.

Like they both were now.

Ortega grabbed the beer and opened it for himself, taking a long pull, then wiping his mustache with the back of his hand. He stepped closer to the two plastic chairs until his legs were practically touching Eli's mother's. His dark eyes had an animal twinkle in them. He kept his gaze on Aurelia.

"I know ways you can make a lot more money, *muñeca,*" he said. *Baby doll.* "Enough so your daughter wouldn't have to work at all."

Eli stiffened. Neither of them had any doubt what he was proposing. Right now, it was a suggestion. A negotiation. But in Eli's and her mother's experience, it never stayed a negotiation for long. What men couldn't get with their charm and conniving, they took with their fists.

The only hope was to soothe his ego. To stall. To pray that Luis showed up much sooner than he'd promised. Aurelia smiled, shyly, like she was flattered by his attentions.

"Señor," she began, staring at her feet, "I don't know what to say."

"You are a beautiful woman. I'm sure men have told you so before." He took another slug of beer and reached down to stroke the wet denim fabric of her thigh. He was close enough now for both to smell the beer on his breath, the nicotine on his clothes, the way it mingled with the sickly sweet scent of his aftershave. Her mother didn't flinch. Eli held her breath.

"I'd have to think about the offer," said Aurelia, her voice high-pitched and breathless. "My daughter is here and—"

"Your daughter is almost a woman herself." Ortega's gaze shifted to Eli. He parted his mouth—just slightly—and licked his lips in a slow, salivating way that chilled her. Chilled them both.

Aurelia sprang to her feet. "I think I hear my brother's truck."

It was a lie. They all knew it was a lie. But events had escalated quickly and, for once, her mother's trusting nature had not overpowered her common sense. Eli sprinted for the door even before her mother uttered the words. She was operating on animal instinct now. It was a survival mechanism finely honed from their journey north. They had seen terrible things. Sometimes, it was only luck that had saved them. Sometimes it was fast reflexes.

Like now.

The door to the trailer was made of flimsy metal. It opened easily and stayed open. But there was a second door, a screened one, that automatically hissed shut on its hinges after opening. Eli got through the screen door. Her mother—a second behind—didn't.

Eli heard a tiny gasp, followed by a suction-like sound as the metal door closed behind her, the rubbery insulation sealing off her mother's escape. Eli turned and flung open the screen door again. She heard another noise now. One that made her heart stop in her chest. A click.

Ortega had locked her mother inside.

Eli pounded on the door with her good right fist. "My uncle's here!" she shouted. "He will kill you if you touch her." But the rain beat down so loud on the tin-roof awning, Eli wasn't even sure Ortega could hear her. She scanned the clearing beyond the trailer. She saw nothing. Just empty, mud-soaked fields. She had to do something. She remembered the plastic sheds in the orchards full of hacksaws and pruning shears and shovels. If she had a shovel, maybe she could break down the door with her good hand and rescue her mother.

Eli dashed into the clearing, lifting her oversized boots out of the mud that threatened to bog her down, her eyes blurred by a mix of tears and rain. She was breathing so hard, she didn't hear the engine at first. Didn't believe it wasn't just the rattle of air through her lungs. But then it drew nearer. Relief flooded her senses as her uncle's big, shiny, blue Jeep came into view. He stopped the car short and hopped out.

"Elizabeth!" He said her name sternly, as if he thought she was running around for fun. "Where is my sister?"

"Señor Ortega . . . the foreman," she choked out, trying to catch her breath. "He locked her in his trailer. He . . ." She dissolved into tears, finally able to surrender this terrible burden of carrying an adult load alone.

Luis slammed the car door and raced to the trailer, cursing under his breath in a mixture of English and Spanish. Eli couldn't keep up. He bounded up the steps, opened the screen door, and pounded on the metal one.

"Ortega! You *hijo de puta*! Open this door right now, *pendejo*!"

A minute later, the door slowly hissed open. Aurelia stepped out, looking pale and shaken. Eli threw her arms around her mother. It felt like hugging a tree. Her mother just stood there with no expression on her face. She didn't lift her arms to return her daughter's hug. Behind her, Ortega stood, finger-combing what was left of his hair into place. He chuckled nervously. "Nothing happened, Luis. I promise you—"

Luis balled up a fist like he was going to hit Ortega. Then he let it drop to his side, as if some invisible force was holding it back. "Go," he said to Eli's mother. "Both of you. Get in the truck." His eyes never left Ortega.

Aurelia's walk was stiff, her steps small and measured.

Eli opened the front passenger door of her uncle's truck and helped her mother inside. Then she climbed in back. A moment later, Luis returned and got into the driver's seat, slamming the door. He made a three-point turn and the Jeep bounced down the muddy road to the paved two-lane.

Aurelia said nothing, only stared blankly at the fog of condensation on the windows. There was no other sound save for the steady thump of wipers and the purr of the engine. Luis never took his eyes off the road.

"The hospital is far," he mumbled. "But there is a clinic about twenty minutes away. Dr. Carrasco is supposed to be pretty good. She treats a lot of immigrants in the area."

Aurelia didn't answer. They drove in silence until the rain slowed to a drizzle, spattering the windshield like someone had sneezed across it. Her uncle's fingers rose and fell on the steering wheel, like he was having an argument with himself. He snuck a glance at Eli's mother, whose gaze stayed straight and unblinking.

"He won't hurt you again, Aurelia. I promise." His voice was hoarse and phlegmy. "He knows I will kill him if he touches you. If he *ever* touches Elizabeth." His eyes turned glassy. He blinked the slickness away.

"It's only for a little while," he continued. "Until you can pay back at least *some* of the money. Then Elizabeth can go to school. Then you can forget about all of this."

Aurelia still didn't respond.

"You have to understand," he droned on. "It's not like I have a lot of choices, okay? Things are hard for me too." Eli had no idea what he was talking about and she was sure her mother didn't either. Luis sounded almost pleading now. "Look, I'll get you a phone. *Today.* Right after we finish up at the doctor's. It will be a pay-as-you-go, but you'll have it so you can call me if that *cabrón* ever tries to grab you again."

"You think a phone is going to change everything?" Aurelia's words, after so long a silence, were harsh and accusatory.

"It will help," said Luis.

"Help your conscience, you mean."

Luis pounded the steering wheel. "What do you know about the pressures I'm under? You know nothing! Things are hard here. In a different way from Guatemala, yes. But they're still hard. They call America the land of dreams. To dream, you have to sleep, and you can never shut your eyes here. Not for one minute, or someone will come along and steal everything you've worked for."

Her mother stared out the window at the smooth, slick, winding two-lane. She had stopped speaking. She used to retreat like this too, after Eli's father had one of his explosive bouts.

"Aurelia, please, I give you my word," said Luis. "It's only for a little while. Things will get better. You'll be okay. You *and* Elizabeth."

Eli wanted to believe him. But she'd long ago stopped trusting the promises of men.

Chapter 16

Every police department has guys like Don Barzak. Clock-watching in Pistol Permits. Dodging paperwork in Traffic Violations. Snoozing in a corner of Evidence Storage or playing with their phones in the Motor Pool. Way, way back, these guys must have wanted the job. Maybe their father or uncle was already on the force and they liked the idea of a steady paycheck and the respect that came with the uniform.

Then, somewhere along the line, they gave up. Some, because they got cynical. Some, because they got scared.

And some, like Barzak, because work was a four-letter word.

As a patrol officer, Barzak was famous for driving around for hours and not spotting a single arrestable offense. Not even a misdemeanor. He eventually transferred to the traffic division, where he did little more than issue parking and speeding tickets when a supervisor got on his case. Real accident investigations were always handed off to someone else because his were sloppy and cursory. If anyone complained about him, he complained to the union.

It wasn't that Barzak was dim-witted or mean-spirited. On the contrary, he was always up for a party to celebrate someone's promotion. He chipped in to the football pools and bought Girl Scout cookies from cops with daughters selling them. He attended all the division picnics and union meetings. He never showed up to work drunk or high. Never made a documentable homophobic or racist or misogynistic slur. He was too lazy to violate someone's civil rights. Too much effort and paperwork.

He did nothing that could be considered a firing offense.

He just did nothing—until he finally landed an assignment where he could do just that. What cops call a "tit" job. The Government Employees' Threat Assessment Unit. GETAU, which sounded a lot like "Get Out." Which was probably what the brass wanted him to do.

Post-9/11 funding had enabled both the state police and the county to fund the unit. The state took the money and left the work to the county. The county took the money and gradually eliminated the warm bodies that handled any real investigative work. Barzak was an investigator in name and a clerk in reality. He collated complaints and sent them on to real detectives if he needed to. The rest of the time, he stayed in his office in the basement, across from Evidence Storage, and gossiped with other cops who came to tender or retrieve items for a case.

That was Don Barzak's greatest asset. He was a walking Wikipedia of every piece of police gossip in the county.

Vega knew better than to visit Barzak first thing in the morning. The man would likely clock in and go immediately out for coffee. Not that Vega could blame him. His office was in what guys called "the dungeon." No natural light. And no matter how carefully controlled the air system was in Evidence Storage, there was always a faint smell of human decay that wafted through the corridor, a reminder that "evidence" included a lot more than guns and knives.

Vega waited until a respectable ten-thirty a.m. to seek Barzak out. It fit better into his day's schedule anyway. He was supposed to meet Kaylee at O'Rourke's this afternoon when she went on break.

Vega found Barzak in his cubicle, staring at his computer screen. From the back, the man looked like Silly Putty that had been poured into the chair, then molded by gravity. His thick neck rolled straight into his fleshy mountain of a back, covered in a dark blue polo shirt that strained at the seams. Vega stepped closer and caught the image of a poker hand on the screen. Barzak quickly clicked out of it and turned.

"Oh. It's just you." He settled back in his chair. "I thought it was the brass. Not that they ever come down here. You need an N95 just to breathe."

"Hey," said Vega. "It's cooler than outside." It was another blistering day. Thunderstorms were slated for later this afternoon. For once, Vega welcomed the rain. He was tired of sweating through every decent shirt he owned.

Barzak pointed to the ceiling. "My condolences, Jimmy. I heard that you got screwed over and Drew Banks got your promotion."

Of course Barzak would know. Barzak knew everything.

"Yeah, well. It happens," said Vega. "Drew's a good officer. I wished him luck."

"If it's any consolation," said Barzak, "*I* made sergeant—God knows how—and it didn't do me squat." He shook his head. "That whole trial is a crock. You know about that ambulance chaser Carver, right? He's got a profitable little franchise going, suing everybody in sight on behalf of nonexistent immigrant relatives."

"So I've heard." Vega didn't want to gripe about the trial with Barzak. It would be in every cop locker room by six tonight. He pointed to a chair stacked with folders full of papers. "Mind if I move these and take a seat?"

"It's a free country. Some of the time anyways."

"I got a couple of questions maybe you can answer."

All of Barzak's chins nodded, each in their own rhythm. "If I can, I will."

"I understand you're what's left of GETAU."

"Yep. Me, myself, and I," said Barzak. "GETAU sounds like one of those drugs they advertise on TV that makes you horny all the time."

Vega grinned. He wondered if Barzak was checking out porn as well as poker on his computer.

"Does the state still funnel everything to you?"

"They're supposed to. No way to know for sure." Barzak shifted his girth until he was leaning slightly back in his chair, his gut out in front of him like a water balloon. "I'm like the night watchman at a nuclear plant. I get none of the responsibility and all the blame if something goes wrong. How about you tell me what you're looking for? Or are you fixing to replace me after Carver makes you the ten-million-dollar man?"

"I'm not looking to replace you." The words came out sharper than Vega had intended. He couldn't entirely hide the fear that if he really *did* lose the lawsuit, there'd be some sort of dungeon in his future.

"Well, that's good," said Barzak with a smile. "Because I'm not looking to get replaced."

"I want to know if you've come across any threats against judges."

"*All* judges? Or one in particular? 'Cause I'll tell you—divorce court's the worst. People threaten to kill each other over the disposition of a sofa. I'm not kidding." Barzak grabbed an open bag of Doritos next to his phone and held it out to Vega. Vega waved it away. Ten-thirty seemed a little early for Doritos. Kind of like popping a beer in the a.m. But hey, to each his own. Barzak dug his fingers inside the bag, pulled out a chip, and popped it into his mouth.

"I'm interested in threats against Julia Spruce."

Barzak stopped chewing. His mouth hung open a second before he thought to close it. He wiped his lips with the back of his hand. "You're working the courthouse shooting with the FBI. Jesus, Jimmy—how the hell did you manage that? 'Cause the brass 'round here wouldn't let you clean a toilet with a toothbrush right now."

"I'm just doing one errand for the feds," said Vega.

Barzak jabbed an orange-coated finger at the ceiling. "Does Waring know?"

"The FBI is walking the paperwork through now."

"Well, well." Barzak wiped his fingers along the armrests of his chair. His body was so thick and fleshy, his arms seemed lost in all that mass. "I'm glad somebody appreciates your talents. But be careful on this one, my friend. Julia Spruce is politically protected."

"By whom?"

"Andrew Locklear. Our beloved state attorney general. He would not be a happy camper if you put her court record under public scrutiny. It could come back to haunt him in the November election."

"I've heard she's anti-ICE," said Vega.

"She's more than anti-ICE," said Barzak. "She's on a crusade."

"Does it matter here?" asked Vega. "A court officer is dead. The FBI is trying to catch a killer."

"Politics *always* matters. Which is why the FBI sent you to me. They know Spruce was the target. They know Locklear needs to do damage control."

For a guy who spent his days underground, Barzak sure knew a lot about how things worked.

"You got anything in your files to back up your theories?" asked Vega.

"My brother-in-law, Vinnie, is an ICE agent," said Barzak. "That's how I know about her record with illegals. And then there's that Juan Rivas case up in Lake Holly."

"Rivas?" Vega had been so preoccupied with preparing for his trial, he'd been out of the loop.

"The Juan Rivas case," Barzak said again. He dug into his bag of Doritos and looked disappointed to find it empty. He pushed it to the side of his desk where it joined an empty coffee cup and two crumpled candy bar wrappers.

"There was a BOLO out for this Mexican dude," said Barzak, kicking back in his chair, relishing a chance to share a little gossip. "A reputed cartel member was wanted in some heavyweight dealing upstate. Somehow, Lake Holly got word that he might be hiding out in their jurisdiction. So they did a sweep of the area. Didn't find the bad hombre. But they picked up this guy who gave his name as Juan Rivas. Didn't speak English. Claimed he was a day laborer in the area, but no one recognized him and he had no ID. One of the local detectives who speaks Spanish frisked him and found a filet knife."

Omar Sanchez. Vega had worked with Sanchez on several occasions. The detective was very by-the-book. Since New York State forbids noncitizens to carry knives, Sanchez would definitely have charged Rivas for the knife possession.

"Rivas tells the detective he uses the knife when he goes fishing. But Lake Holly decides to hold him anyway, seeing as he has no ID and no one knows him."

Vega couldn't see why this very pedestrian arrest would interest Barzak so much.

"I haven't told you the kicker," said Barzak. "Lake Holly tries to run the guy's prints. He has none."

"You mean, he's not in the system," said Vega.

"I mean he has no prints. Nada. Zip. The detective asks him about it and Rivas says they were burned off in a landscaping accident. Landscaping accident, my ass. Vinnie says his pads were as smooth as a baby's behind."

"Wait," said Vega. "How's your brother-in-law involved?"

"He was the ICE agent who issued a detainer on Rivas. Soon as he heard about the lack of prints, he knew: You don't get that from an accident. His prints were lasered off. Nobody does that unless they've got a rap sheet they're looking to hide."

Vega had to agree.

"Bet you can guess the rest," said Barzak. "Rivas, lucky guy that he is, ends up before Judge Spruce. Spruce vacates the charge. Rivas skips before Vinnie even makes it to court."

"Hold it." Vega put up a hand. "Are you saying that Judge Spruce *knew* Juan Rivas had no fingerprints—and still let him go?"

Barzak shrugged. "What other conclusion can you draw?"

"Lake Holly could have forgotten to send a report about the prints," said Vega. "Spruce may not have known."

"Maybe. But hey, Vinnie knew," said Barzak. "So, you have to figure that Spruce saw the print report and ignored it."

Vega massaged his forehead, trying to come up with a reasonable explanation for the blunder. "Is Judge Spruce losing it, perhaps? Early Alzheimer's?"

"Dunno," said Barzak. "Anything's possible. But you can see why people hate her."

"*People?* Or just ICE and the cops?"

"I'll show you." Barzak pushed himself out of his swivel chair and walked over to a file cabinet just outside the cramped cubicle. He grunted as he tugged open the top file drawer. He lifted out a folder and handed it to Vega. The spine fit comfortably in the palm of Vega's hand.

"This is one year's worth of hate mail to all the other judges in the state. I'm talking every level. Family court. Traffic court. Criminal court. People who've had their kids taken away from them. People who've lost their right to drive or been sentenced to twenty years on a drug rap. This folder contains every letter, phone call, Internet comment, or social media post deemed threatening enough for the state or county to funnel to me. And this . . ." He opened the file drawer beneath it and pulled out a much larger accordion folder that took up almost a quarter of the space. He pushed it into Vega's hands. "This is all the hate mail in the last year to Julia Spruce."

"You're kidding," said Vega. It was five times as large. Vega settled back into his chair and opened the accordion folder. "Are all of these letters and emails about her being soft on illegals?"

"Pretty much," said Barzak. "Which is unusual in itself. Most of the mail other judges get is from the families of defendants who are unhappy with their sentences. She has a couple of those. But the majority aren't from anyone connected to her cases."

"Is she pro-defense in all of her criminal proceedings?" asked Vega.

"Not from what I can see," said Barzak. "She seems pretty evenhanded otherwise. She's just got this thing about federal encroachment in her courtroom. Or at least, that's how she frames it. All I know is, it's pissing off a lot of conservatives."

"What do you do with all this mail?"

Barzak must have sensed a criticism in the question. He spread his soft, fleshy arms. "What *can* I do with it? I'm one sergeant. Hey, if the brass wanted to make this a priority, they shouldn't have reassigned all those detectives."

"So"—Vega knew he had to tread carefully—"you just file the papers?"

"I read 'em," said Barzak defensively. "Somebody threatens physical harm, I pass it along to the detectives division. But most of the writers just like to vent."

Vega patted the Spruce folder on his lap. "Are all these

letters from different people? Or is it a couple of trolls, over and over?"

"The letters and emails come from all over," said Barzak. "Even out of state. I think she's a target of the alt-right. They like to bash her on chat sites. If I get a letter or email where the language is pretty much the same as other letters and emails, I just file it. I don't bother wasting a detective's time."

"Why?"

"Because it's just a campaign, you know? Like when people all copy and paste the same letter to their senator. Doesn't mean they're going to *do* anything."

"Have you ever tried to match these letters?" asked Vega. "Maybe see if there's a network of extremists who are connected?"

Barzak exhaled, like he was explaining shoelace tying to a very uncoordinated kid.

"Jimmy—that's the work of the FBI. Not one agent or two, but a whole goddamn unit. I'm one guy. Besides, you know that these chat-site crazies are all disaffected young men, sitting in their parents' basements, hoping to get laid. They're not a *real* threat. I mean, maybe every now and then one of them commits an act of vandalism—"

"Or kills twenty-two innocent people." They both knew Vega was referring to the mass shooting of a group of predominantly Latino civilians by a white supremacist in El Paso, Texas.

Barzak pulled a face. "You can't predict that stuff. Those are lone gunmen."

"Except when they're not," said Vega. "All these guys feed off each other online. If Spruce is hated by so many, isn't it possible that there's a network of extremists out there who might have coordinated an attack?"

"You want to earn your gold star with the feebies and make that sort of connection?" asked Barzak. "Knock yourself out."

"So, can I take the folder?"

Barzak hesitated. "I could be a hard-ass and insist you only look through them here. In my presence. They're evidence, after all."

"*Evidence?* You got a case?"

"I could . . . One day . . ."

"And maybe one day, you'll be chief of department too."

"I got a better chance than you at the moment." Barzak leaned back in his chair. "I'm worried you're gonna find something and end up hanging this puppy on me."

"You just said yourself, Spruce's people want all of this buried."

"Yeah. But I don't want to get buried with it." Barzak threw up his hands. "Ah, what the hell. Take it. But be careful, my friend. You may not make any friends with this folder either."

Chapter 17

The sky had darkened by the time Vega left Barzak's office with his folder of Judge Spruce's hate mail. A breeze kicked up on the pavement, swirling grit and old cellophane wrappers, but once again, the rain never came.

He drove north to Anniston, setting his GPS for O'Rourke's Bar, where Kaylee worked. Two and a half years ago, when he last visited her place of work, Kaylee greeted him from behind a desk where she made appointments for families searching for their forever home. Now, she schlepped drinks in a smoke-filled dive for men with inked bodies and dreams no bigger than their next score.

It depressed him. He'd have to work not to show it.

O'Rourke's sat between a vape store and a tattoo parlor, far from the majestic sweep of the Hudson River. It was sided in faded brown wood, including the door, which was splintered at the bottom from being kicked too many times. A sign above the door advertised the name, along with a shamrock, which seemed to be ever-present when anything sounded vaguely Irish. There was only one window, too small to peer inside. It had a Genesee beer sign glowing in it.

Vega parked up the street, away from the entrance to O'Rourke's so as not to tip anyone off about his relationship with Kaylee. He didn't want anything getting back to

Richter. He texted Kaylee from his phone. **I'm parked in front of the Dollar Store up the street. Let me know when you're on break and where you want to meet.**

He waited. Five minutes. Ten. No reply. He tried again.

Kaylee? I need to know you're okay or I'm walking into O'Rourke's.

The reply came back instantly: **I can't do this.**

Have you been threatened? Vega texted. **We need to talk.**

Go away.

I will go away when you tell me this in person. Name the spot and time and I will make sure there's no risk to you.

Minutes ticked by without an answer. Vega wondered if one would ever come. And then it did: **Longwood Cemetery. Give me 20 minutes.**

She didn't have to give an address or say where she'd be in Longwood. Vega knew. That was the cemetery where her family was buried nineteen years ago. It was a beautiful spot with one of the nicest views in Anniston on a high hill overlooking the Hudson River. Her father, Richard Wentz, had been an unemployed, alcoholic, air-conditioning repair technician. He never could have afforded such a nice plot. It was a gift from an anonymous donor. Personally, Vega would have preferred the donor establish a trust fund for Kaylee. But maybe in the end, this was better. Maybe, when you lose your whole family in the blink of an eye, you need a place to visit them. A place to call home.

This was the closest thing Kaylee ever had to a home.

Vega arrived early but kept back from the grave site, in case Kaylee wasn't alone. He wanted to see her before she saw him. She wore a black miniskirt and a pale pink tank top with white tennis shoes. Her blond hair was pulled back into a haphazard ponytail. Bits of hair hung on either side of her lean face, curling in the humidity. From this distance, the tattoos on her arms made her look scarred.

Maybe that was the point.

She was carrying a large canvas tote bag instead of a purse. It looked like something she'd take to the beach. She pulled a cigarette from inside and lit it as she stared at the two ornate, white marble gravestones that spelled out her mother's and brother's names and epitaphs.

KATHARINE MARIE WENTZ, LOVING MOTHER. MAY GOD GRANT ETERNAL REST.

JORDAN MICHAEL WENTZ, SON AND BROTHER. BLESSED ARE THE INNOCENT.

A ground marker to the left of them simply read: RICHARD ALLEN WENTZ with his date of birth and death. It had been Kaylee's paternal grandmother's wish that the family be buried together. At the time, it had seemed an offense against Kaylee's mom and nine-year-old brother. But now, Vega noticed that all three graves had a few wilted stalks of flowers across them. The grandmother was long dead. The maternal aunt who'd raised Kaylee lived way upstate. These flowers had to have come from Kaylee.

"Hey," said Vega, making sure not to startle her. She turned. The socket around her left eye was bruised. "What the . . . ? That son of a bitch!"

She'd done her best to cover it with makeup, but she'd sweated it off in the heat. "Now you see why I can't do this?"

"Did you tell him about me?" *That would be disastrous*, thought Vega. If Richter was involved in the courthouse shooting—or had contacts who were—they'd be tipped off. Any case the FBI hoped to make would be in peril.

"He doesn't know anything about you or our arrangement," said Kaylee. She turned away from Vega, took a drag on her cigarette, and studied the slow-moving barges working their way lazily along the Hudson River. "I come up here often, you know. It's the only place I can go to get away from Boyd. I've never told anybody that before."

Vega stood very still next to her and said nothing. She'd taken him here, to her secret place, to say something she was struggling to say. He'd let her say it. At her own pace. In her own way. A stiff breeze washed off the river, cooling his face and the back of his neck. The western sky churned with thickening gray clouds, massive and craggy as mountains, sunlit from above. Vega heard a rumble of distant thunder.

The rain was finally coming.

Kaylee took one final drag on her cigarette, then dropped it at her feet and stamped it out. She kept her eyes on the glint of sun through the clouds as it danced across the river. Her voice barely rose above a whisper. "I told him I was thinking of moving out. That's how my mother died, you know. She told my father she was leaving him. She could deal with him hitting her, even deal with him hitting my brother. But when he started on me . . ."

Her voice trailed off, disappearing into the breeze like it had somewhere important to go. Someplace outside Kaylee where it could be stitched into a narrative that wasn't edged with regret.

"My aunt told me that my mother picked the county park because she figured he wouldn't make a scene. She thought it was safe." Kaylee shook her head at the irony. "There was no safe place once she decided to leave my father. None."

Vega put a hand on her shoulder and gently turned her to face him. "You're worried that that's going to happen here."

"It's already happening, and I haven't even tried to leave."

"Kaylee." Vega held her gaze. "Have you ever asked yourself *why* your mother chose to leave when she did?"

"I know why," said Kaylee. "It's because my dad started hitting me. I'm the reason my mother is dead—"

"No," said Vega. "She's the reason you're alive. She gave her life to get you out. Don't you want a safe life for Hunter?"

"Boyd doesn't hit Hunter—"

"*Yet,*" said Vega. "What about the future? What about the abuse that Hunter is witnessing?"

Kaylee reached into her tote bag and pulled out a large manila envelope. She pressed it into Vega's hand. "Listen, I know I promised you I'd see what I could pull off Boyd's computer. I managed to print out some things. I don't know if they're helpful or not, but they're yours. Do with them what you want. Just . . . don't tell anyone where they came from."

Vega tucked the envelope beneath his arm. "This was never just about an investigation, Kaylee. It was about *you.* Let me take you away now. We can pick Hunter up at Little Sprout and get an order of protection right away, especially with that shiner on your face. You'll be resettled in a safe place by this evening."

"No."

"Why?" He searched her eyes. "Does he supply you with drugs?"

She tucked her chin to her chest and stared at her feet. She didn't have to answer. He could see the answer already. "It isn't that," she said finally. "I mean, I want to get clean."

"Then why?"

"I guess . . . I still care for him."

"Aw, Kaylec, Jesus!" Vega threw up his hands.

"I want him to quit all this hate stuff. I do. But . . . I don't want to be alone. I've been alone my whole life."

"You're *not* alone. I'm here. You've got Hunter." Vega could see he wasn't making any headway. He decided to try a different tack. Kaylee had always had a tender heart for other people in need. She could see their agony better than she could see her own. “What if I told you that a little girl was in danger?”

She frowned. “What little girl?”

“A little girl who can identify the courthouse shooter.”

“You don’t really think Boyd would do something like that? I mean, sure, he beats on me. But he’d never go after a stranger.”

“He sounded pretty convincing the other day at the demonstration,” said Vega. “He got arrested for assaulting a cop who tried to rein him in.”

“The police egged him on.”

Not that Vega could see. If anything, the cops were too passive—far more passive than they were when Black folks protested, in his opinion.

“Boyd isn’t behind any shooting,” Kaylee insisted. “And he’d never hurt a child.”

“What if the child was a Latin-American immigrant?” asked Vega. “He doesn’t seem to think that people who look different from him are even people.”

“Not a child,” Kaylee said again.

“Look,” said Vega. “Maybe you’re right. Maybe Boyd isn’t involved in the courthouse shooting. But he’s into some pretty bad stuff. With some pretty bad people—one of whom might be behind this shooting. A guy who does that sort of crime isn’t about to leave a witness behind, child or not. Do you really want that little girl on your conscience?”

“No,” she said softly.

“Just think about what I’m saying,” said Vega. “Think about the escape route I’m offering. You don’t have to do anything that makes you feel uncomfortable or puts you at risk. But don’t just give up. Please. You were always such a strong girl. Don’t crumble now.”

“I’ll think about it,” she said.

“Good.” He felt the first hard drop of rain fall on his

shoulder. The sky was about to open. "Why don't you leave first?" Vega suggested. He knew she needed to get back to work.

"Thanks." She hugged him tightly. Unexpectedly. And then, without a word, she turned away. He thought of something he'd meant to ask her.

"Hey, Kaylee? What did Boyd do in the army?"

She turned back to him. Rain began *tick-tick*ing on the leaves of trees, turning the pavement dark, washing away the heat and grit. "He was with the First Armored Division in Afghanistan."

"But what was his MOS? His Military Occupational Specialty?"

"He was . . ." Her voice trailed off. Something crossed her rail thin features. Reluctance. Disbelief. Her face was now all chin and cheekbones. Every emotion was relegated to her pale blue eyes. Vega noted a slow dawning in them.

"He was a sniper."

Chapter 18

The rain fell in earnest as Vega hopped back into his truck. There was a crack of thunder and then the heavens opened, tapping on the pickup roof like falling rice. Condensation fogged up the windows. He turned on the engine and blasted the air-conditioning. When the glass cleared, he flicked the wipers.

The cemetery parking lot was empty. Kaylee was gone.

He opened the manila envelope Kaylee had given him. Inside were two sheets of paper that had gone limp and velvety with the humidity. It looked like some sort of spreadsheet. On the left side were initials. *CP, MR, GB . . .* In the next column, after each set of initials, was a number: *2.5, 5, 1.5 . . .* Vega suspected those numbers corresponded with thousands: $2,500, $5,000, $1,500. He suspected this because the third column was the most specific of all. It listed makes and models of semiautomatic rifles that anyone familiar with them would recognize: *BM XM-15 . . . SR 556 . . . CQB MRP . . . S & W 15 VTAC.* After each type of rifle—Bushmaster, Ruger, LMT, Sig Sauer, Smith & Wesson—Richter had typed a number ranging from 5 to 15. The second page had more initials, more apparent dollar amounts, and more shorthand notations. In addition to rifles, Richter appeared to be selling pistols, ammunition cartridges, silencers and flash suppressors. Most chilling of all, he was selling illegal bump stocks that turned semiautomatic rifles into automatic ones.

Vega felt a slow dread as he took in the numbers. Richter was a one-stop supplier of high-grade weaponry—some of it, like bump stocks, banned in the United States. Kaylee had mentioned that he built his own guns. Probably from kits or untraceable parts. Which meant his clients were likely people who shouldn't be in possession of them in the first place: Felons. Radicals. People with psychiatric histories or orders of protection lodged against them.

Who were Richter's clients? The initials told Vega nothing, other than the fact that Richter was a very dangerous man. In all likelihood, the people he dealt with were equally dangerous.

The FBI needed to know.

Vega dialed Agent Hewitt's cell. It went straight to his voice mail. Vega hung up and left him a text instead: **In Anniston. CI has provided me with a list of what appears to be potential gun sales made by subject in question. Would like to discuss. Also, I have the requested file from GETAU. Haven't gone through it yet, but it's in my possession.**

Hewitt texted back immediately. **I'm meeting in my office with a DEA agent on a related matter. Can you join us? Bring the materials you mentioned. We'll wait.**

Vega felt a flutter of excitement. Two days ago, he'd lost his sergeant's promotion. Now, he was being invited into the inner sanctum of the FBI on a major federal case.

The elation died when he thought about Kaylee. About the risks she was taking. The risks he was exposing her to. The sooner he got Richter off the streets, the better.

Traffic was heavy by the time Vega left Anniston and headed south to the FBI's field office in Broad Plains. The rain wasn't helping things. On the boulevards, wipers thumped against windshields. Brake lights and stoplights glowed red and green in puddles. The few souls who sprinted along the sidewalks did so hurriedly, beneath umbrellas.

It took Vega twenty-five minutes to reach the federal complex, a brown, ten-story office building that looked like an upended UPS carton. It was constructed in the 1960s and it showed its age. The green speckled marble floors were scuffed. The bronze eagle above the elevator doors had blackened in the folds of its wings. Faded yellow-and-black fallout shelter symbols marked the exits. Vega felt like a salmon swimming upstream at 5:15 p.m. People were rushing to get *out* of the federal building, not into it.

He took the elevator to the tenth floor. The administrative staff were gone. Hewitt let him in. The FBI agent was joined by a lean, good-looking Black man, dressed in a dark knit polo and khakis.

"This is Stanley Devereaux of the DEA," said Hewitt. Vega switched his paperwork to the other arm and shook the man's hand. He wasn't sure what an agent from Drug Enforcement had to do with the case, but it wasn't his place to ask.

He followed the two men down a hallway lined with photos of former FBI directors. Everything in the interior was a sleek, cool gray with lots of glass and chrome. It was leagues better than the furniture at the county police headquarters, which was mismatched because it was always bought piecemeal when there was money in the county budget.

Hewitt's office had two glass interior walls and a sweeping view of Broad Plains, including the courthouse. But what really struck Vega was what was inside the office. In addition to the usual framed degrees and family photos, there was a wall of newspaper clippings that showed Hewitt overseeing various high-profile cases from Oklahoma to Denver to Philadelphia. Bank robberies. Arrests of fugitives on the Ten Most Wanted list. Kidnappings. Pedophile rings. He'd had an impressive career before coming to Broad Plains. *Too impressive*, thought Vega suddenly. What the hell was Doug Hewitt doing running this second-rate field office? It wasn't New York City. It wasn't even the state capital, Albany. Was this assignment a punishment of sorts?

If so, for what?

Vega took a seat across from Devereaux and studied Hewitt behind his desk. The boyishly full, dyed chestnut-colored hair. The gym-honed physique that looked like it took effort to maintain. The white-collared pinstripe shirt and designer suit that tried a little too hard to impress. Something had happened to Hewitt's career for the FBI to transfer him from Denver to Broad Plains. If it had had even a taint of corruption to it, the agency would have forced him to retire. So it wasn't that. More likely, he'd stepped on someone's toes. Gone against a superior or someone highly connected in Colorado political circles.

Hewitt leaned his elbows on his desk and nodded to Stanley Devereaux. "Let's get down to business, shall we?"

Devereaux cleared his throat. "Eight months ago," Devereaux began in a lilting voice with a trace of Caribbean accent, "local police in Sayertown, New York, arrested two bikers at a trucking depot with about 25 grams of methamphetamine."

Vega knew Sayertown. It was a semirural white hamlet on the other side of the Hudson River, outside his jurisdiction. A lot of New York City cops and firefighters lived around there, because of its cheap housing.

"One of the bikers agreed to flip," said Devereaux. "He told the police that the meth ring was small but that it was part of a much larger operation run by a white supremacist biker gang called 'the Puritan Sons.' "

Vega straightened. "Richter is a member of the Puritan Sons."

"Richter's name never came up in the reports," said Devereaux. "However, the DEA did manage to make some inroads into the meth end of the operation. When we processed the busts, we found significant caches of guns."

"How many?" asked Vega.

"In all?" Devereaux stroked the side of his face. A dark shadow of black stubble made a scratching noise along his palm. He looked like one of those men who had to shave twice a day. "About three dozen semiautomatic rifles, eight of which had been altered to automatic. Almost two dozen handguns. Over two thousand rounds of ammo. The guns were all built from unmarked parts or parts where the serial number had been removed. We never found the supplier. We couldn't get anyone to flip on him."

"I'm beginning to think it's Boyd Richter," said Vega. "Take a look for yourself." He opened Kaylee's folder and handed the spreadsheet pages to Hewitt. Hewitt glanced at it with no reaction and then handed it to Devereaux. Devereaux's eyes widened.

"These are some of the same types of weapons we confiscated in the bust," said Devereaux. "The Bushmaster-style AR-15. The Ruger." He slipped the pages back in the envelope and looked at Hewitt. "I think we've got ourselves enough here to secure an order for a wiretap and twenty-four-hour surveillance."

"We'll take the lead on this one, Stan," said Hewitt.

"Wait," said Vega. He couldn't believe they were already marking territory. Lions at a kill. His gut clenched. A wiretap and surveillance would exponentially ramp up the heat on an unstable man who could explode on Kaylee and her little boy at any minute. "Do you know what Richter's MOS in the army was?"

"Sniper," said Devereaux. "We checked his army record while you were driving here."

"He'll make your surveillance in no time," argued Vega.

"It could tip him over the edge. Turn him more violent. He's a dangerous guy. The least you can do is give me a chance to get my CI and her three-year-old out of there."

"It'll take twenty-four hours to set everything in motion," said Hewitt. "That's plenty of time for her to escape." *If she wanted to. Which she didn't.* What, Vega wondered, was he doing here in this room, playing federal agent with these men? Had he been lying to himself all this time? Telling himself he was doing this for Kaylee, when all the while, he was just trying to make up for his own thwarted ambitions? And now, Kaylee might pay for his mistakes. All her life, she'd been paying for men's mistakes.

Vega told himself that he was different. But he was just as selfish and ego driven as the rest of them.

"Look," said Vega. "I get that Richter's probably supplying guns to this white supremacist biker gang. But his involvement could be so much more. He could be the courthouse shooter. He could have other targets in mind. Shouldn't we give my CI a chance to find out before putting all this heat on him?"

Hewitt's eyes narrowed. He wasn't used to being contradicted.

"Your CI is, of course, free to leave the investigation at any time," said Hewitt. "And so are you." He turned to the DEA agent. "We've had a very productive meeting, Stan. I won't keep you any longer. There are a few things I'd like to address with Detective Vega, if you don't mind."

"Certainly." Devereaux rose and shook Vega's hand. "A pleasure." His eyes held Vega's a beat too long. Vega sensed a warning in them to watch his step. It already seemed too late. "I'll see myself out."

Chapter 19

The DEA agent left the office and closed the door. Hewitt tented his fingers beneath his chin and stared at Vega for a long moment, their outlines shadowed against the rain-spattered glass.

"Detective Vega, I invited you into this meeting today. I invited you into this investigation. I didn't have to do either."

"I understand that, sir. And I appreciate it."

"No," said Hewitt. "I don't think you do. I don't think you understand or appreciate that this is a federal case. You don't call the shots here. And you definitely don't *question* them." He pushed back in his chair. "I understand that that's a problem in general for you. Following orders, I mean."

"Sir?"

"I called over to the county police today to inquire about that trial you're involved in. Apparently, the county stands to lose ten million dollars over your actions."

"I was cleared of any wrongdoing back in December," said Vega.

"Yes, well, as any cop will tell you, the ultimate wrongdoing isn't about what's right or what's wrong, but about who you piss off above you."

Vega sensed Hewitt was speaking from experience.

"Kaylee Wentz is a fragile young woman with a tragic history," said Vega. "Do you really want her fate on your conscience?"

Hewitt turned up his palms. Pontius Pilate washing his hands. "She is free to leave Richter at any time. She needs to also be reminded that if she tips off this boyfriend of hers in any way, I will personally see to it that she does some serious time on the meth charge. Her son will be graduating high school before she sees him again."

Vega stared at him. "All this attention could drive Richter and his associates underground. Make it even harder to find out if he or one of them is behind the courthouse shooting."

"I'll take that risk," said Hewitt. He gestured to the accordion folder in Vega's lap. "I assume that's the file of Judge Spruce's hate mail."

Vega patted the folder. "It's more than I expected. I haven't had a chance to go through it yet."

"No matter." Hewitt held out a hand. "I'll take it."

Vega tightened his grip on the folder. "This file is the property of the Government Employees' Threat Assessment Unit."

"Which you said yourself is down to one county sergeant," said Hewitt. "I'll be sure to send a memo to him, explaining that the FBI needs to hold on to it for now. He's not going to get in any trouble, if that's what you're concerned about."

Barzak was right. Vega should have listened to him. "Locklear," he said softly.

"Excuse me?"

"Andrew Locklear. Our state attorney general," said Vega. "He called you, didn't he? He told you to sit on these letters. He doesn't want Julia Spruce's record to hurt him in the November election."

Hewitt opened his mouth to argue, then closed it again. The game-show host smile was gone. His face looked old suddenly. Tired. He pushed himself out of his chair and stood at the window, staring down at the traffic ten stories below. He had climbed high.

He had fallen from higher, Vega suspected.

He pressed his palms to the glass. "I was once like you," he said. "I was the good guy. We caught bad guys. I saw everything in absolutes. But there's a problem with that sort of thinking." Hewitt turned away from the window to face Vega. "One day you wake up and discover that those other good guys you worked with? They weren't so good after all. And now, instead of working *with* them, you're working *for* them."

Hewitt walked over to the chair where Vega was sitting and held out his hand. "You don't really have a choice here, Detective. That folder is going to disappear, one way or the other."

"What if one of these letters ends up being from the courthouse shooter?"

"I never said the FBI wouldn't look at it."

You never said the FBI would either, thought Vega.

"We're going to nail the courthouse shooter," said Hewitt. "With or without the letters. That's a promise. This?" He took the folder from Vega's hands and tossed it on the edge of his desk. "This will just stir up trouble that won't help the FBI at all."

"Or you."

"Or you," Hewitt shot back. "Look, Detective, I want this sniper as much as you do. I want Boyd Richter. But we're going to do things my way. You want to pull Kaylee Wentz out of this investigation, that's your choice. And hers. So long as she keeps her mouth shut."

"What about the girl?"

"What girl?"

"The immigrant girl at the bus terminal who can ID him."

Hewitt shrugged. "We've had no sightings of her. My

guess is she's long gone from the area and unlikely to come forward. Honestly, if we can make a case against Richter or one of his associates without her, all the better. I'm not wild about using some fresh-over-the-border kid as a witness anyway. She'll never stand up in front of a jury."

Chapter 20

The text came right after Vega left the FBI office. It was from his friend, Lake Holly Detective Louis Greco.

If you're still at work, can you swing by Adele's on your way home? I need to show you something.

It had to be about the bomb threat to La Casa. *Was there another?*

Adele lived in a small blue Victorian on a tidy street of postage-stamp lawns in the heart of Lake Holly. An unmarked detective's sedan sat in the driveway, parked behind Adele's Prius, taking up Vega's usual spot. Vega knew it was an unmarked by all the antennas sticking up from the trunk. He parked down the street and walked back, past parents pushing baby strollers on the sidewalks and neighbors chatting over fences. Adele's neighborhood was tight and chummy. It suited her, though Vega much preferred the solitude of his cabin up north.

He unlatched the white picket gate at Adele's and bounded up the steps to her front porch. He could smell burgers grilling on someone's backyard barbecue. It made his stomach rumble.

Adele's front door was open, with only the screen door closing it off from the porch. Vega cupped his hands over the mesh, the interior hazy and indistinct.

"Adele? Grec?"

Adele came to the door, still dressed in a silky cream-colored blouse and dark pants from work, a look of worry on her face.

Vega opened the screen door. "What's going on? Greco texted me."

The Lake Holly detective poked his head into the hallway. His presence filled the space like some giant Victorian hallstand: wide, heavy, and once settled, impossible to budge.

"Jimmy, we got a problem."

Both ends of that sentence frightened Vega. Lou Greco never called him by his first name.

"You're talking about the bomb threat?"

"That was at La Casa," said Greco. "This is more troubling. Go around back. I'll show you."

Vega snaked around the side of the house between the back door and a large, freestanding, wood-shingled garage with a peaked roof and cupola. The garage was loaded with so much junk, Adele never parked in it. The white paint was starting to flake. The area behind it was overgrown with fragrant honeysuckle vines and weedy bushes with rubbery stems and thick green leaves that provided a better natural barrier to the busy, adjoining street than the white fence that surrounded her yard. Some of the branches were recently broken and flattened—by Greco or someone else, Vega wasn't sure. He followed Greco to the rear of the garage. That's when he saw it. In large black letters across the wood shingles. Someone had spray-painted: *Illegals Get Out!*

Vega cursed under his breath. It wasn't the scrawled, unoriginal sentiment that bothered him. Or the fact that lots of residents likely saw the graffiti from the main thoroughfare behind Adele's house—even before Adele. It was the fact that her entire rear yard was fenced in. In order to have gotten access to it, someone would have had to walk onto her property and stroll the length of it, right past her house—likely last night, while she slept upstairs. Alone.

That thought chilled Vega most of all.

"Do you think it was random?" Vega asked Greco. "It looks like the graffiti was intended for passersby more than Adele."

"That's what I'm hoping," said Greco. "I'm hoping we find a couple of clueless teenage vandals who didn't even know whose property they were trespassing on. The other scenario is, obviously"—he raised an eyebrow—"much more troubling."

Greco wagged a finger at Adele. The two had been sparring with each other for more than a decade—ever since Adele started La Casa. It had never been a smooth relationship. But Vega knew, too, that Greco was genuinely concerned. He spoke to Adele in an almost fatherly manner.

"It's your fault, you know," he lectured her. "Having a listed address and phone number."

"I'm not a celebrity," Adele shot back. "I'm a community leader. I need to be reachable."

"You're reachable, all right. You were within two feet of reachable last night." Greco turned his frustration on Vega. "And not for nothing, how come *you* haven't made her install a security system?"

"Don't look at me," said Vega. "I've told her the same. Many times."

"It's too expensive," said Adele. "I like to sleep with my windows open at night. To let in fresh air. I can't do that with a security system. Besides," she insisted, "Jimmy installed dead bolts on all of my doors so I'm safe."

"Not in my book," growled Greco.

"Look," said Adele, "I'm worried too. But it's entirely possible that whoever did this had no idea who I was. I mean, if they wanted me to see it, they picked a bad location. The only reason I learned about it was because people on the main road told me."

"I still don't like it," said Vega. "It feels too coincidental right after the bomb threat. Greco's right. Tomorrow, we should look into getting you a security system. Tonight, I think you should stay with me."

"I have that report to do, Jimmy. My files are here. This is where I need to be."

"Then I'll stay with you."

"And who will feed Diablo and keep him company?"

Vega didn't have an answer.

"You can't stay with me forever," said Adele. "Sophia will be back on Sunday. And besides, Lake Holly's my home."

Greco threw up his hands. "I'll order extra patrols on the house. That's all I can do. Too bad you're allergic to dogs. A nice big rottweiler would put an end to all of this."

Vega thanked Greco for his concern and walked him to his car. When he returned, Adele was standing in her kitchen, staring out the window above her sink at the garage.

"I'll paint over those words this weekend," Vega promised.

"You won't need to. I already have two of my clients coming by tomorrow to do the job."

He came up behind her and gently turned her to face him. His eyes traveled to the bare, tawny skin below her collar bone where her dad's religious medallion used to be.

"You didn't find the necklace at La Casa either, I take it."

"I turned the place upside down," said Adele. "All my clients were looking for it. It wasn't there or at La Casa North."

"I'm sorry," said Vega. "Can I pick up something for you to eat this evening before I go?"

"I'm not very hungry."

"When Sophia's not here, you don't eat," he scolded. "You'll probably just have a bowl of cereal in between writing up that report."

She smiled. He knew her well. "I don't need food," she assured him. "But there is one thing you can do before you go."

"Anything."

"I need a shower," said Adele. "I'd feel better if I wasn't alone when I take one."

"I can join you." He grinned.

"Which sort of defeats the purpose, if both of us are naked."

"All right." He held up his hands. "Can I at least keep you company?"

"I'd love that."

He stood in the doorway of the bathroom and watched her slip out of her clothes, slowly revealing the body he'd come to know and love so well. The shoulders, soft and rounded at the corners, glistening in the steam like maple syrup. The ripe fullness of her breasts. Hips that had a pleasing give whenever Vega put his hands on them. He wanted to make love to her right now, but he understood; she couldn't afford the distraction with this deadline hanging over her head.

She asked about his day. He waited until she'd stepped behind the shower curtain to tell her. He always found it easier to express his feelings when he wasn't face to face.

"I got myself in sort of a jam," Vega began. "The FBI wanted to find out if Judge Spruce has any enemies. The county police have a unit—well, really, just one guy—who looks at hate mail that comes to government employees. I got tasked with fetching the mail. I wanted to look through it; the pile was so big. But the feds made me hand it over before I could read any of it."

"I'm sure the FBI will handle that," said Adele, her voice muted by the stream from the shower.

"I don't know that they will," said Vega. "I can't go into all the reasons why. But I'll tell you this: They're burying everything they can about that woman."

Adele pulled the curtain away from the wall and poked her head out. Her hair was frothy with shampoo. Her face looked like the child Vega had once imagined her to be. Intelligent. Fretful. Cautious.

"Why would they do that? Don't they want to find out who killed that court officer and wounded Judge Spruce?"

"I'm sure they do," said Vega.

"Well then, they need to stop calling it a random shooting," said Adele. "There's nothing random about it. Julia Spruce was the target, whether the FBI wants to admit it publicly or not."

Vega said nothing.

"Don't tell me the FBI is going to protect some right-wing extremist just because they don't like Judge Spruce's politics."

"Nobody is protecting some right-wing extremist," Vega insisted. His hair was growing damp from the steam. He pushed it back from his face. "Adele? I know you've met Judge Spruce at immigration events. You've heard her speak and all. Does she seem . . . fair . . . to you?"

"Of course she's fair," said Adele. "She's the only one on that court who is."

"You don't think perhaps you're a little biased?"

"I'm a defense attorney, first and foremost," Adele insisted. "I believe in the law. And so does Judge Spruce."

Vega heard the squeak of knobs from behind the curtain. The shower water stopped. The drain gurgled as the water dripped off her skin. Adele reached for a towel and dried herself off. Then she pulled back the curtain. Her silky black hair hung in wet clumps at the nape of her neck. Her skin was speckled with water droplets and smelled of lavender and something coconut-scented that made Vega think of a beach. He wanted to forget all about

Julia Spruce. And Kaylee Wentz. And the FBI and the trial. He wanted to crawl into bed with her and never come out.

"She has a reputation for letting defendants with deportation orders off the hook. She routinely lets them skip their ICE detainers."

"First of all," said Adele, drying herself a little too briskly, "whatever Judge Spruce does or doesn't do in her courtroom, she's doing it in the presence of both a prosecutor and a defense attorney in accordance with the criminal codes of New York State. She's not making it up on the fly. And second," said Adele, stepping into her underwear and jeans and zipping them up, "an ICE detainer is not a warrant. It hasn't been reviewed or signed by a judge and, therefore, has no legal authority. Julia Spruce is not only correct in ignoring a detainer, she is legally bound to do so."

Vega pulled a face. "That's liberal-ass bullshit."

Adele stopped toweling her hair and stared at him. "You think the Constitution of the United States is liberal-ass bullshit?"

"I never said anything about the Constitution."

"Detaining people without judicial cause is a violation of the Fourth Amendment. You're a cop, Jimmy. You should know that. If the charges in Judge Spruce's courtroom get vacated or reduced at a bench hearing, the state of New York has no cause to detain the defendant. If the federal government feels otherwise, that's what a warrant is for. No warrant, no detainment. That's not *circumventing* the law. That's *obeying* it."

"Those defendants are in the country illegally," said Vega. "Warrant or no warrant."

"Which has no bearing on their rights as a defendant," said Adele. "Again, the Constitution is very clear on this matter."

"I still think it's wrong."

"You mean, 'the Constitution be damned.'" Adele

slipped on her bra and a pale pink T-shirt that gave her curves in all the right places. "What's that phrase you always say to me?" She snapped her fingers in mock surprise. "Oh yeah. I remember: Just because you don't like a law doesn't give you the right to disobey it."

"Touché." Vega grinned. "I can never argue with you. You always beat me."

She pulled him toward her and kissed him. Then she pushed back and searched his face with a look of concern. Her damp hair left a wet spot on his shirt that cooled as she pulled away. "I don't think Julia Spruce's politics is what's eating you. It's that girl up in Anniston, isn't it? The one you saved all those years ago?"

Vega didn't even realize that was what was weighing most on him until the words left his mouth. "The boyfriend's beating her up," he said slowly. "It's the usual story. She wants to leave but she's afraid. She claims she still loves him. I don't know how to convince her to get out of there."

"I'm on good terms with Evelyn Ramirez at New Beginnings," said Adele. "It's the best domestic violence shelter in the county. She can stay there up to three months while she gets her life together. She'd have her own room and everything."

"I thought you have to go on a wait list for New Beginnings," said Vega.

"Evelyn keeps one small room for emergencies. I know if I explained the situation, she'd help this girl and her little boy."

"Thanks, *nena.*" Vega felt as if a burden had been lifted from his shoulders. "That would be great."

Chapter 21

After Vega left, Adele turned on every light in the house and worked late into the night on her research project. By 1 a.m., it was nearly done, save for one medical clinic in Petersville that Adele still had to visit. She had an appointment to visit there at ten a.m. She'd been putting it off because it was in a rural, out-of-the-way area an hour and a half north of Lake Holly. The visit would eat up a good portion of the day. She consoled herself that the change in scenery might do her good.

She double-checked all the deadbolts on the doors and left her upstairs hallway light on before she turned in. At her bedroom window, she parted the curtain and looked out on the street, reminding herself that old Mr. Zimmerman and his live-in caretaker, Wil Martinez, were right next door. Nosy Mrs. Davies and the sprawling Olivera family were just across the street. She was glad she didn't live in a remote cabin like Jimmy. She felt a spark of relief when she saw a Lake Holly police car cruise slowly past her house. It should have calmed her.

It didn't.

Reflexively, she touched a hand to her chest, her fingers probing for the soft, raised shape of Saint Mariana de Paredes. If she closed her eyes, she could still hear her father's gentle words when he gave her that religious medallion: *This will watch over you when we're at work.* Her parents, teachers in Ecuador, worked nights here cleaning office buildings and delivering newspapers. They had no money for overnight childcare, so they left Adele and her younger sister Grace alone while they worked.

"Don't tell anyone," her mother cautioned. "The police will take you away."

Adele never told. She simply lived with the fear that a burglar might break into their apartment. That a workplace raid might get her undocumented parents deported. She slept poorly, her dreams full of monsters with huge fangs and claws who ripped children away from their parents. She never spoke of her terrors, compressing them so deep that they petrified into something permanent. Something that became a part of her, like a dental filling that blocked the nerve endings from being exposed.

Her father died of a heart attack when she was sixteen. Her mother succumbed to cancer when she was in law school. They'd filled her with courage and dreams but little tangible to draw on when she needed it most.

Like now, when the memories of those childhood terrors came flooding back.

The sky was a bright blue when she awoke the next morning. The humidity had dropped and the breeze filtering in through the windows felt refreshing. She showered and checked her phone messages. There was a text at six-thirty a.m. from Dr. Miranda Carrasco, the director of the Helping Hands clinic in Petersville:

Can we move your visit to 4 p.m. today? I'm going to be doing rounds at the hospital all morning and then I'll be swamped with a backup of patients.

Adele wished Dr. Carrasco had given her some advance warning. She'd scheduled her whole day around being back in the office by two, and now she'd have to rearrange everything again and kill most of her evening.

Any chance one of the other doctors can give me the tour? she texted back.

I wish I had another doctor! Carrasco texted. **It's just me, a receptionist, and two part-time nurses.**

Adele had no idea the operation was that small. There was no website for Helping Hands like the other clinics she'd reported on, just a listing in the Whitepages.

At two-thirty, she left La Casa and drove north, following the directions on her GPS until she reached Petersville, a small farming hamlet bordering rural North Kitchawan, where most of the orchards and dairy farms in the region were located. The main street held a mixture of century-old brick storefronts and shingled Victorians interspersed with more prosaic stucco warehouses.

Helping Hands was located in a former beauty salon on the main street. The clinic's waiting area still sported black and white tile where the wash basins had been. Two Hispanic men in jeans and baseball caps sat on plastic chairs near the windows. One held a wad of cotton against a bloody gash on his arm. A mother bounced a fussy baby.

Adele gave her name to the receptionist, who summoned a nurse. The two women looked like sisters. Both were Latinas in their twenties with charcoal-lined eyes, burgundy lipstick, and dimples when they smiled.

"My name is Carla," said the nurse. "Dr. Carrasco asked me to start the tour for her. She will join us when she gets a chance."

"No problem," said Adele. She had a long list of standard questions that she asked of every health center she visited, from number of patients per week to average length of visit, to types of treatments, and follow-up. She'd found that the staff often knew more than the doctors about such things.

Carla was no exception. She managed to answer everything—perhaps because the clinic was so basic. Two exam rooms. A supply closet. A break room. The doctor's office and an X-ray room.

"The X-ray machine is our biggest expense," Carla explained. "It came from a donor. We'd be lost without it. We get a lot of breaks and fractures."

"You handle them all here?" asked Adele.

"The simple ones, we do," said Carla. "Anything complicated, we send to the hospital. But that's forty minutes away and many of our patients don't have the insurance or transportation to get there."

They were in the supply closet, a half hour into the tour, when Dr. Carrasco breezed in to join them, thrusting out a hand, like she was stepping on stage. Adele supposed she was, in a way. Every new patient is, in their own way, a one-act drama.

"Adele! I've heard so many wonderful things about you," said Carrasco. "I believe we have a lot in common."

The doctor had clearly done her homework. Adele felt chagrined for not doing hers sooner. She'd spent the morning learning from the Internet that Miranda Carrasco was the child of undocumented Mexican farmworkers who'd gone on to graduate West Point and attend medical school at Johns Hopkins on the army's dime. After an impressive career as an army doctor, she retired and returned to her old hometown eight years ago to found this fledgling clinic to help other immigrants like her parents.

"Thank you for making time for me, Doctor."

"Miranda," she offered. "Please call me Miranda."

She was in her early fifties with short black hair that was feathered in a no-nonsense style. She wore jeans and a white lab coat that hung loosely over her solid frame. Her clear plastic-framed glasses highlighted her warm, deep-set eyes. She had a touch of the playful about her as well. Her white sneakers were threaded with Dora the Explorer shoelaces and shoelace charms. Adele noticed them and laughed.

"My young patients love them," said Carrasco. "It's a conversation starter when children are frightened. Come, let's go to my office." She turned to the nurse. "Thanks, Carla. I can take it from here."

Carrasco's office was decorated with colorful Mexican pottery and woven trinkets from Central America. It reminded Adele of her own office at La Casa—all except for the photographs of two golden retrievers on her desk. "My babies," said Carrasco. "Do you have a dog?"

"I'm allergic," said Adele. "But I do love animals."

"I grew up on a farm," said Carrasco. "I originally wanted to be a veterinarian." The doctor chose a seat next to Adele rather than behind her desk. "How can I help you?"

"Carla's done a wonderful job of giving me most of what I need for the report," said Adele. "I just have a few questions that perhaps you can answer."

"By all means."

"Carla said most of your patients come from the orchards and dairy farms in the area. Many are undocumented and don't have any real proof of identity. How do you manage your record-keeping and medical reimbursements?"

Carrasco settled in her seat and took a long, weighted breath. "The short answer is, we don't. We ask patients to fill out an intake form with their name, address, phone contact, medical history, and allergies. One of my nurses takes their picture. We charge twenty-five dollars cash for the visit and do our best to figure out how to cover the rest of the costs of treatment later."

"Do you go through any of the state plans for the uninsured?" asked Adele.

Carrasco laughed. "I wish."

Adele gave her a puzzled look.

"To get state reimbursement," Carrasco explained, "I have to prove that my patients are who they say they are. Many are undocumented and here on false ID. I don't want to turn a patient away because they can't verify their identity. But it makes reimbursement through state channels next to impossible. That's why I still work at the hospital," she added. "Somebody's got to pay the bills."

Adele sat back in awe. She'd done many things to help clients at La Casa. But she'd never had to dig into her own pocket to keep the place afloat.

"You've done this for *eight years*?"

Carrasco shrugged. "If I don't help these people, who will? My parents died young from treatable medical conditions because they had so little healthcare. Every patient who walks through my door reminds me of them."

Adele knew the feeling.

"Just yesterday," said Carrasco, "I had a twelve-year-old girl in here. A really sad case. I treated her for a broken wrist just as the clinic was closing."

Adele suspected the clinic was probably already closed but Carrasco wasn't about to turn a patient away.

"Her mother brought her in," Carrasco continued. "Along with a man who said he was the girl's uncle. When we were alone, the girl told me her story . . . I can't let it go."

"Sexual abuse?"

"I'd have called the police on that," said Carrasco. "This was . . . more complicated." Carrasco frowned at her lap like she wasn't sure where to begin. "She told me her uncle brought her and her mother here from Guatemala. Paid for their passage. But now, he's demanding they work in the orchards to pay him back. He won't let the child go to school until they do."

"She's *twelve,* and her uncle won't let her register for school? Maybe you *should* have called the police."

"And tell them what, Adele? It's August. School won't start for two more weeks. What crime could I possibly call them on? It would only make this child's situation worse. I worry that it's bad already."

"You mean, aside from not being able to go to school?"

A pause. Adele heard babies crying in the waiting area. Carrasco had a room full of patients to see. Adele was conscious of not taking up too much of her time.

"I asked how her wrist got broken," said Carrasco. "She told me a 'bad man'—her words—had broken it. She said he would kill her if she said anything."

"You think she was referring to her uncle?"

"Possibly," said Carrasco. "I didn't get a chance to find out. The uncle walked back in the room at that point and the girl shut down entirely. I gave the mother the clinic's card, but I'm sure she'll never call. She looked totally traumatized herself."

"I still think you should pass along their contact information to the police," said Adele.

"The information is no good," said Carrasco. "I checked after they left. They gave me a fake address. A fake phone number. Maybe even a fake name, for all I know. The uncle said the girl's name was "Maria," but she didn't answer when he called her that. If I go to the police with this, they'll do nothing. Or worse, they'll drive around the orchards and harass the pickers. Who will find out it's because I tipped off the police. Then, next time a child is hurt or abused, I'll never see them."

"Are there any social workers in the area who could help?" asked Adele.

"Una Voz, the closest agency that deals with immigrants, closed its doors last year for lack of funding," said Carrasco. "The state workers are overwhelmed and often put immigrant cases last because they're so hard to work and the people move around so much. Still, that girl is really bothering me. I want to find her and help her. Get her away from that situation and in school where she belongs."

"I can see why." Adele pictured herself at that age. Scared. Alone. Forever afraid that someone—the police, a burglar, immigration—would upend her life. "You don't have any way to track her down?"

"I have her snapshot and intake forms. She's local, I'm sure, but there's no way to find her without asking my other patients. I don't have time for that. Plus, I have to consider how that might look to my patients. They might decide not to divulge something personal to me next time because they're afraid I'll hunt them down."

"What if *I* showed her photo around?" asked Adele. "Nobody knows me in these parts. I could just say I'm a social worker helping you. That way, it wouldn't look so intrusive."

"Oh, Adele." Carrasco looked touched by the offer. "It would mean the world to me . . . But no." She shook her head. "You have so much work yourself. I couldn't ask that of you."

"I'm here already." Adele gestured beyond the closed office door to the waiting area. "It's clear you have your hands full."

"Well . . ." Carrasco tapped a finger to her lips. Her nails were short and blunt. No polish. No jewelry. She was not a woman who had time or patience for adornments. "I'd have to pull some HIPAA sleight-of-hand to make a copy of her photo and records available to you," she said, referring to the federal patient privacy regulations. "You can certainly mention Helping Hands. But please don't say I gave you patient records—"

"I won't."

Carrasco pushed herself out of the chair and walked over to her computer. She tapped some keys until she called up a photo of a girl. "This is her," she said.

Adele peered over the doctor's shoulder. The child looked far younger than her twelve years. She had a round, indigenous face, high cheekbones, and sunburn across her nose, likely from too much exposure in the fields. Her Asian-looking eyes had a haunted look to them. Adele couldn't tell if that was from her time here, her journey north, or perhaps even farther back, a trauma so deep, it was woven into her DNA.

"I'm probably not going to get access to any of the orchards," said Adele.

"No," Carrasco agreed. Then she looked at her watch. It was just after five p.m. "The best place to go would be the grocery store in North Kitchawan," she explained. "Often, the drivers who truck the people from the trailer parks to the farms will also take them to the grocery store during the week. If you show her picture discreetly around the store and tell them you just want to make sure she gets medical attention, you might get some cooperation. But stay away from the drivers."

"Why?"

"They're sort of like underbosses," said Carrasco. She could see Adele was confused, so she explained. "I grew up here, but everything is different now. Back then, my parents worked directly for the farmers. Now, with all the ICE regulations, the farmers are afraid of employing immigrants directly. So, they contract with middlemen—immigrants who have been here a long time and are either citizens or Green Card holders. These middlemen smuggle the workers in, house them, and contract them out to the farms—taking a cut, I assume, every step of the way. The people are basically indentured servants."

"Sounds like a terrible system," said Adele.

"It is," she agreed. "The people live, work, and buy groceries where the middlemen tell them to. They have no real connection to the farmers anymore. And if they complain, someone will call ICE on them. They'll be deported. Or worse."

"*Worse?* What do you mean, 'worse'?" asked Adele.

Carrasco turned away from her computer and looked at Adele. Her voice dropped to barely above a whisper. "My partner works for the county medical examiner's office.

Every year, we have about half a dozen unidentified Hispanics who show up dead by the sides of roads. Strangled mostly. For some, the cause of death is never known. The murders are never solved."

Adele glanced down again at the photograph of the child on the screen. It was a hell of a life. Certainly not what immigrants hope for when they picture life in the United States. Carrasco gestured to the screen. "Can you imagine if someone had told our parents that *we* couldn't go to school? Where would we be now?"

"School was everything," Adele agreed. "Give me a few of your business cards, along with her photo and intake sheet. If I can find her, I will. She deserves our help."

Chapter 22

Adele found North Kitchawan even more sad-looking than Petersville. Just a couple of intersecting streets of tumbledown row-frames with an aging brick elementary school, an off-brand gas station, and a grocery store with beer and lottery-ticket signs in the dusty plate-glass windows. The few people walking the streets or gassing up their cars appeared to be white. The only Hispanics Adele saw were the ones getting out of vans in the grocery store parking lot. They wore dusty jeans and baseball caps. The women carried children by the hand or on their hips.

The drivers never got out. Never even turned off their engines. They kept the windows rolled up, blasting their air-conditioning and Spanish music with equal force. They were better dressed than their passengers. Collared shirts. Buzz-cut hairstyles. They carried themselves like they owned the people they were transporting. Adele thought of what Dr. Carrasco had told her about the immigrants being indentured servants. The whole system felt like an antebellum plantation.

She parked her Prius in a far corner of the lot and pulled the photo of "Maria" out of the manila envelope Dr. Carrasco had given her, along with a copy of the intake report. She left the report in the car and tucked the photo into a cloth tote she snatched off the rear seat. She wanted to look like she was just coming into the store to pick up some milk and bread.

Except she didn't blend in. Not in her silky striped blouse, formfitting slacks, and heeled sandals. She assumed that there would be other people in the store who didn't blend into this crowd either. But when she got inside, she didn't see a single white face—or any face—that didn't look as if it had come from one of the vans. *Where do residents shop around here?* Obviously, not at this grocery store. Adele could see why. The shelves were poorly stocked. The items were prohibitively expensive. There were canned goods and white bread that cost more here than in Adele's local store. The same was true of the rice and beans and some sorry-looking packages of chicken. The food reminded Adele of the dispiriting items her mother used to get at the charity pantry to supplement what the family could afford. Sugary cereals and Pop-Tarts. Ritz Crackers that were nearly past their expiration date. Off-brands of milk and cheese.

She saw almost no fresh fruit. In summer. In a region where people just came from picking fresh fruit.

All around her, Adele heard chatter. Some of it was in Mexican- and Guatemalan-accented Spanish. Some of it was in indigenous languages Adele didn't speak. She scanned the faces of the children accompanying their parents. She saw no one who looked like Maria here. Only one girl even looked to be about Maria's age. She was shopping with her mother. Adele walked up to them and took out Maria's photograph.

"Excuse me, señora," said Adele, addressing the mother in her politest Spanish. "I am a medical worker from Petersville. I am trying to find a girl who needs follow-up treatment for her broken wrist. Have you seen her?"

Mother and daughter studied the picture. Both shook their heads.

"I'm sorry, no," said the woman. "We haven't seen her."

"Thank you anyway." Adele moved on to another woman, purposely skipping over the single men who were less likely to notice a young girl. Again, the woman said she didn't recognize the child. By now, Adele had drawn attention. An older woman with skin like a raisin hobbled over to study the photograph. She stood staring at it for several seconds. Something flickered in her eyes, moving all her wrinkles in unison. She glanced over her shoulder. Adele followed her gaze to the back of the store where a mop stood immersed in a bucket of dirty water.

"You are a medical worker?" the old woman asked, her voice wary. Adele flushed. She was a terrible liar, so she stuck to the parts of her story that were true.

"The girl's wrist is broken. I am here to make sure she gets the follow-up care she needs."

"Care from who?"

"Dr. Carrasco at Helping Hands in Petersville," said Adele. "Do you know where the girl might be?"

The woman hesitated. Adele sensed she recognized the girl but wouldn't or couldn't provide her name. Adele pulled out one of Dr. Carrasco's business cards and pressed it into the woman's callused palm. Her fingers bore the cuts and calluses of a life working with her hands.

"Give this to her if you can," Adele pleaded. "Tell her that Dr. Carrasco wants to help her. We *both* want to help her."

The woman's hand tightened around the card until it disappeared in her fist. She turned away to examine a can of corn. The movement was so abrupt, Adele thought she'd offended her in some way. Adele went to apologize, but she had a sudden sense of being watched. Being targeted. Then an arm darted across her field of vision. A man's arm. With a chunky gold watch encircling his hairy wrist. It was trailed by the musky scent of aftershave as he brushed against her to reach for an item on the shelf: hot sauce.

Adele reared back.

"You are new here, señora," said the man in Spanish. His accent was Mexican, with the rhythmic, chopped sound of someone from the northern border. "Do you . . . live around here?"

Adele could hear the demand beneath his words: *Tell me who you are.*

He wasn't tall but there was something menacing about him. Something that suggested he gauged a person by how much they had to offer and how easily he could take it. Most of the clients who came through La Casa were farmers and tradesmen and shopkeepers in their prior lives. Simple men with simple desires: A safe place to raise their families. Decent wages. An education for their children.

But every now and then, Adele came across a different sort of man at La Casa. A man who had tasted power in his homeland. As a soldier. Or a cop. Maybe even a rebel or a gangster. There was a ruthless streak to them that frightened Adele. An opportunism that preyed on the weak and well intended.

Not every immigrant was a pilgrim in search of the promised land. Some were just looking for their next score.

"I'm a medical worker," Adele said again, trotting out the lie that already felt as thin as a cheap shirt. "I'm looking for a twelve-year-old Guatemalan girl who saw a local doctor about her broken wrist. The doctor needs to see her for a follow-up."

"What's the girl's name?" He asked like he had a proprietary interest in the matter.

"Maria Gonzalez." At least, that was the name the uncle had given Dr. Carrasco.

"You have a photograph?"

Something about the demanding tone in the man's voice, the way other people stayed away from them, made Adele nervous. Still, she'd come to find Maria. It was possible he knew the child. She pulled Dr. Carrasco's snapshot from her tote bag and showed it to him. He snatched it from her hand and turned it to the store's bad tube lights to get a better look. His eyes narrowed. He seemed acutely interested in a way that men like him only were when they sensed opportunity.

"A broken wrist, you say?" The man's scrutiny turned from the photo to Adele. "If you're a worker at the clinic, how come I've never seen you before?"

"I'm new," Adele stammered.

"New, eh?" The man tucked the photograph in a back pocket of his pants.

"Hey. I need that." Adele leaned forward. The man grabbed her in one effortless pull, like he was used to manhandling people. Nobody in the store moved to help her. Not the other immigrants shopping in the aisles. Not the young women at the checkout counters. He had Adele's shoulder bag and tote bag off her in an instant. The tote bag was empty. He dropped it at his feet. He pulled her wallet from her shoulder bag and flipped to her driver's license.

"Adele Figueroa. Two Fourteen Pine Road, Lake Holly, New York." He dropped the wallet back into her shoulder bag and held it out to her with a flourish, like he was returning something she'd lost. "Well, Adele Figueroa of Two Fourteen Pine Road, you are certainly a long way from home."

She grabbed her shoulder bag from him and bent to retrieve the empty tote on the ground. She thrust out a hand.

"I'll take the girl's photo back."

"I think I'll keep it." He smiled. There was something sharklike in his grin. "I'll show it around. See if I can find her. That's what you want, isn't it? To find her?"

"Dr. Carrasco at the clinic—"

"Don't worry about Dr. Carrasco," said the man. "I know where her clinic is. And now, I know where you are too."

Chapter 23

"Go. Out the back door. Into the van," ordered a Mexican man Eli and her mother had never seen before today. Normally, the old toothless Guatemalan drove them to and from the fields in his rusted flatbed truck. But this afternoon, vans took them to town to the grocery store. The men who drove the vans weren't like the old Guatemalan. They wore clean, open-collared shirts and lots of gold jewelry. Some wore cowboy hats and boots, like Señor Ortega. They blasted their norteño music and never spoke to anyone.

"They always drive to this store?" Aurelia asked Encarna, their neighbor with the wax-paper skin.

"Always," Encarna answered softly. "And after, you watch. The men go in with big canvas bags and take a lot of the cash. It's just like Guatemala, I tell you. Everything is owned and run by gangsters."

And now, one of these "gangsters" had pushed Eli and her mother into the back of the van while everyone else was still inside, shopping. Eli watched from the tinted window as a beautiful Latina walked out the front doors. Everything about her looked silky. Her short black hair that curved like parentheses on either side of her face. Her striped blouse and slacks.

"Who is that lady?" Aurelia asked the van driver.

"Immigration," he growled. "She's looking for your daughter. She showed a picture. She wants to deport you both."

"But we have asylum papers," Aurelia protested.

"You took your daughter to the doctor yesterday, right? To fix her wrist?"

"She was in pain."

"Well, that doctor called immigration," said the driver. "Told them you abused your daughter."

"That's not true!"

"Doesn't matter," he grunted. "They think you did. And now, they're looking for you both. Gonna deport you both. So stay down and shut your mouths."

"But I need to buy groceries," said Aurelia.

"Give me the money," said the van driver, holding out a palm. "I'll get somebody to buy some things for you."

Aurelia handed over the few measly bills from their pay that day. They didn't get it all. Señor Ortega said that he'd been instructed to pay the bulk of their wages to Luis and that Luis would pay them.

The driver slid the van door shut. Aurelia and Eli sat inside the hot and stuffy interior. The air was stifling, but at least they could sit for a while. Eli flexed her fingers the way the doctor showed her yesterday when she reset the bone. Her wrist didn't hurt as much anymore but it was immobile now, the entire forearm encased in a plaster cast and wrapped on top in a garbage bag to keep out moisture.

"Mami? Do you really think the doctor called immigration?" Eli thought the doctor was kind and caring yesterday, but now she wasn't sure. She felt guilty for telling her all the things she had. Maybe her words had gotten them in trouble.

"I don't know. I don't know anything anymore," Aurelia mumbled into her lap. "So many things here are not what I expected." Her mother lifted her gaze and stared out the window, her face reflected in the glass. There was something flat and resigned in her dark eyes that Eli had never seen before. Her mother had made no mention of what happened in Señor Ortega's trailer yesterday. Eli didn't think she ever would. And yet it sat between them, this big unknown, walling them off from each other. Eli longed to hug her mother and tell her everything would be okay. But this was a trauma Eli didn't know. A violation her mother had spared her from. She couldn't pretend it away.

"Mami?" asked Eli. "Are you okay?"

Aurelia turned from the window and stroked her daughter's hair. "I'm just glad that all that man did was break your wrist. It could have been so much worse."

"He had a gun. In this black backpack he was carrying."

Aurelia's hand froze on Eli's head. "A . . . gun? He was going to shoot you?"

"I don't know," said Eli. "He was wearing a fake beard. I saw him take it off. I ran. He grabbed me and then I bit him."

"*Jesucristo!*" Aurelia made the sign of the cross.

Some of the immigrants were walking back to the van from the grocery store, carrying brown paper bags. Aurelia turned to her daughter. "Never, *ever* mention this to anyone. Do you hear? We don't know who this man is. Or where he is. You broke your wrist falling. That's what you tell anyone if they ask, yes?"

"Okay." Eli didn't want to tell her mother that it was already too late to keep the secret. At least one person besides them knew the truth: the doctor.

The van driver emerged from the store with a brown bag that looked nearly empty. Eli wondered how much he'd bought and how much he'd pocketed. From her mother's gaze, it looked like she was wondering the same thing.

"I thought everything would be different here," said her mother. "In so many ways, it's exactly the same."

Chapter 24

Adele's visit to North Kitchawan had spooked her. She drove home, checking her rearview mirror the whole way. She didn't feel normal again until she turned in to Lake Holly. It was dark by then, but the streets were alive and happy. Restaurants set out tables under sidewalk awnings. Families strolled the main streets. People sat on park benches, eating ice cream cones while teenagers shot hoops on the courts.

She pulled into her driveway behind a white pickup with the words *E & H Painting* on the side. The painters had come to cover over the graffiti. Adele didn't want to block them in, so she parked down the street and walked back. By then, the men—two brothers from Mexico and clients of La Casa—were sealing up paint cans and throwing tarps in the back of their truck.

"I'm so sorry I wasn't here sooner," said Adele in Spanish. "I was out all afternoon. Were you able to cover the words?"

The older brother, a kindly man named Ernesto with big brown eyes, smiled. "Two coats of primer and one topcoat," he replied in Spanish. "It's fine now. Come. Humberto and I will show you."

They walked her down her driveway to her garage. The entire back side of the garage as well as the side facing the house had been sanded, primed, and repainted. It looked brand-new. Much better than the dingy, flaking paint that had been there before.

"Wow," said Adele. "You did the back and the side? It all looks fantastic. I thought you were just going to paint over the words."

"But now it looks much better, don't you think?" asked Ernesto, wiping his paint-spattered hands on a rag.

"It does," Adele agreed. "Come inside. I'll get my checkbook."

"No, no, señora." Ernesto waved his hands in front of his face. "No charge."

"No, please," said Adele. "I insist. I always pay for work."

"We know you do," said Ernesto. Humberto nodded in agreement. "But this isn't a repair or renovation. What those vandals did is an insult to you. To La Casa. We consider it our duty to paint over those words."

"I don't feel right accepting your generosity," said Adele.

"It was no trouble. Really," said Ernesto. "A few hours' work late in the day. We would feel insulted taking money to fix this."

Adele thanked them for their work, sending both men off with some muffins she'd baked for Sophia when she returned from Cape Cod. She could always bake more.

She went inside and took a shower. When she came out, she didn't feel like fetching her car, still parked down the street. It was fine where it was. The neighborhood was safe.

She called Sophia, who was headed out to see fireworks with her grandparents that evening. The child was having such a good time, Adele wondered if she missed her mother at all. Still, it was good for the girl to bond with her father's family. Adele's own parents were long dead. Her sister Grace had no children and relocated all the time for her high-powered jobs in finance. Sophia deserved more family than that.

Adele called Vega after she got off the phone from Sophia. She could hear a baseball game blaring in the background and Diablo panting on the sofa. Vega was kicking back himself. *Good.* He'd have to go back to court tomorrow morning and face that attorney, Carver, again. He needed the break.

"I called Evelyn Ramirez today, who runs that shelter for battered women," said Vega. "She promised she'd make room for Kaylee and her little boy."

"What did Kaylee say about it?" asked Adele.

"I left voice mails and texts," said Vega. "She hasn't responded. I've got an appointment to see her when I get out of court tomorrow. I guess we'll talk then." He sounded uncertain. Adele wondered if he was thinking the same thing Adele was—that Kaylee was an addict and addicts weren't reliable. "Did you finish your report?"

"Almost," said Adele. "I drove up to Petersville today to research the last one."

"Petersville? That's like, an hour and a half from you."

"That whole area gives me the creeps," said Adele. She told him about Dr. Carrasco and going to the grocery store in North Kitchawan to track down a child with a broken wrist.

"An abuse victim?" asked Vega.

"Probably," said Adele. "I didn't find her, unfortunately. What I found instead was a whole community of immigrant farmworkers who seem to be totally under the control of overseers. Like some sort of modern-day plantation system."

"Huh." Adele heard an announcer talking excitedly in the background. The Yankees had probably just brought in a run. Vega was only half listening. *Men and sports.*

"Jimmy? Did you even hear what I just said?"

"I heard," he said defensively. "Don't know what I can

do about it except to call an investigator I know in the state police and ask him to poke around. But not until the trial is over. That's my priority right now."

"Speaking of the trial," said Adele. "Do you want me there tomorrow?"

"No." The word came out fast and flat. Like he was facing an execution and didn't want to see family members in the audience. "Isadora Jenkins called me earlier. Carver's subpoenaed Captain Lorenzo."

Head of Internal Affairs. Adele knew that wasn't the actual name of the unit, but that's what it was. The policer of police. Vega told her that most officers don't choose to work in a division that rats on cops. They just get assigned there. It was telling that Lorenzo had chosen to make it his life's work.

"He's not going to shaft you, Jimmy. He'd be shafting his own department."

"True," said Vega. "But the jury's going to see that there's no love lost between us. It won't be pretty."

Adele wished she could offer him some pithy advice or great legal strategy. She had nothing but her love and loyalty. "I believe in you, *mi vida,*" she said softly. "I'll say a prayer to Saint Mariana de Paredes for you tomorrow."

"If we can ever find her."

She hung up and spent the next couple of hours finishing a rough draft of her report. Around eleven-thirty, she called it quits, turned off all the lights, and went to bed.

She awoke to a sound like scratching. Like some creature was nosing around her back porch. *A raccoon?* Adele hoped the animal hadn't figured out a way to get in through the screens. All her doors were dead bolted, but it was summer, and she kept the windows opened to let in fresh air.

She sat up in bed and looked at her alarm clock. One a.m. Her bedroom window faced the street, not the backyard. A soft breeze rustled the curtains. Beyond, she saw only streetlights bathing the fronts of darkened houses and cars parked along the curbs. She crept to the window and looked out at her driveway. It was empty. For a moment, she panicked, thinking someone had stolen her car. Then she remembered that she'd left it parked down the street when the painters were here. With all the lights off and the driveway empty, her neighbors probably thought she wasn't home.

She heard the scratch again, more insistently this time. It was definitely coming from the screened back porch off the kitchen. She swung her legs over the side of the bed and dug her feet into the braided scatter rug on the bare plank floor. She felt just as she had when she was small, listening at night for her parents to come home. Only then, the sounds gave her relief.

Here, she wasn't so sure.

She patted the table beside her bed. It took her a moment to make out the outline of her phone in the slash of streetlight. She detached it from the charger cord. She was being silly. Who was she going to call? The Lake Holly Police? About a raccoon? God, she'd never live that down. She ran a hand down her T-shirt and pajama shorts. Her hair was a tangled mess. *Go back to sleep,* she told herself. *It's nothing. You'll solve it in the morning.*

Then she heard it—a sound that took all the breath from her lungs. It made her toes and fingers tingle with pins and needles and brought a slick of sweat to the back of her neck.

The creak of a floorboard. On the screened back porch.

Raccoons don't have the weight to make a floorboard creak. Only a human could do that.

Oh God . . . oh God . . . oh God. Should she shout? Call 911? Try to run? Would her presence scare them off? Or let them know she was a woman alone and embolden them further? Was there one intruder? Or more than one? Did he just want valuables? Or, God forbid, something more?

Never in her life had she felt so vulnerable.

So alone.

She scanned her bedroom for a weapon. She had nothing. No baseball bat. No knife. She'd been a fencing champion as a teenager, but her foils were all in the attic and, besides, they weren't real swords anyway. All she had was a set of manicure scissors. She couldn't escape through a window. Her windows were all covered in screens. Removing them would take too much time and make too much noise. And besides, she was on the second floor. She'd probably break a bone if she even managed to drop to the ground.

Her whole body tensed—even the tendons of her fingers felt stiff and arthritic. Her heart beat so loud in her chest, it rattled about like a marble in an empty tin can. She was glad Sophia was away. Glad she only had to worry about protecting herself. But how? *Think,* she commanded her brain. *Calm down and think!*

Her house was dark. Her car wasn't in her driveway. More than likely, the intruder expected the residence to be empty. Prime pickings for a burglary. Which meant Adele wasn't the goal. She'd defended a burglar or two in her time as a criminal defense attorney. Those guys were all about speed. They broke in, ran straight to the master bedroom, searched for jewelry, electronics, and safes, and then split within five to seven minutes of entry.

So why hadn't this intruder made any move to come upstairs? He sounded as if he were rummaging through the desk in her dining room where she kept papers from work. Then she heard him in the kitchen, opening drawers. Was he looking for a knife?

Dear God, I've got to get out of here!

She was trapped. The dining room was right off the stairs. There was no way she could make it out the front door before he grabbed her. The kitchen was behind the dining room. That door, too, was inaccessible. And besides, her house was old. The floorboards were creaky. The moment she moved he'd know she was up here.

I've got one chance to save myself, thought Adele. Not by running. No. By locking herself in the bathroom and calling 911 from there. The lock wouldn't hold for long. Not if the intruder was determined to break down the door. She just had to hope he'd choose to run instead.

She'd have mere seconds to dash across the floorboards, into the bathroom, and lock the door. She grabbed her phone and touched a foot to the scatter rug, slowly bringing her weight down on it before settling the other foot down too. Then she took a deep breath and crept as quietly as she could into the bathroom and slid the slide bolt across the frame. She crouched on the tile floor, leaning her whole body against the old wooden door, hoping her weight against it could help seal it shut. She dialed 911.

Nine-one-one emergency service. How may I help you?

Adele spilled out her address in one breathless gasp. She heard noise downstairs. A chair in the dining room being pushed out of the way. Footsteps on the landing. Heavy work boots thudding up the stairs.

"Oh God, please! Hurry! He's still in the house!" Adele cried into the phone.

The footsteps stopped, then reversed. She heard them stomping across her kitchen floor. The give of metal on wood as someone tugged her back door open. The slam as they banged it shut.

She heard nothing after that but the beating of her own heart.

Chapter 25

Vega got two calls that night in quick succession. The first was from Adele, telling him, in breathy tones, that there had been "an incident" at her house. She was fine, but a window screen on her back porch had been sliced open.

It took the second call, from Greco, to get the whole story.

"Some bastard broke into her house while she was sleeping upstairs," said Greco. "Cut the porch screen to get in. Rifled through some drawers downstairs, then fled when she called nine-one-one. She's acting brave and all, but I think you should take her back to your place tonight."

"I'm on my way."

There was no traffic on the roads at this hour. Vega made the journey from Sullivan Falls to Lake Holly in under forty minutes. The town was quiet. A raccoon scurried across the street, his eyes like mirrors in Vega's headlights. Two deer grazed by the elementary school playground. Nothing else stirred until he got to Adele's street. The whole block was lit up like a Christmas tree. Every neighbor's exterior house lights were on.

They all must have heard about the break-in.

Two Lake Holly police cruisers were parked across the entrance to Adele's empty driveway. Vega parked his truck farther down the street and walked back, maneuvering past the cruisers, down the driveway to the rear of the house, following the sound of cops' voices and the glow of flashlights that lit up the darkness like fireflies. He saw two uniforms stringing yellow crime-scene tape around the window of Adele's back porch where the screen had been cut. He felt that cut like they were slicing into his own skin. He couldn't believe someone had violated her home. Violated her. It made him furious.

The porch door was open. Every light in the house was on.

He didn't see Adele.

A familiar voice rumbled out of the darkness. "She's next door, with her neighbor, Max Zimmerman, and his caretaker, Wil Martinez, if you're looking for her."

Greco clapped Vega on the shoulder and stared at the slit in the screen, the way it had been peeled back like the chest wall of a body in an autopsy. "What do I keep saying here? She needs a central alarm system. To hell with opening her windows for fresh air."

"I know that," snapped Vega. "Don't you think I know that?" He was mad at himself for not insisting sooner. "Where's her car?"

"Down the street," said Greco. "She said she left it there because she didn't want to block the painters who came this afternoon to paint over the graffiti."

"So, her driveway was empty at the time of the break-in," said Vega. He was trying to piece things together. "Maybe the perp didn't expect to find anyone home."

"That's what I'm assuming," said Greco. "They broke in through the screen and left as soon as they heard her calling nine-one-one."

"One suspect? More than one?"

"No way to know for sure," said Greco. "Adele never saw anyone. But she thinks, judging from the footsteps, it was just one."

"Did they take anything?"

"Nothing," said Greco. "Her handbag was on a hook by the back door. Her watch and wallet were on the counter in the kitchen. It's all still there."

That troubled Vega most of all. He could see it troubled Greco too.

"They apparently rummaged through her desk drawers in the dining room and some drawers in the kitchen," said Greco. "Don't know what they were looking for, but she said nothing was taken."

"That seems pretty specific to me," said Vega. "Like they had something in mind that they were looking for. Have you got any leads?"

"I'm working off the same assumption you probably are," said Greco. "That this break-in may be related to the bomb threat at La Casa and the graffiti on her garage. Can't say for sure, though."

"What do you mean, 'can't say for sure'?" asked Vega. "How can they *not* be related?"

Greco slapped at a mosquito. "Damn bloodsuckers." Moths flitted about in the beam of his flashlight. "At this point, we have no idea how long that graffiti was there. Adele said she never goes back there. It's too overgrown with vines."

"But everyone saw that graffiti for the first time yesterday," said Vega. "Which means it's recent."

"It *means,*" said Greco, "that the owner of the property on the main road behind Adele's got some trimming work done. *Yesterday.* When the gardeners cut the vines on the maple, it exposed the graffiti."

"Are you telling me those words were there all along?"

"It's possible," said Greco. "This time of year, those vines could cover a dead body and I wouldn't see it. Is it related? Maybe. But my priority at the moment is the bomb threat and this break-in. Not a few painted words."

"Any progress on the bomb threat?"

"It was called in through a network of computerized phone exchanges," said Greco. "The origination point appears to be a trucking depot in Sayertown, New York. That's all I have right now."

"Sayertown was the site of a DEA meth bust eight months ago," said Vega. "The dealers had ties to a white supremacist group called the Puritan Sons. At least one of them was at that rally against La Casa North up in Anniston."

"Sounds like you know more about it than I do," said Greco. "You got a contact at the DEA who can fill me in?"

"Stanley Devereaux."

Greco copied down the name. Vega had to spell it three times before Greco got it right. "I'll call him."

"What do you have so far on this break-in?" asked Vega. "Any prints?"

"No prints, no witnesses," said Greco. "The perp probably used gloves and wore a mask. I'm pulling the license-plate reader feeds now. Tomorrow, I'll see if I can match them to any surveillance footage around town."

"*Tomorrow?*"

"Yes, tomorrow," said Greco. "A lot of businesses are closed in the middle of the night. In case you haven't noticed."

Vega glared at him.

"Look, Vega," said Greco. "I know this is personal. I know you're upset. But I have to proceed the same way I would with any case. It will all get done."

"I don't want to see Lake Holly drop the ball on this," said Vega. "Like you did with Juan Rivas."

"Juan . . ." Greco frowned. "What the hell are you talking about?"

"Juan Rivas. You know—the illegal Omar Sanchez arrested for knife possession who had no prints?"

"What's Rivas got to do with this?"

"Sloppy police work, that's what," said Vega. "ICE slapped a detainer on him and Rivas skipped because Lake Holly forgot to send the paperwork about the missing prints to the judge."

"Screw you, Vega. Lake Holly *sent* the paperwork. That snowflake, Julia Spruce, either lost it or pretended to."

"You mean to tell me that a sitting judge *knew* Juan Rivas had no fingerprints—*knew* he'd likely gotten them removed—and she let him go? I don't believe it."

"Oh, you don't believe that," said Greco, throwing up his hands. "But you accuse *my* department of sloppy police work. Maybe it's time for you to go see your girlfriend next door and cool off a little. Because your presence ain't exactly motivating me right now, *capiche*?"

Vega decided to do as Greco suggested. He walked next door to Max Zimmerman's house, and rang the doorbell. Zimmerman answered, looking pretty good for a man of ninety who was awakened in the middle of the night.

"Jimmy! I was wondering when you'd get here." The old man leaned one hand on his three-pronged cane and used the other to beckon him in. He was still square-shouldered and strong as an ox, with thick silver hair and black-framed glasses. "Adele's in the kitchen, eating chicken soup. When all else fails, chicken soup is the best remedy."

Vega followed Zimmerman into the kitchen. It hadn't been updated in at least forty years. All the fixtures were a 1980s shade of avocado. Adele was sitting at a Formica-topped table with Wil Martinez, the young Guatemalan college student who lived with Zimmerman and kept him company. Vega had learned long ago never to call Wil the old man's "caretaker." Zimmerman had survived the Holocaust and being a refugee in three countries. He didn't need anyone to take care of him.

Adele slowly lowered her soup spoon when she saw Vega. Her lip quivered as she fought to compose herself.

"We'll leave you two alone, okay?" Zimmerman gestured to Martinez and they both left the room.

Adele rose from her chair and Vega wrapped her in a bear hug. The only sound in the room was the ticking of a large clock over the sink.

"It was my fault for not parking my car in the driveway," she murmured into his chest.

He pushed her back to face her. "*Nena,* do you seriously think a car is going to stop someone? You're just lucky it wasn't *you* they wanted. You're not spending the night alone until you install an alarm. And buy a gun. Tonight, you're coming home with me."

She sank back down into one of Mr. Zimmerman's padded kitchen chairs, which was framed in polished chrome. The whole kitchen looked to be about forty years out of date. "I'm not getting a gun, Jimmy. Nor am I going to your place tonight. You've got court in the morning. I've got to hand this report in. Detective Greco shouldn't have dragged you all the way down here in the first place."

"Are you kidding?" asked Vega. "You should have explained better what was going on. This is a serious situation, Adele. Someone broke into your house. *While you were in it.* Couple that with the bomb threat to La Casa and the graffiti—all of it on the heels of that protest rally in Anniston—and I have to think those white supremacists from the rally are behind this."

"You think so?"

"You've got other enemies?" His intonations were starting to sound like Max Zimmerman. *Jesucristo.*

Adele smiled. "I guess not. It's just . . ."

"What?"

"When I went up to North Kitchawan today, to inquire

about that child with the broken wrist—the one who might have been abused—there was a man."

"A man? What man?"

"This creepy gangster sort of guy," said Adele. "Mexican. From the northern region, judging by his accent. Well dressed—not a laborer. When I started showing the child's picture around at the grocery store, he took the photo from me. And then he grabbed my bag and opened my wallet. He read off my name and address from my driver's license. He even commented that I was a long way from home."

Her description of the incident gave Vega chills. But logic took over. "We're talking about a tiny town an hour-and-a-half north of here," said Vega. "Why would he care about you? Because of some photo of an abused immigrant kid? Why break into your house and take nothing? It doesn't make sense."

"I guess." Adele stared at the chicken soup growing cold on the Formica table. Vega noticed that the bowl was still full. She'd eaten very little. "All I know is he scared me," said Adele. "A lot. I think he wanted to make sure I don't come back."

"And you won't," said Vega. "Why would you? If this kid's going to be rescued, someone in that community's got to do it. You've got enough on your plate."

"You're right." Adele exhaled. "Mr. Zimmerman already offered for me to stay over. He's got a spare bedroom. I won't be alone."

"You don't want to come back with me? I'll drop you off before I have to be in court tomorrow."

"It doesn't make sense for me to go all that way just to come back again in a few hours," said Adele. "And besides, I want to be near my house. It will make me feel better."

"Okay," said Vega. He leaned down and kissed her. "Try to get some sleep. And tomorrow, we're talking about an alarm system."

Chapter 26

Under the best of circumstances, County Police Captain Greg Lorenzo was not a jolly person. He was a gaunt, grim-faced man who only seemed happy when he was making other cops miserable. He was so obsessed with keeping overtime pay in the Special Investigations Unit to a minimum that he once made an officer come back early from his honeymoon rather than pay another officer overtime to cover for him.

It wasn't surprising that Vega and Lorenzo wouldn't like each other. What was surprising is that it had taken eighteen years for their paths to finally collide. First in December, after the Ponce shooting. And then again in January, when a Lake Holly police officer shot and killed a felon wanted on suspicion of murder and Vega made the mistake of being present without departmental approval.

In police work, there was no higher crime than failing to go through the chain of command.

"Captain Lorenzo," Bernard Carver addressed him on the stand. "You are head of the county police's Internal Affairs unit, is that correct?"

"It's called the Special Investigations Unit," Lorenzo corrected. He was always a stickler for details. Everything about him radiated a by-the-book demeanor, from his starched dress uniform, replete with medals, to his clean-shaven face with a slash of lips that barely moved. Carver could have subpoenaed Chief Lakeworth, who always looked as dazed and distracted as a golden retriever when the cameras weren't rolling. Or Captain Waring, who, as an ex-military officer, would have felt some duty not to throw one of his subordinates under the bus. Lorenzo felt none of this. His duty was to the department, sure. But he earned his pay by depriving cops of theirs. Vega would just be another notch on his belt.

"Your primary purpose, as I understand it," Carver continued, "is to police the police."

"Affirmative."

"You were part of the three-man board that oversaw Detective Vega's disciplinary hearing in January."

"That's correct."

"What was the purpose of the hearing?"

"To determine whether Detective Vega had violated departmental protocol."

"You make it sound, Captain Lorenzo, like Detective Vega forgot to shine his shoes." Carver smiled at the jury, who chuckled appreciatively. They were dressed for the weekend. Shorts and T-shirts. Big tote bags. It was a summer Friday and they were all in a good mood. They weren't thinking about Vega's torched career or Lucinda Ponce's supposed dead husband or how much money Carver stood to make. They were itching to get an early start on the weekend.

So much for Isadora Jenkins's theory that a two-day continuance could disrupt Carver's rhythm with the jury.

"The stated infraction," said Lorenzo stiffly, "was failure to obtain departmental approval for inter-agency police engagement." Lorenzo didn't like the jury laughing. He probably thought they were laughing at him. He had no sense of humor and was suspicious of those who did.

"In other words," said Carver, "Detective Vega decided, without permission, to involve himself in another department's police surrender that resulted in the death of a suspect—"

"Objection!" said Isadora Jenkins. "Your Honor"—she turned to Judge Edgerton—"there is no evidence Detective Vega involved himself in any way in the direct surrender of the suspect. He was an observer. Nothing more. The hearing was to determine whether he should have gotten permission to be present—not whether he'd inappropriately engaged. And may I remind the jury that he was exonerated."

"I'll allow the objection," said Edgerton. "Redirect, Mr. Carver."

"Very well," said Carver. "But I'd like to also remind the jury that Detective Vega was exonerated by a vote of two to one. Two members of the panel chose in his favor. And one believed he was guilty of a serious infraction that should have involved disciplinary action."

Carver turned to Lorenzo and looked him in the eye. "Captain Lorenzo, would you kindly tell the jury your vote in the hearing?"

Lorenzo's gaze narrowed. He didn't like being manipulated, even if the words were his own. The room went silent, save for the thrum of air-conditioning through the ducts and the faint creak of ceiling fans overhead. Isadora Jenkins knew there was no point in objecting. It was all in the transcript anyway.

"I voted in favor of disciplining Detective Vega for failing to seek departmental approval," said Lorenzo.

"Why?"

Lorenzo's thin lips parted and then shut again. He sensed anything he said would come back to haunt him.

"Perhaps I can refresh your memory," said Carver. He walked over to the plaintiff's table where Lucinda Ponce shot glances at her cell phone and pretended not to. He picked up a pair of tortoiseshell glasses Vega had never seen him use at any time before in the trial. He took his time fitting them over his face. This was all playacting for the jury. Vega was sure of it. Carver grabbed a sheaf of papers and made a show of flipping the pages. Then he cleared his throat.

"Captain Lorenzo, on page twelve, paragraph six of the hearing transcript, you state that Detective Vega exhibits, quote, 'a lax attitude about command structure and too much personal involvement in his cases.' What did you mean by those words?"

Lorenzo licked his lips. Carver allowed the tortoiseshell glasses to slip low on his nose. He regarded Lorenzo over them.

"Don't insult the jury's intelligence by trying to walk back your words, Captain."

"I'm not walking back anything."

"So, you stand by them?"

Silence.

"Well," said Carver. "Do you or don't you?"

"I stand by them," said Lorenzo testily. "Detective Vega doesn't follow the rules."

"What do you mean by 'rules'?"

"Procedures. Protocols."

"Protocols such as having backup when he initiates an arrest of a suspect?"

"Objection," said Jenkins. "Mr. Carver is leading the witness."

"I'll withdraw the question," Carver said quickly. But he'd made the connection for the jury. The ten-million-dollar connection: *Detective Vega doesn't follow the rules. That's why this woman's husband—or whatever he was—is dead. It's his fault.* Never mind that the circumstances that night warranted quick action. The jury had been led to a simple conclusion. They weren't about to overthink it.

"Your Honor," said Jenkins, desperate to turn things around. "Captain Lorenzo said Detective Vega doesn't *follow* the rules. He didn't say he *broke* any."

"Semantics, Counselor," said Carver. He picked up an empty Starbucks takeout cup sitting on the edge of the plaintiff's table and threw it to the floor, stamping it with his foot until the rim had folded to the shape of a half-moon. It was a dramatic action and it completely captured the attention of everyone in the room.

"There's a law against littering in the building," said Carver, gesturing to the flattened cup. "Tell me, Counselor. Am I not *following* the rules? Or am I breaking them? Because I don't see a difference. Do you?"

On and on it went. Carver walked Lorenzo through every stinging comment he made about Vega at the hearing. Isadora Jenkins looked like a jack-in-the-box the whole time as she sprang to her feet with objection after objection. None of it mattered. The die had been cast the moment Carver threw the Starbucks cup on the floor. The jury was turning against Vega.

"There are plenty of people on the job who'll tell you I'm not a hothead or a cowboy," Vega whispered to Jenkins. "I have a good conviction rate precisely because I take my cases personally and work hard to solve them."

"If we can rescue the day, I'll try to get some of those people on the stand." Jenkins rose. "Your Honor, if I may point out—"

She was cut off, not by Carver or Judge Edgerton, but by her own co-counselor, Henry Zaroff, who hadn't said a word this whole time.

"Your Honor?" Zaroff rose from his seat. "May I ask for a brief recess so that we may confer privately with Mr. Carver in your chambers?"

Vega shot a panicked look at Jenkins. The fight had left her eyes.

"This is it, isn't it?" Vega murmured to Jenkins. *Zaroff is going to make a settlement offer.*

"I think so," she replied.

Edgerton banged his gavel. "Captain Lorenzo? You are

excused from the stand. Jury will take a short recess. Counselors will meet in my chambers."

Zaroff leaned over and said something in Jenkins's ear, then quickly left the courtroom, pointedly ignoring Vega. Vega waited until the little man had left to speak to Jenkins.

"Can I offer my two cents to the judge?"

"Detective," Jenkins said kindly, as if speaking to a child, "you know that's not how this works. This is between the attorneys. We'll settle on a price and Carver will take it back to Ponce's widow to see if she'll agree."

"Oh, she'll agree all right," Vega muttered. "She's been paid to agree."

Jenkins gave Vega a disapproving look. He felt like he was back in Sister Margarita's office at St. Raymond's. "Get some coffee," she told him. "Take a deep breath until I text you our plans. And for Pete's sake, sew that mouth of yours shut."

Chapter 27

Vega loosened his tie and stuffed it in his pocket. Zaroff looked prepared to settle. Not for $10 million, perhaps. But the sum, Vega was sure, would be in the seven figures. Vega would be paying for this for the rest of his career. He'd lost in the end, not for what he'd done on that December evening. Not for the life he'd taken. But for what he hadn't done in a completely unrelated case some six weeks later.

He hadn't asked permission.

The civil trial hadn't excited anywhere near the press that the original shooting had. Still, Vega didn't want to chance running into any reporters in the common areas or the cafeteria. He needed a place in the building to hide until Jenkins texted him. He recalled that the court clerk area upstairs was quiet. Plus, it was down the hall from the lost-and-found, which was finally open.

He made his way upstairs via a back stairwell, past plastic sheets and temporary walls, following paper signs to a maintenance area where they kept the lost-and-found. One of the court officers let Vega paw through the contents. Umbrellas and sunglasses. Sweatshirts and single earrings. A book on how to fix a marriage. Vega wondered if one of the divorce litigants had left it behind—or, more likely, thrown it at their soon-to-be ex-spouse.

Adele's religious medal wasn't among the items. Vega swallowed his disappointment. He wanted so much to find it for her.

He thanked the officer, then walked down the hall toward the court clerk area. He was hoping Lucille Bouchart might find him a spare cubicle where he could check his phone in private. He wanted to see if Kaylee had gotten back to him to confirm their meeting for later. She was supposed to drop Hunter off at his babysitter's house—Little Sprout was closed on Friday evenings—then head to O'Rourke's where Vega would meet her before she started her shift. He'd texted her twice to confirm. She'd yet to text back.

The offices of the court clerk were down the hall from the judges' temporary chambers. One of the chamber doors opened now and Kent Edgerton stepped out. He turned and began walking in Vega's direction. *Ay, puñeta!* Vega didn't want the judge to think he was eavesdropping on Edgerton's meeting with the lawyers. Isadora Jenkins would have his head. He searched for a quick escape. The only one that presented itself was the men's room. Vega ducked inside. He was thankful when the judge didn't follow.

One man was at the urinal, zipping up his pants. The mirror caught his reflection. Gold-rimmed bifocals. A neatly trimmed gray mustache that partially hid the hint of a smile.

"There are closer bathrooms to the courtroom, you know, Detective."

"Which is precisely why I'm hiding here."

Albert Pearsall walked over to the sink and ran the water. He pumped the soap twice and lathered to his wrists, like he was prepping for open-heart surgery. "I saw your trial listed on Edgerton's docket. My condolences, Detective. But I suspect you knew that there would be some sort of civil action after the shooting. There always is, these days."

"Yeah. Tell me about it." Vega didn't want to get into a gripe session. Not after his attorney's warning. He used the urinal, then joined Pearsall at the sinks. "Is this your first day back?"

"It is." Pearsall dried his hands on a paper towel, then removed his glasses and wiped the lenses with a handkerchief from his pocket. "Keep calm and carry on—isn't that what the British always say?"

"The British don't have to worry about getting shot at by every half-wit in their country," said Vega. "How's Judge Spruce holding up?"

Pearsall returned his glasses to his face and blinked at himself in the mirror. His pale blue eyes looked sad and a little lost. "As well as can be expected, I guess. The earlobe will heal, thank goodness. She might need a skin graft. But physically, she should make a full recovery."

"I'm glad to hear it. Listen," said Vega. "You got a spare cubicle that I can hang out in, check my messages, while I'm on recess?"

"I'm sure I can find you a spot."

The cubicle Pearsall found him had a desk, a chair, and an assortment of extra computer equipment that didn't seem to belong anywhere else. Vega didn't care. It was private, at least. No one paid attention to him, which was just the way Vega wanted it. He let the sound of ringing phones and the clattering of fingers across keyboards wash over him. He breathed in the stale, clammy air from the air-conditioning ducts and promised himself he'd go jogging around the lake tonight with Diablo. The county could take away his promotion and future prospects. But they couldn't take away his life.

He checked in with Adele and told her Zaroff had elected to settle the case.

"Oh, Jimmy," she said, her breath coming out like she'd held it in too long. "I'm so sorry."

"Yeah. Me too." He told her he'd also checked the

court's lost-and-found for her religious medal and it wasn't there.

"Thank you anyway, *mi vida*. I appreciate that you tried." She sounded more resigned than surprised.

"Now you can do something for me," he said in a fatherly tone.

"Anything."

"I need you to get a home security system like I've been begging you to do."

"I'll look into it." A lawyer's response. He'd had enough of lawyers for one day.

"*Nena*—I need a promise."

"Okay. I promise." Vega heard an intake of breath on her end, like she had something else to say. "Jimmy? Did you and Greco have words last night? I spoke to him this morning and he seemed sort of, I don't know . . . abrupt with me. More than usual."

The Rivas case. "Long story," said Vega. "Don't worry about it. I'll talk to him."

He hung up from Adele and walked over to Albert Pearsall's cubicle. He knocked on the fabric partition. "Hey, man, sorry to bother you again, but I have a question."

"Judge Edgerton likes a lot of deference. Yessir and no sir."

"This isn't about my case," said Vega. "It's about another that took place a few months ago. A day laborer with no ID who gave his name as Juan Rivas. Lake Holly busted him for possession of a filet knife. ICE lodged a removal order against him. He came before Judge Spruce and claimed he used the knife for fishing. She reduced the charge to a fine and released him."

Pearsall gave a sympathetic nod. "That's Julia. She doesn't like to see people's lives upended over small mistakes."

"Except the case wasn't that simple," said Vega. "When

Lake Holly busted him, they discovered he didn't have fingerprints. Rivas said they were burned off in a landscaping accident. Except there was no scar tissue. They were smooth—like they'd been lasered off. Like the guy had a jacket he was trying to shake. Something like that should have raised alarm bells with a judge. So why on earth did she release him?"

Pearsall shrugged. "I don't recall the case. My guess is that Lake Holly failed to make Judge Spruce aware of the situation."

"So, you're saying the judge never got the police report about the missing fingerprints?"

"I suspect not. But let me check." Pearsall swiveled his chair until he was facing his computer and typed in the information. "I'm scrolling through the submitted police report now. Was the information about the missing prints in an attachment?"

"Probably," said Vega. "It was probably submitted as evidence. In a separate report."

Pearsall gestured to the screen. "I don't have anything like that in the court record."

"Lake Holly sent them to ICE."

"If they say so. But ICE wouldn't send them to us. We'd have to get them directly from the arresting agency. We didn't. You can't expect Judge Spruce to rule on something she never saw."

"No," Vega agreed. Without the information about the missing prints, Juan Rivas was just a Spanish-speaking day laborer with no ID and a filet knife he claimed to use for fishing. It was even remotely possible he was in the country legally but had other issues—mental illness, alcoholism—that prevented him from having the paperwork to prove it. Vega had heard of cases where American-born Hispanics got deported over such things. Was this just a paperwork blunder? Or was it something more?

"Listen," Vega leaned in close. He could see the razor-sharp creases in Pearsall's pressed slacks and smell the cinnamon-and-leather scent of his aftershave that for some reason brought to mind a British sea captain. "I know you work for Judge Spruce and you're fond of her. But do you sense her . . . I don't know . . . slipping in any way?"

"She's as sharp as ever, as far as I can see."

"Has she become . . . perhaps more strident in her views? Maybe her politics have overshadowed her judicial impartiality?"

"She's against federal intervention in state matters," said Pearsall. "That's always been her position. And it's legally defensible."

"I know." Vega tossed off a laugh. "My girlfriend has taken great pains to explain that to me. But . . . is it possible the judge has gone too far?"

Pearsall swiveled his chair away from his computer. He brushed a finger beneath his silver-threaded mustache and studied Vega for a long moment before he spoke.

"Look, Detective. I respect you as a police officer. But I respect Judge Spruce too. Just because you don't agree with her position on certain issues, doesn't mean she's"—he put his fingers in quotes—"losing it. She's a good judge who makes sound legal decisions. Just look at her overall record and you'll see how balanced she is."

"Overall, yes," said Vega. "But it seems to me she has a blind spot on this issue."

"Police officers don't necessarily view the law the same way judges do," said Pearsall. "What happens on the street is very different from what happens in a courtroom. I'm sure you're feeling the effects of that now in your civil trial. Good intentions don't always translate the same way in court."

"You got that right," said Vega. "So, just to clarify: Judge Spruce never received Lake Holly's report about the missing prints?"

"She did not."

Vega's cell phone dinged in his pocket. It was a text from Isadora Jenkins. **Go get lunch. We're still a million apart. This is going to take a while.**

A million *apart*? Vega's stomach lurched. He couldn't even conceive of the numbers they were throwing around. The enormity of them. With overtime, he currently made about $82,000 a year. If he banked every penny he earned, it would still take him more than a dozen years to earn a million dollars. And that wasn't even the settlement amount. That was just the difference. Not that he was paying, of course. The county's insurance fund was paying. But one way or another, the department would see to it that he paid for this the rest of his career.

However long—or short—that turned out to be.

Vega was too keyed up to eat. What he really wanted was to talk to someone who could understand, as a cop, what he was going through. Someone who could take a pragmatic approach to his troubles. He left the court clerk's area and made his way to the security lot, hoping the fresh air might clear his senses. He hadn't been back here since Monday afternoon, when Darryl Williams was killed. The yellow crime-scene tape was gone. The only sign that a shooting had occurred was a dinner-plate-sized rust-colored splotch baked into the pavement between two courthouse vans.

There was no shade and no place to sit, but Vega welcomed just being outside. He pulled out his phone and punched in a number.

"Did you have lunch yet?" He didn't bother identifying himself. He never needed to.

Her laugh was sharp and breathy. It instantly transported him back to his childhood. "You go weeks without seeing me, *mano,* and all of a sudden I'm supposed to be available for lunch? I already ate at my desk. And besides, I thought the trial was still going on."

"They're working out a settlement. I have to stay near the courthouse."

"*Ay bendito.*" Michelle understood immediately. "I'm so sorry, Jimmy. That sucks. Especially when you *know* this is just one more scam from that silver-tongued ambulance chaser."

"Feels like it," said Vega. "The widow focuses more on her phone than on the trial."

"She was paid to look beautifully bereaved, not interested."

Vega found a narrow band of shade on the corner of the building. He leaned against the brick. It felt marvelously cool on his back. "Speaking of court shams," he said. "You ever hear of a defendant named Juan Rivas? I understand he gave the slip to one of your ICE agents. A guy named Vinnie."

"Vinnie Fiero. Yeah," said Michelle. "I know about the case. It's in our Turn-'em-loose Spruce files." She laughed. "Sounds like a television series, doesn't it?"

"Spruce's court clerk claims the judge never got Lake Holly's police report about the missing fingerprints."

"Can't say yes or no on that," said Michelle. "But I can tell you, there's plenty more cases in our illustrious file just like that one."

"I'd love to see them."

"And like I told you before, *mano,* I'd love to keep my job."

"C'mon, Michelle. This is your brother asking. Do you really think I would do anything to cost you your job?"

"Why do you want to know so bad?"

No way was he going to discuss Judge Spruce's record standing in the courthouse security lot. "I just want to see what you got, that's all. I'm not going public with it."

"I can't remove the files," said Michelle. "But I guess I can take a couple of cell-phone photos of the reports and show them to you."

"That would be great."

Another pause. "Is that what you *really* called for?" She had a Bronx girl's radar, no doubt sharpened by their wayward father and later, her deadbeat ex-husband.

"No," said Vega. "I really called to ask you to lunch."

"Right answer," she said. "I'll get the photos. Meet me at the Broad Plains Diner in ten minutes."

Chapter 28

Every cop and civil servant in the area knew the Broad Plains Diner. It had the best coffee in the area. Which was why there was always a line at the takeout counter.

Vega donned a Yankees baseball cap and sunglasses so nobody would recognize him and requested one of the red Naugahyde booths near the back. He ordered coffee and waited.

Michelle arrived ten minutes late, all drama and chatter about traffic and something to do with a fight between her older son and his best friend at camp. She flopped down in the booth across from Vega. The seats were old, the springs, compressed. She was tall and ropy but the booth made her look small and compact. She rolled her eyes at his cap and mirrored aviator shades.

"Please don't tell me I'm going to have to spend our whole lunch looking at my reflection."

"I don't want to get recognized."

"You're not The Rock, I'm sorry to say. You're yesterday's news. People cared about you when you were the cop who shot an unarmed man. Civil suits don't interest them. Lose the disguise."

He removed the sunglasses but not the baseball cap. The waitress brought two menus.

"I'll take a burger. Medium rare. American cheese. No onions. And an iced tea with lemon," said Michelle.

"I thought you said you ate lunch at your desk?" asked Vega.

"If you're buying, I'm eating."

Vega ordered the same, minus the iced tea. "I didn't think I was hungry. But if you can eat two lunches, I suppose I can eat one."

"Hey, this is my main meal of the day," said Michelle. "Gotta make it count."

She waited until the waitress left. Then she leaned forward, her voice soft. "What's all the interest in Turn-'em-loose? I thought the courthouse shooting was an FBI case."

"It is," said Vega. "But there's a unit in the county police that oversees threat mail to government officials. The special agent in charge asked me to fetch any mail on Spruce—"

"Let me guess," said Michelle. "They needed a special room to contain it all."

"Not quite," said Vega. "But it was a lot. More than any other official. Before I could even go through it, the FBI took it from me. I got the sense it wasn't to look at but to bury."

"That would be our illustrious attorney general's doing," said Michelle. "If the press gets a hold of her record, it's going to reflect badly on Andrew Locklear in the November election."

"She was still a victim in the shooting."

"That she was," said Michelle. "I hope they find the shooter. I'm sure they hope so too. But the power brokers in this state would rather gloss over the why."

"Sounds like there's plenty of why."

"You bet there is." Michelle pulled out her phone. "I'm texting you some pictures of court records right now. I was able to photograph only three cases. But there are more, trust me. Read 'em. Then destroy 'em."

"I won't get you in trouble," Vega promised. The waitress came by to refill his coffee. He waited until she'd left again to pull up Michelle's photos. The first concerned the case of Jorgé Santiago Garcia, alias Jorgé Garcia Santiago, alias Jorgé Guitterez Garcia. Age twenty-five. Birthplace: Guadalajara, Mexico. Police in Port Carroll arrested Santiago after he ran a stop sign, couldn't provide a license or vehicle registration, and blew a 1.7 on his BAC. When the Port Carroll Police ran his fingerprints, they discovered he was in the U.S. illegally and had incurred two previous arrests for the same offense—which, for American citizens, would bump this up to felony DUI. If convicted, Santiago would almost surely be deported.

Except he wasn't. Santiago's attorney—a relatively pricey drunk-driving specialist—argued that the man was the sole support of his two American-born children and had entered rehab to work on his alcohol issues. Spruce knocked the charge down to reckless driving and released him.

Vega was furious. He'd cut many a young shoplifter or first-time drug offender a break. But if there was one charge he always threw the book at people on, it was impaired driving. When he was in uniform, he never missed a court date to testify against a drunk driver. He'd been to too many fatal accidents involving innocent people hit by drunk drivers. In many cases, the victims were children. If he could get one self-centered and reckless asshole off the road—American or immigrant—he was happy. Yet here was Spruce, undoing all of that.

Vega stirred more sugar into his coffee. He'd been so absorbed with the report, he couldn't remember if he'd put in one teaspoon or two already.

"I can see you just read Santiago's report," said Michelle.

"Yeah." Vega went to take a sip of his too-sweet coffee.

The cup perched at his lips. The smell suddenly nauseated him and he put it back down without drinking. Or maybe it was Santiago who nauseated him. He wasn't sure. He moved on to the next case. Of an undocumented immigrant man breaking down his estranged wife's door—a charge that was originally labeled as "menacing," and was bargained down to "vandalism" after the man's estranged wife signed off. *Under duress?* Vega wondered. There was no way to tell.

He closed his eyes. If drunk drivers made him furious, abusers made him apoplectic.

"How can the judge justify what she's doing?" asked Vega. "I get it that she thinks our immigration system is messed up. I do too. I think decent people aren't getting a chance to be productive members of our communities. But that doesn't mean I want to see jerks and criminals running about with impunity."

"Imagine how my agents feel," said Michelle. "We're charged with getting unlawful aliens off the streets. In many cases, these people have committed serious crimes. They're often repeat offenders. Yet we're being sabotaged by our own government."

"Adele says the judge is following the Fourth Amendment."

"Yeah, well, Adele doesn't have to walk into a lockup and interview a gangbanger who hopped the border illegally, raped a fifteen-year-old girl, and then sliced up her brother when he tried to defend her."

The waitress brought their burgers. Michelle tucked in. Vega took a few bites. But his frustration had wiped out his appetite. He reminded himself that Michelle and her colleagues had put together the judge's worst cases—which accounted for only a small fraction of her judicial decisions, even the ones involving undocumented immigrants. He himself had cut breaks to people whose only infraction was illegal entry—sometimes decades ago. A lot of them were mothers and fathers. Outstanding community members and steady employees. There was a place for compassion in the law. But these particular defendants wouldn't be anyone's poster child for that.

"Michelle? Can I ask you something?"

"Sure."

"Do you think there's some other reason for these decisions?"

"What? You mean like, is she corrupt?"

"Or maybe succumbing to early Alzheimer's. Or secretly drinking."

Michelle shook her head. "First of all, you know as well as I do that judges don't pick their cases. The court clerks assign them depending on availability in their docket."

"True."

"She's not corrupt," said Michelle. "She's not losing it either. I've heard her speak and she's a true believer. She thinks she's on a mission to help humanity. If she were doing the work your girlfriend is doing, I'd say okay." Vega heard the slight disparaging lean on "girlfriend." Michelle and Adele accepted one another. But they didn't like each other. "The problem is she's a sitting judge."

Vega studied the third set of records. From the case he was most familiar with: *Juan Rivas*. According to the file, Rivas had given his full name as Juan Nelson Rivas-Gomez. Age: thirty-eight. But that's not what drew Vega's eye. It was the mug shot. Of a pale-skinned man with a faint scar through his left eyebrow that made it turn perpetually up. Lots of Latin Americans didn't fit the mestizo stereotype, just as lots of Puerto Ricans didn't fit the Caribbean one. Some were the clear descendants of African slaves. Others favored their indigenous origins. Others, like Rivas, had a lot of European blood running through their veins.

But that's not what made Vega sit back in the booth, unable to turn his gaze away from the photo. It wasn't the scar or the eyebrow. It was one niggling realization that rippled through him, the way it would any cop who made it a point to never forget a face.

"I've seen him before."

"Rivas?" asked Michelle. "Recently?"

"No," said Vega. "A long time ago."

The sounds of the diner washed over him. Waiters taking orders. Crashing plates. People talking on their phones more than they talked to each other. The jangle of loose change as the cash register opened. Vega barely registered any of it. All he could see was that face. And with it, the knowledge.

Judge Spruce had released a very dangerous man.

Chapter 29

A honey-colored light settled over the orchard as Eli and her mother trudged in from the fields that Friday afternoon. The air had cooled under a bright blue sky. Birds swooped low through the trees, their chatter as animated as that of the workers. Everyone was tired, but Friday nights were still a festive time. Young men spoke about buying beer and cranking up their music with friends. The older ones planned to catch a ball game on TV or rustle up some neighbors for a game of dominos. They'd all be back here tomorrow. Most only took Sundays off. But even so—people tried to put a little fun into whatever free time they had.

Eli and Aurelia returned their mesh bags to the crate and walked toward the truck that would take them back to the trailer park. Eli saw a chrome bumper peeking out from behind the truck. She stepped nearer and saw a shiny blue Jeep parked in the clearing. The driver's door opened, and Luis slid out, dressed in shorts, a T-shirt, and a baseball cap. His broad, clean-shaved face sported a hesitant smile. He braced one arm against the open door and in the other, held out a large canvas bag.

"I want to take you somewhere special," he said. "Come."

"Where are we going?" asked her mother.

"It's a surprise. You'll see."

Aurelia yanked on the hem of her T-shirt, streaked with dirt. "You want us to go somewhere dressed like this?"

"You're fine," Luis insisted, without really looking at them. He opened the rear door of the Jeep. Two dark eyes blinked from the interior. A boy. He looked both older and younger than Eli with his smooth, even skin, soft cheeks, and big glassy eyes. He wore what looked like swim trunks and a T-shirt with pointy creases on the sleeves like it had just been ironed. He smelled of coconut. This had to be Eli's fourteen-year-old cousin, the youngest of Luis's three boys.

"Wilmer," Luis said in Spanish. "Say hello to your *Tía* Aurelia and *prima,* Elizabeth."

"Hi," the boy squeaked out in English. There was a pause while everyone waited for him to say something in Spanish, but he just stared at Eli and her mother like they were exotic animals, something entirely foreign to him—and maybe even a little scary.

Were they scary? Eli wondered. They were dirty and tired and probably didn't smell too good. Eli's left wrist was encased in a plaster cast that had been covered over in a black plastic garbage bag. The bag was shredded now, the edges of the cast by her fingers now gray and dirty. But she didn't think they were scary. *He* was the scary one, with his pressed blue T-shirt, perfect, white, fence-post teeth, and even, unblemished skin. He looked nothing like Eli's other cousins back in Guatemala. It was hard to believe they were related.

"Well," said Luis, clapping his hands together with forced cheer. "Let's get going."

Luis tossed the canvas bag in the trunk and slid behind the wheel. Eli's mother sat in the front passenger seat. Eli climbed in back. Wilmer stared at Eli as she buckled her seat belt, then pretended not to.

"Your arm," he said in Spanish. "What happened?"

"Do you mean my wrist?" she asked, pointing to it.

"Your wrist, yes." His words were shaky, like he had trouble stringing them together. Eli suspected he understood Spanish perfectly, since his parents probably spoke it at home. But he probably didn't have a lot of opportunities to speak it himself.

"I fell and broke it," she lied.

"Ah."

Luis made a three-point turn and drove out of the orchard and onto the two-lane, blasting the air-conditioning, which chilled the sweat on Eli's skin too quickly and caused her to shiver. Her mother pulled down the visor and finger-combed her hair in the mirror. "I must look awful," she said to Luis.

"You look fine," he replied, without taking his eyes off the road.

"Maybe we should shower first. Change clothes," her mother suggested.

"That's not necessary," said Luis. "Really."

He clicked on the radio. American pop music filled the interior. A female voice singing over a staccato beat.

Wilmer gestured to the radio. "Ariana Grande," he said. "Do you know her music?" His sentences in Spanish were choppy, but at least Eli could understand them.

She shook her head. "I don't know her."

"She's very popular in our country." *Our country.* The words startled Eli. Reminded her that Wilmer was an American and she was not. "Do you like sports?"

"I like watching football sometimes," said Eli.

"We call it soccer here," said Wilmer. "Here, football is American football. I like American football a lot—especially the New York Giants. I hate the Philadelphia Eagles and the Washington Redskins. Those are their . . ." He searched for the word in Spanish and used the English instead. ". . . rivals."

"Ah. *Rivales,*" said Eli. "Almost the same." At least they had that one word in common.

"Yeah," Wilmer grunted in English. He made a few more statements about American football in Spanish. Eli could tell he was struggling to string the words together. She wished she knew English and they could talk normally and naturally. There was so much she wanted to ask him. One subject, in particular.

"Where do you go to school?"

"Petersville Regional," he replied. "We only have a primary school in North Kitchawan. After that, everyone goes to Petersville Regional. They got a middle school and a high school on the same campus." He said the words "middle school," "high school," and "campus" in English. But Eli got the gist. The secondary school she needed to attend was in Petersville.

"Is that far away?"

"Twenty minutes, maybe," said Wilmer. "You were there, weren't you?"

"I don't think so."

Wilmer turned and asked his father something in English. Luis hesitated, then nodded. Wilmer turned back to Eli. "You were. That's where the clinic is where my dad took you to get your wrist fixed."

Eli noticed her uncle sink down a little in the driver's seat. He'd told her and her mother that the secondary school was too far away for her to attend when it wasn't far away at all. Eli shot a glance at her mother, but Aurelia wasn't paying attention. She was asking Luis questions about how to use the phone he'd bought her. Eli didn't want to spoil the moment. Her mother seemed happy. For the first time since they'd stepped off the bus in Broad Plains, things felt almost normal. Maybe her uncle and his family just needed some time to adjust to the idea of Eli and her mother being here. Maybe after Aunt Miriam and her older cousins—Christian and Franklin—met them, Luis would change his mind about everything. He would tell her mother that they didn't have to pick that mountain of apples to pay him back.

Maybe in September, Eli, too, could go to school in Petersville—right alongside Wilmer.

Eli closed her eyes and tried not to think about the size of the debt before them, but to concentrate instead on this lovely summer evening and the drive to Luis's house. She assumed that's where they were headed. She recalled pictures of the big white house tacked to the wall above her grandmother's bed in Guatemala. She remembered being fascinated by the front door—those panels of what looked like stained glass running down either side and that carpet of green lawn in front. It seemed to stretch on forever without any fence around it.

Luis flicked on his indicator and made a left down another road that wound up at a wooded hillside. He turned again by a big wooden sign: LAKE PEQUOT STATE PARK. Eli saw her mother tense in the front seat.

"We are meeting Miriam *here*?" she asked.

Luis cleared his throat. "Miriam can't make it today, unfortunately."

"Your other sons?"

"They are working," said Luis. "But we can have a picnic! I brought food and a blanket and Eli can go swimming in the lake!"

"Swimming?" Her mother gestured to Eli's arm. "In what? How? She has no bathing suit. Her wrist is in a cast. She can't get it wet."

"I have a T-shirt and shorts for her in the trunk," said Luis. "She can go in up to her waist if she wants. Cool down and have some fun."

"Fun?" Eli could hear the anger rising in her mother. "Fun would be to not wake up in the dark and spend twelve hours a day picking apples. Fun would be not

standing in the hot sun, fighting off wasps and poison ivy and men who want to grab you all the time—"

"Aurelia!" He held up a hand. "You are spoiling everything."

"What am I spoiling, Luis? Your attempts to wash your guilty conscience?"

"I have nothing to feel guilty about!"

The lake was before them now. Eli could see that it was quite beautiful. Sunlight glittered across its surface like crushed glass. It was surrounded by deep green pine trees. Right off the parking lot was a short trail that led to a sand beach. Aurelia didn't notice. She was waving her arms at her brother.

"What? I'm not good enough to meet your fancy wife? Your stuck-up sons? This is how you treat your family?"

"I brought Wilmer, didn't I? I'm trying!"

"This is trying?" Aurelia folded her arms and stared out the passenger side window. "Take me back to the trailer. I don't need your *trying*."

Eli's heart sank. She didn't want to go back. She wanted to see the beach. She hunkered down in her seat and said nothing. Fortunately, Luis was too mad to turn the Jeep around. Or maybe Wilmer wanted to swim, Eli wasn't sure. Either way, he ignored his sister and pulled the Jeep sharply into a space. He cut the engine.

"I'm going for a swim!" he grunted. "You can wait in the Jeep or not—I don't care!" He got out, fetched the canvas tote bag from the trunk, and stomped off in the direction of the lake. A few seconds later, Aurelia took off after him, leaving Eli and Wilmer in the backseat. Eli felt embarrassed. She sensed Wilmer did too. They sat there in the Jeep, the air growing hotter around them until Wilmer undid his seat belt.

"Do you know how to throw rocks?" he asked her.

"Throw rocks?" Eli frowned. "At who?"

"No." Wilmer shook his head, searching for the word.

He mimed skipping a stone. Eli's face brightened. She gave him the word and he repeated it.

"I'm not very good at it," she said.

"I will show you."

Eli followed Wilmer down the path to the beach. It was a beautiful spot with picnic tables and grills under some shade trees. About half a dozen families were scattered about, mostly white but a few Hispanic—with beach blankets on the sand and coolers on picnic tables. One man was frying burgers and hot dogs on a grill. Eli's stomach rumbled at the delicious smell.

Wilmer kicked off his flip-flops. Eli slipped off the rubber boots she was still wearing from the orchard and put them next to Wilmer's flip-flops. The sand felt warm and soft on her feet. She strolled down to the water and stuck her feet in up to her ankles. The water felt refreshing. It was so clear, she saw the wavy outlines of her feet and little fish swimming around. She wished she could wade farther in but she couldn't. It wasn't just her cast she was worried about. Her T-shirt would get translucent and show her bra. She wasn't that developed—but still.

Wilmer ran up to the wooded area just beyond the sand and began digging for stones to skip. Eli cast a nervous glance around the beach for her uncle and mother. She didn't see them. She saw only happy families. A young Hispanic father in the lake, teaching his little daughter to swim, while his wife splashed water on their younger toddler. A white mother showing her two little boys how to catch and release fish in a net. The white dad at the grill, calling to his children, who came scurrying over to eat.

Watching them all, Eli felt a deep sadness. Here was a life she yearned to experience but knew she never would. A close, normal family, enjoying the simple pleasures of being together. Every family she knew in Nejapa was torn apart for one reason or another. Parents working in the

United States. Children lost to drugs or gangs. Pervasive violence. Nobody she knew in Guatemala had a completely intact family. Poverty made that impossible. The United States seduced the young and ambitious, then remade them into something unrecognizable to their own kin. What was left behind—the old, the sick, the unlucky, and the impulsive—quickly crumbled the way a house might, if a wall were removed.

Her family, Eli realized, was a house with three walls.

Wilmer came back to the beach, carrying a handful of stones. He pressed some in Eli's hand and showed her how to skim them across the water, away from where the children were swimming. They didn't talk much—she understood now that they couldn't really. His Spanish took effort. But it felt nice just being in his presence.

It didn't last. In a wooded clearing to the right of the beach, Eli could hear the unmistakable pitch of her mother arguing with her uncle in Spanish. Luis's voice was lower and calmer. Wilmer hunched his shoulders slightly and frowned at the lake.

"I wish they'd stop yelling."

"Me too," said Eli.

"My father brought food. We were going to have a picnic. I don't understand why your mother can't be a little nicer."

Eli startled. Wilmer's phrasing hurt even more than his criticism. He said "your mother." Not "my aunt." He didn't see Eli and her mother as family.

"My mother is nice," Eli insisted. "You don't know your *tía* like I do."

Wilmer didn't pick up on the correction. He was stubborn like Luis. *Tío* Luis. He was still her uncle, whether or not her cousin saw them as family.

"Well, she's not being nice now," Wilmer continued. "My dad is having a lot of problems with his business. He and my mom are always arguing about money. Yet he still brought you both over to the United States. He's *trying* to help."

Eli closed her eyes and thought again about the debt they were under. The mountain of apples that awaited picking before she could ever set foot in a school. Every muscle in her body ached. Her nose and cheeks stung from sunburn. She shot a sideways glance at her cousin. His soft, well-fed body. Those perfect white fence-post teeth. She thought of all her mother and she had endured to get to this country. The grueling work they'd done since they'd arrived. She thought of Señor Ortega, the way he looked at Aurelia—looked at them both—like they were meals he could order off a menu any time he wanted.

"You have no idea what you are talking about," she said slowly.

"Sure I do," said Wilmer. "I'm older than you."

Eli opened her hand and let the stones slide off her callused palm and into the clear lake water, churning up the sand until she couldn't see her feet. She was invisible beneath the surface. Nothing but a murky island of flesh and bone to the fish swimming around her. Unknown and unknowable.

An intruder in their world.

Chapter 30

Vega sat across from his sister at the Broad Plains Diner, staring at the mug shot of Juan Rivas. Something about the memory chilled him to the core.

"Where do you remember him from?" asked Michelle. "Did you arrest him?"

"My unit did," said Vega. "Or rather, tried to. Back when I worked undercover."

The waitress breezed by, asking if they wanted to order anything else. Vega pushed his plate aside. He felt queasy all of a sudden.

"We'll just take the check," said Michelle. The waitress dropped the bill on the table. Vega waved away his sister's money and slapped a credit card down. The waitress disappeared with it.

"Do you recall anything about the case?" asked Michelle.

Vega wiped his napkin across a spot of spilled ketchup, then crumpled it beside his saucer. "It had to be about six years ago." He knew this because it was around the time his divorce was finalized. Right before Joy's bat mitzvah. Just after Wendy had her twins with her soon-to-be second husband, the man she'd cheated with while she was still married to Vega.

A memorable time all around.

"It was up in Mount Washington as I recall," said Vega. "Near the border with Hudson County. A joint bust with the local police. I remember the guy because he didn't belong."

"Didn't belong how?" asked Michelle.

Vega stared out the diner window, watching the passersby, most of them workers from the courthouse and federal building. He tried to recall this case out of the hundreds he'd worked on in his half decade undercover.

"He was whiter than the other guys," said Vega.

"I've seen plenty of white-looking Latinos, even among day laborers," said Michelle. "Plenty of Black- and Asian-looking ones too."

"It was more than that," said Vega. "He was different in every way. All the other suspects we arrested in the sting were street-corner narcotics dealers. Nickel-and-dime hustlers. I think we booked him for possession of a couple of marijuana joints—just to hold him. We never got more. No weapon. No other drugs. No one confessed to knowing him, although the other guys all seemed scared of him."

"I guess the judge cut him loose," said Michelle. "Was it Spruce?"

"I don't think so," said Vega. "I don't remember. But you need to realize that this was before the big crackdown on illegal immigrants. You can't really blame a judge for fining him and letting him go."

Vega's phone dinged in his pocket. It was a text from Isadora Jenkins. **We're still a half mil apart. The judge said to take the weekend to work this out. Go home. Relax. There's nothing else you can do.**

Vega showed the text to Michelle while he signed the credit card receipt.

"Ugh," she said, handing the phone back to him. "Well, at least you can take the rest of the day off."

"Yeah." Vega tossed off a laugh. "And *relax* this weekend." His whole future was up in the air. There would be no "relaxing."

Vega tucked his phone in his pocket and threw a cash tip on top of the credit card receipt. He stared out the window again. His mind was a million miles away.

"Jimmy? Is it the settlement that's eating you? Or this Rivas guy?"

"Both, I guess," he said. "Only I can't do anything about the settlement." He pushed himself out of the booth. "I can't do anything about Rivas either, I suppose. He probably had fingerprints back then. But I'd have to pore over hundreds and hundreds of records to match his likeness to a name. It's not like he was convicted of anything."

"You know," said Michelle, grabbing a couple of sugar packets and throwing them into her purse. She never passed up anything that was free. Napkins. Mints. Plastic cutlery—you name it. Vega wasn't sure if it was because she was a single mother or because she'd been largely raised by one. Orlando Vega hadn't exactly been father-of-the-year to her either.

"If you booked him after that bust," Michelle continued, "his booking sheet would still be in the county jail's electronic records. If he had prints back then, as you say, they should still be there."

"But I don't have a case number or a date or anything," said Vega. "I wasn't even the arresting officer. I was undercover."

"Do you remember who the arresting officer was?"

Vega thought about it. His captain, Nick Santorini, oversaw the bust. He was head of narcotics, then and now. But he wasn't the arresting officer. That would have been Vega's handler back then. An old-timer who'd started his career with the NYPD and finished it with the county police.

"Sergeant Frank Locuso," Vega told Michelle. "But he retired about a year after I left undercover work."

"Doesn't matter," said Michelle. "If anything, that may narrow the window."

Vega gave his sister an approving look. "I wouldn't have thought of the county lockup."

"That's because you didn't work in corrections like I used to. Jails always have the most detailed records. They have to know who they're dealing with."

Vega said good-bye to Michelle, retrieved his truck from the courthouse parking lot, and drove to the county jail, a low-slung, beige, concrete building rimmed by two sets of razor wire. Vega regularly visited the lockup to interview inmates, so, while he didn't know all of the staff's names, he knew their faces and they knew his. This helped, because what he was asking the corrections officer currently staffing Records Intake was outside his normal scope of duties.

Garner was his name. Latrell Garner. He was a large, soft-spoken Black man who lacked the gruffness normally associated with the job. Which meant either he was very good at getting inmates to obey without it—or he was a total pushover. It was always a tightrope in law enforcement. Stay reasonable, and you got blindsided by manipulative criminals, maybe even hurt. Treat everyone like a criminal, and you ran the risk of alienating people who might be cooperative otherwise.

Garner gave Vega a friendly nod when he approached the bulletproof glass. Vega made small talk about the Yankees, then moved on to what he needed: a booking sheet for an arrest made by County Police Sergeant Frank Locuso about six years ago.

"You don't have a date?" asked Garner.

"I got the year," said Vega. "It was in June or July. I'm not sure which."

"That could be like, dozens of booking sheets."

"Locuso was nearing retirement," said Vega. "I don't

think he was making dozens of arrests while he was planning his future in Florida."

"All right." Garner exhaled. "I'll do my best." He turned to a computer and typed in the arresting officer's name, the year, and the two months. Vega was right. There were only seven arrests during that time.

"Let me buzz you in," said Garner. "It'll be easier than reading everything off the screen."

An ear-splitting alarm resounded from a heavy metal door to Vega's right. He wondered if the corrections officers ever got used to that sound. He opened the door. Garner pulled up a chair so Vega could see the screen for himself.

He found the matching mug shot on the second booking report. Same facial features. Same scar above the eyebrow. Same dead eyes. Vega stared at the name: Oscar Ramon Beltran-Parra. Vega smiled to himself, remembering how his friend Lou Greco once said that dealing with Latin-American names was like reading a bad Russian novel.

The booking sheet gave Beltran's age six years ago as twenty-eight and his place of birth as Guatemala. Both pieces of information might be as phony as the name. But there was one thing Beltran couldn't fake: his fingerprints. They were right on the booking sheet.

"That's him," said Vega. "That's who I'm looking for. Can you print out what you have?"

"Sure," said Garner.

The printer hummed and, within seconds, Vega was staring at Oscar Beltran's arrest. For two marijuana joints in Mount Washington six years ago.

Something had to have happened between then and now for Beltran to have paid to have his fingerprints lasered off.

"Can you run his prints through AFIS?" Vega asked Garner. The Automated Fingerprint Identification System, a national, computerized bank of fingerprint scans available to all law enforcement agencies. "I think there may have been other arrests since this one."

"That's sort of beyond my scope here," Garner apologized. "I'm sure you can do that through the county police."

"Okay. No problem," said Vega. "Just one more thing." He pointed to the printout with Beltran's picture. "This dude got arrested again this past June in Lake Holly for carrying a filet knife. He went by the name of Juan Rivas on the booking sheet. He had no prints but he was brought here. Can you pull up Rivas's mug shot?"

"No prints, huh?" That piqued Garner's curiosity. "We get a few of those from time to time. Career criminals. A lot of them are from the cartels."

"I know," said Vega.

Garner ran through his booking sheets on the computer until he'd found the right one. June 3. Beltran was booked under the name Juan Nelson Rivas-Gomez. He stayed in lockup for four days, then went before Spruce and was released. Garner printed it out and handed it to Vega.

Vega lined the two mug shots up next to each other. There was no doubting it was the same man. The scar through the upturned eyebrow was identical. He'd aged in the six years between photos. His wavy black hair had begun to recede into the characteristic M-shape of male-pattern baldness. His skin had become puffy and blotchy. There were sharp creases at the squint of his eyes, as if he'd been carved up with an X-Acto knife.

A lot had happened to Oscar Beltran in those intervening six years—not all of it in his fingertips.

Vega thanked Garner for the printouts, then left the jail. In his truck, he called his old boss from county narcotics, Captain Santorini.

"Jimmy?" Santorini sounded surprised. "I thought you were wrapping up that, uh, civil case. On the, uh, incident."

The shooting. To a cop, the word had the same weight as "cancer." To say it was to conjure back luck. Every cop who was willing to put his life on the line for others had to be willing to pull the trigger. You were no good to anybody if you couldn't—not civilians in danger. Not fellow cops. Which meant every serious cop was one bullet away from being in Vega's shoes.

"There's been a continuance," said Vega. He didn't want to go into details. "Listen, I need a favor. About six years ago, when I was working undercover busting up that narcotics ring in Mount Washington, we arrested a guy coming out of one of the rooms in that fleabag motel. The one that used to be called the Stardust, I think."

"I remember," said Santorini. "Motel's now called the Roadway Inn. The county uses it to house the homeless."

"Yeah. That's the one," said Vega. "Anyway, the guy we picked up coming out of one of the rooms was a Guatemalan by the name of Oscar Beltran-Parra. Age twenty-eight. Claimed he was a gardener who didn't speak English and was just meeting a lady friend. We booked him for possession of a couple of joints because we thought he had a connection to the narcotics ring. I had our guys arrest me too, to try to draw him out. You remember any of that?"

"It's coming back," said Santorini. "You thought he was a player, I believe, but we couldn't get any traction on him."

"That's the one," said Vega. "Well, get this: He was arrested again a couple of months ago in Lake Holly on a knife possession charge."

"Okaaay . . ."

"Calls himself Juan Rivas now. He had fingerprints then. He doesn't now."

"Huh." Santorini took a moment with that. "You sure it's the same guy?"

"I compared the mug shots," said Vega. "It's definitely the same guy."

"Is he in custody?"

"Negative," said Vega. "ICE lodged an order of removal against him. But the judge never saw the police report about the missing prints and released him."

"Somebody's head is gonna roll," said Santorini.

"Listen, Cap—can you do me a favor? If I text you over the case number from six years ago, can you pull it up and rerun Beltran's prints? See if any other arrests turn up after Mount Washington? I have to think there's more to this guy. Maybe the fingerprint lasering was recent."

"I can do that, sure," said Santorini slowly. "But, uh . . . Jimmy?"

"Yeah?"

"If this is one of your assigned cases, you could do it too." Police rules were strict these days about using the databases for anything not work related. "This isn't about your civil trial, is it? You're not trying to dig up dirt on the judge in some way?"

"Kent Edgerton?" Vega laughed.

"Oh, you have Edgerton. Glad to hear it. Never mind."

"It's not about my trial," Vega assured him. Nothing about Oscar Beltran had any bearing on Vega or his case. He just didn't like the way Doug Hewitt turned him into an errand boy for Spruce's hate mail, then buried the whole thing. "He might figure into something I'm working on. Can I leave it at that?"

"Okay. I hear ya," said Santorini. "Let me see what I can find in the database. If anything turns up, I'll let you know."

"Thanks."

Chapter 31

A weekend. A whole goddamned weekend before Vega would know just how bad the court settlement against him would be. It felt like a death sentence hanging over him. He needed to clear his head and be strong for Kaylee when he saw her later. He picked up his cell phone to give Adele the news. But every time he started to dial the number, the words bunched up somewhere between his gut and his throat. He couldn't do this over the phone.

He got in his truck and drove to La Casa. He knew Adele would still be at work for at least another hour.

La Casa was housed in a one-story warehouse that used to sell wholesale seafood. On damp summer days like today, the place gave off the faint odor of low tide. The staff and volunteers did their best to make it cheerful. The walls were painted in primary colors. There were posters everywhere in English and Spanish, exhorting clients to *Dream Big!* and *Read to your children every day!* Donated computers and white boards lined a classroom for teaching English and computer skills. There was a pool table and snack bar in back for recreation.

The place was always busy, even on a Friday afternoon in summer. Children played games on the computers. Women sat in a small classroom, taking a tailoring class.

Contractors came in, asking for men who could do landscaping or masonry or other warm-weather jobs that demanded a sturdy back. Most clients worked seven days a week when the weather was good.

Ramona poked her head out of the tiny glassed-in office near the front of the building.

"Adele's not here," she said. "She's at the police station with Detective Greco."

"Any breaks in the case?"

"I don't know," said Ramona. The phone on her desk rang. She regarded the flashing light, then let it go to voice mail. Ringing phones were like white noise to the staff. "I have to assume it was something important," she said. "He summoned her."

"I should probably check it out," said Vega. "Thanks."

He found Greco in the stationhouse conference room, talking to Adele.

"We'll be finished in a moment," Greco grunted over his shoulder without looking up from a notepad covered in chicken scratch. "You want to talk to her or to me, it'll have to be when we're through."

Greco's tone stung. "Listen," said Vega, "I know you're sore about last night—"

Greco cut him off. "Take a seat outside. I'll talk to you when I'm through."

Adele shot a look at Vega, then Greco. They were two bulls in the room. She knew better than to interfere.

"I'll be in the hall," said Vega. He backed out of the room and shut the door. He cooled his heels staring at the wanted and missing posters lining the bulletin board in the hallway. Tacked in the center was the FBI one about the girl from the bus station, the grainy video footage magnified to show her frightened little face and Asian-cast eyes, along with the pink unicorn T-shirt she was wearing. He was surprised they'd never found her.

After about ten minutes, the conference door opened,

and Adele stepped out. "Your turn. Good luck," she said darkly.

"Can you wait here for me until I'm finished? I'd like to talk to you before you head back to work."

She read something desperate in his eyes. "Of course."

Greco was writing something on his notepad when Vega stepped into the conference room and closed the door. The big man didn't lift his gaze. His seat was pushed back from the table, allowing his belly to rest as a pillow in between. He put down his pen and rummaged through a bag of red licorice Twizzlers next to the notepad. He didn't offer one to Vega. He already knew Vega hated Twizzlers. They knew a lot about each other—which was what made the tension between them so difficult.

Greco took a bite from his Twizzler, regarding Vega over the soft pillow of belly barely contained beneath his knit polo shirt. "I'll save you some time here. No, we don't have a suspect in the break-in yet."

"Nothing?"

"I pulled the raw data from the license plate readers in town," said Greco. "Got a hit from one of the LPRs over by the First National Bank at twelve forty-five a.m. About fifteen minutes before the break-in. A black Honda Civic was driving past with plates from a Dodge Minivan stolen out of Buffalo six months ago."

"The perp didn't leave behind any fingerprints or DNA?"

"No fingerprints. He was probably wearing gloves. As for DNA, we're not sure. We recovered an item we're scanning for DNA at the moment. When I get more, I'll let Adele know."

Vega noticed that Greco didn't offer to let him know as well. Greco was still sore about last night.

"Look, Grec," Vega began. "I'm sorry about what I said last night. I was upset. I shouldn't have accused the Lake Holly Police of not doing their job, especially on a case I'm not directly involved in."

"You got that right." Greco shifted in his chair. "You want to keep this back door open between us, you gotta respect the house you're walking into. This ain't the county police. It's Lake Holly. I don't tell you how to do your job. Don't tell me how to do mine."

Vega sensed Greco had been rehearsing this speech in his head since last night.

"I understand," said Vega. "And in most cases, you'd be right. Except . . . not this time."

"What?" Greco set the rest of his Twizzler on top of the cellophane wrapper.

"Juan Rivas. The guy Sanchez arrested. His real name is Oscar Beltran-Parra. I know, because my unit busted him in Mount Washington six years ago as part of a narcotics sting when I was working undercover."

"You *know* this? For a fact?" Greco spoke with an edge, like he was interrogating a witness.

"I compared mug shots," said Vega. "It's the same guy. Same scar. Everything. I think he's a player in the narcotics trade, but we couldn't get him back then. I've asked my old boss in narcotics to see if he can dig up anything else on Beltran before he had his prints lasered off. You don't get your prints lasered if you're a nobody."

"You think Beltran's working with the cartels?"

"Maybe," said Vega. "What I don't get is why he's playing the part of a day laborer. Back in Mount Washington six years ago and in Lake Holly now. Those guys like to flash their power, not hide it."

"It gets him off the hook," said Greco.

"Not always," said Vega. "Remember: He had his prints lasered off. So something went wrong for him. Something got him jailed and possibly deported. I just don't know what. If I find out anything more, I can let you know. That is," Vega added, "if you want."

The wariness and suspicion washed out of Greco's face, replaced by something else. Something every real cop understands: curiosity. Greco hated being in the dark about anything.

"That would be good," he told Vega. "And I'll let you know if we get any DNA from the break-in."

"You never said what the item you recovered was," said Vega.

"We found it on the grass right outside where the screen had been slit," said Greco. "I wanted to be sure Adele didn't have some explanation for it, but she said she'd never seen it before."

Greco opened the folder and fished out a photograph. He slid it across the table.

It was a picture of a toothpick.

Chapter 32

Vega couldn't take his eyes off the photo. The chewed-up toothpick looked just like the one he'd found on the roof of the bus terminal. Vega reminded himself that Adele had two painters at her house yesterday afternoon. The toothpick could have come from one of them.

It was a stretch to think that the person who dropped a toothpick at Adele's had any connection to the shooter on the bus terminal roof.

Yet something about the coincidence made Vega's skin crawl. Everything suggested that the shooter on the bus terminal roof was aiming for Judge Spruce. Which meant his motive likely had something to do with her being soft on illegals. Adele was the director of an outreach center with the same sympathies. In the past few days, La Casa had been the target of a bomb threat, Adele's garage had been spray-painted with anti-immigrant graffiti, and now someone had broken into her house.

And all of it either happened or was discovered *after* that mob protest against Adele's new immigrant center in Anniston. Boyd Richter, a white supremacist, was at the center of that protest. Was it possible he was at the center of far more?

Vega's hands curled into fists on the table as he pictured Richter now. That shaved white head like a squid. Those thin pink lips and thick-set muscular arms swimming with tattoos. That leather vest with *Puritan Pride* on the back. Richter, the ex-army sniper. Richter, the punk who battered his girlfriend, and now was terrorizing Adele. Vega couldn't wait to get Kaylee and Hunter out of there so the FBI could take Richter down.

"What's wrong?" asked Greco.

"I think the person who broke into Adele's may be the same person behind the courthouse shooting," said Vega.

"*What?* Get outta here," said Greco.

Vega walked his friend through what he knew. "Richter's got the military background and the ideology to take down Judge Spruce."

Vega watched Greco's face change from skepticism to alarm. "Do you know where this dirtbag is?"

"He lives in Anniston." Vega copied down a phone number and slid it across the table to Greco. "Do me a favor? Call Doug Hewitt at the FBI and tell him what I just told you."

"You're not going to go after Richter by yourself, are you?"

Vega shook his head. "I need to remove someone from his line of fire. And I need to do it right away."

Vega opened the door to the conference room. Adele was standing outside, staring intently at the wanted and missing posters tacked to the bulletin board.

"Hey, Jimmy," she began. "On the bulletin board, there's this picture—"

"I need you to do something for me." He put his hands firmly on her shoulders. "I need you to stay with Mr. Zimmerman and Wil this evening. Until I get back from Anniston."

"Why don't I come with you? I can help convince Kaylee to go to the shelter."

"No," said Vega. "I don't want you anywhere near Anniston tonight."

Vega walked Adele swiftly out of the building. He felt a nervous thrum of energy buzzing through him, like he was going undercover to set up a bust.

"What's wrong?" asked Adele. "Did Greco say something to you about the break-in that he isn't telling me?"

"I'm not sure. I could be mistaken."

"Still, I'd like to know."

At her car, he turned to face her. The late-afternoon sun picked up the sparkle to her cheekbones, lightly bathed in sweat. He took her hand and felt the moist, velvety softness of her fingers in his. "I'm going to tell you something that you can't repeat to anyone, *nena.*"

"Okaaay—"

"The person who broke into your house last night may have been Boyd Richter, that white supremacist behind the Anniston rally. Kaylee's boyfriend."

"Jesus. Why would he break into my house?"

"For the same reason someone in the Puritan Sons likely made that bomb threat to La Casa."

"You're sure they're related?"

"No. But there are connections." Vega couldn't tell her about the DEA bust in Sayertown and how it potentially related to both the bomb threat and Richter's Puritan Sons. And he definitely couldn't tell her his suspicions that Richter was behind the courthouse shooting. "Look, I can't go into details right now, but it's best if you stay with your neighbors until I'm back. I'll only be gone for a couple of hours."

"To get Kaylee out of there?"

"I hope."

Chapter 33

Anniston was picturesque on a summer afternoon. The peeling paint on the Victorians and triple-deckers looked quaint when lit by the golden glow of a waning sun and fanned by a gentle breeze off the Hudson River. The trees—even the spindly ones—were green and lush. The ball fields were packed with Little League games and soccer tournaments. Even the street where the protest against La Casa North had been was now full of kids lining up for the ice cream truck.

Vega drove away from the river. The hilly terrain lost its connection to the water. The streets narrowed. The breezes died. The faces became exclusively vanilla. There was an invisible dividing line on Clemson that made Vega feel like he needed a passport to cross.

O'Rourke's was three blocks over from Clemson and made no bones about who it catered to, from the shamrock on the sign to the stickers on the door frame—put there by management or patrons, Vega couldn't say: *America: love it or leave it* and *We Speak English Only Here*.

It was just past five p.m. Kaylee should be going on duty. Vega texted: **Are you at O'Rourke's?**

No reply.

He'd decided against texting her in advance to warn her

about Richter. He was afraid that in a moment of weakness—or drug-fueled confusion—she might tip him off. Which would give Richter time to dispose of his drugs and weapons. Erase his Internet history. Flee.

And yet Vega couldn't escape the sick sensation that something was very, very wrong. Kaylee hadn't replied to any of his texts over the past few days. She could be on a tweaking binge. She could have decided to pull out of the arrangement. Anything was possible with an addict. He saw no choice but to go in. If she was there, he'd buy a pack of cigarettes and leave. If she wasn't—well, he'd cross that bridge when he came to it.

He parked his truck up the street and walked back. He heard music blasting inside. He expected country and western or perhaps some Irish band, but the vibe was heavy metal with a lot of screaming and guitar feedback.

He stepped inside and let the door shut behind him. It took Vega a moment for his eyes to adjust to the dim wattage. The ceiling was low. The walls were painted black. There was a faded and nicked wooden counter to the left, some booths and standing tables to the right, and a pool table in back. The air stank of fried food, sweat, and spilled beer. It mixed with the reek of tobacco smoke that wafted in from just outside the door where patrons obviously went to smoke.

There were plenty of people at O'Rourke's at five p.m. on a Friday. All white. All male, save for one waitress washing glasses behind the bar. The bartender looked like the crowd. Pink and greasy as a side of raw beef, with a bleached ponytail and full sleeves of tattoos that ran from the top of his neck to the tips of his fingers. He wore a black T-shirt with an outline of an automatic rifle in the center and the words, *This Is Your Trigger Warning*. He was drawing down beers for the pool players in back. The waitress washing glasses had hair like clay—reddish brown and stiffly plastered to her scalp like doll's hair.

Vega didn't see Kaylee.

He walked over to the bar and tried to catch the waitress's attention. She didn't look at him. She was serving beers and whiskey chasers to three men talking to one another at the other end. One had long hair, tied off in a bandana, and a scraggly goatee. The other two had shaved heads mostly hidden beneath baseball caps and paint-spattered jeans. They shot sharp looks in Vega's direction but said nothing.

Vega waited, eying the selection of booze behind the bar. There was the usual assortment of whiskeys and bourbons. Some cheap vodka and gin. Nothing too fancy. Above the bar, next to the television, sat a corkboard with nearly two dozen motorcycle patches tacked to it. Vega saw skulls and wolves and flags and Celtic crosses. He swept another gaze around the place for Kaylee. She wasn't here. He pulled out his phone.

I'm inside O'Rourke's, he texted Kaylee. **If you're not coming, tell me. I'm not exactly getting a welcoming vibe.**

She didn't reply. Had she taken Hunter and fled already? That was a possibility. If so, Vega was wasting his time. What's more, he was buying Boyd Richter a chance to escape. The waitress with the clay hair walked to Vega's end of the counter to scoop some ice into a drink.

"Whatever you think you're doing here," she muttered, "it's a bad idea." She kept her eyes on the ice bin as she spoke. She looked older than Kaylee, probably in her late thirties, with puffy skin and bags under her eyes. The stiff red-brown hair looked like some home dye job that she did late at night when she finally put her kids to bed.

"I'm looking for someone," said Vega. "Kaylee Wentz."

She slammed the lid on the ice bin. "She quit."

"When?"

"Yesterday. Her boyfriend called. Said she wasn't coming to work no more." The waitress gave an exasperated look at two men by the pool table in back, shoving each other playfully while they spilled their beers on the floor. More work for her. "You'd better go."

"Did she ever talk about quitting?"

The woman offered a husky smoker's laugh. "Who doesn't?"

"Why did her boyfriend call? Why not her?"

"I don't know. You'd have to ask him."

The man from the far end of the bar with the bandana and scraggly goatee sauntered over, still carrying his half-empty Genesee bottle. *Upstate redneck beer,* thought Vega. *Only good for getting loaded.* Clearly, it was not the man's first "Jenny" of the evening. He was swaying slightly as he walked. He slapped the bottle down next to Vega. His clothes smelled of diesel fuel and stale cigarettes. "You bothering the lady?" His words had a slurred edge to them.

"Just asking a question," said Vega.

"Well now," said the man. "Maybe I can answer your *question.*"

Goatee's two friends stumbled over behind him. They looked like they'd had even more to drink. Or maybe they couldn't handle it as well. One was skinny with bad acne. The other had blubbery arms and a soft chin. No way was Vega going to mention Kaylee to any of them. "I was just asking for directions," said Vega.

"Seems to me, hombre," said Goatee with a smile, "you are definitely in the wrong part of town."

The blubbery man braced a sweaty hand on the counter behind Vega, boxing him in. As a boy in the Bronx, Vega never would have let that sort of challenge go. You let one go, and pretty soon, you're everybody's punk. But he wasn't a boy anymore. He needed to leave, quickly and quietly, so he mentioned the first place in Anniston that popped into his head.

"I was looking for Longwood Cemetery."

"The cemetery," said Goatee. His two friends—Blubber

and Zitface—sniggered. The waitress with the clay hair moved away from them to help another customer. Vega suspected she was beginning to sense trouble and wanted no part of it.

"Well," said Goatee, stroking his chin hairs, "there's two ways to visit it. One, is to drive there." Goatee winked at Blubber with his arm behind Vega. The man moved in a little closer. Vega could smell onions and booze on his breath. He understood at once what was about to happen. He was supposed to ask what the other way was.

And then, they would show him.

Vega knew from experience that an elbow was a very lethal weapon when pulled straight back, capable of breaking a jaw or nose, depending on the angle. Blubber was definitely within jaw-breaking range. But Vega wasn't looking to get into a brawl with three wasted drunks. So he turned to the chinless loser.

"You like getting up close to other men? I didn't think you swung that way."

Blubber let go of the bar and stumbled backward. "I'm no faggot," he slurred. "You're a faggot." He hauled back a fist to punch Vega. He was bigger and possibly stronger. But Vega was sober and in better shape. He swiped Goatee's half-empty beer bottle off the counter. When Blubber tried to connect, Vega grabbed him in a headlock, shoved his face into the counter and emptied the rest of the beer down the man's paint-spattered jeans. Then he released him, holding the empty bottle out as a weapon, in case Goatee and their other friend, Zitface, got any ideas.

Goatee glared at Vega but didn't move. He was obviously the type who preferred others to do his bidding. Zitface pointed to Blubber's soggy jeans, now reeking of beer.

"You look like you pissed your pants."

"Shut up," said Blubber. He hiked up his jeans. He couldn't sit down anymore. He looked to his friends to help him, but Vega still had the beer bottle raised. No one made a move. Vega pulled a five out of his wallet and slapped it down on the counter.

"Thanks for the Jenny. I put it where it belongs."

Then he backed out of the bar and hightailed it up the street to his truck. He had no illusions that these guys wouldn't sober up and assemble a mob to come after him. He tossed the bottle in a trash can and looked down at his slacks. The slacks from the JC Penney suit he'd been wearing every day to court. He'd spilled beer on himself in the confrontation, and now he smelled like a brewery. He drove a few blocks to a small grocery store parking lot where he dialed Doug Hewitt.

"Vega, where are you?"

"I'm trying to find my CI and extricate her before the FBI turns up the heat."

"You're too late," said Hewitt. "Richter's got her. He's holding her at gunpoint in their apartment. He's got the boy too."

Vega stared out the windshield at the warm, sunny afternoon. At people pushing grocery carts through the parking lot with children in tow. One mother had bought a large plastic ball in the store and her little boy was holding it tight to his chest, his greatest new possession. Vega could barely process the images. His mind's eye was locked in that park nineteen years ago. On another warm summer afternoon where another man had chosen to obliterate everything he once loved rather than allow it to exist without him.

"Have any shots been fired?"

"Richter fired on responding units when they arrived about an hour ago," said Hewitt. "But as far as I know, there have been no reported injuries to emergency personnel or civilian bystanders. Everyone in the building except the girlfriend and her son have been evacuated. County SWAT and our hostage negotiator are on their way. Fiske and I are driving up now."

"Do they know"—Vega could barely get the words out—"if Kaylee and her son are still alive?"

"There's been one confirmed sighting since the gunshots," said Hewitt. "And no further shots, so the assumption is they're still alive."

"What in God's name set him off?"

"Word is," said Hewitt, "she told him she was leaving."

Chapter 34

He should never have come back into her life again. He should have left her alone.

Vega argued with himself as he sped over to Kaylee's street. He had messed with the universe, altered imperceptibly the course of her fate. The first time, that intervention had been good. It had saved her life. Given her some good years, perhaps. A fiancé. A child. Some hope for the future. He hadn't put Boyd Richter in her life. She'd done that to herself. But he'd messed with the trajectory, and now she might die. She and Hunter both.

Vega couldn't help but feel a certain responsibility in all that. He was a police officer. He'd handled hundreds of domestic violence calls over the course of his career. He recalled only four that involved an armed standoff and only two of those were with a gun. The rest typically involved a fight where either a witness or one of the parties called 911. Sometimes the calls involved visible injuries, sometimes not. Often, both parties were leveling charges of battery, even when one—typically the man—was the instigator.

So much had changed for victims of domestic abuse over the course of Vega's career. Back when he was starting out, a victim had to be bruised and bloody for cops to take her seriously. Women like Kaylee's mother, Katharine, didn't stand a chance.

Vega didn't understand the dynamics when he first came on the job. He'd grown up with a strong single mother and grandmother who would never have allowed a man to knock them around. Even his deadbeat father was a lover, not a fighter. The subtleties of toxic couple interactions mystified him. He once responded to a DV call and witnessed an abused wife go silent after her husband emerged from the bathroom with a towel draped over his arm. Vega couldn't understand it. He'd seen no bruises on the woman and yet she was terrified of the man and nearly catatonic after he emerged with the towel. Fortunately, Vega's partner, a man who'd grown up with an abusive father, noticed the connection right away and took the woman outside. It turned out that the husband always covered his wife's head in a towel before he beat her—to minimize bruising. The towel draped over his arm was a warning: *You're getting a beating if you say anything.*

There was so much the police didn't understand back then, when domestic violence was still viewed as a "personal" matter. Years ago, there were fewer female officers on the job and the ill-trained males asked clueless male sorts of questions. The kind that demanded answers you can see, hear, and touch. *Did he strike you? With a fist or open hand? Where is the injury? How often does he hit you? Why haven't you tried to get away?*

They didn't understand all the considerations that go into leaving an abusive partner. *My children are in school and I can't disrupt their lives. He has all the money. He owns the cars. How will I gather my belongings? Where will I put my pets? How will I explain this to my family?*

It was no wonder many victims never filed charges.

The process had become much better over the last two decades. Cops were better trained. Restraining orders were automatic. Judges, more sympathetic. There were more shelters for battered women, with more services. And yet still, so many never got away—or tried to run and never made it.

In Vega's experience, battering escalated over time, but extreme escalation like this only happened when the abuser believed he was losing control. Was it because Kaylee told him she was leaving? Or did he know that the FBI was closing in on him? It would certainly explain why Richter could have broken into Adele's house last night. Vega shuddered to think that this whole scenario could be playing out with Adele as his hostage if she'd confronted him instead of locking herself in the bathroom and calling 911.

Vega tried to get inside the mind of Boyd Richter and the anger he harbored—not just at people of color, Jews, and immigrants, but at women as well. What resentment formed the seed of all this hatred? Was it fear that fed his fire? Or a desire for power? What made a woman like Kaylee fall prey to it? What made her stay until it was too late to leave?

A SWAT helicopter hovered overhead as Vega got nearer, its blades beating down against the leafy trees. He parked a block away, knowing the street would be cordoned off, and made the rest of the journey on foot, following the staccato flash of emergency lights and the thickening crowd of bystanders. Most seemed to have no idea what was going on. *It's a burglary gone wrong. It's a drug bust. It's a man who wants to commit suicide.* Even those who thought it was a hostage situation didn't think it was a local man holding his live-in girlfriend and her son.

Everybody wants to believe that evil comes from somewhere far away. Never in one's own backyard.

Armored vehicles blocked off Kaylee's street. County SWAT officers in flak jackets, goggles, and special helmets took up barricaded positions behind police cruisers. Snipers crouched at the corners of roofs. Nothing moved, save a cat who sauntered defiantly across the empty street.

Vega noted a converted Brinks security vehicle with an FBI logo on the side parked well back from the police perimeter. He didn't see Hewitt or Fiske, only a white woman in her thirties with a freckled face and kinky red hair pulled back into a ponytail. She was dressed in faded jeans with holes at the knees and a navy-blue T-shirt with an FBI emblem. Not exactly work attire. Certainly not for the FBI. He guessed she'd been called from home. Without warning. Flown here by helicopter perhaps. There was only one type of agent that would demand such a response.

An FBI hostage negotiator.

Vega walked up to one of the SWAT officers at the perimeter and showed his badge. They both worked for the county police, but SWAT was its own little fiefdom. Vega didn't know all the SWAT officers and they didn't all know him.

"Special Agent Hewitt of the FBI sent me," said Vega. Not true perhaps, but it wasn't like Hewitt ordered him *not* to come either.

"I'm assuming SWAT knows Richter was an ex-army sniper."

"Affirmative," mumbled the officer. "Although his two shots were air-bound. They hit nothing.

Vega suspected they were warning fire only. A trained sniper like Richter wouldn't blow a shot. Then again, if he was behind the courthouse shooting, he likely blew his shot with Spruce. Maybe he was drinking heavily. The shakes will wreck a shooter's aim.

"I need to speak to the FBI negotiator. I know the female hostage inside. I have a long history with her."

The officer looked dubious. "Agent Callahan only communicates through the chain of command." Which was normal, Vega knew. A negotiator had to juggle a lot of competing interests at a hostage scene—the erratic demands of the hostage-taker, tactical considerations, strategic goals that might differ by agency, and most of all, any fallout with the media.

"I know things she needs to know," said Vega.

"Stay here, I'll get Captain Speers." The county police's SWAT team captain. Vega knew Speers, at least. Hyper-defined shoulders, even without his Kevlar padding. A squint like he was always standing behind a spotter scope, waiting to make his next kill.

Vega stood at the barricade. Normally, police scenes are noisy affairs with cops barking orders, dispatch radios blaring, and civilian onlookers asking questions. But not here. Radios were on mute. Cops spoke in hand signals and whispers, their bodies and voices tense and low as they scanned the street.

Vega looked up at the triple-decker with the pitted vinyl siding and the air-conditioning units leaning precariously out of their frames. He still didn't know which floor Kaylee and Richter lived on. He had to assume it was the top floor because all the windows there had dark curtains covering them. If so, that might be good news. If a SWAT team member could just get to the roof, he might be able to rappel over the side and into a window.

Vega watched Callahan on her headset. The FBI hostage negotiator looked like a kid home from college break in her T-shirt and ripped jeans, loose strands from her frizzy red ponytail curling around her freckled face. Everyone around her was sweating. She wasn't. She looked calm and composed, like she was in a little bubble, far from the action.

"Vega?" Speers stopped in front of him, like a tank brought up short. "What is your business here?"

Vega told Speers about his history with Kaylee. He didn't mention that she was his confidential informant. Maybe Richter already knew. But if he didn't, in the heat of a standoff, it could push him over the edge.

"I think I can offer some perspective to Agent Callahan," said Vega. "If I could be granted access."

"Wait here," the SWAT captain grunted. "I'll relay the information. If she wants you, I'll let you know."

Vega stared down at his clothes. He was wearing his striped dress shirt and suit slacks from court, now sweaty and creased and splashed with beer from his run-in at O'Rourke's. He didn't exactly present the image of a seasoned professional. Then again, in her ripped jeans and T-shirt, neither did she. Vega watched Speers relay his request. He waited for it to play across her face. He saw nothing. No expression at all. She turned in Vega's direction, gave him a long, hard look, and then turned away. *Coño!* No dice.

Speers walked back to Vega. "She'll give you five minutes."

Vega blinked in surprise. "Man, she'd be great at poker."

Her name was Shana Callahan. It said so on the card she handed Vega. Her handshake was cool and professional. Her voice, on the other hand, had a warm underglow to it. It was the voice of a woman who would render forgiveness, even if the recipient deserved none. Vega felt he could be talked into almost anything by her.

"I understand you have a history with the victim," said Callahan.

"Yes, ma'am." Vega kept his words to a minimum so as not to disrupt her rhythm. A hostage negotiator runs the show—with good reason. They hold lives in their hands. One false move could have dire consequences. Last year, at a training session, Captain Waring played a tape of a New Jersey cop telling a suicidal teenager to "shut up and man up" after he barricaded himself and his mother inside his house. The teenager killed the mother and himself shortly after.

"Does Boyd know about your relationship?" she asked.

That dirtbag would never be "Boyd" to Vega, but he understood that Shana Callahan had to do everything she could to humanize the hostage-taker and establish rapport.

"I'm hoping he doesn't," said Vega. "Richter is a white supremacist. There's no telling how he'd react. Plus, there's something you should know." Vega took a deep breath. "Kaylee was working for me as a confidential informant. The relationship had only just started, but I have no idea whether he discovered it."

"He hasn't said anything to indicate he's aware of that."

"Good."

Their conversation was interrupted by the voice of Boyd Richter on the receiver. "Christie?"

"Christie" was Callahan. Negotiators never gave their real names.

Everyone went silent. Callahan picked up. "I'm right here, Boyd. How is everyone doing? I'll bet little Hunter's getting hungry."

Beneath the show of concern, Vega, the cop, saw all the strategies at play. She was making sure Hunter was alive. She was offering something that could, in turn, be used in negotiation. And she was keeping the conversation away from anything that might escalate his anxious state. So much of hostage negotiation involves playing for time.

"We don't need the government's poisoned food," he growled.

We. He'd just told law enforcement that at least one of the hostages was still alive.

"I want the power back on. I want the air conditioner working." His voice was slurred. He sounded drunk.

"You must be hot in there, Boyd," she cooed. "Why don't you open a window and get a little fresh air?" Callahan probably didn't think Richter would be stupid enough to do the deed himself and give SWAT a clear target. But if he sent Kaylee, at least they'd know she was alive. At least they'd know she was ambulatory.

"Nobody's going near any windows!" Richter shouted. "You think I'm stupid?"

"I just want everyone to be comfortable," she replied. "It's better for you and Kaylee and Hunter."

Again, she was trying to make sure they were alive. Again, Richter rebuffed her.

"I'll tell you what's better for me," said Richter. "You turning the power on." He was getting agitated. They could all hear it in his voice. Callahan stayed ice-cold calm.

"That's going to take a while, Boyd," she replied. "I will relay your request to my superiors. Absolutely. I'm sure they will do their best to make you comfortable. In the meantime, if you open a window—"

He was through with her suggestions. "You turn the power on, or I start shooting!" he shouted. "I've got plenty of ammo up here. There's no chance I'll run out."

Chapter 35

Shana Callahan spent the next five minutes talking Richter down in her steady, reassuring voice. Vega could see she was a pro in the way she juggled so many competing goals at once. De-escalating his emotional state. Verifying that the hostages were alive. Obtaining information on their whereabouts in the apartment. She had to convince Richter to surrender while at the same time affording SWAT every opportunity to take him out if necessary.

She was his best friend and potential executioner all wrapped up in one.

Callahan clearly had a knack for establishing rapport. In Richter's case, she focused on his military background. She told him her brother Danny had been in the 101st Airborne, stationed in Afghanistan as well. Vega had no idea if it was true, but he suspected someone close to her had been in the 101st. She was too conversant with the facts for them not to have been partially true.

"I'm always so awed by veterans like you who served there," Callahan gushed. "Nobody really understands all you went through."

"Yeah." He opened up a little after that, listing some of the regions where he'd served. His voice was scratchy and hoarse. He stumbled over syllables. Vega hoped that maybe he'd just pass out at some point. Then again, drunks were impulsive. There was no telling what he might do.

Callahan kept up the banter, trying to move him toward surrender while she relayed her information to SWAT command. She asked to speak to Kaylee and Hunter. Richter refused.

"I need to know they're alive, Boyd. That's important. I believe you wouldn't lie to me, but I need you to prove it."

Richter said nothing, but Vega could hear footsteps and a creak of a mattress, which told him that Kaylee and Hunter were on a bed. Possibly bound and gagged. Kaylee seemed to cough and spit out a muffled "I'm okay." The child sobbed. Vega could hear the bastard doing something to them again—probably retying the gags. But they were alive, at least. He thanked God for that.

"Hey, Boyd," said Callahan. "My brother Danny's watching this on TV. He's worried for you. He doesn't like to see a brother-in-arms going through this. There are so many places these days where a service member of your caliber can get help."

"I don't need help," Richter growled. "All that psychological bullshit. It's part of a Zionist conspiracy. A government mind-plot to replace the white man." Richter went off on a tirade, calling Kaylee a "backstabbing bitch" because she wanted to leave him, and then prattling on about Jewish world domination and the invasion of "lesser people" on white soil.

He didn't mention anything about Kaylee being a confidential informant or about the FBI closing in on him for his gun sales. He said nothing about the courthouse shooting or breaking into Adele's last night. Vega felt relieved. But only for a few seconds. Richter's next words chilled Vega to the bone.

"Soon as nightfall comes, they're dead. Her and the boy."

Callahan's voice stayed smooth and even. "You don't

want to do that, Boyd. What will your army buddies say? You killed a three-year-old child?"

"He ain't mine."

"But he's just an innocent child." Callahan thought a moment. "A white child. The future of our race. You don't want to kill him. We need him. We need them both."

Vega gazed up at an adjoining roof. Several officers were attempting to cross onto the roof of Richter's building.

"What's that noise?" Richter demanded.

"You want it cooler in there, right?" asked Callahan. "That's what we're trying to do, Boyd. Give you what you asked for. You want us to back off? Keep the power off?"

It was a risky move. If he said yes, she'd have no wiggle room. On the other hand, offering to back off would convince him she was telling the truth.

Vega stared up at the sky again. The salmon color was fading. There was a velvet hue at the edges. Nightfall would be coming soon. They didn't have much time.

"I want the power back on," he said.

"Okay, Boyd. Okay. I'm trying to work with you here. The Anniston cops cut it pretty sloppily before we got here. It's taking time to repair."

Vega was a handy guy. He'd done most of the electrical work himself to bring his summer cabin up to year-round living standards. So he knew that the Anniston police hadn't physically "cut" the electricity. They'd simply turned it off. Probably with a call to the local utility. Either Richter didn't know that, or in his inebriated state, he hadn't made the connection. It was a bargaining chip the police were using—one among many.

Callahan tapped out a message, no doubt to Captain Speers, for the unit to proceed. Then she swiveled her head and studied the sky. The sun had just set over the western edge of rooftops. The sky was striated orange, like raw salmon. Vega texted Adele. He didn't expect to be back in

Lake Holly for hours. Then again, the man she most likely had to fear was right here—and he wasn't going anywhere.

He wasn't even talking anymore. Speers walked over. Callahan muted the receiver.

"We've got snipers in place," said Speers. "We could use flash-bang grenades to distract his attention, try for a grab. The problem is, Richter's a trained weapons expert. He's not going to go without a fight. One or both of the hostages could get hurt. Ideally, we need someone inside already who can isolate Richter from the hostages before we go in."

Vega looked up at the building. "You haven't gotten the power back on yet, have you?"

"Negative," said Callahan. "We like to stall as long as possible on requests."

Vega nodded. He'd once heard about a plane hijacker who gave up because it took four hours for the FBI hostage negotiator to get him a cup of coffee and, when it arrived, it was cold and didn't have the sugar he'd requested. Petty frustrations had undone many a would-be assailant.

Vega stared up at the darkened windows, still covered with drapes. In twenty minutes, the light would leave the sky completely. If Richter was serious, Kaylee and Hunter would be dead soon after.

"Does the building have electric stoves or gas?" Vega asked Speers.

"My guys saw gas hookups," said Speers. "Why?"

"What if you told Richter that the electrician had to turn the power on from the circuit breaker box in the basement and then manually relight the pilot in the gas stove?"

"I'd have to send a guy into a dark building without any body armor or weapon," Speers replied. "And even if he managed to get into the basement, what makes you think Richter would let him relight his stove? I don't think he's thinking about frying up some bacon right now."

"You could tell him that if the electrician doesn't relight it, the gas could accumulate and create an explosion," said Vega. "That can't happen with newer stoves, but it's a scenario that he might buy."

"Even so," said Speers, "we'd need whoever went in there to be able to get to Kaylee and Hunter on a moment's notice. We don't know if she'd trust him and the little boy certainly wouldn't."

"Send me in," said Vega. "Kaylee trusts me. I rewired my house so I know my way around electricity. Best of all, he's unlikely to see me as FBI."

"Has he seen you before?" asked Speers.

"I don't think so," said Vega. "I hung back at that protest rally in Anniston. He got arrested before I made contact with Kaylee."

"How about the boy?"

Vega froze. *Hunter.* Hunter knew him. He was a small child. Would he tip Richter off? Or would he be too scared to say a word?

"You'd have no protection," Speers noted. "No gun. No body armor."

"I'd have authorization though, right?" Speers was a captain in the county police. His authorization was more than a matter of semantics or protocol. If Vega got injured or killed, Speers's authorization guaranteed Vega's participation would be viewed as line-of-duty. Joy would get the life insurance if something happened to him.

"Are you sure you want to do this, Vega?" asked Speers. "We'll have SWAT on the roof. They'll know you're in there, but you won't have a radio or any way to coordinate with them."

Vega stared up at the building. He had ten minutes,

maybe less, to save Kaylee's life. He'd had less than that nineteen years ago. He wondered if he'd get lucky twice.

"I've got one question before I go in," said Vega. "It's for Callahan."

"What?" she asked.

"Was your brother really in the 101st Airborne in Afghanistan?"

"No," she said. "I was."

Chapter 36

Vega didn't text Adele about what he was doing. He didn't want her to worry. And besides, he wasn't sure she'd understand. She might think it a betrayal for him to want to risk his life to save Kaylee's. She would never understand that he wasn't choosing Kaylee over her or Joy; he just needed to be able to look himself in the mirror again. To see the man he used to be. The man he'd lost in those woods on that terrible December night.

It wasn't about whether he won or lost the trial. Or got or didn't get the promotion. Neither of those things would alter the fundamental rent in the fabric of his being. Right or wrong, he'd taken a life and, right or wrong, he had to offer himself up as a replacement.

He texted Joy, but it was a short directive only: **Do me a favor? Go to my house and stay with Diablo tonight? I'm stuck at work. Love you, Dad.** He was going to call her by her childhood nickname, Chispita—Little Spark, in Spanish. But he worried that might tip her off that something was wrong. He was relieved when she texted back: **OK. You owe me a dinner.**

That was a debt he hoped he could repay.

Speers set up the basics. They had to move fast. Darkness was muscling the light from the sky. Already, streetlights and porch lights were flicking to life. Lamps winked behind closed curtains. They found a neighbor about Vega's size who lent him a T-shirt, jeans, and a pair of work boots. The work boots were vital. Vega was convinced that the first thing Richter would look at were his shoes. If Vega was wearing the black, dress lace-ups he wore to court, he'd be a dead man. Speers fitted Vega with a high-powered microphone that slipped underneath the crew neck of the T-shirt so it was undetectable. The SWAT team would be able to hear everything going on in the room below with Richter. The FBI secured a set of master keys from the landlord and handed them to Vega, along with a small toolbox outfitted with a snub-nosed .22 caliber pistol hidden inside a box of drill bits.

"Lose the pistol," said Vega.

"Are you crazy?" asked Speers.

"You really think if things go south in there, I'll have time to open the toolbox, pull out the drill bits, and access the gun? There's a greater likelihood that Richter will search the box and find it than that it will help me. And besides, you've got enough firepower out there to overthrow a small developing country. This twenty-two is only going to get in the way."

Speers grumbled, but removed the gun. Vega turned over his own wallet, keys, and cell phone to Shana Callahan. Again, he couldn't chance anything tipping Richter off.

"You'll start by unlocking the front door and entering the main hallway," Speers explained. "Go to the end of the hall and unlock the door to the basement. Don't go down. It's too easy for Richter to trap you down there. Wait a few minutes, then say, 'It's connected.' That will be our cue to the utility to restore power to the rest of the building, *except* Richter's apartment on the third floor."

That was part of the plan, as Speers had outlined it. They wanted to keep Richter in total darkness until the moment when SWAT flipped all the lights, allowing the

SWAT team good visibility of the suspect while temporarily blinding Richter, who would need a moment or two for his eyes to adjust.

"After the lights come back on in the rest of the building," said Speers, "you're going to enter the subject's premises. We believe Kaylee and her son are in the bedroom, gagged and tied, perhaps to the bed." Speers looked up at the curtained windows. Something softened in his face. Vega wondered if he, too, had a daughter. Kaylee had always felt like a second daughter to Vega.

"Get Richter over by the stove in the kitchen. Make some sort of excuse about how hard it is to get to the pilot light. Ask him to help you pull out the stove. Whatever it takes to keep him away from the bedroom. When you've pushed him as far as you can go, say the word 'power.' We'll commence rescue."

Vega knew what rescue would be like. He'd seen county SWAT in action. Flash-bang grenades. High-powered rifles. Lots of shouting and mayhem—and a chance he could be shot by friendly fire. These guys were pros, but still. Nothing ever goes according to plan. Speers knew this too when he clapped a hand on Vega's shoulder. "Anything feels off or you need us to come in sooner, just say 'power.' And believe me, you'll get it."

Callahan got on the phone to Richter and explained the need to get into his apartment to reignite the pilot light on his stove.

"Nobody's coming in!" he screamed. He'd become more volatile over the last hour, Vega noticed. The stress was getting to him. Maybe the darkness and heat as well. He knew the light was fading. He knew if he killed Kaylee and Hunter, the police would have no incentive to bring him out alive.

"We can't reconnect the power otherwise," Callahan explained to him. "The gas will build up and cause an explosion from the slightest bit of friction."

"Nobody's getting in here! I'll blow them away if they walk through that door."

"Then the ignition from the gunshot will set the gas alight, Boyd. You'll all die. In the most horrible way."

Silence. Callahan tried again. "Listen to me. My brother is on the other line. He's begging me to save your life. I'm trying, Boyd. But you've got to let me help you. It took my boss almost an hour to find a handyman even willing to set foot in the building."

"Yeah. Some FBI asshole who's gonna blow me away."

"He's just some Spanish dude who services a couple of apartment buildings in town." Callahan shot Vega an apologetic look. "I don't think he even speaks English. He agreed to do it if we pay him really well."

"I don't want some wetback beaner in here."

"He's the only handyman who was willing to do it. Look, Boyd, he's not armed. All he's going to do is walk down to the basement, reconnect the power, and then come upstairs to work on your stove so you don't get blown up."

There was a long pause. Vega heard nothing but heavy breathing on the line. Then a sound like Richter taking a long pull on a bottle. The drink was probably turning his reasoning fuzzy, which was good. But it was also magnifying his paranoia.

"Boyd," Callahan sighed. "You can't hurt this man. You have to promise me—soldier's promise—that you'll let him do his job and leave. I could lose *my* job if you don't let him leave. Promise me."

Silence.

"Promise me, Boyd," Callahan said again.

"The beaner doesn't mess with me, I won't mess with him." Richter hung up.

Vega frowned at Callahan. "A, his promise is worthless. And B, I'm not leaving Kaylee until SWAT has steel bracelets on this guy."

"*You* know that and *I* know that," said Callahan. "But he's got to believe you're just a civilian who wants to get out of there alive. Jesus!" She massaged her temples. "I told him you speak Spanish. You *do* speak it, right?"

"Fluently."

"This could work in our favor," said Callahan. "Richter doesn't speak a word of Spanish and I speak it passably. We might be able to keep up some communication if you pretend to talk to yourself in Spanish."

The triple-decker was bathed in shadow, the sky behind it to the east already a deep blue. Streetlights turned the sparse grass in front a glossy gray color, like Vega was staring at a black-and-white photograph. He moved slowly, right hand on his toolbox, left in the air to show he was unarmed. There was no sound on the street, save the scrape of his borrowed work boots on the pavement. His feet felt weighed down by concrete blocks. His chest burned like someone was scraping sandpaper across his lungs. A Tupac Shakur rap song about taking a bullet thrummed inside of him, a drumbeat to his heart. It felt like Tupac was delivering his eulogy.

He looked up to the curtains on the third-floor bay windows. The edge of one flickered. Richter was watching, most likely through a series of mirrors. SWAT probably knew this too—knew Richter wouldn't be stupid enough to make himself a target.

Vega made it to the stairs and slowly climbed them to the porch. He pulled out the master keys and unlocked the entrance door. His hands were shaking and he tried to still them. But no. It was okay to be scared. A handyman would be scared. Fear might keep him sharp—so long as he didn't give in to it entirely.

He stood to the side of the door frame, listening to the creak of the door swing open. He tried to mimic his mother's own Spanish accent. As a boy, he sometimes did this to tease her.

"Alo?"

Right then and there, the whole plan went out the window.

Chapter 37

Richter appeared at the top of the stairs. He had a tattooed arm wrapped around Kaylee's neck and a semiautomatic pistol jammed in her ear. Kaylee had her arms wrapped around Hunter in front of her. Vega could see right away that both Kaylee and Hunter recognized him, even in the dim light. Kaylee's eyes widened into two bottle caps. Her mouth formed a perfect O. Hunter thankfully said nothing. The boy was only three, but Vega suspected that survival was a powerful impulse, even in children. Some part of him knew not to speak.

Vega patted the air with his left hand. "*Cálmate, señor. Cálmate.*" Then he added, in Spanish, for Callahan's edification, "You didn't have to bring the lady and child onto the landing with you and stick a gun in her ear."

"I don't speak that damn beaner language," growled Richter. "Speak English!"

"*No hablo inglés.*"

"Great. Just great! A goddamn wetback. Figures the feds would stick it to me." Richter took his gun off Kaylee's head and pointed it at Vega. "Hands against the wall."

Vega stood still. He was shaking, but he had to will himself not to understand. Richter cursed and awkwardly walked down the stairs. He slammed Kaylee against the wall with Hunter and ordered them to stand next to Vega.

Then he turned Vega around and patted him down. He picked up Vega's toolbox and dumped the contents on the floor.

It would have been all over right then if he'd let Speers hide the gun in there.

Richter kicked around the mess of tools and looked satisfied that there were no weapons. "Pick it up and go to the basement," he ordered.

Vega gave Richter a blank look, forcing him to mime his words. *Good,* thought Vega. *He's having to work for every ounce of communication. This will slow things down and give SWAT time to reconsider their plan.* Vega knew it would be tricky. SWAT could use a two-pronged approach and enter their apartment from the roof and the front door while they were down in the basement. On the other hand, Richter could simply barricade them all down there. Vega too. He kept thinking about what Speers had said about not going down to the basement. But what choice did he have? Richter held all the cards here.

Vega gathered up the scattered tools. He pondered whether he had time to thrust a screwdriver into Richter's gut. But no. There were too many moving parts at play here. Patience was a virtue in situations like this. He forced himself to remember that others were out there, waiting for the right moment to strike. He put the tools away, all except for a heavy-duty Maglite flashlight, the kind he always carried on his duty belt. Good for bashing someone's brains in, in an emergency.

"I need to use my flashlight if we are all going to the basement," said Vega in Spanish. He wanted to make sure Callahan knew where they'd be and what sort of weapon Vega might be able to rely on. Also, he wanted to let the SWAT team know that he was the one holding the flashlight, in case any overly ambitious sharpshooter decided to play hero.

"Shut up and get moving, asshole," said Richter. He

grabbed Kaylee and jammed the gun back to the side of her head. He ordered her to grab Hunter. Then he gestured for Vega to unlock the basement door and go down the steps. Vega wished he had a radio so he could know what was happening outside. But that was impossible. He'd have to rely on his own initiative here. He didn't want Kaylee and Hunter in the basement, below ground level. That would make the only means of egress the basement stairs. It would force a do-or-die situation. He reached in his pocket for the keys and tried to remember which one opened the basement door. It had a square top to it, as he recalled. He pretended to drop the flashlight.

"Sorry for dropping the flashlight, *señor*," said Vega. As he picked the flashlight up, he slipped the square key off the ring and into his sock. The darkness was his friend right now. He wasn't sure for how long. Then he took the remaining keys and slowly tried each one in the lock. He spoke again in Spanish. "None of the keys can unlock the basement door. We cannot get into the basement."

Richter was getting frustrated. He took his gun off Kaylee and stepped up behind Vega, close enough that Vega could smell his sweat and boozy, sour breath. He grabbed the keys from Vega and pushed him aside. "Goddamn worthless border-hopper." Richter leaned over and began trying to jam the various keys into the lock.

Vega saw his moment. There was no time to yell "power," and no way SWAT could get to him fast enough in this narrow hallway if he did. Instead, he raised his heavy-duty flashlight over his head and brought it down full force on Richter's.

"Run!" He yelled in English to Kaylee and Hunter. "Power! Power! Power!" he shouted into the microphone on the inside neckline of his T-shirt.

The lights flickered to life but even so, the hallway wattage was dim and gelatinous. Certainly nothing that would blind an attacker. Kaylee grabbed Hunter and backed away from Richter. The boy was like a piece of petrified wood, frozen stiff and unable to move his legs.

Richter wasn't knocked out—not by a long shot. He whirled on Vega in the gauzy light, the gun still in his hand. Vega swung the flashlight again and managed to knock the gun out of Richter's grip. It skittered under a radiator on the other side of the hallway. But Richter didn't need a gun to unleash his fury. All he needed was his two strong hands. He pushed Vega down on the floor and kicked the flashlight from his hands. Then Richter wrapped his thick, stubby fingers around Vega's neck and began to squeeze.

Vega's neck felt like it was on fire. But worse was the sensation of not being able to breathe. He gasped, but no air entered his lungs. He heard sounds coming from every direction, but it all sounded like chatter on a beach to a drowning swimmer. He thought Kaylee was crying, but he wasn't sure. He hoped he was hallucinating. She was supposed to be out of here. Gone. Safe. With the boy.

Vega tried to wriggle free, but Richter's grasp was too strong. The hallway began to close in, the air around him thick with the smell of dust, damp clothes, and sweat. A voice kept crying, "No!" At first, Vega thought the voice was his, but he couldn't talk. He couldn't even breathe.

And then a sound came out of nowhere. Like a champagne cork popping. *Pop*. Just one brief noise. And then nothing. Muffled silence. Vega heard it with the same clarity as those shots that December night in the woods. Those shots that had forever rewritten the narrative of his life. Only this shot didn't come from Vega's hand or Vega's gun. As his vision swam back to life, he saw at once whose hand it came from. He saw her now, not as the woman she was, but as that six-year-old with the blond curls and seed-pearl teeth clutching that Tickle Me Elmo in the back of her father's sedan. She was a victim then.

No more.

Chapter 38

Although he'd never blacked out from alcohol, Vega suspected that oxygen deprivation was basically the same thing. He was aware of nothing, then vaguely aware of only the most lizard-brain sensations—the burning pain on his neck. The heaviness of Richter's body on his chest. Loud voices. Rubber-soled boots. The glare of flashlights pointed at his face. Gradually, his other senses returned.

He felt like someone was sticking razors into his brain.

"You're gonna be okay, brother. We got you." Vega had no idea who the husky-voiced SWAT team member was talking to him. The guy was covered head to toe in body armor. He realized that someone had moved Boyd Richter off his chest. Alive or dead, he didn't know and didn't care. He only cared about one thing.

"Kaylee," Vega choked out. *Where's Kaylee?*

"She's fine. Her and the boy both," said the masked officer. "She made sure that son of a bitch will never bother her again."

Two EMTs maneuvered into the narrow hallway. Vega didn't want to exit the building on a stretcher. That might get broadcast on the news. He didn't want Adele and Joy seeing that.

"I'm okay," said Vega. He tried to sit up. His head swam.

"You need to get checked out at the hospital."

Vega looked at the female EMT and noticed her lips weren't moving. That warmly soothing, maternal voice belonged to Shana Callahan, who looked especially out of place in this hallway in her T-shirt and ripped jeans. With her freckled face and bushy red ponytail, she felt more like a kid who'd stumbled into a bust while she was coming home from school than a crackerjack hostage negotiator. But something about her, Vega noticed, made the SWAT team all keep their heads down, as if in the presence of a commanding officer.

"I can't go out of here on a stretcher," Vega told her. "My daughter and girlfriend don't know I was involved in this. If they saw it on the news . . ."

Callahan spoke into her radio. "Bring the armored truck into the lot. I need a privacy cordon for the ambulance." She rattled a paper bag that jingled. "You want your wallet, cell phone, and keys back?"

"Yes, ma'am." Vega held out a hand. Callahan turned the bag over to the female EMT.

"Give these back to the detective when he gets to the hospital."

"But—" Vega went to protest.

"You heard the agent," said the EMT. She placed the bag in her pocket and wrapped a cervical collar around Vega's neck. "You need to get checked out."

"But I want to see Kaylee."

"I'll have an officer bring her over to you," said Callahan.

"But—"

"Don't argue with a former army major, Detective. I outrank you." Then she leaned over the stretcher where Vega was now immobilized by the collar. "That was great work back there, Vega. Truly exceptional. Give the FBI a call sometime. We'd like to see more of you." She straightened. "I'll have an officer bring Kaylee over."

The EMTs loaded Vega into the back of an ambulance.

He watched them start a saline drip, but his mind was still processing Shana Callahan's words. Was she just flattering him? Or did she have more power within the FBI than he realized?

A few minutes later, Kaylee climbed into the ambulance and sat across from Vega with Hunter in her arms.

"Hey," Vega choked out. He had no words.

Kaylee leaned forward and buried her face on Vega's chest. For the first time he could ever recall, she began to cry. He stroked her hair. Women's tears normally frightened him. But here, he felt so good to finally see that release from Kaylee that he welcomed them. The damp patch on his borrowed T-shirt. The slight heave of her body.

"It's over," he said hoarsely. He suspected he'd be hoarse for a while. "You saved my life."

She straightened and shook her head. "I finally saved my own." She palmed her eyes. "I'm going to get clean. I promise."

"I'll help you," he said. "Only, you gotta be honest with me. No more vanishing acts. We're gonna work this out and get your life back together, okay?"

She nodded and exited the ambulance with Hunter. The female EMT closed the rear doors. Only when they were moving did she give Vega back the paper bag with his wallet, phone, and keys inside. Plus, something else. Something he wasn't expecting. Shana Callahan's business card. Vega tucked the business card in his wallet and checked his phone. He saw a voice mail and text from Adele. She'd clearly heard about the standoff in Anniston from news outlets and knew he was here. She'd worry if she heard his hoarse voice, so he texted her instead. **Richter is dead. Kaylee and Hunter are safe. I have a slight injury that EMTs insist I get checked out. Can you meet me at Riverview Hospital? I won't have my truck.**

He ignored the follow-up ring on his phone from Adele.

He figured he'd do better to explain things in person. He did the same with Joy, texting her with the briefest, scaled-down version of events and thanking her again for staying the night with Diablo. He had a dog walker take him on long hikes every day, but Diablo didn't like being left alone at night.

The ambulance sped down the streets of Anniston and was at the emergency room of Riverview Hospital in minutes. Being an on-duty cop, Vega was ushered into a private triage room where a doctor was waiting. The Anniston Police stationed an officer outside the door to get him anything he wanted. He was breathing normally on his own with no changes in blood pressure or heart rate. He knew those were good signs. The doctor insisted on getting a CT scan of Vega's neck, though Vega was pretty sure it was just a bruise, not a fracture.

When Vega came out of radiology, Doug Hewitt and his silent Nordic sidekick, Fiske, were waiting for him. His neck was sore and his voice still sounded like he'd been gargling with Drano. But otherwise, he felt back to normal.

"That was an impressive rescue, Detective."

The words were Fiske's. Vega wondered if he finally merited the man's conversation.

"Thank you," Vega croaked out. He looked at both men. "I know you're here to take my statement, but can I ask if you've found anything that ties Boyd Richter to the courthouse shooting?"

"We've confiscated a massive amount of weaponry inside the apartment," said Hewitt. "We're securing search warrants for his computer and phone now, so it will be a while on that end before we know more."

"Did you do a cheek swab on Richter?" For DNA. Vega wanted the FBI to compare Richter's saliva to the saliva on the toothpicks recovered on the bus terminal rooftop and at Adele's.

"Affirmative," said Hewitt. "We will let you know if it's

a match. I suspect it will be. We just came from interviewing Kaylee Wentz. From what she's telling us, it appears Richter spoke often about shooting up that new immigrant center in town, La Casa North."

Vega felt relieved that Richter would never get the chance—and sick because one of his associates still might.

Fiske pulled out a small tape recorder and Hewitt asked Vega to recount, as accurately as possible, what was said and done inside the house. A lot would be on the recorded lines, in English or Spanish, but he was still a witness to the shooting and his impressions were fresh.

"I just want you to know now, upfront," said Vega in his scratchy voice. "Kaylee Wentz saved my life. If she hadn't shot Boyd Richter, I'd be dead. I want to make that absolutely clear."

"She's being treated as a victim at this point and not likely to be charged," said Hewitt. "We'll keep you in the loop. For now, rest up. The worst is over."

Ten minutes later, a nurse walked through the door with Adele in tow. Vega was propped upright on a gurney. Adele's eyes traveled straight to his neck. Fortunately, with his skin tone, the bruises weren't too obvious. She buried her head in his lap. He supposed the top half of him looked too fragile at the moment. He patted her hair.

"I'm okay, *nena*. You're safe now. Kaylee's safe. You don't have to worry anymore." Vega told her about the FBI getting the cheek swab from Richter for DNA testing. "He was a dangerous guy. He wanted to shoot up La Casa North. He's dead, but there are others out there. You and your people need to be careful."

"Oh God." Adele shook her head. "What a world we live in."

They spoke awhile about extra security measures for both La Casas until the weight of all this worry got to them both.

"Hey," he said. "They're not keeping me tonight. Joy's

staying with Diablo. Why don't we go back to your house? Sophia's not coming back from Cape Cod until Sunday evening, right? We'll have Saturday all to ourselves. We can do something fun."

"But your neck," said Adele.

"My neck's just a little sore. The weather's supposed to be great. We can drive upstate. Maybe take a winery tour. Go apple picking. You name it. I'll just need you to take me to my truck when I finish up here. Then I'll follow you home."

"Are you sure you can drive to Lake Holly?" she asked.

"I'm fine," he assured her.

Traffic had thinned and the drive from Anniston didn't take long, despite Vega's sore neck. He was relieved to see her little blue Victorian just as Adele had left it. Lights on all over the house. The doors locked. She was still getting that security system, as far as he was concerned, but for now, the threat was over.

He was too sore for a shower, so Adele drew him a bath in her old, claw-footed tub. Then she sat with him, steam rising in the old-fashioned black-and-white-tiled bathroom. She poured water over his head and shampooed his hair. He playfully splashed her.

They were having fun, Adele getting soaked and Vega getting horny. His neck hurt too much for them to make love, but he enjoyed her caresses.

"How can you pick apples tomorrow?" she chided him. "You can barely move your head."

"You'll pick 'em for me," he said. "Or we can just have a picnic at a winery and get sloshed."

Her eyes suddenly lost their playfulness.

"What?" asked Vega.

"I was just thinking about that little girl I tried to track down where all those farms are located. The one I told you who had a broken wrist?"

"You never found her, did you?"

"I don't think the police did either."

"You told the local police about her?"

"No," said Adele. "But while I was waiting for you at the Lake Holly station house, I saw her picture. Or at least, I think it was her."

"Where?"

"On the bulletin board in the hallway."

"Those are wanted and missing posters, *nena.*" The bath water suddenly didn't feel as warm and cocoon-like. Vega slowly pushed himself to his feet and grabbed a towel.

"I could be mistaken," said Adele "It could be a different girl. Dr. Carrasco gave me her picture, but that man I told you about at the grocery store took it from me."

"He took the picture. Of the girl. The same girl you saw on the poster in the station house."

"I think so," said Adele. "Dr. Carrasco gave me her medical intake chart too. Except I can't find that, either. I put it on my desk in the dining room after I got back from Petersville. I haven't seen it since the break-in."

Chapter 39

Dr. Miranda Carrasco hated turning away patients, even at closing hour. The hospital emergency room was a good forty-minute drive from Petersville. It would be packed on a Friday evening. And besides, the man's hand was clearly infected. The skin around the wound on his left palm was red and swollen. The patient didn't speak a word of English, but he told her in Spanish that it was a bite from a stray dog who'd wandered into the orchard where he worked.

"I can stay and help," Carrasco's nurse assistant, Carla, offered. But Carla had a baby at home and a husband who worked opposite shifts at a local utility. He might get in trouble or be docked pay if he showed up late.

"No. You go," Carrasco assured her. "I can handle this myself."

Carla pulled the doctor aside. "Are you sure that's a good idea?" she asked in English. "You're a woman. Alone. We've never met this man before."

Carrasco studied the man. He was more European-looking than most of the laborers she encountered, with pale, blotchy skin and a receding hairline that he shaved short beneath his baseball cap. But he was dressed like he'd just come off work: jeans, a zippered hoodie, and work boots. He was clearly in pain. She couldn't abandon him. "I'll be fine," she assured Carla.

Carla left and Carrasco handed the patient an intake form in Spanish to fill out. He gave his name as José Gonzalez and listed his age as thirty-four, though he looked older. His skin was uneven in color, flushed with broken capillaries on the nose and cheeks but grayish around his eyes. Carrasco suspected he was a heavy drinker—she had several patients who were—though she detected no alcohol on his breath, even when she moved in close to take his photo for their records. She saw nothing to suggest he used intravenous drugs. *Good.* That was her primary concern: that he was here to steal drugs.

She didn't want to give voice to her other concern. Carla had done enough of that already.

On his intake sheet, Gonzalez checked off that he had no known medication allergies or previous surgeries. He scribbled a local address and a phone number and indicated that he had no insurance, which was typical for Carrasco's patients. She charged him her usual copay of $25, which he paid in cash. She didn't bother putting the money in the safe. Best not to open it right now.

"Do you have ID?" Carrasco asked him in Spanish. "I see you drove here."

Gonzalez shook his head. "I borrowed the car. I hope the police don't stop me. I don't have . . ." He waved his good hand sheepishly. He didn't have a driver's license.

"How about a library card, an electric bill—something?"

Gonzelez shook his head. "Last month, my trailer caught fire. Everything is gone." He seemed to realize suddenly what having no ID might look like. "Please, *Doctora.* I swear," he said, "I mean you no harm. I just need help."

"Of course." She gestured for Gonzalez to walk into the first examining room. She followed him in, leaving the door wide open and her cell phone in her pocket. She patted the exam table. He hoisted himself onto it and held out his infected palm. Carrasco kept one eye on him while she washed her hands at the sink. Then she slipped into surgical gloves to examine the wound.

"A dog did this?"

"*Sí, Doctora,*" he replied. "I went to pet him, and he bit my palm."

The bite looked human.

Carrasco examined both of Gonzalez's hands. He had the smoothest hands she'd ever seen on a farmworker. Aside from the bite, they were free of calluses and cuts. The nails were trimmed and even. All the farmworkers she'd seen—even the very young ones—had rough hands and broken nails. Some were missing parts of fingers.

She removed a bottle of betadine solution from a shelf and thoroughly cleansed and debrided the wound. It wasn't deep, fortunately. She decided against stitching it up, reasoning that it would heal more naturally if she just covered it with ointment and gauze. She explained this to him. He nodded.

"Whatever you think is best, *Doctora*. No pain you give me is worse than the pain I'm already in."

"With your hand?" She looked surprised.

"With my heart." He touched his chest with his good hand. "A few weeks ago, my wife left me and took my daughter. I don't know where they went."

"I'm very sorry to hear that," said Carrasco. She took out a tube of antibacterial ointment and slathered it on the open wound, then pressed gauze on top and began to bandage it. Gonzalez watched her.

"The worst part," he continued, "is that she left with a man. A bad man. I think he's abusing my daughter. Physically and maybe"—he kept his eyes on his bandaged hand—"other."

"Why do you say that?"

"I just hear bad things about him," said Gonzalez. "Only I can't find him. I can't find any of them."

"Have you talked to the police?"

Gonzalez studied his hand without replying.

"If this man is sexually abusing your daughter, the police will intervene."

"I don't know if they will listen to someone like me."

"Are you referring to your immigration status?" asked Carrasco. "The police are not allowed to ask about your immigration status if you're reporting a crime."

"I am so worried about my daughter. Yes." He nodded. "Maybe I will call."

"Good." Carrasco pulled a syringe out of a drawer. "I'm going to give you a shot of penicillin," she explained. "And write you a prescription for dicloxacillin tablets. One every six hours for seven days. That should clear the infection."

"Gracias, Doctora."

He removed his zippered hoodie so she could reach the skin on his upper arm. She noted a thin scar that appeared to be at least a decade old from some sort of laceration. He had a small scar in his left eyebrow as well. She wondered if they were both from the same occurrence. An accident. An encounter with the wrong person. Many of her patients had scars. Not all of them were immediately visible.

She swabbed his upper arm with an alcohol wipe and administered the shot. He kept his eyes on her the whole time. He had dark, penetrating close-set eyes that rarely blinked. He made her self-conscious, though she couldn't say why. She turned away after administering the shot and threw the syringe in her red biohazard container on the counter.

"People in Petersville and North Kitchawan say you are a good doctor," he said slowly.

"Thank you."

"They say you know all the farmworkers."

"Not all," Carrasco reminded him. "I don't know you."

"Maybe you have seen my daughter. Her name is Maria."

"I know many Marias," said Carrasco. "How old is she?"

"Twelve."

"I see." Carrasco thought about the twelve-year-old in her office the other day with a broken wrist. She'd sensed from the outset that something was wrong with the child's story. Even so, she was still bound by patient confidentiality. She couldn't just release information without being sure. She tapped some keys on her computer and pulled up a photograph of the girl on the screen. She turned the computer so he could see.

"Señor Gonzalez—is this your daughter?"

"*Dios mío*, that's her. Is she all right?"

"I treated her a few days ago."

"For what?"

Carrasco hesitated, then relented. The father needed to know. "A broken wrist."

"My poor little Maria. She didn't have a broken wrist last time I saw her. Did she say how it happened?"

"I've already divulged more than I'm legally allowed to," said Carrasco. "I'm sorry."

"Do you know where I can find her?"

"The address and phone number I was given are incorrect," said Carrasco. "That's why you need to go to the police."

"But the police will take their time," said Gonzalez. "My daughter is in danger. She needs me now."

"I understand," said Carrasco. "But there is nothing I have that can help you. I'm sorry."

"Perhaps you know where her mother works?"

"You don't?" Carrasco raised an eyebrow.

"She left the farm we both work at," said Gonzalez. "I

don't know where she's working now. If I knew, I could tell the police where to find her. It's the only way to rescue my daughter."

"I can't—"

"Please, *Doctora.* This man may be abusing her. How else am I going to find her and put a stop to this?"

Carrasco hesitated. She'd been so suspicious of this poor man when he first came in. And now, it was clear, he wasn't going to hurt her. He was just a distraught father searching for his child—the same child Carrasco had asked Adele to find. This was the break they'd both been looking for. Maybe Gonzalez would contact the police who would rescue his daughter. Maybe now the girl could attend school.

"Maria mentioned Watkins Farm," said Carrasco. "She and her mom pick apples there."

Carrasco's phone rang in her pocket. The caller ID said "Carla." Carrasco couldn't ignore it. Her nurse was probably calling to make sure Carrasco was okay.

"Excuse me a moment, please," she said to Gonzalez in Spanish. She picked up the phone and spoke to Carla in English.

"I'm fine. Honestly, Carla. He's harmless," said Carrasco. "I'm about to write him a prescription and then he'll be leaving. As a side note, do you remember the girl with the broken wrist? He says she's his daughter."

"Wow," said Carla. "I guess the visit was meant to be. Too bad you don't have an address to pass along."

"I told him where they work," said Carrasco. "I hope I made the right decision. I mean, how do I *know* he's her father?"

"How do you know the uncle was her uncle? Or the mother, her mother? You don't," said Carla. "You wanted to find her and get her help. Now, you have."

"I suppose," said Carrasco. "I'd feel better if he'd produced even one shred of evidence to prove that the girl is truly his daughter. A picture. Anything."

"You can ask him."

"Maybe I'll do that." She hung up and finished writing the prescription. Then she turned and handed it to Gonzalez.

"You need to take one pill every six hours, okay?"

"Yes. Thank you." He tucked the prescription in his pocket. "I'm sorry I don't have a picture of Maria to show you," he said in Spanish. "Or some other shred of evidence. As I mentioned before, everything was burned up in the fire."

"*Pizca.*" Carrasco mouthed the word slowly. It was Spanish for "a pinch." To describe the evidence she was looking for. She'd used the word "shred" in English and he'd translated it perfectly. Carrasco stared at him openmouthed as the realization sank in.

José Gonzalez had understood every word of her call.

Chapter 40

"Hey, Jimmy—did I wake you?"

It took Vega a minute to place the voice on his cell phone. He rolled over, blinking back the sunlight that streamed in through a crack in the curtains. The air felt delicious on his skin. He was thankful to be alive, thankful to be lying with Adele in her bed on a Saturday morning. He would have slept in a little longer, if his old commander, Nick Santorini, hadn't ruined it.

"Cap? What's up?" Vega asked hoarsely. His voice was still rubbed raw from last night. He wondered if Santorini had heard that Vega had been involved in the hostage standoff in Anniston, but the captain's tone suggested he hadn't. Not that Vega was surprised. It was an FBI operation—not a county police one. Which meant that anything Vega did there was of no political value to his own department.

"You asked me to do a search of Oscar Beltran-Parra's rap sheet. I did. You'll never guess what I found."

Vega wasn't sure it mattered anymore. Whatever mistakes had transpired in Judge Spruce's courtroom over Beltran/Rivas's missing fingerprints, it was over. The FBI believed Richter was behind the courthouse shooting and were targeting the dead man's associates in the Puritan Sons. Spruce's activist leanings would be swept under the rug. Still, Vega had asked this favor of his old boss. He couldn't brush him off now.

"Can I catch up with you about this on Monday?"

"I'm leaving for some R and R on Monday," said Santorini. "Two weeks in the Rockies. If you want to wait until I get back—"

Vega caught Adele staring at him and turned away. "Are you in your office?"

"Affirmative. Got to catch up on some paperwork before the vacation."

"I'll be there in thirty minutes."

Adele sat up and gave him a sour look as he hung up. "How can you do this? We had plans for today—"

"We still do. But Captain Santorini's doing me a favor. I can't crap out on him now. It'll take twenty minutes, tops." He kissed her forehead. "We'll be on the road by ten. I promise."

The narcotics unit was just down the hall from major investigations and the homicide task force. Santorini was hunched over a computer in his glassed-in office. Vega's former boss was movie-star handsome: lean, chiseled features. Thick salt-and-pepper hair. A boyish smile. It was only when he turned full-face that people could see the faint port-wine stain that ran from his cheek to his left eye. It made him look like he'd fallen asleep on one of those old mimeograph machines. It also made him unsuitable for undercover work. His face was too memorable.

"I should probably warn you," said Santorini. "They got a big *Congratulations Drew Banks on Making Sergeant* poster in the break room. Not only will you have to sign it, you'll have to stare at it until his promotional party on Friday."

"I figured as much," said Vega. "It's all right. Banks is a good guy."

"So are you." Santorini leaned back in his chair. "I just

heard about the standoff in Anniston and how you took the perp down."

"Actually, the victim took him down," said Vega. "I just provided the distraction." Vega closed the door and took a seat. "I'm surprised it's going around. It wasn't a county operation, except for SWAT."

"Some agent at the FBI is making sure everyone knows."

"Doug Hewitt?"

Santorini shook his head. "A female. Don't recall her name, but I understand she's connected. Her dad is among the top brass in the agency."

Shana Callahan. Vega wondered if this would help or hurt him.

Santorini fished a thick folder out of a pile on the corner of his desk. "I printed Beltran's whole jacket for you."

"*Whole?*" Vega opened the folder. "How many arrests does this guy have?"

"Five, counting the Mount Washington bust six years ago," said Santorini.

"I'm surprised he wasn't deported."

"He was. It's all there."

Vega looked down at the first page, to the Mount Washington arrest. They'd busted Beltran for marijuana possession. The amount was only two ounces—misdemeanor weight. Santorini's crew weren't interested in the pot. They were interested in what Beltran was doing there, and whether he was implicated in the heroin dealing going on in the parking lot. Vega wasn't surprised when the judge—not Spruce, another judge—dismissed the charges. Beltran had a clean record, even if his story sounded suspicious. Nevertheless, the arrest meant that Beltran's fingerprints, name, and date of birth had been entered into the federal database, assuring that ICE would be aware of his presence in the country and could issue a detainer for any subsequent arrests.

There were many.

A year and a half later, in Paterson, NJ, Beltran was picked up for driving without a U.S. license. He gave his name as Ramon Parra and produced what turned out to be a forged Mexican driver's license. If not for the fact that his fingerprints were already in the system under a different name and nationality, the cops might not have picked up the forgery. Instead, they arrested Beltran and notified ICE . . .

Who failed to issue a detainer that would have caused him to be jailed and deported.

Vega smacked the report. "They had him. Right there. All ICE had to do was act."

"You wanna be the cop who goes on the nightly news and tells people why a gardener should be deported for driving without a license? 'Cause that's all the Paterson PD had."

"They had a man with fake ID who couldn't give them a real name, let alone a consistent nationality," said Vega.

"Things were looser back then," said Santorini.

Vega moved on to the next police report in the folder. This one was from Waterbury, CT, about three and a half years ago. For trespassing on private property. Again, Beltran claimed to be Guatemalan. Oscar Parra was his alias this time, though his prints linked him to his rap sheet. Again, the judge dismissed the charges. Only by this time, the political climate had changed and ICE did issue a detainer . . .

Which the judge ignored after he vacated the charges.

Vega moved on to the next arrest. Again, for trespassing. This one, three years ago in Wilmington, DE. The pattern from Waterbury was repeated. Cops sent Beltran's prints to ICE. ICE issued a detainer. The judge dismissed the charges and ignored the ICE detainer.

"This guy keeps getting breaks," said Vega. "In different states. With different judges. Why?"

"Dunno," said Santorini. "My guess? The more politicized immigration became, the more some left-leaning state judges believed they needed to counter what they considered to be federal overreach. It's a standoff of sorts, I suppose," said Santorini. "Each side thinks they're the good guys acting on the country's behalf."

"Where do we fit in?" asked Vega.

"That's easy." Santorini laughed. "We're *always* the bad guys."

Vega looked down at the folder again and read Beltran's final police report. From Utica, NY. A little more than two years ago. Someone had shot and killed a local drug dealer. Police were scouring the area for witnesses and suspects. They came across Beltran, questioned him, decided they had probable cause to frisk him, and ended up confiscating a small amount of cocaine. He was arrested. His prints were sent to ICE. The agency once again issued an immigration detainer.

But this time, Beltran wasn't so lucky. The Utica judge who heard his case honored the detainer. Beltran was jailed and deported back to Mexico, where presumably, he spent at least a small portion of those next two years getting his fingerprints lasered off. A costly procedure. Certainly not the sort of thing a recreational drug user and low-level gardener would seek out.

"And now he's back, with a different name," said Vega, closing the folder, like he'd just finished reading a book with an unsatisfying ending. "I knew he was dirty all those years ago. I just knew it."

"It's worse than you imagined," said Santorini.

"How so?"

Santorini swiveled to his computer, his profile now obscuring the smudged-ink hue of his other cheek. "We've recently been partnering with the DEA to look into a splinter group of one of the Mexican cartels that has been making significant inroads into the narcotics trade in the mid-Atlantic region."

Vega cursed under his breath. "And Beltran's part of this—is that what you're gonna tell me?"

Santorini clicked a few buttons. "You be the judge."

Vega walked around Santorini's desk to the screen and looked over the captain's shoulder. On the screen was a map of the mid-Atlantic region of the United States, from Delaware to Connecticut. There were big stars on Mount Washington, NY, Paterson, NJ, Waterbury, CT, Wilmington, DE, and Utica, NY.

"You've starred all the places where Beltran has been arrested," Vega noted.

"Affirmative," said Santorini. Then he clicked on a second screen, with a big *CONFIDENTIAL: PROPERTY OF THE DEA* across the top. It showed a zigzag pattern with lines and bull's-eyes all over it.

"What the DEA has told me," said Santorini, "is that this splinter group of the Sonoran Cartel has found a profitable business model that involves the distribution of heroin and fentanyl in target neighborhoods throughout small industrial cities in the mid-Atlantic region. This splinter group calls themselves Los Demonios."

"The Demons," said Vega.

"That's right," said Santorini. "They go into a place and muscle out the local dealers."

"You mean kill them?"

"Not always. But yes—when they have to," said Santorini. "Since all their markets are small, these killings have been chalked up to local warfare over turf. The killings go unsolved and the local cops, pressed for manpower, are mostly relieved when things calm down."

"*Do* they calm down?"

"Most certainly," said Santorini. "Think about it as if Walmart set up across from like, six or seven mom-and-pop stores, then put them out of business. These guys are suddenly the only game in town." Santorini held down a button on his keyboard. "Now look at this." He slid the zigzag pattern with the bull's-eyes over the map of Beltran's arrests.

"*Coño,*" said Vega. "It's a match."

Santorini nodded. "Oscar Beltran—alias Ramon Parra, alias Juan Rivas—is likely part of the Demon cartel."

"Except the cartel doesn't appear to have business in Lake Holly."

"No," said Santorini. "My guess is that Beltran just found himself in the wrong place at the wrong time. Maybe he was doing some reconnaissance in the area. Maybe he was visiting a girlfriend."

Vega straightened, trying to take it all in. "What I don't get," he said, "is why all the moving around? If Beltran's a narcotics supplier, how come the cops have never caught any product on him?"

"He's probably a boss," said Santorini.

"No." Vega shook his head. "A boss doesn't get swept up by cops after some rival dealer gets gunned down. A boss doesn't do reconnaissance. A boss isn't even on the scene."

"So what is he?"

Vega stared at the map. The Demons were like Walmart. They carefully scouted their locations. They had strong supply lines. And once they moved in, they drove their competition out of town. Unless the competition didn't want to leave. Then the Demons could do something Walmart couldn't.

"The Utica cops picked Beltran up after a dealer had been gunned down, right?" asked Vega.

"Affirmative," said Santorini.

Vega flipped through the police reports for Waterbury and Wilmington. The pattern was the same. The police came across Beltran while they were trying to find witnesses and suspects in a drug dealer killing.

"That's it," said Vega.

"What?"

"Beltran's not a boss or a supplier," said Vega. "He's a *sicario.*" *A hit man.* "That's why he moves around all the time. That's why his prints have been lasered off. Because he can't afford to leave them behind and link himself to any of the executions."

Santorini stared at the screen. "Jesus . . . If you're right, we've got to get the DEA in on this. We've got to take this guy down."

"Except," said Vega, "because Judge Spruce released him, nobody knows where he is."

Chapter 41

Vega and Adele decided to skip apple picking. Vega's sore neck couldn't take the strain. They settled instead on a winery tour.

It was a beautiful day—the sort that feels more like early fall. The air was crisp; the sky, blue, with just a thin ribbon of white cirrus clouds running like the string of a kite along the horizon. They blasted the radio and rolled down the windows, letting the breeze blow across their arms and mess up their hair like they were teenagers. Vega promised himself he wouldn't mention the case or the trial or anything work-related for the rest of the day. He'd already checked on Kaylee. She was staying at her aunt's house with Hunter. Vega could breathe again. He didn't even need his gun on him. He'd left it in a spare lock box he kept at Adele's house for when he came over.

They followed the handmade signs for Sun Haven Vineyards, turning into a long gravel road that climbed up a gentle slope, past fields of corn and a barn where a swaybacked horse swished his tail lazily in a field. Two big wrought iron gates stood open at the end of the road. An artist had soldered a large, copper, smiling sun to the gate above the vineyard name. Adele liked the artwork. Vega thought it was cheesy. He suspected the wine was second-rate and the wine tour little more than a sales pitch. But they weren't here for the quality of the booze or the tour. They were here because Sun Haven offered picnic lunches in the vineyard with panoramic views.

They took the tour, along with two other couples. The vineyard's main building looked like a French Normandy castle, with cobblestone walls that stayed cool and damp all summer, and cathedral ceilings framed in mahogany beams. Everything smelled darkly fruity. Their guide, Jennifer, was a young, doe-eyed woman who spent more time talking about what went into designing the wine labels than what went into the wine.

Vega was never a wine connoisseur, preferring beer with meals. But he happily pretended to know what he was doing when he swirled the half glass samples of pinot noir and chardonnay provided and listened to Jennifer talk about letting the wine "breathe" and determining its "bouquet." He extended his pinkie and playacted knowing what he was doing. Adele giggled.

"You'll always be a beer kind of guy," she teased him.

"Least I don't have to let my beer breathe," said Vega. "Whatever the hell that means."

They bought their picnic baskets of bread, cheeses, fruit, and cold cuts, along with a bottle of the vineyard's chardonnay, and walked out to an arbor where picnic tables had been set up. The view was magnificent. The land spread out before them in patches of green and gold like a chessboard, along softly undulating hills. The air smelled grape-sweet with a fine, musky scent that Vega could detect in the wine.

Adele clinked her plastic cup against Vega's. "To a better future."

Vega clinked back, thinking about the trial. "To *any* future."

"You're a hero, Jimmy," Adele insisted. "Even if the county gives Carver a big settlement, your department can't ignore that you uncovered the courthouse shooter. You stopped a white supremacist from possibly carrying out even more deadly missions. Isn't that what the FBI is saying?"

"The FBI's saying it," said Vega. "Not my own department."

"Your SWAT team commander was there. He okayed your participation. He's bound to tell Captain Waring and Chief Lakeworth how well you did."

"You don't *tell* people anything in my job, Adele. You write them up. Speers has no incentive to write me up. I'm from a different unit. I'm not politically connected. And I'm not a popular guy right now with several millions in settlement hanging over my head."

Adele sipped her wine and said nothing. She could see his logic. "Still, Kaylee's safe. Richter's dead and the FBI's likely to bust up his ring of associates. Which means that little girl with the broken wrist doesn't have to fear this neo-Nazi coming after her anymore."

Last night, after Vega's bath, he'd told Adele what that FBI poster of the girl on Lake Holly's corkboard had been about. The child was the only person who could potentially identify the courthouse shooter. But now that the FBI could access Richter's computer records and his weapons stash, they didn't need her testimony anymore.

"I wonder if Dr. Carrasco will ever know her real name," said Adele.

"You don't think it was Maria Gonzalez?"

"Dr. Carrasco didn't. I have to assume she's right. She said the child was scared. I wish we could find her again just to get her out from whatever situation she's in. Imagine, being twelve years old and finding out you might never go to school again."

"That's not legal," said Vega.

"Of course it's not legal," said Adele. "But I got the sense that up in that community, the people in charge make the rules and everyone else just has to obey—legal or not. I suspect most of the white Americans in those towns have no idea this is even happening. I mean, how would they? It's all hidden. The social service net is weak. The police don't want to get involved, especially since it might open up a whole can of worms for the farmers. Cause their entire labor force to be deported. There's just no accountability and no one who wants any."

Vega drained his plastic tumbler and looked out across the hills. "It's such beautiful country, you know? Driving through, all you see are dairy farms and vineyards and orchards. Nobody sees the people who do the work or the toll it takes." He rolled his empty tumbler between his fingers. "It's not just the immigrants either. Remember that story a few years ago? About the dairy farmer who shot like, fifty of his cows, and then shot himself?"

"I remember," said Adele. "He was having financial issues, as I recall. He was afraid the bank would take everything away."

"I look out there, I see land and freedom," said Vega. "I guess a lot of these people look out there and see nothing but obligations and endless toil."

Vega's cell phone rang in his pocket. He looked at the number in case it was Joy. He knew she'd be leaving later and Vega would have to be home this evening for Diablo. But the call wasn't from Joy. It was from Doug Hewitt.

"Let it go, Jimmy," Adele pleaded.

Vega nodded. "Whatever he wants can wait until Monday." The phone stopped ringing. Then Vega heard a ding. Hewitt had sent him a text. Then a second ding. Another Hewitt text.

"I should at least see what he wants."

"Jimmy—"

"It will only take a minute."

The text had three words, all in capital letters. **CALL ME ASAP**.

Vega showed Adele, then dialed Hewitt back before she could object.

"The search warrant came through for Richter's computers," said Hewitt. "We've got a treasure trove of information on gun sales, white supremacist contacts, and potential targets of violence—including an antigun rally in Albany."

Vega shuddered. On the one hand, he felt relieved that the FBI might be able to put a stop to all that now that they had the information. On the other, he knew that Richter was one cockroach in a swarm. Just because he'd been eliminated didn't mean the threat had been removed. There was still so much work to do. But it wasn't his work. This was an FBI operation and his connection to the case died with Boyd Richter.

"Vega." Hewitt's voice turned grave. "There's something else you should know. The DNA results came back on those toothpicks. They're a match. Whoever was up on that roof where the shooting took place was the same person who broke into Adele's house."

"That's good news, isn't it? A two-for-one on Richter."

"Except the DNA isn't Richter's. He's not our suspect."

"*What?*" It took a moment for Vega to process the words.

"He was a bad dude, no mistaking," said Hewitt. "He was selling guns to white supremacist biker gangs. He was planning attacks. But we have nothing that places him on the bus terminal rooftop or at Adele's house."

"You think it was an associate?"

"That's our theory," said Hewitt. "It's going to require a lot more digging. The DNA's not a match to anyone in CODIS." The FBI's Combined DNA Index System. Vega immediately understood the implications: The FBI was looking for a perp who'd never been convicted of a violent felony or sexual assault. Those were the standard parameters. Misdemeanor offenders did not get their DNA entered into CODIS.

"We can try getting a judge's permission to go through genealogy databases," said Hewitt. "But that's a tricky area these days and it could take time. Right now, we're going to have to pursue more standard methods of investigation. Running down Richter's contacts and seeing who else might fit the profile."

Vega glanced at Adele. She had no idea from Vega's end of the conversation what had just transpired. She looked so happy and relaxed, the sun glinting off her glossy black hair. They both thought she was safe now. Her ten-year-old would be back from Cape Cod tomorrow. Everything was supposed to be okay.

She was at more risk than ever.

But why? wondered Vega. What was the connection between Adele and the courthouse shooting? Sure, her politics were the same as Julia Spruce's. But that was true of everyone in the immigrant community. She'd been behind the opening of La Casa North in Anniston, but Julia Spruce had had nothing to do with that.

Vega felt he was missing something. Something significant. The same person who'd taken a high-powered rifle to the bus terminal had taken a knife to Adele's back porch screen. The perp clearly had the ruthlessness and tactical experience to have killed Adele. But he didn't. He didn't seem to want Adele. Most likely, given that she'd parked her car down the street that evening, he didn't even know she was home. Which meant he didn't want her. He'd wanted something she had.

Did he get it? Or would he try again?

"You should probably let Adele know," said Hewitt. "That's why I'm calling you mostly. When I hang up, I'll make sure the Lake Holly Police know as well so they can put extra patrols on her house."

Adele's not the only person still at risk, Vega suddenly realized. But he didn't want to express his thoughts to Hewitt. Not yet. Not without being sure.

"Thanks for the information," said Vega. "Will you call me if anything changes?"

"I'll keep you in the loop."

Vega hung up and turned to Adele. "*Nena* . . ." He took a deep breath. He felt the weight of his words, the darkness they were bringing back into Adele's life. And to someone else's as well. Someone who might be in even more danger.

A little crinkle furrowed her brow. "What is it, *mi vida*?"

Vega took her hands and told her what Hewitt had just told him.

"But that can't be." She pulled away. "You said it was Richter. He's dead. Sophia's coming back tomorrow night. I can't have my daughter—"

"I know," said Vega. "I think she should stay with her dad for a while. You can stay with me. Or maybe with your friend Paola if the dog dander gets to be too much—"

"I'm not abandoning my house," said Adele. "I agree about Sophia—at least until school starts. But I'm not abandoning my house."

Vega thought she'd say that. He'd fight that battle later. Right now, he had a more pressing concern. "Adele, are you *sure* the photo Dr. Carrasco gave you of that girl is the same girl in the FBI bulletin?"

"I'm not certain," said Adele. "She looked very similar. But I don't have the photo anymore. Dr. Carrasco would, though."

"Where's her clinic?"

"In Petersville," said Adele. "About ten miles north of here. But she doesn't have any way to contact the child. All she knows is what the child told her."

"Still," said Vega, "if we took a ride up there, maybe Dr. Carrasco might remember something else about her."

"If we try to find her," said Adele, "we might put her in danger."

"If the courthouse shooter is still out there, she's in danger already," said Vega. "Besides, we can blend in. Keep things on the down-low. Better we get in there before one of Richter's buddies decides to find her and take her out."

Adele turned away from Vega and stared out at the patchwork of green and gold hillsides. "You can't get the FBI involved in this, Jimmy. Not until we know more. These poor people are so scared. Bringing in the FBI could expose this child to even more risk. More abuse."

"All right. I understand," said Vega. "We'll go ourselves. Talk to Dr. Carrasco. Even if she can't help us find the girl, maybe she knows if anyone has been poking around those parts, asking for her."

"Do you really think the shooter could get to her?"

"A child like that isn't on anyone's radar," said Vega. "So yes, if our assailant knows she's still out there, he will definitely find her."

Chapter 42

Saturday morning dawned cool. A thin veil of mist drifted like gauze over the stubby trees stretching up the hillsides in perfect lines, broken here and there by trailer beds full of wooden fruit bins emitting the overripe scent of apples.

All the workers were quiet as they got off the truck. Eli shivered in her thin flannel shirt, T-shirt, and blue jeans, the sleeve on her left arm cut and rolled up to accommodate her bulky wrist cast. The cast had started out white and shiny on Wednesday evening, but now it was a dirty greenish gray, especially at the seams. The part near her fingers had a soft and spongy feel to it.

It was impossible to keep anything dry here. The leaves and fruit were always marked with morning dew, even if it hadn't rained. The water painted Eli's rubber boots a glossy black all the way to her ankles and speckled them with bits of grass and mud. People slipped all the time. They tried not to do it when they were on a ladder.

She'd gotten used to working with the cast, at least. And although she couldn't pick with her left hand, she could use the arm to cradle the apples until she could ease them into the bag. It made the work harder and slower, but at least she could still contribute.

The workers shuffled over to the trailer area and grabbed

the big white sacks to sling across their bodies. The stronger men grabbed old wooden straight-back ladders. The best pickings were high in the trees, but they were also the most dangerous since it was easy to slip and fall, especially with a full bag of apples weighing you down. If you fell and damaged the fruit, you wouldn't get paid—never mind that you might break something and not be able to work for weeks.

Señor Ortega barked out commands, then disappeared. The only sound after that was the shuffling of feet. Some of the men had pocket radios, but their batteries ran out if they used them all day, so they often saved them until the afternoon when everyone needed a little boost of adrenaline.

Reach. Pick. Pick again. Gently place into the bag. Repeat. Over and over. You were supposed to pick two to three apples with every reach. But Eli's hands were too small, and it was impossible anyway, with her left wrist in a cast. She tried for two when she could and settled for one when she couldn't.

The hours passed. She knew this from the sun. From where it was in the sky and how hot it felt on her shoulders. She no longer counted the hours or made up math problems in her head. Her back and neck and limbs were sore in a way that she now thought of as part of her. As if there had never been a time she hadn't felt this way. Her mind was blank, like a turned-off television.

Sometimes, she heard someone humming a tune she recognized, and her thoughts would chase the music. But the work was too hard to focus on anything for long. The ladders required attention to balance. The apples needed to be delicately handled. There was the ever-present danger of wasp nests and poison ivy. The sun burned. Insects swarmed around her nose and mouth, sometimes her ears. She had to make sure her skin didn't come into contact with the insecticide powder on the leaves and fruit. The other night, her entire arm had turned red and itchy from something she'd touched.

These things occupied her thoughts now. These and nothing else.

She and her mother worked side by side in one of the main fields where the trees were as tall as two men and a child standing on each other's shoulders, and so dense, you couldn't see a worker on the other side. Eli and Aurelia were careful to stay away from Señor Ortega. They stuck together, using the outhouse only when they were desperate. They ate under a tree with other workers.

But even with all these precautions, Eli could see the change in her mother since that afternoon in Señor Ortega's trailer. She talked much less than she used to. She never smiled. She rarely said more than one or two words to the other workers. She flinched if Eli bumped up against her unexpectedly. Eli suspected this wasn't just about Ortega. Her mother had endured men like Ortega her whole life.

No. It was what Luis had done that broke her. Broke something her mother had been building all her life—ever since Luis sent his first photographs back from the United States. Of his sharp clothes and new sneakers. Then later, his bright, shiny car. And still later, his well-fed wife and sons in front of his big white house.

The photographs had filled Aurelia with hope. The cheapest thing to possess. The most expensive when it dies.

Eli heard Señor Ortega's ATV zipping along between the trees, the motor revving up and stopping and revving up again. She'd heard some of the teenage boys joke that he didn't know how to drive anything faster than a mule.

The ATV pulled up behind Eli and her mother. "I need someone to clean out the plastic bins in the back forty," said Ortega. "That's a woman's job, but the pay's better. A flat one hundred for the both of you for the rest of the day."

Aurelia blinked at Eli. Cleaning the bins was dirty work, but they wouldn't be paid by the piece. They wouldn't have to climb a ladder or worry about insects and poison ivy.

They'd be alone back there too. The pickers would be in the fields below.

"Who else is going to be cleaning?" asked Aurelia.

"No one." Ortega shrugged. "You want it or not? Because I can ask someone else."

"My daughter can't get her cast wet."

"There are gloves back there. And more plastic bags. I'm sure you can figure something out."

Aurelia looked at Eli. She clearly wanted Eli to make the decision, which frustrated the girl. She didn't want to carry the burden of worrying about their safety all alone back there. Safety or money—it always came down to that.

"We'll do it," said Eli.

They walked their apples over to a bin. They'd only managed two bins so far today. Ortega peeled off two $20 bills for their labor and promised them the other $100—directly—at the end of the day for cleaning the bins.

They removed their bags and climbed behind Ortega on the ATV. Aurelia was forced to hang on to the señor's shoulders to avoid falling off as the wheels bumped along the rough dirt path. Eli could feel her mother trembling. Neither of them could stand being this close to the foreman, taking in the sickly scent of his aftershave mingled with sweat.

He revved the engine and turned onto a slightly wider path in the orchard, grinding the ATV up a hill, where the orchard ended. There was a rusted wire fence, broken and twisted in places, and beyond it, a steep path down through the woods. Eli wondered where the path went. She knew it wasn't to the farmer's house. That was up on a hill when they entered the orchard—a big white house with a front porch and long windows that glowed golden at the end of the day.

Eli turned her attention away from the path. Her mother was staring at the three large trailer beds parked end-to-end along the rusting wire fence. Each was full of plastic bins, grimy from the detritus of rotted bits of apples, leaves, and mud.

"You said one trailer full of bins," said Aurelia. "Not three."

"I didn't specify," said Ortega. "Do you want the job or not?"

"We can do it," Eli assured her mother. She was exhausted from the picking. Just having a different sort of muscle task felt appealing.

Aurelia and Eli got off the ATV. Ortega showed them where the water spigot was, along with buckets, sponges, rubber gloves, and soap.

"Is there an outhouse?" Aurelia asked.

"Not back here," said Ortega. "That's what the woods is for." Then he drove back down the hill, the ATV stuttering out of sight.

They were alone. But it was a nice alone. The air wasn't humid today. There was some dappled shade from the trees. Insects buzzed, their chorus rising and falling in waves. Eli's mother found a big plastic bag and wrapped her cast as best as she could. They both slipped into gloves and started to work.

The bins had been sitting back here a while. The dirt and fruit juice stuck to their surfaces and needed to be scrubbed off by hand. But the work was more pleasant than picking. Less physically and mentally demanding. Eli's mind could wander.

They'd been working for about forty-five minutes when Eli needed to pee.

"Just do it here," said her mother. But Eli was shy. They

were on a hill. What if the workers in the orchards below saw her?

"I can go into the woods," she said. "It won't take a minute."

"Okay."

Eli stepped over the rusted wire fence and followed the dirt path on the other side. Sunlight faded under the umbrella of thick trees. Birds flitted in the canopy overhead. Weeds and thorny bushes choked the land on either side of the path. Eli didn't want to chance walking into a patch of poison ivy.

Up ahead, she noticed a clearing. A patch of dirt with only a few scrub weeds around it. She squatted and peed, pulling her underwear up quickly when she heard voices. Two men chattering in Spanish. She couldn't hear what they were saying, only the occasional hard barks of laughter.

The sounds were coming from below. From the other side of a steep drop-off. Eli peered over the edge. At the bottom sat a grouping of cabins with peeling white paint and dark green window trim. Eli didn't think they belonged to the orchard. Rather, they looked like something that people might have vacationed in long ago. But no more. The windows and screens were all broken. Weeds sprouted from the planks of swaybacked porches and partially caved-in roofs.

The two men were leaning against their vehicles in a gravel parking area next to the cabins. One of the men was Señor Ortega. Eli could see his broad-brimmed cowboy hat and the side of his pickup truck. The man he was talking to had his back to Eli. His arms were folded, his elbow propped against an old blue sedan. His left hand was bandaged as if from an injury. His legs were set wide apart. He said something to Señor Ortega who laughed with a nervous trill to his vocal cords. It was the same sound she'd heard when her uncle raised a fist to Ortega after he locked her mother in his trailer.

Ortega was scared of the man with the bandaged hand.

And yet, he didn't run away. He stood there until the man thrust some bills from his shirt pocket at Ortega. The foreman shoved them quickly into his pocket without even counting the amount. Then he backed up to his truck, anxious to leave.

The man with the bandaged hand turned. Eli saw his face for the first time. Her breath felt like she'd swallowed a handful of gravel and it was tearing up the lining of her throat. She didn't have to see the scar in the man's eyebrow to hear his voice in her head again:

If you tell anyone about me, I will kill you.

She backed up to the path, then raced up the hillside, tearing her jeans as she lifted her leg over the rusted fence. Her mother was hosing down the inside of a bin.

"Mami!" she huffed, her chest burning with fear and effort. "The man! The one with the gun in the bus terminal! He's here! He found me!"

Her mother stopped scrubbing and straightened. "How? How could he find you?"

"I don't know. Maybe it was that pretty lady asking about me in the grocery store," said Eli. "I saw him near some cabins on the other side of the hill. We've got to get out of here."

Aurelia blinked at the orchards below. They were a good mile from the highway. She patted the two twenty-dollar bills in her front pocket. It was all the money they had. She seemed frozen by the enormity of their predicament.

"We should call my brother. Luis will know what to do."

"Luis hasn't helped us since we got here," said Eli. "Why do you think he'll help us now?"

Aurelia turned to Eli, her eyes glassy with tears. "We are his family, Eli. His blood. Surely he'd protect his blood."

Chapter 43

Vega and Adele headed north to Petersville. Adele pulled out her phone while Vega was driving and dialed Dr. Carrasco's clinic. She gave the receptionist her name. "Please tell Dr. Carrasco I need to speak to her right away."

"I'm sorry," said the receptionist. "She's with a patient. I can have her call you back if you'd like."

"I'm less than half an hour drive from the clinic," said Adele. "Will she still be open?"

"She's open until six this evening."

Adele looked at her watch. It was three-thirty. "Great. We'll be there by four."

Vega picked up his speed as they followed the directions on their GPS. The winding road that had felt so freeing before now swallowed them in a silent prism of worry.

"She'll be okay," Vega assured Adele. "This is just precautionary. If we can't find her right away, I don't think the shooter will either. And at least it narrows our search area."

"Narrows it to a strange community where the immigrants don't talk to *any* outsiders," said Adele. "Let alone the police."

Vega kept both hands on the wheel, navigating the hairpin curves, past bars with no name and trailers with BE-

WARE OF DOG signs tacked up in windows. Past old storefronts long empty and gas stations with their pumps removed. The area had the feel of death about it. It was like driving through a beautiful historic cemetery, all of it quaint and all of it long buried in another time.

He was glad he hadn't liked the wine enough to finish the bottle. The alcohol content was low, anyway. He felt sober enough to keep his wits about him as he nosed the pickup past a volunteer firehouse with the garage door open and two white men in navy-blue T-shirts sitting in lawn chairs, taking in the afternoon sun. He drove a little farther and suddenly found himself on the main street of Petersville. There was a small brick-face post office with an American flag out front, a scattering of low buildings of various vintages—none of them built in the last twenty years. He saw a few pickups and SUVs parked outside a VFW hall. At the end of the street, he found Carrasco's clinic in a former beauty salon with a red cross on the window, covered over in blinds, and the name above painted in English and Spanish: HELPING HANDS/MANOS AMIGAS.

Vega parked in the lot and walked inside with Adele. The place was packed. There were about ten plastic chairs and almost every seat was taken. Women shushed fussy babies. Toddlers played hide-and-seek between seats. People hunched over cell phones, tapping out messages. Vega wondered what all these people would do without Dr. Carrasco. The closest hospital was over a half hour's drive from here.

Adele walked up to the receptionist, a thoroughly Americanized Latina. Blond-streaked curls and a nose stud. She was different from the one Adele had met the other day. Maybe Carrasco had different staff on weekends.

"Wow. It's busy," said Adele.

"Dr. Carrasco doesn't like to turn anyone away."

"Can we see her before her next patient?" asked Vega.

"It's important." He didn't say "police business." Nobody but Carrasco needed to know that. And besides, he didn't look like a cop today. He was dressed in faded jeans, sneakers, and a T-shirt. He wasn't carrying his duty belt or gun.

"I'll try to fit you in."

Ten minutes later, an exam door opened, and a mother and baby walked out. The nurse—also a different one from the other day—beckoned Adele and Vega to follow. The salon had clearly once been two big rooms, but had since been partitioned into the waiting area, storage, doctor's office, X-ray and exam rooms with the use of sheetrock walls, now painted, like La Casa, in bright colors. The nurse led Vega and Adele past Dr. Carrasco's office to the first exam room. The doctor was bent over the exam table, ripping off the creased waxy paper from the last patient and replacing it with a fresh part of the roll. The tearing sound made Vega think of a sandwich being wrapped at a deli.

Dr. Carrasco straightened. She was a stout and nononsense-looking woman in her white lab coat, clear, plastic-framed glasses, and bowl-style haircut. Vega imagined he could have picked out Miranda Carrasco from her fifth-grade class photo and she wouldn't have looked much different.

"Adele! So nice to see you again. And who is this?"

Adele introduced Vega. The doctor was pleasant but reserved. Police officers made her nervous, it seemed. Or maybe she'd just adopted the natural fears of her patients.

"What can I do for you?" she asked as she wiped down a counter with disinfectant and removed some bandage wrappers. She was doctor-nurse-and-janitorial-staff all in one.

"I'm back about the girl," said Adele. "It turns out that she might be more than just an at-risk child. She might be able to identify someone who committed a serious crime."

Carrasco stopped cleaning. "A crime? What crime?"

Vega took control. "If you don't mind, Doctor, I'd like to see your intake photo of the girl. I have a download of a picture from a flyer I'd like to match against it."

"Of course. My computer's in my office."

Vega and Adele followed her into the small room, decorated with colorful Mexican pottery and Central American worry dolls. The walls had paintings of Mexican plazas and village markets. It reminded Vega of the stuff Adele kept in her office. Carrasco typed in a code and called up the photo on the screen. Vega had no doubt as soon as he saw the picture that it was the same girl, but he pulled up the flyer anyway and held it next to the screen.

The doctor cursed. Not the reaction Vega had expected. "What's her name?" Vega asked Carrasco.

"The man who brought her in said her name is Maria Gonzalez. He said he was her uncle, but I don't know if any of that's true. He wrote down an address and phone number on her intake forms that doesn't check out." Carrasco stared at the screen, as if the forms could tell her something now that they hadn't before. "I should have pressed harder for proof," she said, more to herself than to Vega and Adele. "I shouldn't have believed him."

"Her uncle?" asked Adele.

"No." Carrasco turned to face them. Vega read something that looked like fear in her eyes. He didn't get the sense that Miranda Carrasco was afraid very often.

"A patient was in here last night—just as I was about to close. He had a bite wound on his left palm. It was infected, so I treated him. He told me his wife had taken his daughter and run off with another man who was abusing the child. As we talked, I discovered that the child he was talking about was this girl."

"That's good news," said Vega. "We trace the father, we can trace the child."

Carrasco didn't look reassured. Vega realized he'd made the wrong assumption. "You don't think this patient was her father?"

"I don't know," said Carrasco. "I can't say why exactly, but he . . . frightened me. He didn't *do* anything scary. His wound needed attention. He paid me, but . . ."

"He wasn't a white guy, was he?" asked Vega. "The person of interest we're looking for is likely white."

"No." Carrasco laughed. "We don't get many white people in here."

Vega felt his insides relax a little. Whoever this guy was—the father, a male relative, or perhaps, a jilted boyfriend—he wasn't their suspect.

"What was it about him that scared you?" asked Vega.

"Well, first off, he said he didn't have any ID," said Carrasco. "He said it had all been destroyed in a fire. He'd driven here in a car, so that already seemed suspicious, but he said he'd borrowed the car from a friend."

"He could have a rap sheet," said Vega. "The wound could be from an assault—maybe a rape—and he didn't want a record of it."

Carrasco nodded like that made sense. "At first, I thought the name he gave me, José Gonzalez, was fake. But then he said he was looking for his daughter. He perfectly described the child I'd treated two days earlier. He even gave the same name: Maria Gonzalez."

Vega could hear the cries of fussy babies beyond Carrasco's closed office door. He could see that Carrasco, too, wanted to get back to her patients. But something was bothering her.

"He told me he worked at a farm," said Carrasco. "But his hands were smooth. Not the hands of a laborer. I wondered if he was lying about something. But I was just so relieved he wasn't there to steal drugs or attack me . . . When he mentioned Maria, I felt bad for him."

"Can you share his intake sheet with us?" asked Adele. "I know you're not supposed to. But maybe we can contact him and find this girl from there. He obviously knows her."

"All right," said Carrasco. "I have a photograph of him too. He was reluctant, but as I mentioned to you, I always keep a picture of my patients with their files. I'd just have to print it all out for you and then ask you both to please keep this to yourselves. I'm not supposed to share patient information, as I'm sure you can understand."

"Certainly," said Vega.

Carrasco turned back to the computer and entered a password. "I remembered something about the girl when Gonzalez was here."

"What?" asked Adele.

"The child said that she and her mother worked at an apple orchard. Watkins Farm in North Kitchawan. It slipped my mind when you came in the other day. I remembered it when Gonzalez pleaded with me for information about his daughter. I told him about the farm. But as soon as I did, I regretted it."

"Why?" asked Adele.

"Because my other nurse, Carla, called me up from home to make sure I was okay. We spoke in English. When I hung up, Gonzalez clearly understood everything I'd said."

"A lot of these people speak and understand more English than they let on," said Vega. "They play that game with cops all the time."

"Perhaps," said Carrasco. "But when he first came in, he made it seem like he couldn't speak a word of English. Plus, I keep going back to those hands of his. Those were not the hands of a laborer."

Carrasco clicked on a screen and scrolled down. It was a listing of patients by date. She highlighted her last patient of the day yesterday and opened the tab that read: *José Gonzalez.*

Vega didn't need to read the chart to know that every single thing about José Gonzalez was a lie. He didn't need to ask why this man had an interest in Maria. It was all there, clear as the scar running through his left eyebrow.

José Gonzalez was Oscar Beltran-Parra.

Chapter 44

Oscar Beltran-Parra. Alias Juan Rivas. Alias, the man with no fingerprints. Vega just hoped that between last night and now, there was still time to get to Maria and her mother before Beltran did.

Maria. Vega suspected that wasn't even the girl's real name. She was so tiny; it was hard to believe she was nearly twelve. The surveillance video had been grainy and blurred. Carrasco's snapshot showed the child more distinctly. Those big, sad eyes, slightly upturned, with little puckers of flesh beneath them. The brown, sunburned skin that peeled along her nose. Her chapped lips were pressed together, almost like she was fighting to hold back pain. *Physical pain? Or something else?* Her dark eyes had the hesitant and knowing look of a girl who'd already experienced too much in her short life.

"I don't understand," said Adele as she followed Vega to his truck. He was moving so fast, she had to race to keep up. "I thought we were looking for a white supremacist. Who is Oscar Beltran-Parra?"

"A *sicario*," said Vega. "A hit man for a Mexican cartel called Los Demonios. He's not Maria's father. He's tracking her down to kill her. She's the only person who could potentially place him in the bus terminal at the time of the shooting."

"Wait," said Adele. "Yesterday, you were convinced the shooter was Boyd Richter. And *now* you think it's a cartel hit man?"

"There would be no other reason for a guy like Beltran to track her," said Vega. "That's what he does: He kills people for a living. She's the only person who saw him at the bus terminal without his disguise. That's why he broke into your house. To get Maria's medical records so he could track her down and kill her. Except the address and name were a fake. So he had to invent that story about being her father to get information from Dr. Carrasco."

Adele opened the door to Vega's truck and collapsed on the passenger's seat, dropping her face into her hands. She was still processing the most personal part of his assertions. "A Mexican hit man was in my *house*?"

Vega said nothing. He didn't want to contemplate what might have happened had she confronted Beltran. This was a guy who took no prisoners.

"But how would a Mexican hit man even know Maria was up in North Kitchawan?" asked Adele.

"You showed her picture around," said Vega. "You told me some creepy guy took it away from you. He read your name and address off your driver's license. Whoever that was had a line to Beltran."

"Oh God." Adele massaged her forehead. "I'm responsible."

"You're not responsible," said Vega. "You didn't even know the FBI was looking for her. If anything, we caught a break here." Vega studied the copy of Beltran's intake chart that Carrasco had printed out for him, along with another copy of Maria's photo. "I'm betting the cell number on here is real, just as his bite was real. He'd want Carrasco to be able to contact him if Maria showed up again."

"So?"

"So, the police can track his phone and get to him before he gets to Maria."

Vega pulled out his own phone and dialed 911. As soon as the dispatcher came on the line, he identified himself as a police officer and asked for the state police. He didn't want the locals on this one. They didn't seem aware of all the lawlessness going on in their midst—or maybe they did but it was more convenient to look the other way. The FBI was too far away for such a time-sensitive matter. Plus, Vega had a close friend in the state police. The bassist in his side band, Armado: Officer Brandon Cruz.

The 911 dispatcher patched him through to a state police sergeant. Vega identified himself and explained the situation. He needed an immediate police presence at Watkins Farm in North Kitchawan to find and secure a Guatemalan immigrant mother and child who were employed as orchard workers on the farm. Vega gave a description of them, along with the child's alias, Maria Gonzalez. In addition, he needed the staties to put out a BOLO on Oscar Beltran. Vega gave all of Beltran's aliases, plus the cell phone number Beltran had scribbled on his intake sheet. Then he asked the sergeant for his cell number and texted the shot of the photo Dr. Carrasco had taken of him.

"This guy likes to pose as a laborer," said Vega. "He's a cartel hit man. He's armed and dangerous. Plus, I have reason to believe he's behind the fatal courthouse shooting in Broad Plains. Proceed with extreme caution."

"Would you know him on sight?" asked the sergeant.

"Affirmative," said Vega. "I've had contact with the suspect before."

"Can you meet the responding units at the farm?"

Vega cast a sideways glance at Adele in the passenger seat. He was unarmed. Out of uniform. Most importantly, he was with Adele. He absolutely wouldn't do anything that put her in harm's way.

"I'm up in Petersville," said Vega. "Who can I contact if I make it there?"

"Not sure yet," said the sergeant. "If you can get there, get there. Your name will be in the initial report."

Vega hung up and turned to Adele. He took her hand and laced his fingers between hers. "I need you to do me a favor."

"Anything."

"I need to drive over to Watkins Farm. I'm the only one who knows Beltran on sight."

"Okay," said Adele. "Let's go."

"*Nena.*" Vega squeezed her hand and looked at her. "I need you to stay here. At the clinic. With Dr. Carrasco and her staff."

"Why can't I come with you?"

"Because this is a police operation. They won't let a civilian within a hundred feet of the command post."

"I'll stay nearby."

"Which would make me so nervous, I wouldn't be able to focus on anything else. This guy's already been in your house," Vega pointed out. "He knows you. Please, *nena*. I won't go otherwise."

"All right." Adele exhaled. "I want them safe too. Do what you have to do."

"Thanks." He leaned over and kissed her. She put a hand on the door to get out of his truck, then thought of something.

"Jimmy?"

"What?"

"Why would a man like that want to assassinate Judge Spruce? It makes no sense."

She was right. The only time Spruce and Beltran had crossed paths, to Vega's knowledge, was when Betran came before the judge as Juan Rivas, the laborer, in June. Knowingly or unknowingly—the judge had set him free. Nothing about that encounter marked her for death.

"I don't know the answer to that," said Vega. "Only Beltran does."

Vega watched Adele disappear inside the clinic. Then he pulled out of the lot and set his GPS for Watkins Farm in North Kitchawan. The road wound past cornfields eight feet tall and red barns with hay bales rolled up like carpet padding beside them. At the orchard, the workers were probably coming in from the fields for the day. If there had been a shooting at the farm, the state police sergeant would have informed Vega. Which meant Maria and her mother were safe.

For now.

All the police had to do was trace Beltran's phone and arrest him. Once in custody, they could get a DNA sample from him and compare it with the samples from the toothpick found at Adele's house and on the bus terminal roof. If it was a match, Beltran was their guy.

Yet Vega couldn't quiet the question Adele had asked. It played over and over in his head as he drove the winding roads to North Kitchawan: Why would Beltran want to assassinate a judge who set him free? It didn't make sense. Nothing in Darryl Williams's past suggested that he was the target. It had to be Spruce. But why?

Maybe Spruce figured out that Juan Rivas was Oscar Beltran. But no—even if she had, belatedly, she wouldn't be a risk to him. She couldn't find him. No one could. And besides, to admit her mistake publicly would be a political embarrassment, not only to her but to the attorney general.

Could the judge be on the take after all? Again, Vega found that hard to believe. Judges had no say in which cases they got except to bow out on conflicts of interest. *No.* Spruce likely freed Rivas because of her beliefs. The United States was not a Third World country. The system was set up to make it difficult for judges to affect a case on a bribe. Then again, Vega couldn't discount the missing police report about the fingerprints. Greco insisted Lake Holly sent them. Spruce's clerk, Albert Pearsall, insisted they weren't in the record. Vega had to assume they'd gotten lost somewhere and nobody wanted to admit to it.

He saw the flashing lights of state police cruisers as he cleared the next bend in the road. They winked at him through a field of stubby fruit trees, identical in height, planted in perfect rows along an undulating hillside. Vega turned at the sign to Watkins Farm—an old wooden sign with peeling paint. This was not the sort of farm for tourists or pick-your-own. The road alone told him that. It was cratered with potholes and ditches. He turned in and drove up to a state police SUV parked along the side of the path.

A state trooper got out and put out his hand for Vega to stop. He wore mirrored sunglasses and a broad-brimmed felt campaign hat that made his square-jawed white face indistinguishable from every other state trooper. Vega powered down his window, acutely aware that as a Hispanic man in a T-shirt and jeans, he did not fit this guy's idea of "cop." He made sure he had his police ID out before the man stepped up to his window.

"Detective James Vega," he said. "I called this in. I need to speak to your incident commander."

The trooper studied his ID. "You're out of jurisdiction, Detective Vega."

"I'm out of uniform too. This was supposed to be my day off." Vega reached for the folder of photographs and Carrasco's intake sheets. "I need to get these to your incident commander."

"I can relay them to him."

Vega suspected this might be a problem. Once a police agency takes control of a scene, they hate interference.

"I've arrested Oscar Beltran before. I know the particulars of this situation better than the state police. You need to let me through."

The trooper pulled out his radio and read Vega's name off to someone on the other end. Then he clicked off the radio and leaned on the frame of Vega's open window. "Captain Michael Ross is the incident commander. He said to meet him at the command post next to the foreman's trailer."

"Okay. Thanks."

Vega nosed his pickup slowly along the rutted path until he came to a clearing. He saw a broken-down trailer on cinderblocks surrounded by pickup trucks. Several dozen laborers were gathered around the trucks, all of them Hispanic. Most were men and teenage boys, but Vega also noticed a few women and teenage girls. All of the women and girls seemed to be connected to families.

None of the girls looked like Maria.

The farmworkers wore grass-stained jeans and long-sleeved shirts, caps and bandanas to keep the sun off their skin. They kept to themselves, far from the police officers in uniform, all of whom were white. Two of the officers were talking to a short, burly Hispanic man in a light brown cowboy hat.

Vega parked his truck behind a state police SUV and walked over. The younger of the two officers was interviewing the cowboy-hatted man in stilted, textbook Spanish. His name tag read: *Ketchum*. He turned to Vega.

"Estamos llevando a cabo una investigación aquí."

"I know you're conducting an investigation here," said Vega. "I'm Detective Vega and *I* called it in."

Ketchum flushed. The man in the cowboy hat stifled a grin. Vega felt certain he spoke English—he was just enjoying watching this state trooper painfully negotiate his way through the interview in Spanish.

"I'm looking for Captain Ross," said Vega.

The older officer nodded. "I'm Captain Ross."

Vega extended a hand. "Pleased to meet you. And by the way, I suspect this man you're interviewing understands English very well."

"No, no," the man in the cowboy hat said in response. "I no speak English good."

Vega cocked his head at Ross. It made sense to conduct an interview in any language a person wanted. But it was equally important to know if they understood English. It could affect what else the police said around him.

"How's your Spanish?" asked Ross.

"Spoke it before I spoke English."

The captain gave Ketchum a signal to back off. "This man is the foreman of the orchard," Captain Ross explained. "His name is Adalberto Ortega. He says the woman and child we're looking for walked off the job early this afternoon. He doesn't know why. And he's never seen Oscar Beltran."

"Did you get the real names of the subjects we're looking for?"

"He says Aurelia Rosales is the mother. Her daughter's name is Elizabeth. They have temporary asylum papers. An uncle secured their employment, but Ortega says he doesn't know the uncle's name. We're trying to track that down now through immigration. It's most likely in their asylum papers, since he's probably their sponsor. But it's going to take time."

"Do you have a location on Beltran?" asked Vega.

"We've tracked his cell to Saratoga Springs," said Ross. An upstate New York town about fifty miles from North Kitchawan. That was good news at least, since it indicated Beltran might have left the immediate vicinity. "We've got a state police unit moving in there to arrest him."

"Good." Vega turned to Ortega and spoke in Spanish.

He began by showing Ortega the photograph of the girl. Ortega confirmed that the picture was of Elizabeth Rosales.

"Where were they working in the orchard?" asked Vega.

"In the back forty," said Ortega. "Washing the fruit bins. I offered good money. And they walked out on me!"

Vega showed Ortega the photo of Beltran. "Have you seen this man?"

"I don't think so. I don't remember him."

"So, you're saying he was never on the property?"

"I don't remember any man like that."

Vega noticed that Ortega looked nervous. He kept removing his cowboy hat and wiping his brow.

"This mother and daughter are in physical danger," said Vega. "You understand that if something happens to them and the police find out you are lying, you could be considered an accessory."

"I'm just a poor man who manages an orchard."

"Right." Vega didn't like the old man. His simpering manner. The dark looks he shot his workers, who seemed terrified of him. Everything that came out of his mouth felt like a lie. Vega lifted his gaze to Ortega's trailer. "And you don't know the name of the uncle?"

"I don't remember."

"So, you are paying Aurelia and her daughter directly?"

"I . . . Yes, yes. I am paying them directly."

Vega turned to Ross and the other officer and spoke in rapid-fire English. "I think this guy knows more than he's letting on. I think perhaps you should secure a warrant for his phone and anything else in the trailer."

A warrant would take time. Time they didn't have. Also, Vega doubted a judge would agree to a warrant with so little to go on. But his words weren't for Ross and Ketchum. They were for Ortega, who immediately understood the implications.

"That's not necessary," Ortega insisted. "His name is coming back to me." He said his next words in clear and careful English. "I remember it now. Monroy. Luis Monroy."

Ross turned to Ketchum. "Get me everything you can on Luis Monroy."

Vega raised an eyebrow at Ortega. "I see your English is coming back to you too."

Chapter 45

Luis Monroy didn't want to be driving around the back roads of North Kitchawan, searching for his sister and niece. But Aurelia had called him in a panic, begging to be picked up. He couldn't say no, especially after their fight yesterday at the lake and a distressing call just now from that creep of a foreman, Adalberto Ortega.

"Your sister is crazy!" Ortega shouted into the phone. "She ran off a job I'd already paid her for! She owes me money!"

"What did you do to them?" Monroy demanded. "If you touched my sister again—"

"I didn't do anything," Ortega insisted, stifling a nervous laugh. "She's paranoid, I tell you. She ran off for no reason. Do you know where she is? Has she spoken to you?"

"She called me," said Monroy. "She asked me to pick her up, but she didn't say why. I swear, if you touched her—"

"*Cálmate,*" said Ortega. "I didn't touch her."

"Then why did she take Elizabeth and run?"

"I don't know. She's mentally unbalanced," said Ortega. "An investigator from the state came by. He wanted to know if your niece was registered for school. That's all.

Your sister must have seen me talking to him. And she ran. She imagines things! She talks nonsense!"

Monroy wondered if all the talk of Aurelia being crazy had less to do with some government official and more to do with Ortega being worried about what Aurelia had told him about the trailer incident. In truth, Monroy was too ashamed to ask. He felt a burning guilt that he'd put his sister in that situation to begin with. He argued with himself in his head. *I didn't invite her here. Our mother pressured me and I gave in. Over the objections of my wife, I gave in.*

"Just tell me where she is," said Ortega. "We can figure this out. She can keep the money if that's the problem. I just want to know where she is. I have records to keep for the Watkins family. How is it going to look if I can't tell them where two employees have disappeared to?"

That sounded like Ortega. He didn't care about Aurelia or Elizabeth. He just didn't want to get in trouble.

"I'm driving around now, trying to find her," said Monroy. "All she told me is that she's at a church."

"The closest church is probably that vacant one on Hagerstown Road," said Ortega.

"That's what I figured," said Monroy. The Green Valley Baptist Church was a nineteenth-century, white clapboard structure walking distance from the farm. It was on a winding two-lane dotted with trailer homes on wooded setbacks with NO TRESPASSING signs in the front yards and barking dogs behind chain-link fences in the back. It hadn't been in operation for years. "I'm heading over there now."

"Can you call me when you find them? This official . . . he really needs to see her." Ortega offered up that annoying laugh again. He sounded like a seagull with its head bashed in. "Tell her she can keep the money."

"I'll get back to you." Monroy hung up, frowning at his

dashboard cell-phone holder like Ortega was sitting next to him. He'd known that scheming *cabrón* for years—even worked for him briefly long ago. He was a liar and a cheat who never did a favor without looking for something in return. Monroy didn't believe for an instant that Ortega was telling the truth about why Aurelia and Elizabeth fled. Most likely, he'd tried something with Aurelia again—or God forbid, Elizabeth—and they ran.

I'll find them other work, Monroy vowed. He should have done it the moment Ortega laid hands on his sister. But well-paying jobs were hard to come by for immigrants and it wasn't like he could just forgive the loan. He was behind on his payments to business creditors. Behind on his mortgage and car loans. When he first came to this country from Guatemala at seventeen, he owned what he could carry on his back. A change of clothes. A plastic bottle of water. A couple of tins of sardines. He wore cast-off clothes and slept under the stars. He ate whatever he was paid to pick: Apples and berries. Lettuce and carrots. He was rope-hard and stone-cold, unafraid of anybody.

Little man, little problems.

He'd built a life from the sweat of his brow. Seven days a week. Twelve hours a day. He'd been in the United States for fifteen years before he took a vacation. He rose from a farm laborer with a third-grade education to a naturalized American citizen who owned his own business, supplying workers to the farms. He owned real estate and parts of other local businesses. When it went well, it made him a rich man. And when it didn't?

Big man, big problems.

It had started out innocently enough. When immigration laws got restrictive and Monroy couldn't find laborers for his fruit-tree-pruning business, he tried going through the government's temporary worker visa program. The paperwork was costly—and slow. He stood to lose his whole business if he couldn't find a faster way to import workers. Desperate, he contacted an old friend back in Guatemala and arranged to smuggle some workers in. It was only a few people, but it worked. His business thrived while others went under.

He didn't understand the full measure of the risks he was taking. Not until that day a few months later when a well-dressed Mexican man approached him. Monroy knew men like him back in Guatemala. Men with hands that never got dirty and smiles that faded as soon as you turned your back. The man presented him with a business opportunity. He and his "friends" would set Monroy up as a "labor contractor." His job would be to recruit other Guatemalans to come work at the dairy farms and orchards in the area. In return, Monroy would get a cut of whatever the farmer was paying. If Monroy chose to house the workers, he could earn even more money.

Monroy didn't need to ask what would happen if he refused. At the very least, this man and his associates could tip off ICE that Monroy had smuggled workers into the country. He only had a Green Card back then. He could easily be deported. There could even be consequences to his family. These were not American men. They did not play by American rules. And besides, the money was attractive. He'd earn a kickback for every worker he brought in. If he bought land and built housing, he could earn money on that too. He could be rich.

Who was he hurting?

Not the laborers who desperately wanted to escape the violence and poverty of Guatemala. Not the farmers. Every year, it was getting harder and harder for them to find enough people to legally harvest the fields and milk the cows. Nobody wanted the fruit to rot. Nobody wanted the cows to grow swollen and ulcerated. So he contracted the smugglers and brought in the labor. He bought land and built trailer parks. He hired workers to truck the people back and forth to the fields. The farmers were happy.

The money rolled in. Monroy had to kick back some of it to the investors who'd put him in power. But he could afford it . . .

. . . for a while.

But that's the thing about money, Monroy realized. *No matter how much you have, you always want more.* The Mexicans kept demanding a bigger slice of the pie. The farmers wanted to kick back less. Wages didn't rise but the cost of living did. The United States increased regulations, which made the operation more expensive. The noose kept tightening.

His sister thought he was a rich man who could part with $15,000 for their travel like he was buying a cup of coffee. She had no idea the sort of pressures he was under. And not just from his business either. His wife fought with him for a whole week after Monroy announced that his sister and niece were coming to live with them. *They are strangers to you,* Miriam insisted. *You haven't seen your sister since she was a small child. The girl will be a distraction from the boys' studies.*

Monroy was torn between appeasing his wife and appeasing a sister he hadn't seen in decades.

He had to live with his wife.

Worry was making him sweaty. He cranked up the air-conditioning in his blue Jeep Grand Cherokee and pulled at the buttoned-down front of his white, cotton, short-sleeved shirt, a birthday gift from his wife. She'd bought it from a catalog called L.L. Bean, where all the models try to look like they're always outdoors, even if they're never sunburned or dirty. A white shirt was very impractical. In Nejapa, only people who didn't work for a living wore white.

He found the Green Valley Baptist Church easily enough. It sat on a hill, well off the road, on a long stretch of buckling pavement shot through with weeds. Plyboard covered the arched windows. A rusted chain and padlock secured the double front doors. The white paint had flaked so much off the clapboard that the bell tower was now entirely gray. Monroy turned in. He drove all the way to the cemetery in back where the gravestones were covered in moss and lichen. He cut the engine and scanned the trees beyond. Nothing moved. The buzz of cicadas rose and fell in waves across the land.

He got out of his SUV. The church had a single-panel back door down a half flight of steps. It was ajar. Monroy walked over and opened it.

"Aurelia?"

Monroy saw only empty wooden shelves, dusty with age, bathed in the light coming through the door. Everything smelled damp and moldy. There was an old coal bin in the corner. He supposed that the worship hall had a coal stove.

On the other side of the storage area, a door squeaked open on its hinges. Aurelia blinked into the darkness, her round face silhouetted by light from the worship hall. For a moment, she looked just like the giggly little cherub Luis used to carry on his shoulders.

"Are you alone?" she whispered in Spanish.

"Of course I'm alone," Monroy replied, not bothering to whisper. His sister really did seem crazy. "Who else would I be with?"

She didn't answer, only opened the door wider. Elizabeth was with her.

"What's going on?" Monroy demanded. "Look, if that *pendejo* Ortega touched you again—"

"He didn't touch me," said Aurelia.

"Then why did you run? He says you owe him money."

"He *called* you?"

"Of course he called me," said Monroy. "He figured I would know where you are."

"You didn't tell him, did you?"

"Aurelia . . ." Monroy was getting annoyed. "What is this all about?"

"Eli saw Ortega talking to a man. A very bad man who wants to hurt Eli."

Monroy exhaled in annoyance. "Why would anyone want to hurt Elizabeth?" He didn't wait for his sister to reply. She really did seem delusional to him. "Ortega told me about the man—"

"He did?"

"He said he's some sort of government official, probably sent by that doctor at the clinic, to check up on Elizabeth."

"You believe him?"

"No," said Monroy. "I don't. But I don't think you're acting rationally either."

Outside, Monroy heard a car slowly bumping along the buckled pavement up the hill, toward the church. Aurelia's face drained of color. She clutched Elizabeth tighter to her chest.

"You stay in here," said Monroy. "Let me find out what's going on."

He left the storage area and walked back outside. It took his eyes a moment to adjust to the glare of the late-day sun. He cupped a hand over his brow and stared past the gravestones to the driveway. There, parked next to his vehicle, was an old and unremarkable sedan. Dark blue, perhaps. Maybe a Nissan. A man got out of the driver's seat. He wasn't dressed like a government official. He was dressed like a farmworker, in a T-shirt, baseball cap, and baggy jeans. Maybe Ortega sent him to look for Aurelia and Elizabeth.

"Señor," he said in a respectful voice. "I'm so glad I found you. Your sister and niece—are they okay?"

"Who are you?" Monroy demanded. The man's left hand was wrapped in a bandage. His clothes didn't fit his demeanor. There was something calculated about him. The way his eyes were casing the church. The economy of his movements. "What do you want?"

"Señor Ortega is worried about them."

"Tell him they're okay."

"They're in the church?"

Monroy hesitated. He felt a trickle of sweat creep down his back as he stood facing this man with his dark, calculating eyes. He didn't see the gun leave the man's waistband. He only heard it. A loud pop that stopped the cicadas from buzzing. His last conscious thought as he dropped to the ground was that he was going to mess up his perfect white L.L. Bean shirt.

Chapter 46

The sound of a single gunshot pierced the quiet of the empty church. Eli flattened herself next to one of the pews that smelled of damp wood and rot. She saw dust motes sparkle in a shaft of light.

There were whole worlds in the quiet that followed. It reminded Eli of the time when she was small, and someone set off a firecracker too close to her ear. There was a boom and then . . . nothing. Lips moved on the adults near her. People jostled her. Shone lights in her eyes. She saw it all from a great, disinterested distance. She'd forgotten how to breathe.

She turned her gaze to her mother. Seeing Aurelia cowering behind one of the pews snapped Eli out of her daze. She stood on the pew and peeked out one of the boarded-up windows. Her uncle was lying on the pavement, twitching, blood pouring from his ears. The man with the bandaged hand kicked him aside like a bag of garbage and began walking in the direction of the cemetery.

In the direction of the rear door of the church.

"Mami. The man," Eli whispered. "He's coming for us. What do we do?"

Aurelia balled herself up in a corner, shivering. Her eyes had the look of a stray dog who had been beaten into submission. There was no time to try to figure out her mother's phone. Eli had no idea who she would call anyway or whether they would understand her Spanish. Within minutes, the man from the bus terminal would walk in that back door, find Eli and her mother cowering behind the pews, and shoot them the same way he'd just shot her uncle.

Her only hope was to fight back. But with what? Her left wrist was still in a cast. Her body had grown sinewy and tough from work in the fields. Still, she was a little girl in size and strength. Plus, the man had a gun. She couldn't imagine how she'd be able to defend herself.

She scanned the interior of the worship hall in the dim light. There were discarded cups and candy wrappers on the floor between the pews. Eli saw nothing else except a big black potbelly coal stove that jutted out from a wall between two pews. The stove was so old, the paint was rusted orange in places. The hearth beneath was scratched and streaked with soot. There was no coal bucket or shovel or poker for the fire.

The rear door to the storage entrance slowly creaked open. In a matter of seconds, the man would walk across that small room, up the three steps, and into the worship hall. He would shoot them as easily as he'd shot her uncle. It was a horrible way to die. In Guatemala, Eli had once witnessed a shooting. Two young men were arguing over a girl. The young man who got shot lay on the pavement, screaming in pain. It seemed like an eternity before an ambulance came to help him. Eli later heard he'd died.

Eli willed her hands to keep working, keep searching for a way to fight back. She opened the stove and shoved her hands inside, feeling them cake with a powdery blend of soot and dust that turned her hands and her cast black with the effort. She felt around for anything removable. She heard a scrape, then felt a lift of something heavy in her good hand. Her right hand.

A removable grate. It looked like a giant waffle on a stick.

She pulled it out of the stove, feeling the weight and heft of it, the momentum as she swung it in her right hand. It felt like a cast iron frying pan. She flattened herself against the frame of the door that sealed the storage area from the worship hall. She waited, her breath balled so tight in her chest that her lungs burned with each breath. Her entire body thrummed with a nervous energy. If someone asked her to run ten kilometers barefoot on glass right now, she believed she could do it.

The door handle turned slowly. And then all at once, the man kicked it open. The door swung back on Eli, toppling her off her feet, causing her to drop the grate, which clanged loudly on the wooden floor. She should have been dead right there, but the man must have mistaken the sound for something that dropped off a wall when he kicked the door in. He froze and listened. Aurelia was whimpering behind a pew.

The worship hall was dim. The man moved slowly, his eyes taking time to adjust to the shadows. Eli crouched behind the door, still on her hands and knees, feeling for the heavy cast iron grate before her. She was too small to hit him in the head or even the shoulders. She didn't have the strength to lift the grate high over her head. What she needed most of all was power. The power to bring him down and hurt him. So she settled for the one thing she knew she could do with just one good swing of her right arm.

Hit him in the back of his knees.

She swung the grate hard. The man crumpled before he could turn. He dropped to the wood floor and squeezed the trigger of his gun. The shot went wild, splintering the back of one of the pews. Eli paid no attention. He was on the ground now. She swung and swung again. The man didn't move. She was glad it was dark in the church. She didn't want to see the details of what she had done. She flinched as her mother put a hand on her shoulder.

"It's okay. It's okay, *cariño*. Leave him. We need to help Luis."

Eli dropped the grate. She was breathing like she'd run up the mountain behind Nejapa as she walked with her mother out of the church and into the light. Eli looked down at her hands, black with soot and flecked with blood. She couldn't believe they were hers. She stood staring at them in the sunlight. She hadn't been scared when it was happening, but now, she shook violently. Her mother, ironically, seemed to have snapped back to her senses. She was kneeling over her brother, pressing down on his blood-smeared neck.

"He's alive," she said to Eli. "We've got to get him to the hospital." Aurelia pulled out the cheap phone Luis had given her, but they couldn't get cell phone reception.

"I can't leave my brother here to die," said Aurelia.

"What can we do?" asked Eli.

Aurelia fished out Luis's car keys from his pocket. "I'll drive him. To the clinic in Petersville. That doctor can help us. It's not far."

It was true her mother had driven in Guatemala. But only rarely. She didn't know her brother's car or the American roads.

"Please, Eli, help me," said her mother. "We can't stay here near that man's body. Who knows what the police will say? Luis needs help."

"Okay," said Eli.

"Dr. Carrasco will know what to do," said Aurelia. "We have to try."

Chapter 47

Vega was still at Watkins Farm interviewing some of the laborers when the state police got a report of gunfire near a residence on Hagerstown Road.

"Where's Hagerstown Road?" Vega asked the state police captain, Ross.

"'Bout a mile from here," said Ross. "Used to be the main road to Petersville before the Route Forty-three bypass. Only one shot was reported. Could be hunters taking game out of season."

"You gonna check it out?" asked Vega.

"Heading over now," said Ross, motioning to the younger trooper, Ketchum. "We're about done here anyway." Ross had put out an alert on Luis Monroy's vehicle. He'd dispatched a state police cruiser to his house. They had the mother's and daughter's real names now. They had the uncle's address. It was only a matter of time before they tracked them down.

"I have to drive back to Petersville anyway," said Vega. "Mind if I tag along behind you?"

Ketchum said nothing. He was probably still smarting from making a fool of himself speaking stilted Spanish in front of the English-speaking orchard foreman. The captain jutted out his chin. Like most cops, he didn't love outsiders in his jurisdiction. "Just don't get in the way."

Vega followed the dark blue state police SUV out of the orchard. Ketchum was behind the wheel, Ross riding shotgun. The roads were twisty and unmarked. Vega was glad he was following them. Hagerstown Road was the definition of rural. It had a creek meandering alongside it. Woods and fields were interspersed with run-down cabins and trailers. Two miles in, the state police vehicle slowed next to a trailer home set back in a field littered with old car parts and—surprisingly—two new ATVs.

Ketchum turned onto the residence's long, gravel and dirt driveway. Vega thought about parking in front, but he'd be too far away from the house to know what was going on, so he followed the troopers up the driveway. Ross got out of his vehicle and motioned for Vega to stay in his truck. Fine by him. At a pen that enclosed a portion of the property in back, two large rottweilers barked and bared their teeth.

Ross and Ketchum were welcome to do the honors.

The trailer home appeared to be reasonably well cared-for, with a wooden deck and awning out front and an American flag on a flagpole surrounded by a planting of red and white flowers. The awning bathed the entry in shadows. Ketchum opened a screen door and knocked. It took a long time before it opened, revealing an older, heavyset white woman with a cane. Ross asked her some questions. She opened her screen door wider and gestured to the land behind the pen where her rottweilers paced. After a few minutes, she closed her door. Ketchum returned to the SUV. Ross ambled over to Vega's truck.

"She called it in, all right," said the captain. "One shot. It came from the direction of the Green Valley Baptist Church just up the road."

"A church?" asked Vega.

"It's vacant. Long abandoned," said Ross. "She thought it could be hooligans—her word." He smiled. He had a kind face when he smiled. Like he much preferred shooting the breeze with civilians to arresting them.

"I'll follow you."

Ross shook his head. "Don't need an escort."

"I'm heading that way anyway."

Ross exhaled pointedly. Vega could see him weighing the value of turning this into an argument. "All right, Vega. But that's the last stop on this tour bus. After that, you cut loose."

"Gotcha."

Vega gave Ketchum enough room to exit first. He followed. Within minutes, he was at Green Valley. He could see where it had once been a beautiful New England–style church. It sat on a rise, overlooking the road. The bell was gone from the bell tower. The arched windows were boarded over. The white clapboard had weathered to gray. The buckled driveway was empty. No cars. No people. There was a wooded area behind the church. Vega wondered if the shot had come from there.

The state police SUV stopped short of the small parking area on top. Ross and Ketchum jumped out, their felt trooper hats bathing their faces in shadow. They were alarmed by something in front of their vehicle. Vega drove up behind them and got out. At first, he saw nothing. A gentle breeze fanned the hillside. The sun dipped below the undulating land to the west. Only the tops of the tallest oaks and maples shone with a fierce orange tinge. The rest of the land had softened and been bleached of color like an old sepia photograph.

"What did you find?" asked Vega, coming up behind Ross and Ketchum. Their faces were solemn.

On the cracked blacktop, Vega saw a pool of blood.

It was about the circumference of a snare drum, still gelatinous and glistening. There was also a path of blood about the width of a human body trailing off from the pool and then abruptly stopping a short distance down the driveway, as if something had been dragged to that point and then deposited into a vehicle.

"Still think it's hunters off season?" asked Vega.

Ross turned away from Vega and paced the driveway, his eyes scouring the pavement.

"No shell casing," Ross noted. "I don't know of many hunters who retrieve their shell casings after a kill." Ross mumbled something to Ketchum, who walked back to their patrol car. He was probably calling in the state police's crime-scene unit.

"We should check out the church," said Vega.

"*We?*" Ross bristled, then reconsidered. Three cops are better than two. "Ketchum and I will do the interior search. You can do the exterior."

Vega had investigated enough violent crimes in his life to know that blood could mean anything. It could have come from a perp who already took off—or a victim still alive, collapsed somewhere in the bushes or inside the church. He started with the area closest to the church, figuring a wounded victim wouldn't go far. He saw nothing. No blood. No fibers snagged on broken branches or matted depressions in the weeds. Nothing to suggest someone had crawled there for help.

He wandered the graveyard to the sound of bird chatter, stepping over crumbling headstones so old, the names and dates had worn away. Behind the cemetery was a thick line of trees, now dark and blurry in the waning light. A good place for an attacker to disappear. But if so, where was the victim?

"Hey, Vega," Ross called to him from the back door of the church. "Come over here."

"You find a body?"

"Something else."

At the door, Ross handed Vega a pair of blue surgical gloves. He slipped them on and stepped inside. It was a storage area of some sort, illuminated by the cracks of faint light wafting in from the worship hall. Ross shone a flashlight on one of the shelves. Vega could see a bloody handprint, along with a trail of spatter on the floor that led up the three steps on the other side of the storage area to the worship hall.

Or led down *from* it. He couldn't say just yet.

Vega was careful to maneuver around the stains as he entered the hall. The church was already beginning to rot from within. Vega saw specks of black mold along one wall and watermarks on the pitched ceiling. The pews were bathed in shadows, their dark hulks like stalwart parishioners, facing an empty dais.

Vega followed Ross's flashlight beam to a bloodied piece of cast iron that looked like some sort of grating. His eyes went straightaway to the potbelly stove between two sets of pews. The door to the stove was open.

Ketchum walked over to the stove, knelt down, and poked his flashlight inside. "That grate's from the stove all right, Cap."

Ross walked between the pews, shining his flashlight under the seats. The floorboards creaked in response. "We have a report of one gunshot that may or may not be related. We've got evidence of a violent encounter inside the church and more of the same on the driveway. What we don't have is a victim."

"I can't believe it's not somehow related to the Rosales girl and her mother taking off," said Vega.

Ross turned to Ketchum. "Check in with Saratoga Springs. See if they've caught up with Beltran."

"Yes, Captain."

Ketchum walked out of the church, his duty boots echoing in the cavernous space. The blood was drying in the heat, giving off the stink of rotting meat. Flies had found their way inside and were now buzzing and settling around the smear. Vega waved them away as he bent over the grate.

"Something isn't right here," said Vega.

"What do you mean?"

"We have evidence of a bloody encounter inside the church and an even worse one on the driveway," said Vega. "But they're separate and distinct. There's no trail connecting them."

"You think two different attacks occurred?"

"Possibly," said Vega. "One person was attacked in the church and the other, on the driveway. Maybe the person on the driveway was attacked in retaliation. But then, who removed him? There had to be a third person at the scene. Someone lucid enough to drive the injured away."

Ross walked Vega out of the church. The bird chatter had vanished. The gravestones were fading into long shadows on the mossy ground. An evening breeze kicked up, cooling the sweat on Vega's skin. Adele had to be wondering what had happened to him. When Ross excused himself to speak to Ketchum, Vega texted her.

Got delayed. Sorry. Checking out an abandoned church. No sign of mother and daughter. Be at the clinic inside 25 minutes. XXXJ.

Vega waited for Adele to respond. She didn't. He checked his LIFE 360, the networking app that they'd programmed to show each other's locations. It showed that she was still inside the clinic. Maybe she was helping out in some way and couldn't get to her phone.

"Vega!" Ross was leaning over the driver's side of his SUV where Ketchum was sitting.

Vega walked over. "You get a lead on the mother and daughter?"

"Nothing," said Ross. "Not on the uncle either. But there is something you should know." Ross's serious tone loosened something in Vega's gut. "One of our units tracked Beltran's cell phone to a UPS truck. He must have tossed it inside. We have no idea where he is."

A second state police cruiser pulled onto the driveway,

its light bar flashing red and blue against the weathered siding of the church. This was a crime scene now. Something bloody and terrible had gone down here. The people involved had left in at least one vehicle. *To get help? To get away?* Vega couldn't say. He felt like someone was trawling a razor down his back. The slightest shift in his body—the most incremental exhale—might draw blood.

Vega cast a glance at his phone. Still no reply from Adele.

"This road," said Vega. "You said it leads to Petersville?"

"That's right."

"There's an emergency medical clinic in Petersville," said Vega. "Helping Hands. A doctor by the name of Miranda Carrasco runs it."

"You think whoever got wounded here might have driven there?"

"It's a possibility," said Vega. "My girlfriend's there now."

"Can you call or text her and find out if anyone's come in?"

"I just did," said Vega. "She's not picking up."

Chapter 48

Adele was sitting in the waiting area of the medical clinic, talking to two farmworkers, the last patients of the day, when the front doors burst open. A woman raced in, her jeans and T-shirt drenched in blood.

"I need Dr. Carrasco, please!" she said frantically. "My brother's in the car with a gunshot wound to his head."

The receptionist buzzed the intercom to explain the situation and then immediately dialed 911. Dr. Carrasco and her nurse emerged from the back seconds later. The nurse had an emergency kit in hand as they bolted for the parking lot, following the woman to her car.

That's when Adele saw her. The girl from the photograph. She was even shorter than Adele had imagined, with a face that looked both younger and older than her nearly twelve years. She, too, was covered in blood. And something else. Something that looked like soot. It was all over her hands and arms, worked into the creases and under the nails. There were smudges on her cheeks and chin. Her black hair had loosened from her ponytail, dangling down one side of her face.

The two farmworkers, sensing they wouldn't get treatment and might even be questioned by police, left the building. It was just Adele now. Adele and the girl and the receptionist on the phone to 911.

The girl stood in a corner, staring down at her filthy hands and the blackened cast on her left wrist. Adele walked over to the child and crouched in front of her.

"*Mija,*" Adele said tenderly. "I have been looking everywhere for you. You and your mother. There are people who want to help you. Please tell me what happened."

The girl stared at her hands and said nothing.

"Dr. Carrasco is a friend of mine," Adele explained. "She is here to help. We both are. My name is Adele. What is your name?"

"Eli." Her voice felt more like an exhale than a word. Adele wasn't sure she heard her.

"Eli?"

The girl nodded.

"Can you tell me what happened, Eli?"

The girl's eyes never left her hands. "A bad man drove to this church where we were hiding and shot my uncle in the head."

Adele's chest tightened. The words ricocheted through her brain, bouncing off all the contradictory information she'd been processing these past few days. Vega said a cartel hit man was after the girl. Vega said the hit man was in Saratoga Springs, fifty miles north of here.

"Where is this bad man?" asked Adele.

"He's . . . dead."

"Dead, where?"

"At the church with the boarded-up windows," said Eli. "He shot my uncle and came after my mother and me. So I . . . there was this metal thing in the coal stove and I . . . I hit him with it and killed him."

Adele straightened just as Carrasco and the nurse walked the mother back in. The mother was sobbing. The nurse walked ahead, removing a set of bloody gloves from her hands, wrapping them one inside the other. Carrasco did the same, balling the inside-out gloves in her pocket and putting an arm around the mother. Her pace had lost its urgency. She leaned over to the receptionist. "Tell nine-one-one the patient coded." Adele didn't need anyone to tell her the uncle was dead. "We need the police here before we can do anything else."

The nurse reappeared with a sheet that she took out to the parking lot, presumably to cover the body. Adele heard a ding on her phone. *Jimmy.* Now she was the one with an urgent matter. He'd have to wait. Adele took Dr. Carrasco aside and told her what Eli had said about the dead man at the church.

"Wait," said Carrasco. "Someone *else* is dead too?"

"Can you print out a copy of the photo you took of José Gonzalez the other day when you treated him?" asked Adele.

Carrasco's face drained of color. She seemed to sense that there was a lot she was missing here—and it all circled back to that patient she'd treated with the bitten hand. She dashed back into her office and emerged minutes later with the head shot of Gonzalez.

"Eli," asked Adele, "is this the bad man? The man at the church you killed?"

The girl nodded. Her mother spoke in a rapid, breathless tone, wiping tears with her bloody hands. "He shot my brother on the driveway. Left him to bleed to death, then came inside the church after us. He has been following my daughter ever since she saw him in a bus terminal days ago."

"His name is Oscar Beltran-Parra," said Adele. "He shot and killed a court officer in Broad Plains and wounded a judge. Your daughter saw him at the bus terminal shortly after the shooting. He was planning to kill your daughter to keep her from talking to the police."

"*Dios mío!*" Aurelia made the sign of the cross. "But what will happen to us now? My brother is dead. The police will take us away and deport us for this. We will lose our bid for asylum."

"That won't happen," Adele assured her. "You and your daughter are crime victims—not criminals. My boyfriend is a cop. Let me text him and tell him what's going on." Adele pulled out her phone. She read the text Jimmy sent her a few minutes earlier:

Got delayed. Sorry. Checking out an abandoned church. No sign of mother and daughter. Be at the clinic inside 25 minutes. XXXJ.

No sign of mother and daughter.

Adele stared at the words. Vega had to have gone to the same church Eli was referring to. And yes, as a cop, he could be close-mouthed. But if he'd seen Beltran's body there, wouldn't he have mentioned it?

"Eli," Adele said evenly. "Are you *sure* that you killed this man?"

"I think so," said the child. "I don't know."

"He wasn't moving," said Aurelia.

"Did he have a car?" asked Adele.

"A car? Yes," said Aurelia. "We left it there."

Then where was it? Why hadn't Jimmy mentioned it? Why hadn't he mentioned Beltran?

"How fast do you think the police will get here?" Adele asked Carrasco.

"They usually respond within ten minutes," said Carrasco. "Why?"

"That may not be fast enough."

Chapter 49

Vega heard the 911 dispatch report over Captain Ross's radio. A woman and child had brought in a gunshot victim to the clinic in Petersville. Male. Hispanic. Dead on arrival. Police response requested.

Vega didn't have to know more details than that. He could fill in the blanks from there for Aurelia Rosales and her daughter, Elizabeth. They'd driven to the clinic, probably in the missing uncle's car. Which meant the gunshot victim was likely the missing uncle. There was only one person who could have shot him:

Oscar Beltran.

If the mother and child had made it to the clinic, Beltran couldn't be far behind.

A sick sensation swept through Vega. He'd left Adele at the clinic so she would be safe. And in so doing, he'd put her in the path of a killer.

"Aurelia and Elizabeth Rosales are the mother and child," said Vega. "They're in danger. So's my girlfriend. She's there too."

Ross patted the air. He seemed to think Vega was overreacting. "Sounds like whoever got shot was the danger," said Ross. "And he's dead."

"Ask," said Vega. "I'm betting the victim was the uncle we were looking for: Luis Monroy."

"We'll get a victim ID as soon as the police arrive."

Vega suspected that Ross was used to a different pace of police work in these parts. His cases were likely people he'd already had contact with in the community or investigations that took many months.

"Captain, listen to me, please," Vega begged. "Oscar Beltran's a professional killer. A *sicario*. He's made some big mistakes here, sure. But he's not going to stop until the job is done. He knows the clinic. He probably knows that's where they'd head to try to save the uncle's life. We don't have much time."

Ross's expression changed. A light kicked on in his eyes. "Update dispatch on the situation," he told Ketchum. "Advise our department to send a SWAT team ASAP."

"Will do," said Ketchum. He folded himself into the driver's seat and got on the radio. "The local police are on their way. ETA, three minutes," he called out. "I'm getting an ETA on SWAT now."

Vega fumbled for his phone and frantically dialed Adele. He heard her recorded voice, honey-smooth, asking him to leave a message. He wanted to reach through the receiver and grab her. Pull her to safety. Beltran was going to kill them all unless the police killed him first. There was simply no other way out of this.

He left a message about Beltran, did the same on a text, and then opened the Life 360 app. He saw her little face on the icon—that picture he'd snapped of her at the beach earlier this summer, with her sunglasses on top of her head and a sheen of sunscreen picking up the glint of sun on her nose. The icon was still at the clinic. He hoped that was a good sign.

"Ketchum and I are heading over to Petersville," said Ross. "Everyone has been apprised of the situation. You can follow in your truck if you'd like."

Petersville was twenty long minutes away. "Okay," said

Vega. "If you get anything on the radio, can you call me on my phone?" Vega gave Ross his number and took Ross's.

The men retreated to their vehicles. Vega made a three-point turn and followed the state police SUV. Ketchum flipped the lights and sirens, then roared through a forty-five-mile-per-hour zone at twenty above the limit. Vega followed in his wake. He had his cell phone in a holder on his dashboard. He pulled up his Life 360 app again and hit the icon for Adele.

He had to take his eyes briefly off the road twice to be sure he was seeing what he was seeing.

The icon was moving.

It was heading north. Away from the clinic at a high rate of speed. Which meant she was traveling by car. *Whose* car? Had Adele hitched a ride out of the danger zone with someone? Carrasco perhaps? But why wouldn't she call Vega and tell him?

Maybe she can't.

The thought chilled Vega. There was no reason for Adele to leave the relative safety of the clinic unless someone was forcing her to.

Vega asked Siri to dial Captain Ross's number. He hit the speaker button. "Cap, I need a status update."

Silence. Vega thought maybe the call had been dropped. He hated cell service in these areas. But after a few seconds, Ross's voice came on the line. It was hoarse and tentative, almost like he was formulating the words in a foreign language.

"Vega? You were right about Beltran."

Vega lifted a hand to his neck and felt the tender bruised flesh from yesterday. It hadn't bothered him all day, but it ached now. Vega felt like he was watching himself from a great distance, this little, powerless speck of a figure racing through these dark, back-country roads, every minute a minute too long. This was the moment he would revisit over and over again for the rest of his life. No matter how many years he lived, he would wake at night and feel the sweat on his back, the way it plastered his T-shirt to his skin. He would feel the pins-and-needles sensation in his fingers, the ossified weight of his bones. And he would bargain with God for those few hours back when he could remake the decision to leave Adele at the clinic.

"Where is Beltran?"

"SWAT is tracking his vehicle. We'll get him. Don't worry—"

"Goddammit, Captain! Answer my question."

"He went to the clinic and took the Rosales females hostage," said Ross. "He took your girlfriend with them."

Chapter 50

Stay calm. Wasn't that what Jimmy always told her? *Panic makes for bad decisions. Breathe. Stay in the moment. Think only a few steps ahead.*

Adele tried to take a breath, but it felt like breathing through a cocktail straw. Dr. Carrasco's white Honda Pilot SUV that Beltran was forcing her to drive smelled of rubbing alcohol and wet dog. Adele wished she wasn't allergic. It was one more complication she didn't need, accelerating along an unfamiliar, unlit road at twilight in what was now a stolen vehicle. Her eyes began to tear.

"Stop crying!" Beltran barked in perfect English from the seat behind her.

"I'm not crying. I'm allergic to dogs."

Beltran cursed in Spanish. He tightened his right arm around Eli in back and waved the gun in her face. The girl whimpered. Her mother mumbled prayers in the front passenger seat, crossing herself with hands still encrusted with her brother's blood. Beltran had calculated correctly that he didn't need to train the gun on three women. He just needed to train it on the girl in the backseat with him. Her mother and Adele would do nothing to jeopardize the child.

Adele snuck a glance at her captor in the rearview mirror. Blood crusted his face and scalp and the front of his shirt. His left eye was swollen shut. The palm of his left hand was wrapped in a dirty bandage. She noticed something else too. The whites of his eyes were turning red. He was sneezing and tearing.

Oscar Beltran was also allergic to dogs.

Could she use this in some way? He was already a damaged and desperate man, barely able to see. Still, Adele knew that desperate people do desperate things—not all of them logical. He could be more dangerous, not less, in his current weakened state.

The road had been wooded and darkly claustrophobic as they drove out of town, save for one gas station and the lights of a couple of broken-down trailer homes. Now it opened into thick, impenetrable fields of corn pockmarked by the shadowy outlines of swaybacked barns. Occasionally, a car roared past in the other direction, its headlight beams strafing her field of vision. But otherwise, Adele felt utterly alone.

No one could help them now. If they were going to survive this, they would have to do it by themselves.

Beltran took the gun away from Eli's face and waved it between the front two seats. "Give me your phones," he demanded in Spanish, between sneezes.

Adele's heart sank. She knew Vega had been trying to call and text her. He was likely following her location on the app they shared. Beltran probably figured as much. Adele made no move to retrieve her phone, so Beltran snatched the whole bag and threw it out the window. He did the same to Aurelia.

Adele tried to locate her voice. It spoke to her rapid-fire in her brain, in both English and Spanish. Yet when she tried to place the words on her tongue, they came out halting and distorted. All she could manage was: "Where are we going?"

"I will tell you when we get there," said Beltran in English. Then he leaned forward, his sour breath steaming up the back of her neck. "You have a lovely house, by the way. I considered staying and showing you how a real man does things. But . . . I had a job to do. There was no time for play."

He caught her eyes in the rearview mirror. Adele tried to swallow back the fear his words unleashed in her. He was doing it on purpose. To control her. Her logical brain understood that it made no difference now what he might have done then. *Stay in the moment.* But still, she couldn't hold back the terror it unleashed in her. Her skin felt brittle and chilled. The saliva drained from her mouth. Her tongue tasted like she'd been sucking on a rusty nail. And then she heard it—the sound of a helicopter whirring overhead. In her rearview mirror, she caught the flashing red-and-blue lights of a police cruiser drawing closer.

They weren't alone anymore. She couldn't decide if this was better or worse.

"Keep driving," said Beltran. He ducked low in the rear seat and powered down the window. He shoved his gun out the open window and fired three shots. Eli yelped in response. The cruiser eased up on the accelerator, staying just out of range. Adele saw the dilemma they were in. The police couldn't rescue any of them without first killing Beltran. Beltran knew this. Maybe that was the point. His failures—beginning with the botched shooting at the courthouse—would not go unnoticed by superiors. He was going to die one way or another. But he was not going alone.

"Turn! Here!" Beltran shouted suddenly.

The only "here" Adele could see was a dirt road between two eight-foot-tall rows of corn. She turned sharply right, the car dipping and rebounding as the wheels fought for footing on the rutted path. The brightness of the headlights bleached the tangle of vegetation before her.

"Drive! Drive!" Beltran commanded, jabbing her with

the barrel of his gun. She pushed her foot down on the accelerator and lurched forward, listening to the thump of stalks hitting the sides of the vehicle, their long, downturned leaves brushing against her windshield like ghostly appendages. Vega's words pushed through the chatter in her head. *Think only a few steps ahead.* What was ahead? A barn perhaps? Was he going to lock them all inside? Force a standoff with police?

She drove on, the potholes tossing them about like they were on an amusement park ride. They crested a small hill and her high beams picked up the faded red siding of a barn.

"Turn off your headlights," hissed Beltran.

Adele fumbled to find the switch. She was shaking. This wasn't her car. Beltran, impatient, leaned forward. Eli spotted her chance. She threw herself against the passenger door and pushed it open. Her mother reacted instantly, springing from the front seat and grabbing her daughter like they were still umbilically attached. She threw the girl in front of her to shield her from Beltran and raced them into the leafy jungle of corn. Within seconds, they had vanished.

Beltran grabbed Adele around the neck and shoved the barrel of the gun up against the side of her head.

"You, señora," he murmured, "are staying with me."

He ordered Adele out of the car and dragged her into the cornfield. She stumbled to keep up. The stalks closed in around her, cutting off the light. The crunch of dried leaves mimicked her own hard breathing. Above, helicopter searchlights raked the field, their rotors beating down, violently swaying the deep green and yellow fields of just-harvested corn. Sirens wailed somewhere in the distance. Adele heard cars pulling up short, spitting gravel. Doors slamming. The click and slide of weaponry.

A police officer spoke through a bullhorn in American-accented Spanish. "Oscar Beltran. We know you're out there and have you surrounded. Release your hostages."

Hostages—plural. Wherever Aurelia and Eli were, they hadn't made themselves known to police.

"Say one word and I will kill you," Beltran whispered into Adele's ear.

"I can help you," Adele pleaded softly. "I can negotiate your surrender and keep you alive."

"You *are* keeping me alive," said Beltran. "You're my hostage."

"The police aren't going to let you walk out of here."

"Then neither of us are walking out."

His words stilled the breath in Adele's lungs. This was it. His final showdown. She could see through a clearing where they were headed now. *The barn.* He would hold Adele until he couldn't anymore, and then both of them would die—by his hand or the police's, he didn't care.

Adele didn't fear death at that moment. What she feared was the pain she'd cause Sophia, who would grow into womanhood without a mother. It made Adele angry and the anger sharpened her wits.

Stay in the moment, she reminded herself again.

She felt Beltran's body flinch as he pulled her to his right. The jolt was unexpected, like something had spooked him. She saw his swollen eyes dart nervously to a long, slender handle of something—a broom or shovel that a worker had left in the field. It was lying on its side, bathed in shadow.

In the dim light, with his limited vision, Beltran must have thought it was a snake. She was sure of it. She'd found his weak spot. *Snakes.* He was afraid of snakes.

She tried to slow her breathing. She would have only seconds to make this work. She waited until the helicopter had passed over them again and retreated. Then she turned her head to the left—his bad side: bad eye, bad hand. "*La culebra!*" she shouted, hoping the word for "snake" in his native tongue would elicit a more visceral response.

He recoiled like he'd been bitten. She used the momentum to push away and pitch herself forward into the thick stalks. She ran blindly, leaves slicing through her shirt, corn silk and tassels in her hair. She could see only as far as her hands. She knew a bullet could travel farther and braced herself for the impact, unsure whether the absence of pain was from adrenaline or luck.

She couldn't see the barn anymore. She tried to follow the pulse of red-and-blue flashing lights on the corn stalks, but she couldn't gauge direction. Her lungs were burning. She had a stitch in her side. The thrum of the helicopter drowned out every other noise. She had no idea if she'd lost Beltran or if he was right behind her.

And then she felt it. The vice clamp of a man's large hand squeezing her wrist. She tried to pull away but he grabbed her from behind and dug his nails into her skin. Then he pushed her, face first, onto the soft muddy ground between the rows of stalks. Her mouth and nose filled with dirt and bits of leaves. He pounced on top of her and wrapped his hands around her neck.

"No! Please!" she choked out. She twisted her neck to try to breathe. The corn stalks swayed above her, shadowy against the deepening sky, like old women in shrouds, their arms clasped in prayer.

One of the shrouds had a shovel.

Adele blinked. She saw the figure now. Not a shroud. A woman in a blood-stained T-shirt. She hoisted the shovel high in the air and brought it down on Beltran's head. Adele heard a muffled thud, like a car door closing, and then Beltran collapsed and rolled off her body.

Aurelia Rosales lifted the shovel again and again brought it down on his head. Once. Twice. Three times, until her daughter Eli took her by the elbow and gently pulled her away.

Aurelia was breathing hard, tears streaming down her blood-smeared face. She gripped the handle of the shovel tightly and stood between her daughter and Beltran's body.

"No man will make us unsafe again," Aurelia said softly. "No man."

Chapter 51

Adele sat for a long time in the back of an ambulance, a thick blanket wrapped around her trembling body with Vega beside her, clutching her hand. Night had fallen, but the cordon of emergency vehicles made it feel like daylight outside. She was too shell-shocked to form more than a few words of thanks to Aurelia Rosales and her daughter Eli for saving her life before they were whisked off to a state police SUV with tinted glass windows and driven away.

"Where are they going?" Adele asked Vega.

"I don't think we'll get to know that," said Vega. "The girl's still a witness."

"Against a dead man?"

"The girl and her mother are vulnerable if they stay here," said Vega. "My guess is they will be resettled someplace where the cartel can't find them."

"Will she get to go to school? Will they be able to have access to their family?"

"I'm certain the FBI will make sure those things happen."

They spent Saturday night at Vega's cabin and Sunday at Adele's. Neither of them slept much. They held each other and made promises. To work less. To enjoy life more. When Sophia arrived back home Sunday night from

Cape Cod, Adele hugged her so tight, the child squirmed out of her grip.

"Mom! I didn't get eaten by a shark, you know!"

On Sunday night, Isadora Jenkins called Vega and told him that the county had settled the suit for $1.5 million. He accepted the news quietly. It was what it was. He had taken a life. He had tried to atone in all the ways he could—including offering up his life to save someone else.

He was ready to move on.

"Be at the courthouse by ten a.m. Monday," Jenkins told him. "Judge Edgerton will officially accept the plea bargain and seal the case. Which at least guarantees that Carver can't speak to the press."

Vega supposed he had to be thankful for small favors. In truth, he had bigger things on his mind.

He showed up to the courthouse at eight-thirty that morning with two coffees and a bag of doughnuts. He walked straight downstairs to the surveillance room in the basement and waited for Officer Daley to show up.

Vega had bought all the major newspapers that morning. He skimmed them while he waited. None of them mentioned the deaths of Oscar Beltran or Luis Monroy. The crimes were too far away, the players, too seemingly insignificant. Hewitt had briefed Vega last night and told him that Oscar Beltran's DNA matched the toothpicks found at both the bus terminal and Adele's house. But the FBI was sitting on that information. Yes, they believed that Beltran was the courthouse shooter. But they had no idea why. Everything pointed so neatly to Richter or one of Richter's associates. Yet all they had on Richter was his trail of gun sales to felons and extremists—one of whom called in the bomb threat on La Casa.

Beltran's motives were an enigma.

Vega was out of both investigations. He understood that. And yet, it bothered him on some elemental level that, even in death, Beltran had managed to slip away again. He was a professional hit man. He didn't shoot people he wasn't ordered to shoot. So why go after a judge who had freed him?

At 9:05, Daley sauntered to the locked surveillance-room door, his shoulders as slack as ever, his paunch barely contained beneath his Kevlar vest and uniform shirt. His lizard eyes tightened at the sight of Vega.

"Whatever it is, I already gave it to the FBI."

"Ten minutes—that's all I'm asking." Vega held out the coffees and the bag of doughnuts, hoping that might persuade him. "I just want to review the video of the shooting one more time."

"Why? From what I hear, they got some neo-Nazi for it. The case is solved."

Vega blinked his surprise. He'd expected Hewitt and his people to be very tight-lipped on the subject of both Richter and Beltran since both would be ongoing investigations. He was taken aback that someone would be floating the wrong version of the story. He wondered if that was intentional. At least until the November elections, it might be better for the FBI to be the heroes foiling a white supremacist assassin rather than pointing out a cartel hit man whose murky motives might undermine the judge—and by extension, the attorney general who supports her.

"Ten minutes, Daley. I won't bother you again. You have my word."

Daley grumbled, but relented, given the coffee and bag of doughnuts Vega was proffering. He accepted the offerings, then turned on the computer and keyed in a password. He clicked on a screen and drew the arrow over to the correct footage by time and date.

"Ten minutes," he said, taking the coffee and doughnuts with him. "I'm gonna take a leak, have my breakfast, and check my phone. I come back, you better be finished."

"Gotcha."

Daley left. Vega settled himself at the computer screen and pulled up the video, rewinding to three minutes before the shooting. He set the speed at normal from that point forward and watched the security lot come into view. He saw the two vans parked in the lot. It was otherwise empty.

He hunched forward and waited until the small white golf cart puttered into the frame, traveling north from the records building to the courthouse. He took in the last moments of Darryl Williams's life. His loose and easy posture as he sat behind the wheel. The way his shaved head glistened in the sunlight. He noted Judge Spruce directly behind Williams, that white streak of hair flowing prominently down the left side of her face. To her right sat her clerk, Albert Pearsall, hands in his lap, sitting stiffly back against the seat. Everything about Pearsall had that erect and proper bearing. With his small gray mustache and gold-rimmed spectacles, he looked more like a member of the British Parliament going to vote than a court clerk.

Nothing about the three figures looked out of the ordinary. Nothing gave off any hint of what was to follow. Vega slowed down the video speed as Williams stopped the golf cart near the rear entrance door to the courthouse and exited the vehicle. He stood beside the vehicle and pivoted to the rear, facing Spruce.

From what Vega now knew about the angle of the shot from the bus terminal roof, Williams presented a perfect shot right now if Beltran had wanted to kill him. His entire body was out of the vehicle, perpendicular to the line of fire. Beltran could have shot him cleanly from the right at any time from this point forward. He didn't need to wait until Williams bent down to make the same shot.

Which proved from a geometry standpoint, at least to Vega, that Williams was never the target.

Williams extended a hand to the judge to help her exit the vehicle. Spruce took it. Then Williams did something totally unexpected.

He leaned in.

Maybe Spruce needed more help. Maybe he wanted to tell her something. Vega couldn't say. But it was that lean in that killed him.

Vega followed the geometry lines of the shooting. He worked backward with the logic. Beltran had a perfect shot of Williams anytime he wanted to make it. But he also had a pretty good shot of Spruce too. True, she wasn't yet out of the vehicle. But she was seated directly behind Williams. Beltran was a professional. He knew how to shoot from a great distance. A lot of these guys are trained from early adolescence.

Beltran could have shot her as soon as the golf cart stopped. He could have shot her as she got out.

If he was aiming for her. If he'd *ever* been aiming for her.

Vega pulled out his phone and dialed Doug Hewitt's cell.

"I don't have any updates," said Hewitt.

"But I do," said Vega. "I've got to go into a proceeding at ten." He didn't say "settlement." He didn't want Hewitt to know the details. "Can you meet me after? I'd like to go over the shooting footage one more time with you."

"Why?" Hewitt sounded overwhelmed and irritated.

"You'll see."

There were just six people in the courtroom this time besides Vega and Judge Edgerton. The court officer. The court reporter. Bernard Carver and his client, Lucinda Ponce. Plus, Vega's two lawyers: Jenkins and Zaroff. The jury had been dismissed. There was nothing to do but listen to the judge sign off on the $1.5 million settlement and perhaps say a few words that might look good on his reelection record.

The whole sorry situation reminded Vega of his divorce proceedings. He had the same knot-tight stomach that overflowed with a combination of grief and anger for all the mistakes he'd made along the way and her betrayal at the end. He felt the same drowning sensation when he looked at the faces of everyone else in the room and realized that he was the only one with any skin in the game. Everyone else—Lucinda Ponce included—seemed to just want it over. Wendy had been like that too. She was, by that point after all, pregnant with another man's children and planning their marriage. She was moving on.

That's what everyone around him seemed to do on a regular basis.

Edgerton peered down at the paperwork before him. "I'm aware that both sides have agreed to the settlement amount," he said. "And while I may not always agree with the outcome of such cases, I feel myself duty-bound not to set the decision aside."

Edgerton looked up from the paperwork. "However, in this case, I am going to add a stipulation to the settlement." The judge turned to Zaroff. "Mr. Zaroff, I am going to order the county to pay the full amount of the settlement into an escrow account, to be paid in full as soon as Mr. Carver and Mrs. Ponce produce additional documentation that she was Mr. Ponce's lawful wife—"

"Your Honor," Carver sputtered. "My client doesn't have—"

The judge cut him off. "Mr. Carver, I am not asking for official documentation. I understand your assertion that such things are hard to come by in Honduras. I will accept photos, mementos, written statements from members of Mrs. Ponce's family—particularly members residing in the United States. In short"—Edgerton stared down at him—"I will accept *any* independently verifiable proof that Lucinda Ponce is his widow."

Edgerton turned his gaze now to Vega and his attorneys. "This escrow will be kept for one year. If, during the year, Mr. Carver brings this court acceptable proof, the full escrow amount will be released to the plaintiff and attorney. If not, after one year, the full amount will be returned to the county and Mr. Carver will be liable for all court costs."

Vega stared openmouthed at the judge. Edgerton never looked directly at Vega. But Vega felt something pass between them. The judge wasn't blind to Carver's manipulations. Nor was he unsympathetic to a genuine widow who'd lost her husband. He just wanted to be sure.

That felt fair to Vega. That's all he wanted in the end. He'd taken a man's life. No amount of money could change that. When he fired those shots, he had every reason to believe his life was in imminent danger. It was a mistake. Legally defensible. But a mistake, nonetheless. One way or another, Vega would carry it with him until he breathed his last breath.

"This isn't over," sneered Carver as he stomped out of the room. But Vega sensed by the way he left poor Lucinda Ponce standing there that it might be.

"Come," said Jenkins. "I'll buy you lunch. My treat."

"Another time, I promise," said Vega. "Right now, I've got someone I need to see."

Chapter 52

It was late afternoon by the time Vega finished up his meeting with Doug Hewitt and headed back to the courthouse, to the court clerk's temporary headquarters on the second floor. He expected to find Albert Pearsall diligently typing away beneath his assortment of British kitsch.

The desk was empty. The partition walls had been stripped. Vega found Lucille Bouchart in one of the adjoining cubicles. She was wearing teardrop silver earrings today. Another of her daughter's collection, he suspected. "Where's Albert?" asked Vega.

"You might still be able to catch up with him in the downstairs parking lot," she said cheerfully.

"He's cutting out early?"

"He's already said his good-byes."

"His . . . good-byes?"

"Oh." She blinked at him. "I thought you were coming to do the same. Albert put in his retirement papers this morning. He just finished cleaning out his cubicle."

"I didn't think he was retirement age," said Vega.

Bouchart leaned in confidentially. "Disability," she whispered. "The shooting was just too much for him, poor man. I know an officer such as yourself has to deal with such things. But . . . the truth is, we're all a little shaken."

"You say he's in the downstairs parking lot?"

"He left maybe five minutes ago with a box," she replied. "We're planning a big party for him when everyone gets back from summer vacation. We're going to invite a lot of the detectives who worked with him as well as all the court staff. I'll let you know the date once it's settled. It should be in the next week or two."

"A surprise party?"

"Just a party," she said. "Albert preferred it that way. If you miss him now, you can catch up with him later, I'm sure."

Vega took the stairs, two at a time. Court employees worked nine to five, so at 3:45, the downstairs garage was empty, save for Pearsall, who was stuffing a cardboard box into the rear of a dark gray, late-model Lexus SUV, carefully maneuvering it between two others. For a moment, Vega didn't think he was looking at Albert Pearsall at all. His gray hair was dyed ink-black. His mustache was missing. His gold-rimmed glasses had been replaced by a pair with black plastic frames. Vega had known Pearsall for probably more than a decade and the only thing about him that had changed in all that time was the deepening gray of his hair.

Vega walked softly toward him. Pearsall was so focused on getting the boxes to fit just right in the trunk that he didn't notice Vega until Vega was practically on top of him. His face seemed to pale under the harsh glare of the fluorescent lighting.

"Detective." He seemed momentarily flustered. "What are you doing down here?"

"I just heard upstairs that you're taking early retirement. You never mentioned it when I saw you the other day."

"I'd been thinking about it for a while. And then, after the shooting . . ." Pearsall's voice died in his chest. Vega noticed a thin band of sweat gathering on his upper lip where his mustache used to be.

Vega stepped closer to his trunk and noticed a white

form sitting on top of one of the boxes. A U.S. Postal Service form that Vega used himself when he wanted to suspend his mail delivery because he was going on vacation. Pearsall had filled it out already. He'd listed the "hold mail" period for thirty days from tomorrow—the longest amount of time the post office will hold mail.

Bouchart had just told Vega that they were having a retirement party for Pearsall in the next two weeks.

Vega gestured to the form. "Taking a break?"

"Um . . . yes. Getting away. Clearing my head."

"Where you going?"

"Going?"

"On vacation," said Vega.

"Oh, um—I don't know yet."

"And you'll be gone a month?"

"A month. Yes." Pearsall's words had a nervous, staccato delivery to them.

Vega pointed his finger at the ceiling where heating ducts and pipes snaked between the suspended light fixtures. "You know, upstairs, they're planning a party for you in something like two weeks."

"Yes, well. I guess I'll have to reschedule."

"You didn't tell them you'd have to reschedule."

"I forgot."

Vega leaned a hand on one of the SUV's taillights and closed the space between himself and Pearsall. "Oscar Beltran may be dead," said Vega, "but you can't run. They'll find you. One way or another, they will."

Pearsall didn't ask "who." They both knew. Vega braced himself against the bumper of the Lexus. "What I want to know is why?"

"Why?" Pearsall expelled a defeated breath.

"Why Beltran was ordered to kill you," said Vega. "You'd rearranged the docket so he got Spruce. Like you did for so many other gangsters who got picked up on petty offenses. You made sure the police report of Rivas's missing fingerprints never made it to Spruce's desk. You did everything Beltran's people asked of you. So why would they want to kill you?"

Vega glanced down at Pearsall's hands. They were shaking.

"Somebody caught on to what you were doing, didn't they?" asked Vega. "If you talked, the feds might start looking at other court clerks in other jurisdictions. They might start to realize they have a real problem on their hands. You were never the only one."

Pearsall pulled off his glasses and wiped beneath his eyes. "Beltran's people are going to kill me," he whispered. "I have to get away."

Vega leaned in close. "Who found out, Albert? Who was on to you?"

"No one."

"No one knew what you were doing?"

Pearsall shook his head. "They just . . . saw the undeclared money. They were going to follow it."

Vega suddenly understood what Pearsall was saying. "The IRS caught up to you. They were going to trace the money. You figured Beltran's people had some way to put a stop to their investigation. Instead, Beltran's people decided to put a stop to you."

Pearsall sank down onto the edge of the bumper. He pinched two fingers to the bridge of his nose. He didn't look like he had the strength to stand. "They're going to kill me if I don't get away."

"They're going to kill you if you do," said Vega. "Your one option here is to tell the feds everything. It's bigger than you are, Albert. Beltran alone has been suspiciously able to get past a number of judges in different states. You are probably the tip of the iceberg."

Vega sank down next to him on the bumper. "Come

with me, Albert. Let's sit down with an FBI agent I know and straighten this out together."

"You're talking about arresting me." Pearsall worked with cops. He knew the lingo. They never said "arrest" to a suspect until they had him in handcuffs. "And if I refuse?"

"I'd like to walk you out of here with dignity," said Vega. He patted the small microphone button on his shirt. "Either way, this is happening."

The door to the downstairs garage opened and Doug Hewitt, Richard Fiske, and two more of their associates spilled out. Strength in numbers. It was always the way cops did things. To Pearsall's credit, he seemed resigned to his fate. He slipped his glasses back on his eyes and took a deep breath as he slowly rose to his feet. He turned to Vega.

"Tell Julia I'm sorry. I know her intentions were never anything but well meaning."

"I'm sure they were," said Vega. "The road to hell is paved with them."

Chapter 53

September rolled around. The summer people at Vega's lake packed up their cabins. Gone were the plastic buckets and shovels on the beach, the chatter and woodsmoke that wafted nightly through the trees. Joy returned to college. Sophia started her first year of middle school.

Adele finally caved and installed an alarm system on her house. She didn't sleep any better. It would take time, Vega supposed. Time, and something else. Something that all the alarm systems in the world couldn't buy.

They were up at his place, having a quiet dinner on his deck, watching Diablo chase after squirrels, when Vega slid a small blue-velvet-covered box across the patio table to her.

"What's this?" she asked.

"Something that may help you sleep better at night."

She studied his face, trying to read him. For once, she had no idea what he was thinking.

"*Nena,*" he coaxed. "Just open it."

She cradled the velvet box in her palm and tugged at the lid. The hinge sprang open all at once, revealing a small fourteen-karat gold disk on a delicate linked chain. On the front of the disk was a raised etching of Saint Mariana, her head bent in prayer. Adele's eyes grew wide. She pulled back, bringing a hand to her lips. "Oh, Jimmy," she whispered. "It can't be."

"Before you get too excited," he said, not wanting to disappoint her, "it's not your dad's medallion. I looked everywhere and never found it. I had this one made up as a replacement."

She undid a small pin holding the chain to the box and pulled it out. She draped it in her hand. He knew she had to see the differences. Saint Mariana's halo wasn't partially rubbed away. The links of the chain were a little larger; the clasp was different. Not a lobster claw, but a barrel-type clasp, which Vega thought would hold better. But the words inscribed on the back were the same. *El Señor es contigo—The Lord is with thee.*

"It's so close to my dad's," Adele marveled. "How did you . . . ?

"I'm a cop." Vega shrugged. "I'm trained to recall details. All the times I've lain next to you, you think I wouldn't remember it? I drew a picture for the jeweler. I was probably the most pain-in-the-ass customer he's ever had 'cause I wanted it perfect."

Adele stroked the medallion. Her eyes turned glassy. She brushed away tears. Vega's stomach lurched. He felt a sudden ripple of worry. Was this replica a discredit to her father's memory? "I know it's not the same," he stumbled. "Maybe . . . maybe because it's not the same . . ."

She got up from her chair, the medallion still in her hand, and wrapped her arms tightly around his shoulders. "Oh, *mi vida*, it's the best present in the world."

"But you're crying."

"I'm crying because I can't believe you did this."

"Yeah, well . . ." He wasn't sure what to say. He was not a man of words. But when he opened his mouth, he spoke what he felt—what he knew he'd feel for the rest of his life. ". . . Your dad can't be here to watch over you anymore. But I will, *nena*. Always. That's a promise."

When his neck injury healed in early September, Vega went back to his cubicle at the county police and tried to ignore talk about the promotional ceremony coming up the following week. He went to Drew Banks's sergeant's party, drank to his success, and ignored the gossips in his department who tried to rile him up with pity and indignance in equal measure.

He didn't need anyone's pity or indignance. Life was good. Joy was doing well in school and talking about transferring to a more prestigious college after her sophomore year. Kaylee, too, was doing well. Vega had spoken to a judge on her behalf and gotten her diverted into a drug treatment program. She was staying sober, bunking at her aunt's house for help with child care while she concentrated on getting well and going back to school for her Realtor's license. Vega checked in with her regularly and she always texted back.

He was sitting in his cubicle, working his way through a license plate printout for a hit-and-run when Captain Waring called him into the conference room. Not his office. The conference room. Vega entered with trepidation. There, on the other side of the table, sat the chief of department, John Lakeworth, flanked by Vega's boss, Frank Waring, and Captain Lorenzo. Lakeworth looked pleased about something, like a puppy with a new bone. Lorenzo was scowling. Waring was inscrutable as always.

"Have a seat, Detective," said Lakeworth.

"Am I in some kind of trouble?" asked Vega.

"No trouble," said Lakeworth. "We just wanted to inform you that Sergeant Barzak is retiring."

Vega pushed back from the table slightly and tried to contain his enthusiasm. *Barzak—retiring?* Vega had to assume the man had found a way to finagle a disability pension. That's the only way they'd get him out of here. Which was great news for Vega. Barzak's retirement meant there would be an opening in the sergeant's ranks. The county SWAT commander had written up a very nice commendation for Vega over the Kaylee Wentz hostage situation. But that might not play here, given that Vega had been up there primarily on FBI business. His superiors didn't know all the details about Albert Pearsall and Oscar Beltran. The FBI was keeping that under wraps while they explored the case.

"In answer to your unasked question," said Lakeworth, "no, you will not be getting that sergeant's promotion. It's going to Tracy Romano."

The next name *down* from Drew Banks on the sergeant's list. Vega felt like he'd been lifted in the air to be slammed down even harder on the pavement. He looked over at Lorenzo. His scowl had briefly flickered into a smile. He was clearly enjoying this moment.

"Vega," said Waring, redirecting his attention. "We didn't call you in here to tell you you're being passed over again."

"It sure seems like it."

Lakeworth shook his head. "Yesterday, I received a call from someone in the FBI. It has come to their attention that you've been doing stellar work as a liaison for the bureau. They asked if the county could make that part of your permanent duties."

"The FBI wants me as their liaison?" Vega was floored. Hewitt hadn't said more than two words to him since Vega turned Pearsall over. "Who recommended me? The Broad Plains field director?"

"Someone higher," said Lakeworth. "It went through channels."

"Still, I'd like to thank him."

"It's a her."

Shana Callahan. Vega recalled her invitation to contact

the FBI. He'd been so focused on the hostage situation, it never occurred to him that she was serious.

"The problem," said Lakeworth, "is that to be a liaison, you need to attain at least the rank of Lieutenant Detective."

"Oh." Vega couldn't even get bumped up to sergeant. No way were they going to bump him two levels to lieutenant.

"As far as pay grade goes, you will need to test for lieutenant on the next promotional exam and achieve the complete pay grade raise at that time," said Lakeworth. "As far as rank, as chief of department, I can sign off on a probationary promotion, contingent upon the next test."

"Wait." Vega couldn't believe his ears. "Are you saying that I'm being promoted? To lieutenant detective?"

"You will receive the formal promotion at the ceremony next week," said Lakeworth. "You will also be working joint cases with the FBI as part of your duties, effective immediately."

Vega took a deep breath and let his lungs exhale with satisfaction. His whole body felt fizzy with excitement, like a can of just-popped soda. This was his second chance—the second chance he never thought he'd get. All his life, stuff happened to him and he reacted, for better or worse. Fatherhood. Marriage. Giving up his musical career. Becoming a police officer. His life was mostly about stumbling into things and only understanding them in the rearview mirror. But here was something he'd wanted to do for more than a decade: work with the FBI. Here was his chance to make a choice about his future. This time, he would greet the road ahead of him—not look back in longing at the one behind.

"Thank you," said Vega. "I will make the most of this opportunity."

"I'm sure you will," said Waring, offering a rare smile.

"Congratulations, Lieutenant Detective Vega, on a job well done."

Eli awoke to her first-ever snowfall in late November. It looked like God had draped a sheet across their new little town. Everything was shrouded—cars and rooftops and sidewalks. She walked to school that morning, her new boots crunching on snow, leaving behind a pattern of swirling grooves wherever she stepped. Snow softened the sharp edges of things, covered up the ugly parts. They were still there, of course. Bad things never really disappeared. But it gave the illusion of a fresh start.

When the teacher in Eli's ESL class asked her where she came from, she said simply, "Guatemala." She made no mention of the journey from Nejapa or how she and her mother ended up in this tiny town near the Canadian border. The government agents said they'd be safe here. That was all that mattered.

Her mother got a job making sandwiches at a deli within walking distance of their apartment. On Friday nights, they gathered with other Central Americans at a church hall. The older people would play music they remembered from home. The girls would ignore them, weaving friendship bracelets and fixing up their hair to look like Ariana Grande. Eli knew who the singer was now; she listened to all her music. But even here, among others far from home, she never spoke of her journey. Nor did they.

Some parts of your life you learn not to tell. You simply let them scab over and hope the scars will soften with age.

On the wall of their kitchen, Eli's mother had taped a photo, sent by her grandmother through the government agents after they moved to their new apartment. The picture had yellowed with age and turned white and spongy along the creases. It showed a good-looking, lanky, teenage boy giving a piggyback ride to a little girl in braids, her tongue protruding slightly between the space where her front baby teeth had fallen out.

Eli recognized the photo. It had sat in their own little house in Nejapa until their journey north. The boy in the picture had been the hero of all her mother's stories. In death, he'd become a hero again, giving up his life for theirs.

At least, that's the way her mother told it.

Eli suspected this wasn't entirely true. More likely, Luis had been in the wrong place at the wrong time. Still, she understood her mother's need for this fairy-tale image of her brother. Otherwise, she'd have to accept the ugly truth that the border had changed him. Hardened him. Broken the bond between them that she held so dear. She couldn't do that. And maybe, in those final moments of Luis's life, neither could he.

Family is that string that always pulls you back to the place you came from, even if you can't go there anymore.

Eli wondered if this might be her legacy one day as well. She would likely not return to Guatemala for many years, if ever. She would be cleaved in two—not quite American enough for here and never Guatemalan enough for there. She would know things that only a person who has undergone such a journey could know. This would be her strength and her sorrow. As it was for her uncle. As it is for so many who have come before her.

And the many yet to come.

Acknowledgments

Thank you to all the people who have made this book—and series—possible. To my editor, Michaela Hamilton, and Kensington CEO Steven Zacharius for sticking with the series when so many other publishing houses might have dropped it. I hope that your faith is ultimately rewarded. Thank you to Vida Engstrand for publicity, and to my first reader and independent editor, Rosemary Ahern, for always keeping the narrative on track.

I'm indebted to Gene West, as always, for his uncanny sense of plot and dialogue and total command of everything related to law enforcement. As a former journalist, I pride myself on accuracy and, Gene, you always deliver.

Thanks to my agent, Stephany Evans, and Ayesha Pande Literary, for their support and guidance. Thank you most of all to my family: my husband, Tom, and children, Kevin and Erica, who always keep me grounded.

The Jimmy Vega series grew out of a university-sponsored project I undertook in 2012 to recount the true stories of undocumented immigrants. Our world never evolved enough for the people I interviewed to step out of the shadows. Regardless, I am forever grateful and honored that they shared their stories with me. I hope I've done them justice.